THE DEAD MAN'S MIND

TED TORGERSEN

THE DEAD MAN'S MIND

TED TORGERSEN

TABLE *of* CONTENTS

FORWARD/ ACKNOWLEDGEMENTS

Firstly, I would like to apologize to all the authors who have written eloquent forwards or prefaces to their novels, because I never take the time to read them. More importantly, I want to say a few words about my book. I began this story at the age of sixteen with no knowledge of my ideas. I simply picked up a pen and wrote with no research, no plan, and no idea of where my plot was headed. I certainly wish I could still write with so little effort. I feel the need to confess that I only really started trying to understand my own story about three quarters of the way through the book. I have worked hard to remember my own story over these four years when I had virtually no time to write. At the age of twenty I am quick to judge my sixteen year-old self as simple minded and childish, and sadly the twenty year old me is at times not particularly proud of this book. On the other hand the sixteen year old in me is immensely proud of it, and of course doesn't give a — what anyone else thinks of it. I feel the need to explain the context in which I created this book and the events of my life that caused me to almost abandon the project on many occasions, however in the end I hope all of this will be irrelevant. I have spent far too much time qualifying myself and my work, but I will leave you with one last qualification: many of my characters are much older and wiser than I. I have done my best to understand them.

I would like to thank my great friend Ania for her help with this book and the character of Marissa, even if neither of us can remember exactly what she helped me with. I would also like to thank the real captain for his help with some of the concepts in the book, although he is nothing like Captain John Carl. I want to acknowledge the bartender at the real Sharktooth Tavern in Tampa Florida, which I discovered only after I came up with the name. Finally, I want to thank you, the reader, for reading this forward which I so kindly kept under one page.

PROLOGUE

It was Friday the thirteenth, not destined to be a good day in the eyes of many overly superstitious fishermen on the dock. It was a gloomy day. The sky was scattered with dark clouds and a misty fog hung over the ocean.

"Doom and gloom again," said Captain John Carl Thomason unenthusiastically, as he watched his crew unload the catch onto the dock. "The price is in the toilet again. What happened to the way things used to be around here?"

"Probably gone along with his mind," muttered a short balding man who looked worthless in every respect.

"Shut your trap, Remi," snapped John Carl.

"Yes Cap," said Remi. He sounded like he had memorized the responses he gave to his captain's commands.

John Carl Thomason looked as though he would be very good looking if it were not for the fact that he always looked as though he was having the worst day of his life. "Is that a banana you're eating, Remi?" asked John Carl casually.

"Yes Cap," said Remi automatically.

"Well, guess what, mate?" said John Carl, his voice colder now.

"What?" asked Remi, not catching his captain's cold tone.

"Bananas are bad luck, that's what," yelled John Carl. He grabbed the banana out of Remi's hand and shoved it in his face. "DO –YOU– REALIZE –WHAT –TODAY –IS?" he yelled, pronouncing each word with deadly emphasis.

"No sir," spluttered Remi, who looked quite the idiot with banana all over his face.

"IT'S FRIDAY THE THIRTEENTH, YOU WORTHLESS IDIOT," roared John Carl. "We have enough bad luck without you making things worse with your stinking slimy banana." The Captain threw the banana peel on the dock and stormed away, swearing loudly.

Remi stumbled towards the truck, carrying a large box. He stepped on the banana peel and fell flat on his face. "Hey, Remi," called a young man named Sono, "how long does it take from when you step on the peel to when you hit the dock? One banano-second!" There was a roar of laughter from the other crewmembers on the dock.

"Nice one, Sono," said another young man called Browen.

Sono and Browen were brothers, ages nineteen and eighteen. They looked very much alike and had very similar personalities. They seemed to be able to read each other's thoughts, and were, therefore, exceptional liars. They could always talk their way out of anything, even with their captain, who was not easily fooled. Remi was not a challenge for them. They had taken the job working on the boats because neither of them was very academically inclined. They were, however, very good at making jokes, pulling pranks, and having as much fun as possible while on the job. They stopped at nothing to insult anyone who displayed a lack of intelligence or physical prowess.

Remi Nelson was a short, chubby, balding man, who had never really been able to make anything of his life, or at least it never seemed like he had. He was thirty-five, but looked forty-five, at best. Sono and Browen thought he was at least fifty. Everyone always made fun of Remi, but he still seemed to feel important and useful. This only seemed to make things worse for him, although he never seemed to understand that.

"Just imagine being stupid enough to eat a banana in front of Cap on Friday the thirteenth," said Sono loudly.

"Imagine being stupid enough to slip on the peel and fall flat on your face," said Browen.

"Imagine doing this job 'till you're fifty," said Sono.

"I'm thirty-five," snapped Remi, who had stood up and was wiping banana off his face.

"Really?" said Sono mockingly. "I had no idea guys went bald and got beer bellies that soon. You might want to tell Cap to get a move on, he must be at least thirty or thirty-five. I don't see him looking like that".

"Looks aren't everything, you know," muttered Remi.

"Clearly, or you wouldn't even be alive," sneered Sono.

"Get to work," snapped John Carl coming up behind them.

"Yes Cap," said Remi immediately

"Sorry *sir*," said Browen emphasizing the last word. "We just found out that Remi's only thirty-five and we're, you know, shocked."

"We thought he must be at least fifty with the way he looks," continued Sono.

"It's quite understandable," sneered John Carl.

"We're sorry sir" said Browen again. "We'll get to work right away."

Browen and Sono moved away down the dock.

John Carl Thomason stood on the dock staring out to sea. He was tall, slim,

and handsome with dark hair and eyes. He did not look quite as handsome as he was simply because he wore a permanently depressed, defeated, and stressed out expression. He was thirty-three, but looked older. John Carl was the captain of a fishing boat that went out on ten-day trips and then came in for a week to sell. John Carl had been on the boats since he was nineteen and captain since he was twenty-nine, but he still never seemed to have a good day. There was always something wrong with someone and something. If there wasn't an obvious problem, the captain would find one.

John Carl's cell phone rang in his pocket. "Damn phone," he snapped, flipping it

open. "Yes?" he snapped. Suddenly his voice changed. "Oh right, um…sure". He sounded nervous now. "Um…well, I'll be there, of course, of course I will, it's no problem. Um…thanks. Tell her I'll be there real soon. Thank you." He closed the phone. John Carl stood motionless. He was scared. Not today, he thought, not on Friday the thirteenth.

*   *   *

Tamera Nickelson always thought it was ironic that the best day of her life had been a Friday the thirteenth. She was married to a man who feared the day, and had come to dread it somewhat herself. She knew her husband had been more afraid than she the day her daughter was born. John Carl always said they were lucky everything had gone alright, but for Tamera it was the most perfect day she could imagine.

On that day, November thirteenth, Tamera had given birth to her only child. She had wanted a child for many years before that day, and finally had a daughter. The birth of Katerina Alicia Thomason was a dream come true for Tamera.

The birth had even softened her sometimes harsh husband, John Carl Thomason. Tamera had not changed her last name to Thomason when she married John Carl ten years previously at the age of twenty-six. She really didn't know why she hadn't. Tamera Thomason just didn't sound right. She had wanted to give her daughter the name Nickelson, but something told her that Thomason was her daughter's rightful last name.

"She's beautiful," the doctor had said when Katerina was born. And it was true. Katerina had dark hair like her father and very white skin. The most unusual thing about her appearance was her eyes. They were not dark brown like her father's or light blue like her mother's, but a very deep shade of green.

Tamera sat in an armchair in front of the fire, rocking back and forth, her baby daughter in her arms. "She's a funny baby," said John Carl softly. He was sitting in an armchair opposite his wife.

"What do you mean, funny?" said Tamera sharply.

"She never cries," said John Carl. "She didn't cry when she was born and we've had her three days. I haven't heard her cry once."

"Well, I guess you're right," said Tamera. "But that's good isn't it? She must be happy."

"She doesn't wake up crying at night," continued John Carl.

"I know," said Tamera, "but she does wake up. She wakes up every few hours, but she doesn't need to cry. I always know when she wakes up."

"How do you know?"

"I don't know how I know," said Tamera, "I just do."

"I suppose we're just lucky," said John Carl. "Do you think I can go back to work in four days?"

"Yes," said Tamera, "I can handle things".

"Alright, business as usual then," said John Carl. "I think my luck is changing," he continued. "I finally had a good Friday the thirteenth. It might have been the best Friday I ever had. It's weird how things happen. I guess that's just life."

*   *   *

Rain was pounding on the back of Sela's head. She crouched under the window, listening to the conversation going on in the house. There was a man and a woman talking about their baby. The man had said that the baby was unusual, but what parent didn't think their child was somehow special? Sela didn't see the significance of the conversation at all. Her back was sore from crouching under the window. She had waited hours for the couple to come home, but now that they had finally arrived she was only half listening to their conversation.

Sela crossed the yard and slipped out through the fence like a shadow. Her footsteps made no sound on the ground where she walked. She was dressed in a full length black coat with the hood up, so her face was obscured.

Sela was beginning to dislike her job. She felt this new anger as she made her way up the road, her body aching from the cold rain. What was she getting out of it? She risked so much and was told so little. Why was it important that she get this information? Could there be a connection between this and her other job? Perhaps he was using the two sets of information toward a common goal, but he had not told her anything, only that the job was important and that the information was useful, but not why. Then again, he had never told her about the other job, either. There were always so many questions, and so few answers. Sela was tired of working in the dark, or at best, the semi-dark.

The rain had let up slightly, and Sela stopped at the corner of the road and lowered her hood. She had long, straight, reddish blonde hair with light highlights, framing her narrow face. Her eyes were a very light shade of brown. Sela was eighteen, but looked much older. Everything about her gave her the look of someone who was very cunning. She had an unknown job and an unknown past.

Sela did not make many mistakes and she was not easily fooled. She was not afraid, she had been through too much in her life to be afraid. She would give him a chance, but only one.

Sela looked up and down the street. It was a normal street for any middle class neighborhood. The houses were all medium size with small yards and low fences. Looking at the houses brought back memories of things Sela was trying hard to forget. She checked her watch, wondering what she could find out in a short amount of time. She was not sure how tardiness would be treated. Dare she do anything beyond the confines of her orders? She had never done anything against orders in her nearly six months of this job.

*   *   *

Rain poured down and the wind howled, sending huge waves crashing against the rocks. In the distance, on the hill, the many lights of the city were blurred by the rain. Sela stood on the bluff, staring out at the dark, stormy sea. If any "normal" man or woman stood where Sela was standing, all they would see was a large rock island on the horizon. Sela, however, could see a massive structure built on this rock island. A soft glow of silver light came from the upper windows of the huge circular building. The waves rose and fell all around the rock island, but never touched the structure that stood upon it. If a person could see it, he or she might wonder if it was a prison. It was not. It was the headquarters of a very powerful and secret society of organized crime, or a least that was what some people said.

Sela climbed down the bluff onto the beach, the wind tearing at her coat. She climbed onto a pointed rock and pressed her left palm against the side. There was a soft hiss and a flash of silver, then the rock split open to reveal a hole wide enough for a person to pass through. Sela lowered herself into the rock, and the opening immediately closed over her head. Sela was in a rock tunnel that stretched on without change. It was very dark, but Sela could see in low light better than most people. She was used to the dark, and moved down the tunnel like a shadow, her strange light brown eyes seeming to glow in the dark.

When Sela came to the end of the tunnel a blank stretch of rock lay before her. Sela touched her hand to the rock. The rock spilt in half to reveal a stone staircase, at the top of which stood two large double doors. The handles were long, silver, and diamond shaped. Sela slipped through the doors and entered a narrow hallway.

The lamps that lined the walls cast a silver glow over the hall. At the end of the short hallway were two doors, one leading to the left, the other to the right. Sela took the right, and entered an identical hall lit by the same silver lights. On Sela's right was a sleek stone wall, on her left was the side of a huge circular silver column that ran from floor to ceiling. The hall curved in a half circle around the column. At the end of the hall was a large black door with the silver diamond outlined in gold. Sela paused in front of the door, her gaze fixed on the doorknob. There was a time when Sela had been afraid of what lay behind that door, but Sela no longer felt fear. Slowly, she raised her hand and knocked.

Lord Talson sat in a high backed chair in front of the fire, listening to the rain pounding against the walls. The room was circular, with a desk in one corner and two chairs in front of the fireplace. The room was lit by silver lamps and the golden glow of the fire. Lord Talson was a small man with dark hair and sharp facial features. He had the body of a young man, but the presence of someone much older. He had very bright yellow eyes that gave him a cruel, almost inhuman look. There was a deep, piercing look in his eyes that was almost cold, almost sad, but not quite either one. It was impossible to tell his age, and only Lord Talson knew his true identity, choosing not to reveal his mysterious past even to those who worked alongside him. It was said that Lord Talson had never truly been close to anyone.

Lord Talson heard a knock on the door. "Enter", he said, his voice was soft and somewhat lazy. The door opened and Sela entered. She took off her black coat which was wet from the rain.

Sela", said Talson smoothly. "Sit down." He gestured to the chair opposite him.

"Thank you," murmured Sela, hanging her coat on the back of the chair and sitting down.

"I trust you got the information I needed," said Talson, his voice was soft but sharp.

"Of course," said Sela. "The family had a baby a few days ago."

"Yes, I thought so," said Talson softly. "Did you get the name of this child?"

"Yes," said Sela. "It's a girl, named Katerina Thomason." For a moment Sela

thought she saw Lord Talson's eyes gleam in the dim light, but a second later his eyes were as cold and expressionless as before.

"Yes, very well," said Talson. "You have done well, Sela. Is there anything else you would like to tell me?"

"Well, yes," said Sela softly. "The child's father said Katerina is an unusual baby because she hardly ever cries." Sela hesitated, as though she was slightly afraid to continue. "I don't know if that is significant to you. I mean, I wouldn't know if those sorts of details are useful, but if they are, I can certainly provide."

Lord Talson's yellow eyes bored into Sela's face. Her expression was hard to read. "Yes, that could possibly be significant," he said slowly. "I thought she might be unusual. Yes, that means I would be right in doing so…yes," he muttered, much more to himself than to Sela.

"That was very useful Sela," Talson said, coming back to the conversation. "You have done very well, you may go if you like."

"Thank you, I am always glad to be of use," said Sela. "Good night."

Sela did not allow herself a smile until she was back at the beginning of the hall and had gone through the door on the left side. She was in a large circular room with a fireplace in the center, around which were nine chairs arranged in a circle. The room was deserted. Sela walked over to a table and took a cup, filling it with water from a large jug. She crossed the room and sat down in a chair by the fire. She smiled to herself as she thought about her meeting with Lord Talson. *He's right*, she thought, *I have done very well.*

Lord Talson wasn't sure he liked his options. He couldn't continue to assume that she would be as useless as her father, could he? No, she was bound to be better than him. What if…? He could take her. But no. He could kill her. Better plan. But, what if…? He could not pretend this wasn't happening. He rose from his chair and began to pace back and forth in front of the fire.

Lord Talson was legend. Mothers could be heard saying things like, "If you don't behave, Yellow Eyes will come and eat your brains." Most of those parents didn't know that Lord Talson was not simply a popular character in the stories told in dark closets to scare young children. He was reality. Lord Talson, or Yellow Eyes, as he was often called, wouldn't literally eat your brain, but that wasn't far from the truth. He did not need guns or knives to kill. Lord Talson killed with his mind alone, never physically touching his victims.

Death at the hands of Lord Talson was undoubtedly the cruelest way to be killed. It was long, drawn out, and painful. Lord Talson had killed many. Some had taken years to finish off, but he didn't care. Lord Talson liked doing things slowly, especially killing. He liked to watch as a person's mind was slowly destroyed from the inside.

Lord Talson paced back and forth, thinking hard. He could not kill her yet, he would have to wait and see what she would become. Had he not seen enough these years? What was the chance? But then there was him, that useless fool. Lord Talson wanted to kill him quickly, because he knew he could not bear to draw it out. He would grant him a painless death, something he had never deserved. For what he hasn't done, not for what he has done, Talson reminded himself. Do not kill in anger.

Maybe this time, Lord Talson thought. He smiled to himself and his yellow eyes glinted in the firelight. There were some who knew that Lord Talson was more than legend. Some knew what he did, but no one knew how he did it.

CHAPTER 1

EAVESDROPPING

People were screaming, feet ran past her on all sides. The smoke of a burning house was in the air. The mob, the crowd, the panic, everyone running in chaos. Two huge yellow eyes, bright and cold stared into her face. She could not look away. She felt something cold on her neck. The yellow eyes gleamed in the darkness for a moment, then went dim. Someone was screaming in pain.

Katerina's green eyes snapped open. She was breathing hard as though she had been running. She sat up in the darkness and reached for a flashlight on her bedside table, shining it on the ceiling so the room was bathed in light.

The bedroom was small, with two windows. The girl sat on the bed, against the wall. There was a small dresser, a toy chest, and a chair covered in stuffed animals of all shapes and sizes. It looked like a normal bedroom for any young girl.

Katerina, or Kat as she was called, was six years old. Today, November thirteenth, was her birthday. Kat looked at the clock on her bedside table. She was thinking about the dream she had been having before she awoke. Five, ten, fifteen, twenty, she counted. The little hand on the five, the big hand on the seven. Twenty-five, thirty, thirty-five. That's it, thought Kat, 5:35 in the morning.

Kat lowered the flashlight and leaned back against her pillows, staring at the ceiling. It was not the first time she had had that dream. That cold on her neck, those huge yellow eyes, and that scream. No one has yellow eyes, thought Kat. People have brown eyes like my dad, or blue eyes like my mom, or green eyes like me, but not yellow. Maybe some people do, thought Kat. I've never seen someone like that, but there must be.

Kat rolled over and felt something cold touch her neck. She sat up quickly, remembering the dream. She looked down at her neck, shining the flashlight at it. Oh, just my necklace, thought Kat, disappointed. Around her neck she wore a silver chain with a small silver elongated diamond, outlined in gold, hanging from it. Kat held the necklace in her hand, wondering where she had gotten it. She had had it as long as she could remember. She liked it, but sometimes it scared her, or made her angry. Even then she never took it off. Something told her to always wear it, no matter what. But where did I get it? Kat wondered. Surely, her mother would know. I'll ask her when she wakes up, thought Kat. She rolled over and tried to fall asleep, but she could not. She had to know, she couldn't bear to wait even a few hours for her parents to wake up.

Kat climbed out of bed, took her flashlight and stepped into the hall outside her room. She crept down the hall to the door of her parents' room. She paused at the door, listening.

Kat was tall for six years old. She had black hair that came just below her shoulders. Everyone always thought she was older than she was. Her face and eyes projected more maturity than was expected from a child of six.

Kat stared at the door, wanting an answer. For some reason she thought that her parents were not going to tell her about the necklace she wore. They wanted to keep it a secret, which made Kat angry. Suddenly, a woman screamed behind the door. Kat stood frozen, listening, but there was silence. Kat turned and walked quickly back to her room.

Why had her mother screamed? What happened to her? Kat did not understand why her father had not said anything. It was like he had not heard her. But he must have. Maybe she was having a scary dream, like me, thought Kat. Her mother's scream reminded her of the scream in her dream.

Hours later Kat heard movement downstairs. She sat up and looked at the clock, trying to figure out the time. Seven…twenty… eight. She got out of bed and crossed the room to the door, her small, long fingered hand on the knob. The memory of the scream made a cold feeling rise in her chest.

Kat walked down the stairs and into the kitchen. Her mother, Tamera, was at the stove cooking breakfast. She was thirty-nine, and looked nothing like her daughter. She was tall with long light brown hair and soft blue eyes.

Kat's father, John Carl, sat at the kitchen table drinking coffee. Kat resembled him very much, except for her eyes.

"Happy Birthday, Kat," he said when she entered.

"Thank you," said Kat politely.

"Happy Birthday," said Kat's mother as she carried a tray with breakfast toward the table.

"Thanks," Kat sat down opposite her parents.

"Do you want to open your presents before your dad leaves?"

"Oh yes. Are you going to work soon?" Kat asked, turning to look at her father. She spoke very clearly for a six year old.

"Yes," her father replied. "I know I should be home on your birthday, but we are scheduled to go out and I don't want to take today off."

"That's okay," said Kat. "It's just another day."

She unwrapped her birthday presents. Her father's present was not wrapped, he had gotten her a bicycle, something she had always wanted. In her excitement about the presents, she almost forgot that she had wanted to ask her parents about the necklace and the scream she had heard in the night. It all came back to her, however, when they started eating breakfast. Kat kept looking at her mother, wondering what had happened to make her scream. She was slightly hesitant to bring up the subject, but finally decided to just ask her mother directly.

"Mom, did something happen to you last night?" Kat asked.

"No, nothing happened to me last night," replied Tamera looking perplexed. "What are you talking about?"

"You screamed."

Tamera looked across the table at Kat, then at her husband. "I...I didn't scream last night," she said finally.

"Didn't you hear her?" Kat asked, looking at her father.

"No, Kat," replied John Carl. "Your mother didn't scream, I would have heard her. You must have been dreaming."

"No, I wasn't," said Kat. "I woke up at 5:35 this morning. Everything was quiet and then I heard a scream."

"Listen, Katerina," said John Carl more forcefully. "No one screamed."

"Yes they did," said Kat, returning her father's harsh tone. "I heard it. TELL ME THE TRUTH!" Kat yelled the last three words.

There was a time when John Carl would have lost his temper if someone spoke to him the way his daughter had just done, but the captain was more patient now.

"I am telling the truth," John Carl said calmly.

For several minutes Kat glared into her father's face. His dark eyes stared back at her. His expression gave no indication of anger or annoyance.

"I believe you," said Kat reluctantly. "It just seemed really real, that's all." She did not believe him, but she knew that her father was not about to share any of his feelings with her at that moment.

"Can I ask you something?" asked Kat, hoping to take advantage of a chance to get her other questions answered.

"Ask away," replied her father.

Kat held up the diamond hanging from the chain around her neck. "Where did I get this?"

Suddenly her father's face hardened. His dark eyes narrowed, giving him a harsh, somewhat cold look. The expression only lasted a very brief moment, then his face relaxed and he looked as calm as before.

"I don't know," he said slowly.

"How long have I had it?"

"A long time," said her father softly.

"You don't know?" Kat was somewhat surprised, she had been sure her parents would know.

"No, I don't," replied her father.

Kat looked at her mother questioningly. Tamera shook her head without speaking. "Sorry Kat," she said. "I...I don't know either."

Kat looked at her parents. Something about her mother's hesitation and her father's momentary hard expression made her doubt whether they were telling the truth. Kat thought they seemed tense, maybe even scared.

"Do people ever have yellow eyes?" Kat asked, deciding to push her mother and father now that they had been so unhelpful. Her father's eyes flared suddenly. He stood up very quickly, looking up at the clock.

"No, Kat they don't," he said sharply, without looking at her. "I've got to go or we'll be the last ones out." He fumbled for his coat and grabbed his bag. He seemed to be suddenly rushing to get out the door.

"I'll see you in four days," he said quickly. "We're going on a short trip this time. Happy birthday Kat," he said, still not making eye contact. "I'll see you in a few days." He left, closing the front door sharply behind him.

Kat looked at her mother, who did not return the glance. Instead, she got up from the table, taking the plates, and stood at the sink with her back to Kat. Kat slipped out the kitchen door silently and went upstairs to her bedroom. She stood in front of the mirror staring at her reflection, her own green eyes stared back at her. She tried to imagine what she would look like if her eyes were yellow. So many questions were running through her mind. Why did it make him angry? Why didn't he tell her? Why did the necklace scare them? Why didn't they tell her what they knew? Kat felt hurt and angry. Why do they lie to me? Do they think I can't see what they're thinking? Kat did not understand. She had so many questions and the only people she knew of who could give her the answers had refused her.

Kat went back downstairs. "Can I go over to Tina's house?" she asked her mother. "I could ride there on my new bike."

"Yes, but I have to go with you," replied her mother.

"I don't need you to come, I can go alone. It's only a couple of blocks."

"I would rather come with you," said Tamera. "I was going to ask Tina's mother if Tina can have dinner with us, and maybe she can stay the night for your birthday. Would you like that?"

"Oh yes," said Kat, smiling.

"You should call her first and ask her if you can go over to her house. It's only polite."

Kat knew she didn't have to, but her father had always told her that politeness could go a long way in life. He also said that in fishing, rudeness could go a long way. Kat grabbed the phone and dialed Tina's number. She had her best friend's number memorized, having called it many times.

"Hello," said a woman's voice.

"Hello, this is Katerina."

"Oh, hello Katerina," said the woman. "Happy birthday."

"Thanks, Tracy," said Kat. "Can I_" Kat began. Then she remembered that Tracy liked people who spoke very properly, and thought very highly of those who used correct language. "May I speak to Kristina, please?"

"What a well spoken young lady," said Tracy, delighted. "Of course, Kristina's right here."

"Hi Kat, Happy Birthday," said a young girl's voice. "That was awesome with my mom."

"Thanks," said Kat. "My dad says politeness goes a long way." They both laughed. "You were listening on the other phone while I was talking to your mom, weren't you?"

"Yeah," said Tina. "I always do that. Listening in on people goes a long way."

"It's called eavesdropping," said Kat.

"Right," said Tina. "Do you wanna come over?"

"Yeah, my mom is going to ask your mom if you can come over for dinner and then spend the night at my house, but I want to come over there first," she lowered her voice so her mother wouldn't hear her, "I've got to tell you something."

"Okay," said Tina. "I'm glad you, you know…with my mom." Tina dropped her voice, "now I know she'll let me come."

"Yeah," said Kat. "That was the plan."

"Nice plan. I'll see you soon."

"Okay, see you," said Kat. She hung up the phone.

"Kat, are you ready," asked Tamera.

"Yes, let's go," said Kat.

Kat and her mother pushed Kat's new bicycle out the front door. Kat mounted the bicycle and her mother ran alongside her, holding the bike. Then she let go. Kat peddled down the sidewalk, her mother walking behind her.

Tamera remembered the first time her daughter had ridden a bicycle. Just one year ago Kat had only been able to ride with training wheels. Tamera didn't know many six year olds who could ride a bicycle without help, but Kat had been determined to learn. Kat was different from others her age. She was always determined to be the best, and whatever she wanted to do she seemed to be able to accomplish.

Kristina Louis had blonde hair and light blue eyes. Tina was two months older than Kat, and like Kat, she looked older than she was. She lived with her mother, Tracy, two blocks from Kat's house. Kat and Tina had known each other since they were babies because Tamera and Tracy were long time friends. Tina and Kat were both only children. Tina's father, Barton Louis had been the first mate of captain John Carl's crew. Tina did not remember her father at all. He had died when she was only six months old.

"What are you going to tell me?" asked Tina as soon as they were in her bedroom. Kat told Tina about her dream, which she had described to her friend once before. She told Tina about her conversation with her father, how he had denied knowing anything about the necklace and how he had reacted when she had asked about people with yellow eyes.

"You don't think there really are people with yellow eyes, do you?" Tina asked when Kat had finished.

"Well…I don't think so, but…in my dream_"

"Yeah, but, dreams are weird sometimes. They're not real."

"My dad looked scared."

"Maybe there is someone with yellow eyes who's really scary," suggested Tina.

"Yeah, maybe, but who?"

"I don't know"

"What about this necklace?" asked Kat.

"Your dad said he didn't know where you got it?"

"Yeah," said Kat, "but I think he was lying." Kat had not meant to say that. The words had just fallen out of her mouth.

Tina's eyes widened in surprise. "You think your dad would just lie to you like that?"

"Well, I don't know, I think my dad must know. I mean, my mom said she doesn't know either, but—"

"You think they were both lying." Tina finished Kat's sentence.

There was a pause, then Kat said, "I think that cold feeling on my neck in the dream is this necklace."

"Maybe it's a dream about how you got it," said Tina.

"Maybe," agreed Kat.

"I just don't get why your mom wouldn't admit that she screamed. I can't believe they pretended it didn't happen."

"Yeah, but the thing is, my dad didn't say anything to her at the time. I was standing right there."

"So, he really didn't hear it. That means they were telling the truth."

"No, he heard it."

"Are you sure?" asked Tina, looking slightly confused now.

"Positive," replied Kat giving no further explanation.

There was a knock on Tina's bedroom door. "Kat, Tina," said Tamera's voice. "Are you guys ready to go?"

Tina opened the door. "We're ready," she said.

"Your mother said it would be fine for you to stay with us tonight."

"Awesome," said Tina and Kat together.

"Nice bike," said Tina as they headed outside.

"Thanks," said Kat. "My dad got it for me."

Tina got on her bicycle and they rode to Kat's house together. Kat and Tina went in Kat's bedroom to play with dolls, board games and every card game they knew. They didn't talk about what had happened to Kat the previous night or about Kat's feelings toward her parents' reaction.

It had begun to rain very hard outside, and although it had been a very pleasant day, the wind was now howling against the windows.

"My dad might have to come home tonight," said Kat.

"It must be really scary out in the ocean right now," agreed Tina.

Just then they heard Tamera calling them for dinner. They ran down the stairs into the kitchen. While they were eating dinner Kat asked her mother if her father was going to come home that night.

"I hope so," replied Tamera. "It must be awful on the water right now. I just hope everyone is alright."

Tamera brought out a birthday cake with six candles on it. Tina and Tamera sang happy birthday to Kat.

"Make a wish, Kat," said Tamera.

I wish I had someone who would answer my questions instead of pretending not to know anything, Kat thought as she blew out the candles.

"I get the first piece," said Kat, eagerly holding out her plate.

When they finished eating cake, Kat and Tina went upstairs to watch a movie. They were lying on the bed in Kat's parents' room when the telephone rang. Kat who liked to answer the telephone, jumped up to get it, but her mother had already picked it up downstairs. Kat paused for a moment, then grabbed the remote, paused the movie, and picked up the phone. The connection was crackling and breaking up.

"I'll be home in an hour or so," John Carl was saying. "It's just too rough."

"Oh, good," said Tamera. "I'm glad you're coming home. I was worried, and besides," she lowered her voice, "I think we need to talk about this morning."

"Alright, I'll see you soon."

Kat hung up the phone and looked at Tina. "My dad is coming home in an hour or so. He said it was too rough. But then my mom said she thinks they should talk about this morning."

"Wow," said Tina. "That means they must have been lying to you earlier."

"Probably," said Kat. "We have to listen in when my dad gets home. I have to know."

"Okay," said Tina, "but it's called *eavesdropping*."

Kat smiled, "You always have to get me back, don't you?"

"Always," said Tina.

Suddenly, Tina's eyes widened. "Wait a minute," she said softly. "Our teacher from kindergarten, Mrs. Piper, she used to say it all the time. She would say, 'be good or Yellow Eyes will come'."

"Yellow Eyes?" whispered Kat. "How do you remember stuff like that?"

Tina shrugged. "I don't know, I just remember those days really well."

"Wow," said Kat, "now we really have to listen in, I mean eavesdrop."

Kat and Tina sat in Kat's bedroom, listening to the rain pounding against the windows. They were supposed to be asleep, but they were determined to stay awake until Kat's father arrived. Finally, Tina looked at the clock on Kat's bedside table. "What time is it?" She asked Kat.

Kat shined the flashlight at the clock for a moment, counting in her head. "9:45," she said.

"How do you read that thing?" Tina's clock was digital.

"See the little hand?" said Kat. "It's on the nine, so that means the hour is nine. Then the big hand is on the nine too, and you count by fives to figure out the minutes. The one is five, the two ten, the three is fifteen, like that."

"I like my clock better," said Tina, making no outward attempt to understand Kat's explanation. *So, the nine is forty-five and the ten is fifty. When it gets to the twelve it's the next hour. So, in fifteen minutes it will be ten o'clock, right?*

"Yep," said Kat. "My dad probably won't be back till about twelve o'clock. You wanna play cards in the dark while we wait?"

The hour hand was just closing in on the twelve when they heard John Carl's car pulling into the driveway. They heard the door open and the sound of voices drifted up the stairs. "He's home," whispered Kat, "let's go." They crept across the room to the door. Kat turned her flashlight off.

"How will we see without that?" asked Tina.

"With our eyes, I know my own house even in the dark. Come on."

They tiptoed down the stairs, and down the hall to the livingroom door. It was a door that Kat's parents almost always kept open, but tonight it was closed. Kat and Tina leaned against the door, listening.

"We thought we might not make it in," John Carl was saying. "The swell is huge, we had waves crashing into the boat the whole way in. The guys could hardly bail us out fast enough."

"I'm just glad you got in safe, and everyone's alright," said Tamera.

"Yeah, we were lucky."

"I was thinking that we should talk about what happened this morning with Kat," Tamera said, sounding slightly nervous now.

Kat and Tina sat down on the floor leaning their backs against the door. The storm outside had quieted somewhat, and the voices carried easily to the children.

"I just don't understand how she could have made that connection," Tamera continued.

John Carl sighed, sounding tired. "Well, I wondered what made her ask about them together too, but I thought maybe it was her friend Tina who told her about it. Do you know how much Tracy has told her daughter?"

"No, I don't," said Tamera. "I don't think she's told her anything, I mean, they're children, they're not ready for that. Imagine how it would frighten them."

"Yes," said John Carl, "but someday we will have to tell Kat and Tracy will have to tell Tina."

"Yes, we will, but six is too young."

"I agree, but how much does she already know?"

"I'm sure she doesn't know any of it. It's natural that she would wonder about that necklace and lots of people talk about Yellow Eyes. She might have heard someone tell a child to be good, or Yellow Eyes will come. You know how Kat always takes things seriously, she probably thought it was real."

"Maybe," said John Carl skeptically. "Somehow it seems like she did connect them. I think you might have been right when you said that. And then there is the scream she thought she heard. You don't think she…she's got…" his voice trailed off.

"You never did," said Tamera. She sounded scared now. "No one in your family did, how could she? That's not possible."

"I know, but, but, what if she… what if that's why he didn't…"

"No, that's impossible."

"My first mate, Barty, was a good man, he didn't deserve… I doubt Tina has any idea what happened to him, not that anyone else does."

"We know," said Tamera.

"Listen," said John Carl, dropping his voice. "No one knows what happens to people once Lord Talson decides to kill them."

The silence stretched on endlessly as the wind howled and the rain pounded on the roof. Crouched in front of the livingroom door, Kat and Tina stared at each other in the darkness. There was a strange glint in Kat's green eyes.

"That was my dad they were talking about," whispered Tina. They had crept back upstairs, and were sitting on Kat's bed. "My mom told me his name was Barty, Barton Louis."

"Yeah," said Kat. "My dad's first mate on the boat. He died a long time ago."

"Yeah, I don't remember him at all," said Tina. *Who's Lord Talson? He's the one who killed my father.*

"I don't know. I wonder if he was the one with the yellow eyes."

"You mean Lord Talson?" Tina looked confused. "Yeah, your dad made it sound like that."

"This proves that they were lying before, they do know. But why not tell me? Why not tell you how your father died?"

"They think we'll be frightened, you heard what your mom said."

"But we're not," said Kat defiantly. "I'm not scared."

"I'm not scared either," said Tina, "but I'm mad that my mom never told me and I'm mad that he killed my dad."

"Well, I'm mad that they lied to me," said Kat. "But now it also makes sense that my dad was mad when I asked about people with yellow eyes."

"Yeah, and why they looked scared," said Tina.

There was silence, apart from the storm still raging outside. Kat's flashlight cast an eerie glow over her face. Her father's words kept repeating themselves in her mind. 'You don't think she's got... What if she... What if that's why he didn't...'

"What if I've got what?" whispered Kat. "What if that's why he didn't, what?"

"I don't know," muttered Tina.

What happens when Lord Talson decides to kill someone? wondered Kat. "Who is Lord Talson?"

CHAPTER 2

THE LETTER

It was a clear June day, and the sun was shining brightly on a neatly kempt schoolyard. Two eleven-year-old sixth graders sat talking on a bench near the playground. Kat and Tina were the best students in their sixth grade class. Unlike many of their classmates, they were more interested in their personal pasts than the latest gossip. Today, like many days, Kat and Tina were discussing the content of the discussion they had overheard five years previously. Not much had changed in five years, Kat and Tina were older, taller, and wiser, but they were still asking the same questions.

"We've been talking about this same stuff since we were six, and we still don't have any good answers," said Tina.

"I'm still waiting for my parents to tell me," replied Kat. "I don't want to tell them that we listened in on them five years ago."

"Eavesdropped," said Tina smiling.

"Shut up," said Kat.

"You don't have to tell them about that to get the job done," said Tina. "They kept saying how they didn't understand how you could have connected things, so—"

"I could tell them about the dream, without admitting that we eavesdropped," Kat interrupted Tina.

"I was getting to that."

"I'm going to tell them about it tonight, since my dad's home right now. I'll fill you in on what they said tomorrow at lunch."

"Yeah, if they tell you anything," said Tina. "They might just lie again and say they don't know what the dream means."

"I'd like to see them try," said Kat coldly.

"I want to tell you something," said Kat. She and her parents were sitting at the kitchen table eating dinner.

"Alright," said her father. John Carl looked older, now at age forty-three.

"I keep having this dream," began Kat. "I'm laying on the ground, and people are running everywhere, then these huge yellow eyes appear in front of me and I feel this cold thing touch my neck. There is someone screaming in pain."

For a moment Kat saw the same anger in her father's eyes that she had seen on her sixth birthday. A moment later, John Carl sighed, he looked tired. "Listen Katerina," he said finally. "What you see in that dream really happened, at least part of it. There really is someone with yellow eyes, or at least there was then. I'm sorry I didn't tell you the first time you asked, but you were only six, and it's hard for me to talk about it."

"So, who has yellow eyes?"

"People call him Lord Talson," said John Carl quietly. "He is a terrible murderer."

"You mean I've seen him?"

"Yes, he attacked us when you were a baby."

"But, why didn't he kill me, you, and Mom?"

"He tried to kill me, but I don't think he could remember how to kill the quick way."

"What do you mean, the quick way?" asked Kat.

"Lord Talson does not kill like other murderers, he does it a different way. It is the cruelest death possible."

"What is it?"

John Carl did not reply immediately. When he did, there was a tone of hatred and anger in his voice. At the same time Kat could see an expression of sadness in his eyes. "Lord Talson kills the mind," he said softly. "He twists the mind, causing the victim to slowly lose control of himself. It is slow and horrible to witness. Sometimes it can take months or even years to kill a single person."

"But you said he tried to kill you quickly," said Kat, "why?"

"I don't know, but he failed."

"Obviously," said Kat, "but why didn't he kill me?"

"I don't know," said John Carl, shaking his head.

There was a long silence between them. "What happened to him?" Kat asked finally. "Is he still alive?"

"Yes, I think so," whispered her father, "but he has been lying low for a while

now. A lot of people would like to think he died."

"But you don't think so?"

"Put it this way Kat, he's not the man legend says he is."

"Why did he kill people in the first place?"

"Hatred," muttered John Carl. "Weird stuff kept happening to people, and no one knew who was behind it. He had followers that helped him kill people, but they were never caught either. They said people died of old age, or Alzheimer's disease, or cancer, they never figured out how his power worked."

"How does his power work? How does he destroy people's minds?" Kat asked quietly.

John Carl stared at the wall behind Kat, not really seeing it. "No one knows how Lord Talson does what he does," he replied softly.

Kat awoke to the sound of her alarm clock on Tuesday morning. She slammed her hand down on the snooze button angrily. Not already, she thought. She had not fallen asleep until the early hours of the morning, and when she had her sleep was disturbed by her recurring dream.

Kat rolled over and stared wearily at the ceiling. She wondered if Lord Talson really was alive. If he was, what was he waiting for? The same unanswered questions rolled over and over in her mind. Why didn't he just kill us?

"Let me get this straight," said Tina. "This guy, Lord Talson, is a murderer who attacked your family when you were a baby, and he's still out there somewhere right now." It was lunch, and she and Kat were sitting at a small table in the corner of the school cafeteria.

"Yep," said Kat. "He kills people slowly, and he failed to kill my dad because he tried to do it too quickly."

"He's the one who killed my dad," said Tina.

"Yeah, he is," said Kat. "He destroys people's minds somehow. My dad said he has followers who help him kill, or at least he used to."

"How does your dad know all that stuff?"

"I don't know," said Kat. "The weird thing is that he didn't kill me or my mom when he attacked us, but he killed your dad right around the same time."

"Yeah, well, it sounds like my dad died the slow way," said Tina. "I wonder why he didn't kill my mom."

"I wonder why he didn't kill you," said Kat. "Not that I regret his decision or anything," she added smiling.

"Tina," continued Kat, "do you remember what my dad said that night when we were eavesdropping? Do you remember when he said, 'what if that's why he didn't…'?"

"Yeah, I do," said Tina. "You don't think he was talking about why—"

"Why Talson didn't kill me, yeah I do," Kat finished Tina's thought. "Then he was talking about me hearing that scream, and he said, 'what if she's got…'?"

"That means he thinks you have something that made Lord Talson decide not to kill you."

"It definitely sounds like that," replied Kat.

"Your dad didn't mention the necklace, did he?"

"No, but I still think he knows about it. He wasn't telling me everything, but I just didn't want to push him because he was angry."

"At you?"

"No, at Talson for what he has done. He's scared of him and he hates him."

"He told you that?"

"Well, he told me that it was hard for him to talk about it," said Kat, "and I could just tell that he was angry about the whole thing."

"You can always tell stuff about people," said Tina. "It's pretty amazing."

Kat shrugged. "Yeah, well, people don't speak the truth, but they think it."

Tina and Kat sat in silence for a few minutes, then Kat said, "There must be a reason why Talson didn't kill us. We have to make the most of our lives, because he didn't kill us, we're alive."

"I wish he hadn't killed my dad," said Tina. "I think I would be stronger if he was alive."

"Sometimes the things that appear to make us weaker actually make us stronger," said Kat.

"Yeah, I guess. How do you know all this stuff?"

Kat smiled, "I don't know how I know, I just do."

"I'm glad you do," said Tina, smiling.

Lord Talson sat in his usual chair by the fire. He was feeling stronger, and every day his mind felt clearer, but Lord Talson was in no hurry to regain his power. He did things slowly, letting life come to him. He had learned to wait, and then wait a little longer. Lord Talson closed his eyes, the sea breeze softly blew across his face. He could still see those deep green eyes. The greatest mistake he had ever made was now something he could use to his advantage. Things always happen for a reason, and we always meet failure on the way to success, thought Talson. He liked the idea of using his own downfall to his advantage. It reinforced his belief that the greatest human strength was the ability to use one thing to achieve its apparent opposite.

Talson rose from his chair slowly and crossed the room. He leaned on his desk and looked at his reflection in the mirror on the wall behind it. Looking at his face now, Talson struggled to remember how he had looked thirteen years previously, when Sela had come to tell him of the birth of Katerina Thomason. His face was gaunt and somewhat sunken now, and his eyes were slightly dimmer than they had once been. His once agile body was now very thin and weak. Talson reminded himself that he looked and felt much better than he had just a few weeks previously. I should have died, he thought, remembering the skull-like face that had stared back at him in that mirror for over a decade. As he remembered the days when he had struggled to lift his own arm, he realized that the simple fact that he was standing there, alive, was something he could never take for granted.

There was a soft knock on the door. "Enter," said Talson, turning to face the door. A tall slim woman entered, closing the door behind her. Talson walked around his desk and sat down behind it.

"Sela," he said softly, "sit down." He indicated the chair across the desk from him.

"How are you?" Sela asked, sitting down.

Talson shrugged, "I'm better, I suppose."

"You look better," commented Sela.

Sela looked much older than she had when she had reported to Lord Talson thirteen years before. She was thirty-two years old now, and had been working for Lord Talson for nearly thirteen years. Sela had seen Talson at his strongest, and at his very weakest. She still resented the fact that she was not told why the information she collected was useful, but she knew she was in a good position at present, and did not want to risk changing that. If she made Talson angry, he would not give her the assignments she wanted. As it was now, she was getting the most important tasks, and was closer to Lord Talson than any of his other agents.

Lord Talson's agents were called the Silver Shadows. Talson liked silver because he believed that it represented the thoughts created in the mind. Silver was also the opposite of gold, the color of Lord Talson's eyes.

"So, Sela," said Talson slowly, "I trust that you have gained the necessary information?"

"Yes, I did," said Sela. "The girl does that very often." *Why in the world does he care if some kid goes outside to get the mail every morning?*

"Because," said Talson, "I want to make sure she can receive something without her parents knowledge. Do you think there is a good chance of that?"

"Yes, there is a good chance of that," murmured Sela. She did not seem surprised that Talson had just answered her unspoken thoughts, she was used to that. What surprised her was that Talson had just confided in her about why the information was important. He had never done that before. Sela could not help wondering why he wanted to send mail to a thirteen year old girl, but she was not prepared to ask Lord Talson any more questions. She did not want to seem ungrateful for the trust he had already shown her. She kept her face expressionless, not allowing Talson to see what she was thinking. Of all the Silver Shadows, Sela was the hardest for Talson to read, especially now.

Sela left Lord Talson's office and walked across Headquarters to the common room. She sat down by the empty fireplace, pondering what Lord Talson had just told her and what she had seen. *Obviously he wants to mail something to this girl.* What Sela didn't understand was why he cared so much about this kid. Sela had been sent to that house thirteen years before to find out if a baby had been born in that family. It was evident to Sela that there was something special about that family, something Talson wanted. Sela wished that Lord Talson had given her another assignment with this family. Sela wondered if he had sensed her curiosity and therefore was not going to allow her to find out more. Sela suspected that Talson was feeling slightly better than he said he was.

The door opened, interrupting Sela's thoughts. A small shifty eyed Latino man with a goatee entered, and took a seat on the opposite side of the circle from Sela. "Good evening Romez," said Sela.

"Good evening, Sela," said Romez, in a somewhat wheezy voice.

Sela liked to think that she and Romez were finally even. She did not trust him, despite the fact that he had been honest with her in the past. Roco Ramirez had been in jail several times for illegal gambling and petty crime before he had gone to prison for an illegal gambling operation that he had been running in the back room of The Sharktooth Bar. He had been running the bar as a front for his gambling operation. Fishermen would come into his bar for drinks when they came in after long trips. Once they were drunk, Roco Ramirez would get them to gamble, often cheating them out of their winnings. That money had earned him a spot in the ranks of Lord Talson, along with the nickname Romez. With that money Lord Talson had gotten into the habit of paying his agents for their work. When Roco went to prison Talson was no longer able to pay his followers, and as a result, he had lost supporters. Fortunately for Romez, his loss was felt by Lord Talson, who gave his remaining supporters, which consisted of Sela and two others, the task of breaking Roco out of prison. They succeeded, but Romez was no longer able to supply money to Talson's operations. That job had been assigned to another man. Roco wanted revenge on the fisherman who had busted his gambling operation. Because of that man, Romez had spent two years in prison, lost his top spot in Lord Talson's ranks along with his job, and was now forever indebted to Sela, Dead Paw, and Tiro for breaking him out. Roco Ramirez wanted revenge on Captain John Carl Thomason.

*   *   *

"This summer is going to rule," said Kat.

"Yeah, it is, and next year, playing in high school is going to be awesome," said Tina. It was the last day of school and the June sun was shining through the classroom window. The outdoors seemed to beckon the students stuck in the stuffy classroom. Kat and Tina, along with their eighth grade class, would be going into high school when school resumed in the fall.

Kat and Tina were looking forward to the summer, when they could go to the beach, hang out at the arcade, and play baseball in the park. Kat and Tina had played three sports in middle school, and were looking forward to doing the same in high school. Kat was the valedictorian of the eighth grade class, and Tina was the salutatorian. They were, by far, the best students in their class, both academically and athletically.

Kat and Tina were sitting in history class. Today was supposed to be a day of fun, and all of the teachers were playing games in their classes, all except for Mr. Langdon. Mr. Langdon, the history teacher, was the driest, most uninteresting person Kat had ever met. Today he was giving a lecture on something in history, but Kat really had no idea what. She had listened to him all year, taking notes and trying not to fall asleep in his classes. Today, she simply did not see why she should make the effort to engage herself in the lecture.

Kat was staring at the back of Candace Peterson's head, who was sitting in the row in front of her. Although Kat was generally popular around her schoolmates, especially her teammates, Candace Peterson hated her. Kat was somewhat proud of this, often referring to Candace as her "high-class enemy."

Candace was of medium height with dark brown hair and eyes. She lived in the hills outside the city, where the houses were much fancier than in the area where Kat and Tina lived. Candace often judged others by how much money their parents made, and bragged about how much money she had to spend on anything she wanted. She was very jealous of Kat, however, who always out performed her in school and in sports. Candace was not a bad student, or a bad player, but she was not an exceptional student and athlete, like Kat. Kat was always just a little bit better than Candace at everything.

Candace was the unquestioned leader of a group of girls that called themselves The K Klub. All the girls' names began with K, except for Candace. It was unclear whether she was excused from the club's primary requirement, or if no one in the club had noticed that Candace began with a C. Candace had hoped that Kat and Kristina would join her clique. Kat remembered the day when Candace had come up to her and Tina, surrounded by the members of the K Klub, after basketball practice one day in the winter of their sixth grade year.

"Hey girls," she had said, "you want to come to the mall with us this weekend? We're going to have lunch, and I'm paying the bill. My mom always gives me money so the girls and I can have some fun on the weekend. Krista can't come because she's grounded, so I thought I'd invite you girls."

Kat smiled to herself as she remembered her response to Candace's invitation.

"Money can't get you better friends, but it can get you a higher class enemy, didn't anyone ever tell you that?" From that day on Kat had referred to Candace as her high-class enemy.

Those were the days, thought Kat, remembering all the great times she and Tina had had because of Candace. "That's Candace, Kat's high class enemy," Tina had said, when she had been given the job of telling a new student, Sherry Littman, the names of everyone in their first period math class. Tina had gotten a detention from their very strict math teacher, Ms. Piper, for that, but she and Kat agreed that it had been worth it just for the laughs they still had over it. Kat put her head in her hands to keep from laughing aloud as she remembered that day in the beginning of the school year. She pictured the back of Candace's head in her mind's eye, that's Candace, she thought, Kat's high class enemy.

Kat's thoughts were interrupted by Sherry Littman, who had raised her hand two seats to Kat's right. Sherry was a small girl with mousey brown hair and glasses. A lot of people thought Sherry was stupid, and Candace always made fun of her for being quiet and because her family was poor. Kat did not think Sherry was stupid, on the contrary, Kat and Tina felt that they owed a lot of their fun times to Sherry for being the new student who needed to learn who everyone was. Kat knew that Sherry was smarter than she looked, but was shy and lacked confidence.

"May I use the stapler please, Mr. Langdon?" Sherry said in a small voice.

"Yes, you may," replied the history teacher in an expressionless voice.

Sherry got up to get the stapler on the front desk, but Candace stopped her. "I'll get it for you," said Candace.

"Oh, thanks," said Sherry, sitting back down. She, like many other girls, was scared of Candace.

"Oh, no problem," said Candace, smiling. She took the stapler off the desk and walked back toward Sherry. Behind Candace, Kat frowned. She knew better than to believe Candace was just being nice.

When Candace reached Sherry's desk, she held out the stapler. As Sherry reached for it, Candace grabbed it in both hands and pushed down hard. Sherry screamed in pain as the staple went into her hand. Blood poured from Sherry's palm.

"Oh, I'm so sorry," said Candace in a convincingly concerned tone. "Are you okay?"

Kat glared at Candace, she could not imagine why Candace would do something like that. Kat continued to glare at Candace, her green eyes boring into her face. Candace was so cruel, she thought. She would deserve something really painful for what she did. What could a person like Sherry possibly have done to deserve that pain? Candace was the one who deserved that. Still Kat stared at Candace. Candace stared back, smirking, as though to challenge Kat.

What are you going to do about it?

Suddenly, Kat heard a scream of pain. She looked around, but no one seemed to have noticed, just like no one seemed to have noticed that what Candace had done was intentional. Everyone was crowded around Sherry. Mr. Langdon was holding Sherry by the arm.

"Everyone stay here while I take Sherry to the nurse," he said. "Come on," he said to Sherry, "you'll be alright, it was just an accident."

Kat turned back to look at Candace. She was still looking at Kat, but was no longer smiling. Kat glared back at her. *An accident, yeah right.*

Suddenly, Candace's body went rigid and she collapsed onto the floor. She screamed in pain and then lay still.

Kat stared down at Candace. "What the—?" she muttered. Everyone was staring at Candace.

"What happened to her," gasped Candace's friend Krista. She knelt down beside

Candace, and shook her. Slowly, Candace opened her eyes and rolled over. "Are you okay?" whispered Krista.

"Kat," hissed Candace. "Kat did that."

"What are you talking about," said Kat. "I didn't even touch you."

"You were looking at me," said Candace, pushing herself up on one elbow.

"Oh, yeah," said Kat sarcastically, "I can make people fall over just by looking at them, didn't you know?"

"Shut up, Kat," said Krista. "What happened to you?" She asked Candace.

Candace did not reply immediately, she looked scared. Finally she spoke. Her voice shook slightly. "I… I don't know. My mind… it was like… I don't know how to describe… It hurt, it hurt worse than anything I ever felt. I don't know what happened." There were tears in Candace's dark eyes.

"You deserved it," said Kat quietly.

"How did you do that?" asked Tina. It was lunch and they were sitting at their usual table in the corner of the cafeteria.

"Do what?"

"Make Candace— whatever it was that happened to her. You're right that she deserved it, but how did you do that?"

"I, I didn't," stammered Kat. "Are you sure it was me?"

"No, I'm not, but, you were staring at her and then, well, you saw what happened."

"Someone screamed," said Kat.

"Yeah, Candace screamed when she fell down."

"No, before that. Candace was still standing there, sneering, and Langdon was helping Sherry to the office. Right then someone screamed." Tina was staring at Kat.

"What?" demanded Kat.

"Sorry," said Tina, "but I didn't hear anyone scream then. The only scream I heard was when Candace fell."

"Are you serious? You really didn't hear anything?"

"No, I didn't," said Tina.

Kat stared at her, her heart beating fast. "How can I hear something that no one else hears?"

"I don't know. It's just like, how do you make someone fall over without touching them?"

"Listen, Tina," said Kat. "I didn't mean to… I mean, I didn't know that would happen. I wasn't trying to do that. Are you really sure I did that?"

"Well," said Tina. "It kind of looked like it to me, and Candace obviously thought it was you. What were you thinking when it happened?"

Kat thought it was an odd question. "I was just thinking about how cruel that was of Candace, because I knew she did that on purpose. I thought that she deserved something to happen to her for that."

"Well, so was I," began Tina, "but, maybe… I mean, do you think that what actually happened to her is what she deserved?"

Kat paused, thinking. "Yeah I guess I do," she said finally. "I mean, I don't feel sorry for her, or anything. I said it then, she deserved it."

Well that's it then.

"Do you think I made her collapse and scream in pain just because I thought she deserved it?"

"Kat," said Tina, "do you remember what Candace said? My mind, it hurt worse than anything I ever felt. Kat, you don't think you can… I mean, isn't that what… what Lord Talson does?"

Kat stared at Tina, her father's words repeating themselves in her mind. 'What if she can…? What if she's got…? What if that's why he didn't…?'

"Tina, no way," she whispered. "When my father said… You don't think he meant… How could I… It's not possible."

"I know," said Tina, "but you can do stuff that no one else does."

"Like what?"

"You know what people are thinking even when they don't say it."

"Yeah, so, I'm just good at understanding people."

"Maybe too good," said Tina.

It was nearly midnight, and Kat was sitting in her dark bedroom, shining a tiny penlight at the ceiling, thinking hard about what had happened that day. Her father was at work, and wouldn't be back for a couple of days. Tamera had listened to Kat's story, but she did not seem to think that Candace's fall had anything to do with Kat. Kat was not in a mood to argue her point. She herself would have preferred to think it was not her doing, but Tina had not given her that option.

If the situation were not so serious, it would have been funny, the fall of Candace, Kat's high-class enemy, or something like that. Now, sitting on her bed, Kat tried to think of an explanation for Candace's collapse. There was none. Tina's words kept going through Kat's mind, 'isn't that what Lord Talson does?' That's impossible, thought Kat.

Kat remembered her mother saying the same thing seven years previously. Both her father and Tina seemed to think it *was* possible. What if I can do what Lord Talson does? What if that's why he didn't kill me, and why he couldn't kill my father? It was an impossible thought, but Kat could think of no explanation for how she had made Candace feel such pain without touching her, and even without truly intending it to happen. 'You can do stuff that no one else does. You do it all the time.'

Kat awoke the next morning with the warm June sun shining through her window. She got out of bed, dressed, and went downstairs to the kitchen, where her mother was sitting at the table drinking coffee.

"Good morning," Tamera said, when Kat entered.

"Good morning," said Kat. "It looks like a beautiful day outside."

"It certainly is, and now that school's out, you will have time to enjoy it."

"The mail's here," said Kat. A mail truck had just pulled up in front of the house, and the postman dropped the mail into their mailbox. "I'll get it."

She walked out the front door into the warm summer morning. Kat opened the mailbox and removed a large stack of envelopes. She leaned against the fence, casually flipping through the mail. Telephone bill, credit card bill, fishing receipts, insurance bill, Macy's summer sale, discount fishing tackle, dentist appointment reminder, all the usual stuff. Kat was about to walk back to the house to give her mother the mail, when a small silver envelope at the bottom of the pile caught her eye. She pulled it out of the stack and turned it over. Written on the front in small curvy gold letters was the name Katerina Thomason. Kat was surprised, she hardly ever received mail addressed to her. There was no return address on the left corner or on the back. Kat ripped open the envelope and pulled out a small piece of silver paper. Unfolding the paper, Kat saw the same curvy gold writing.

In the place where the trees grow in a circle there is a house you have never seen, in that house I will wait for you tonight at ten o'clock. Come to the room on the second floor at the end of the hall, you need not knock. It is important that we meet, for I need to tell you the truth that will change your life.

Kat stared at the silver paper, reading the note through several times. The place where the trees grow in a circle, she thought, could it be the place where she and Tina had gone to play when they were younger, the place they had called the hideout? To Kat's knowledge, there was no house there, but the note had said 'a house you have never seen.'

Kat slipped the mysterious letter under her shirt and went back into the house. She handed her mother the mail, minus the silver envelope, and went upstairs to her bedroom so she could make a telephone call to Tina without her mom overhearing her. She told Tina to come over to her house. "I've got to show you something," she said.

Tina was at Kat's house fifteen minutes later. Once they were in Kat's bedroom,

Kat showed her the letter in the silver envelope. Tina read the letter several times before looking up at Kat, her eyes wide. "Are they talking about the hideout?"

"I think so," said Kat.

"I've definitely never seen a house there," said Tina, "but then again, it said you've never seen it, so..."

"Do you think this is some sort of trap?" asked Kat. "Do you think it's someone we know?"

"Yeah, it has to be someone we know," said Tina. "How else would they know we used to hang out there? As far as it being a trap, you have some slick enemy if it is."

"Are you saying you think it's Candace?"

"No," said Tina immediately. "I don't think this is her style, and besides this seems a lot more serious than that. That note said 'the truth that could change your life'. Candace may be a high-class enemy, but I doubt she knows anything that can change your life. I think it might have something to do with, you know, what should I call it, your power."

"My power?" said Kat incredulously. "Are you for real? I don't have any special power."

"You wanna bet?" asked Tina grinning.

"No, not really," said Kat, "but I don't really believe that I…"

"I know you don't," said Tina, "but, I think that deep down you know that you do, and you know it was you yesterday, and you know that you meant to do it. Am I right?"

Kat paused, looking at Tina. "Yeah, you're probably right," muttered Kat. "Are you saying that I should go tonight, or that I shouldn't?"

Tina had been dreading this question. She did not want to tell Kat to go if it was a trap, but at the same time she did not want to tell her not to go if it was something important. But Kat was asking her, and no doubt was facing the same dilemma in her mind. "Kat," said Tina finally, "you always know whether to trust someone, or something. Go with that feeling, and trust yourself."

"What if I can find out the truth about the dream, my necklace, and my past? I know it's a big risk to take, it might be exactly what the person wants me to do, but I have to know. Maybe I'll even find out something about the power that I don't really believe I have."

Tina smiled slightly. "I understand what you're saying," said Tina. "Are you going to tell your parents?"

"My dad's not here," said Kat. "I'd probably talk to him about it if he was, but my mom will get scared if I tell her. No, I'm just going to have to sneak out tonight. My mom goes to bed early, so I'll be able to leave by 9:15, that way I'll be there early, and I might be able to see who the person is before they see me."

"Okay," said Tina. "I can come over here at around 8:30 and stay until you leave, if you want."

"Thanks," said Kat. "I want you to come."

Tina came at 8:30, as she had promised. They sat in the livingroom talking until nine o'clock, at which time Tamera said she was going to bed. "Good night girls," she said.

"Good night," muttered Kat without looking at her mother.

Tina and Kat sat in silence in the livingroom until 9:15. "We'd better go," said Kat finally, "I guess I should leave my mom a note, you know, just in case," she added quietly. Kat took a scrap of paper and quickly scribbled a note that she knew would never suffice if she did not return, but that was the way it had to be.

Kat and Tina walked outside together, closing the unlocked door softly behind them. A soft summer breeze was blowing as Kat stood on the sidewalk gazing at the millions of stars scattered across the clear night sky. Kat lowered her gaze, and looked down the empty street, then at Tina standing beside her. Tina looked silently back at her. There was so much Kat wanted to say to her, but the silence between them said more than words ever could. Slowly Kat undid the clasp on her necklace and handed it to Tina. She could not remember a time when she had not worn it, but now felt like the right time to take it off.

"Keep this for me, will you?" she said softly. "I just don't think I should wear it right now, for some reason."

Tina nodded and slipped the necklace into her pocket.

"Thanks for everything, Tina," said Kat. "You don't even know how much it means to me."

"Yeah, I do," said Tina, "that's why I'm here right now. You'll be okay, just go with your feeling, and be smart."

"Yeah, I will," said Kat quietly. "I'll see you, tomorrow or down the road somewhere." She hugged Tina. They let go very quickly, knowing it was not goodbye. Kat turned and started down the dimly lit street, toward the place where the trees grow in a circle. Tina watched her go for a moment, then she turned and began walking in the opposite direction.

C H A P T E R 3

THE TWO WITH THE POWER

"Shut up and get to work, you worthless fool," John Carl yelled at his deck hand,

Remi Nelson.

Remi had been complaining about something or other, John Carl didn't really care what it was. Today was one of the best fishing days of the year, and the captain was in no mood to listen to excuses. Everyone was on deck working as fast as they could.

At least Sono and Browen are worth something, thought John Carl. The two brothers, at ages thirty-one and thirty-two, were the best of the captain's crew. It was days like this when John Carl felt the loss of his first mate, Barton Louis, the most. Barty was a good man, he didn't deserve that, thought John Carl as he drove the boat, following the fish. Suddenly, the anger that permanently lived in the back of John Carl's mind came to the surface. The feeling of hatred for the man who killed his first mate gripped his chest. There was nowhere to expend his anger, only his crew, the fish, the boat, and the water.

John Carl could remember the last months of his first mate's life, before anyone knew what was happening to him. He could remember the last days, and the final moments of Barton's life. No one deserves that, he thought. Then he remembered the night after Barton had died, and how close he had come to death himself. For the first time in many years, John Carl felt lucky to be alive, lucky to have his boat and his crew.

39

He thought of his daughter, and how she had helped him realize the worth of his life. Maybe I'm gone too much, he thought, maybe I need to spend more time with her. Maybe I should tell her everything that happened that night, maybe I should show her how…before he does. He wouldn't, though, he couldn't do that.

*   *   *

Kat walked down the silent street, feeling the breeze on her face. After about five minutes of walking, she reached the park where she and Tina had always played as children. Behind the park was the circular grove of trees that Tina and Kat called the hideout. Shining the flashlight in front of her, Kat made her way around the perimeter of the park toward the trees. When she reached the trees she shined the light around, not expecting to see the house described in the note, but to her surprise she saw it immediately. In the center of a small group of trees, almost completely hidden from view, was a small two-story house. Kat approached the house slowly, holding the flashlight higher to get a better view. It was made of rough unpainted wood. The windows were all painted black so no light could come through.

The house was clearly old and Kat could not understand why she and Tina, who had been coming to the hideout for eight years, had never noticed it. When the children from the neighborhood had played hide and seek at the park, Kat had always hid in that group of trees because no one ever thought to look there. She and Tina had called it the advanced hideout. Kat was sure that there had never been a house there.

Kat stared at the building. Maybe this is some kind of magic place, she thought. Maybe that's why no one ever found me when I hid here. This is not a fairy tale, Kat reminded herself, there are no magic houses, this is real life. Kat took a deep breath to steady herself and approached the door. She wanted to slip silently into the house; she knew that the door's rusty hinges would creak loudly. She reached into her pocket and pulled out a tiny bottle of bicycle oil. Tina had always insisted upon silent entrances even when it wasn't necessary, therefore Kat was always prepared to oil door hinges.

Once the hinges were thoroughly oiled and Kat pushed the door open, it swung silently on its hinges. Kat pulled her tiny penlight out of her pocket and turned off her flashlight. The tiny beam of light was enough for her to see the floor in front of her and was less noticeable if someone was already in the house. Kat stepped over the threshold, closing the door softly behind her. Kat left her flashlight standing on one end directly in front of the door.

Kat could tell that she was standing in a narrow hallway. As her eyes adjusted to the complete darkness, she could see that there were two doors on each side of the hall, giving Kat the impression that the house was divided into two separate sides. A dark narrow staircase lay ahead of her. The stairs probably creak, thought Kat.

Kat slowly tiptoed up the stairs, taking care not to put her weight down too fast or too hard. As she reached the top, she stepped over the step second from the top.

She found herself in a hallway much like the one on the first floor. This hall, however, only had doors on the left side. Kat fought to control her fear. She wanted to turn and run away from the house, but she knew she couldn't. What would she find at the end of the hall? The mysterious person who had written the note, or something else? Perhaps even the truth that would change her life.

Kat stopped in front of the third door at the end of the hall. This must be it, she thought. She took a deep breath, and slowly pushed the door open. She shined the tiny light around the room. It was a small circular room, with rough wood walls. It was empty except for two chairs that stood in front of a small fireplace. There was no one there. Thinking that it probably was not yet ten o'clock, Kat entered the room, closing the door silently behind her. She wondered if she should hide somewhere in the room. The room was scantily furnished, and everywhere was in view of the door. There was really nowhere to hide.

Kat crossed the room and stood next to the tiny window, leaning against the wall. She turned off her light and stood in complete darkness, waiting.

From below her, Kat heard the chime of a clock. She counted ten chimes. If someone were coming, they would be there any moment. There was complete silence when the clock had finished. The silence was so intense it seemed almost unreal, as if the house around her had disappeared.

Suddenly, Kat heard a crash downstairs and the sound of something rolling across the floor. Someone had opened the door, knocking over the flashlight. Kat's heart was beating fast. She listened hard, and heard a tiny creak of the stairs. Kat waited, leaning against the wall. Her hands gripped the windowsill, reminding her that the house was still there. Slowly the door opened, and the room was suddenly bathed in silver light. A small figure dressed in black stood in the doorway, holding the light. The person moved into the room without looking at Kat. Kat was guessing it was a man by the way the person walked, but the hood of his coat obsured his face.

The man walked over to the fireplace, struck a match and threw it into the fire. Apparently, a fire had already been laid because Kat could see flames beginning to creep up the sides of the fireplace. The figure raised his head and looked directly at Kat. Suddenly, Kat was struck by an incredible feeling. His gaze, even from under the hood, projected extreme power. Kat felt like the person's eye contact was inside her. She stood frozen against the wall, unable to take her gaze off the figure holding the silver light.

As the light from the fire spread over the room the man removed his hood. He had extremely white skin, and very dark hair. He had a very thin, gaunt face and flaming yellow eyes.

"Lord Talson," breathed Kat, staring into the man's deep-set, yellow eyes.

The man stared back into Kat's green eyes, he seemed to be imagining something.

"It's Talson," he said finally. He sounded almost happy, almost sad, but not quite either one. "Thank you for oiling the door," he added, smiling slightly, "it's very quiet now."

He moved toward the fire and sat down in one of the chairs. "Sit down, Katerina," he said softly. His voice was halfway between a request and a command.

Kat crossed the room slowly, and took the seat opposite Talson. She looked into the yellow eyes she had seen so many times in her dreams.

"Are you going to kill me?" she asked quietly.

For a moment Lord Talson merely looked at her. Finally he spoke. "An interesting question, I suppose I should have expected nothing less from you. It is something I have already attempted."

"I know," said Kat.

"Or at least I planned to attempt it. Then I realized that it was not the best plan and I abandoned it. I thought it was the best plan at the time. You see, I did not realize what I was facing."

"What do you mean?"

"I mean that I did not realize what you had. When I realized it, it was almost too late for you, and even for me. I took an extreme risk, and withdrew myself from you extremely quickly, damaging my own mind. It has taken more than twelve years to heal the damage. Anyway," he continued, "in answer to your original question, no, I am not here to kill you."

Kat stared at Talson, wondering what he had meant when he said, *'what you had.'*

"By that I mean that you possessed a power and used it in a way that I did not think you would."

Kat was startled, realizing that she had not spoken her question out loud. "Can you read my mind?"

"The mind is not a book, Katerina, it is not something that is read," replied Talson. "I cannot read your mind, I can experience your mind."

Kat frowned, "What do you mean, I possess a power and used it in a way you

didn't think I would?"

"That is the reason I wanted you to come here," answered Talson. "I am here not to kill you, but to tell you about your power."

"What is it?"

"It goes by many names, some call it the sight, the feeling, the grasp, or the touch. I like to think of it as the touch, but it can manifest itself as a sight or a feeling. In essence, it is the ability and willingness to connect with and experience another person's thoughts and mental dialogues. It is a very rare combination of ability and desire. As of now there are only two individuals in the world who possess and use the complete power, and both of them are sitting in this room."

Kat stared at Talson in the firelight. "You and me," she whispered. "No one else can—? Why?"

"It is not always clear why things are," replied Talson softly.

"Why do I have it?"

"I am not sure," said Talson. "It is apparent to me that you have the power for the same reason that I have the power, however, it is not clear whether you have the power because I have it. I believe that we both have the power for the same reasons, however, these reasons are independent from each other."

"I don't understand," said Kat, puzzled, "what does that mean?"

"It means that you may choose to use your power differently from the way I use mine. Even though the reason we have the power is the same, we as individuals can make the choice to change that reason, and therefore change our own power. To say it very simply, you're Katerina and I'm Talson, you understand now?"

"Yes, and you use your power to kill," said Kat.

"Yes, I have used it to kill, I have also used it for many other things."

"But your goal is to kill people."

"At times it has been," said Talson casually. "At other times my goals have been completely different."

"Like when?" demanded Kat, becoming angry at Lord Talson's overly casual tone. She was afraid for a moment that she might have gone too far. To her surprise, however, Lord Talson smiled.

"Like right now," he said.

Kat decided to change the subject, she knew Lord Talson had won that particular dispute. "How do you know I have this power?"

"I know because I touched your mind when you were a baby and you used your power against me."

"I did? How?"

"You prevented me from entering the mind of another by grasping my mind. I then realized that I was facing someone who would use the power, but I guessed wrong as to whom it was. When I entered your mind, however, I realized my mistake. I realized that I had entered the mind of the person who was blocking me, not the other way around, as I had first thought. It was a mistake that almost cost both of us our lives, and it is why both of us are here tonight."

"Can you prove it to me?" asked Kat. "How can you know for sure that I can connect with other people's minds? I can't do what you can do. I can't tell what other people are thinking."

"You can't? Are you sure?"

"Well, not exactly what people are thinking," said Kat. "Not like you."

"The only reason why you can't do what I can do is that you are young and have not trained your mind. Your mind has the ability to do everything my mind can do."

"I suppose," said Kat. "Sometimes I know what people are about to say before they say it, and sometimes I can tell when people are lying, or telling the truth."

"Yes," said Talson, "that is a sign of your power. I wonder, do people ever remark to you about your ability to tell the way others are feeling?"

"Yes," said Kat, "my friend always asks me how I know stuff about people, but does that really prove anything?"

"It proves that you possess certain aspects of the power," replied Talson. "And remember, you need only to prove it to yourself. I have had enough proof of your power, living with a damaged mind for nearly thirteen years."

"I'm sorry," muttered Kat. She suddenly felt remorse for what she had done, and although she could not remember it, she felt that she needed to apologize for what she had put Talson through. "I didn't mean to," she added.

"You most certainly did," replied Talson, "but I accept your apology on the grounds that you had reason to be angry with me, since I was attempting to destroy your family. If anything, you have the right to be angry just because I underestimated you, thinking that you would not use the power you were given."

"Well," said Kat, "it's just that I don't remember it, so I can't really say that I did the right thing. If I could do it over—"

"I'm almost positive that if you could have that night back, you would do no different, but now I want to ask you a question. I believe it is my right, since I have already allowed you to ask me more questions tonight than I have been asked over the past thirteen years."

"I'm sorry," said Kat again, "it's just that there are a lot of things I want to know, and no one ever wants to answer my questions."

"It is quite alright," replied Talson, "it's just that I have never had anyone who I could talk to about the power. I have many unanswered questions myself, and have rarely had anyone who could answer them. That is why I am here, to help you discover your power, hopefully in ways I never could."

There was a silence in which the somewhat sad expression in Talson's yellow eyes seemed more evident. Kat realized that Talson was hoping to learn something from her, just in the way that she was so eager to learn from him. "What was it you wanted to ask me?" she asked quietly.

"Oh, yes, I almost forgot," said Talson. "Have you ever made anything happen to anyone?"

Kat thought it was an odd question. "What do you mean?"

"Can you recall a time when you made something happen to someone, when you really wanted something?"

Kat thought for a moment and then said, "Yes I did, once."

"What happened?"

"I made a girl scream, and fall on the floor," replied Kat.

"You were angry at this girl, I assume."

"Yes, I was," said Kat, "but I didn't mean it to happen."

"When you look back on the incident, do you think the girl deserved what you did to her?"

Kat found it somewhat odd that Talson had asked the same question that Tina had asked when she and Kat had discussed the experience. Kat's answer was the same. "Yes, I think she deserved it, what she did was cruel. I just don't understand how I did it."

"Tell me what you were thinking moments before the girl fell," said Talson.

"I was thinking that I hated her, and that she deserved to have something painful happen to her."

"Exactly," said Talson, "and you gave her what you thought she deserved, did you not?"

"In a way, I guess I did," replied Kat.

"That is proof of another aspect of your power. The experience you described is similar to a situation I once experienced when I was still unclear about my abilities. That was when I really began to realize that I had a unique ability, and I have spent much of my life trying to discover what it was and how to use it. And now I have one last question," continued Talson. "Have you ever heard a sound that appeared to be unheard by others?"

"Yes, a scream" said Kat. "I heard it twice, but why can't anyone else hear it? What is it?"

"Others cannot hear it because it is not an audible sound. It is the scream of the mind, heard only by a person who touches the mind of another with the intent of hurting that person. For example, you heard the scream moments before you caused Candace Peterson to collapse because you grasped her mind with the intent of hurting her. And, I should add that she is the type that tends to do things that prompt harsh actions."

"You know her?" said Kat in surprise.

"I do now."

"Sorry," muttered Kat. "It's just that I never told you her name."

"No apology necessary," replied Talson, "the name is in your mind, as is all the information about the incident. When I ask you to recount it, I can get all the information you have whether you choose to tell it to me or not. The real secret to using the power is knowing how to ask the right questions, you understand?"

"I think so," said Kat, "but I heard the scream once when I wasn't trying to hurt anyone. It was early in the morning, my mom was sleeping, and I wanted to ask her something. I was standing at the door of her bedroom when I heard the scream. Later that morning I asked her what happened, and she said she didn't scream. My father didn't hear her either, but I wasn't trying to hurt her, I just wanted to ask her something."

"I assume that you wanted an answer to your question very badly," replied Talson casually.

"Well yes, I guess I did," replied Kat.

"Not surprising, considering that you have the tendency to demand answers to your questions, as you have shown me on several occasions tonight. You may say that it is not your intent to hurt people, but I have already pushed you from my mind tonight when I was unable to provide you with satisfactory answers."

"I tried to hurt you?"

"Once or twice," said Talson casually, "you tried to force me to do what you wanted, that is, to give you the answers you wanted. I am able to push you from my mind only because I am able to use the power to protect myself. If that was not the case, and I could not block you, you would have heard the scream of my mind."

"But I don't know when I do it, I can't feel it."

"Yes, you can," said Talson, "you just don't know what it feels like, and therefore you cannot recognize it."

"But how can I tell if I do it to you again?"

Talson smiled, "next time you do it, I'll let you know."

Kat felt her fear rising again, she did not think she wanted him to let her know.

"Don't be afraid," said Talson softly, "I won't hurt you."

Kat looked at him in the firelight, "I didn't mean to hurt my mother that morning," she said softly.

"No, but you were willing to do almost anything for an answer to your question, and you were afraid that she would deny you that answer, am I right?"

Kat was astounded at how right he was. Those were exactly the thoughts that had gone through her mind when she had stood outside her parents' room seven years before. How was it that he understood her better than she understood herself?

"Because, Katerina, I have done all of these things, and had all of these feelings many times myself. I know that it is your nature to demand the truth from others, because you are willing to do almost anything for knowledge. Your thirst for knowledge is the reason you came here tonight."

"You knew I would come, didn't you?"

"No, but I knew I would come."

"You mean, you know that you would come if you were in my position, right?"

"Right," said Talson, "but I didn't need to say that, did I? For people like us

thoughts speak louder than words, Kat."

Kat sat looking at Talson, unable to think of anything to say. She was in awe of his ability to answer her unspoken questions, and make her understand his unspoken thoughts. She wondered if looking up to Talson was a mistake. Maybe her thirst for knowledge had made her cruel.

"It is not necessarily cruel. After all, knowledge is power and power is knowledge. You should remember that cruelty is only as cruel as the person subject to it."

Again, Kat could think of nothing to say to this. She wasn't sure if he wanted her to answer or not, so she asked a different question. "Why did you try to kill my father thirteen years ago? Why did you plan to kill me?"

Talson looked at Kat for a moment before he spoke. "These questions I will not answer, I have my own reasons."

"But why did you damage yourself to spare my life?"

"Do you regret my decision?" said Talson coolly.

"No," said Kat quickly, "I just wondered."

"It is not clear why, it is only clear that I made a decision and now live with it, as

do you."

Kat had expected a more satisfactory answer, but Talson's answer was not better than the explanation her father had offered. Suddenly Kat felt pain, unlike any pain she had experienced in her body. It was as though an invisible hand had grasped her mind and shook it, scrambling her thoughts together so all she could feel was the pain. Then it stopped. Lord Talson was looking directly into her face. "I told you I would let you know," he said softly.

"Does that mean I just tried to touch your mind?" Kat asked weakly. "Is that why you..."

"Something to that effect, yes," said Talson sounding almost bored. "But this time instead of gently pushing you away, I forced your attempt to enter my mind back at you, causing the power to reverse so you were affected instead of me. It is a way to block and rebound the power at the same time."

"But," said Kat, "I didn't want that to happen to you."

"No, but you wanted the result of it. If you hold a person's mind in your grasp, it is possible to bring information to the front of that person's mind against their will. It can also be done simply to cause pain, as in the case of you and Candace Peterson. If you had been able to hold her longer you could have killed her in that way, although if that had been the goal, it would have been a rather ineffective way to accomplish it."

Kat's mind was racing, trying to take in the massive amount of complex information she had gained. Talson had told her so much, but he was yet to inform her as to the reason he had brought her to the house. Kat knew that he was waiting for her to ask, but she was reluctant to do so. She feared the answer she hoped she would get. "What do you really want from me?" she asked finally, breaking the silence.

"Ah, yes," said Talson, "I had almost forgotten. I want to ask you a favor, but it is also an opportunity for you. I am the leader of an organization called the Silver Shadows. The Silver Shadows do many things, the most important of which is gaining information for me. I ask them to collect information on people, places, and other things, and I use it in various ways. There are various places that we meet, including this house and our headquarters. I want to offer you a position among the Silver Shadows, and if you accept my offer I will give you something in return."

"Do you always give people something in return when they join you?"

"It is an interesting question," replied Talson. "Not always, but since you are different from the rest of them, I am offering you something extra."

"What are you offering me?"

"Anything you want within reason, except for perhaps money, or of course, anything else I don't have."

"Why don't you have money?"

Talson smiled slightly, "because, dead people can't get jobs."

Kat almost laughed, she wasn't sure how Talson qualified as dead. "I don't want money, I want to control my power. Will you teach me how to use the power if I join the Silver Shadows?"

"Yes, I will," said Talson casually. It was as if he had known all along what Kat would want. "I do not expect you to make your decision yet," he continued. "You can return here in one month, same time, same place, if you accept the agreement. If you come I will begin working with you to help you with your power. If you decide not to accept, then there will be no reason for you to return here. I will know if you do not come. Is that clear?"

"I'm going to come," said Kat.

"Obviously," said Talson casually, "but giving a person the option to decline an offer is only polite. If you don't people will think you are what they call evil. I think you will find that politeness can go a very long way when you need it to."

"Can I ask you one more thing?"

"Oh yes, I thought you would ask that," said Talson before Kat could ask aloud. "You were able to see this house tonight because I allowed you to see it. It is another aspect of my power, that is, our power that one can develop. People see what their minds allow them to see, or in this case what my mind prevents them from seeing."

Kat paused, it scared her somewhat that Talson could answer her unspoken questions, and even control what she could and could not see. "How did you know I used to come here when I was younger?"

"It's all in your mind, Kat, everything you've done, everything you know, and many things you don't know," said Talson, sounding annoyed and almost bored again. He stood up slowly, looking into the fire that had burned down to coals during the course of their conversation. "Let's go," he said quietly, his tone was, again, somewhere in between request and command.

Kat stood up quickly and followed Talson out of the room and down the stairs. The house gave Kat an odd feeling, as though she was seeing something that was not real. When they reached the door, Talson bent down, picked up Kat's flashlight, and handed it to her. "It was clever how you put that in front of the door," he said.

"Thank you," said Kat, taking the flashlight from him.

Talson opened that now silent front door, and stepped into the warm night air. Kat followed him, looking up at the house once she was outside. It seemed hard to believe that Talson could make it invisible to her; it seemed unreal. Kat wanted to ask Talson if it was real, but it seemed like a stupid question. It must be, she thought, or he would have already answered it.

"There are truly only two ways to look at things like that," said Talson, surprising Kat. "One can either assume that everything they see is real, or that nothing they see is real. All of life is pretty much that way, it is really quite simple when you don't think about it. If, however, you do happen to think about it, everything is completely different. That's when the happy, simple life becomes the sad complicated life."

"But," began Kat, "never mind," she said, realizing that Talson was undoubtedly right.

"It has been a true pleasure meeting you Katerina," said Talson. "I have learned a lot from you tonight."

"Thank you for answering all my questions," said Kat quietly.

"You're welcome, as always," replied Talson. "And until we meet again," he held out his left hand, "we shake lefty."

Kat nodded, and they shook hands. For a moment the girl and the man stood staring at each other, then they dropped hands and the eye contact was broken. They walked around the park to the street in silence, the man in front of the girl. At the corner of the sidewalk, Talson pulled the hood of his coat over his head and turned right. Kat turned left, looking back over her shoulder, watching him go. Talson rounded the corner and disappeared from view.

C H A P T E R   4

LOYALTIES

Kat walked down the silent street, watching the beam of her flashlight in front of her. Her mind was racing with doubts and questions. Part of her wanted to tell someone everything that had happened, yet she was afraid of the reaction her parents, or Tina, might have to what she was about to tell them. She knew she had to tell someone, she could not keep it to herself forever, but she herself was not yet able to accept what she had just heard.

Tina would be the easiest person to talk to, after all she was the one who had come to Kat's house to be with her before she left on this mysterious mission, and she already knew about the letter. She had given Kat advice, and shown the loyalty of a true friend. Kat thought it would be wrong to keep Tina in the dark considering how much she already knew.

Kat knew that eventually she would have to tell her parents about Talson. She dreaded this. She could still hear the anger and hatred in her father's voice when he had spoken about Lord Talson. Kat didn't think her father would ever listen to her. Blinded by his hatred of Talson he would no doubt never fully accept Kat's decision, regardless of the reasons behind it. Kat knew that her mother would always be there for her, the way mothers always are, but she doubted whether her mother would ever understand or relate to the situation.

Kat could not forget what her father had said about Tina's father, Barton. Lord Talson had killed him. Kat was afraid of how Tina would react when Kat told her that she was considering joining the man who had killed Tina's father. What if she turned against Kat for being a traitor? Kat trusted Tina and knew that she would hear her out, but

Kat was not sure that Tina would ever accept her decision, either. Tina believed in the power, she had even called it the power. Tina had to listen; Kat needed her to listen, even if no one else did.

Lost in her thoughts, Kat had reached her house without even realizing where she was going. Kat slipped through the unlocked front door. The air was heavy with the deafening silence of night. The realness of the power comforted Kat. She turned off the flashlight and locked the door behind her. The door of the livingroom was open; the unread note lay on the table. Kat picked it up, the words filling her mind even though she could not see them in the darkness. *It was something I had to do, I had to know. I hope you understand.* Kat crumpled the note in her left hand, but the words did not fade from her mind. Her own words remained burnt in front of her eyes, even as the note curled into ashes in the dying fire. She wondered if they would ever understand.

Kat awoke the next morning to the sound of her neighbor's lawnmower. Why do people have to cut their grass so early in the morning? She rolled over and got out of bed. It was 7:30, and the summer sun was shining warmly through the window. For a moment Kat stood in the middle of her bedroom staring out the window, wondering why she felt the way she did. Then the memory of the previous night came flooding back to her. The sun shone through the window, mocking her, telling her everything was the way it always was, every morning. Kat pulled the cord on the blind sharply and it came crashing down onto the windowsill, blocking the laughing face of the sun.

Kat crossed the room and picked up the phone. She stared at it for a moment, then slowly she dialed Tina's number. She listened to the phone ringing, waiting for someone to answer, wondering what she should say.

"Hello," said a woman's voice.

"Hello, Tracy," said Kat. "I'm sorry I called so early on a weekend."

"It's alright," said Tracy Louis.

"May I speak with Tina?" asked Kat, aware that she sounded anxious despite her attempt to sound casual. Just the fact that she had called so early on a weekend was odd enough for her. She could have been much more tactful, she thought, if she had waited a few hours. Kat remembered her father saying that there are times when being tactful is impossible. This was clearly one of those times.

"I'm sorry Katerina, but I think she's still asleep, it's quite early you know."

"No, it's okay, mom," said Tina's voice in the background.

"Oh, alright, she's here Katerina, you may talk to her," said Tracy.

"Kat," breathed Tina, when she picked up the phone.

"Yeah, what's up?" said Kat, this time she succeeded in sounding extremely casual.

"Kat," said Tina exasperatedly, "don't even play that game. Don't act like nothing's happening."

Kat laughed, "Okay, you want to come over? I've got a story to tell you."

"I'll bet you do," replied Tina, "I'll be right over."

"Take your time, you don't want your mom to think something weird is going on."

"You weren't so worried about waiting to call here," said Tina, "and you weren't exactly tactful."

"Yeah, I know I wasn't," said Kat, "but it's never too late to make things look better."

"Kat, why do you always have to cover stuff up and make things look good? Why do I have to be the tactful one?"

"You won't be asking me that once I tell you what's going on," replied Kat. "It would look weird if you just went running out to see me at like seven something in the morning, everyone knows how late you always sleep."

"How about you?" said Tina, challenging Kat, "you're the one who is never awake before ten on weekends."

"Look," said Kat feigning annoyance, "the guy next door was mowing his lawn and it woke me up."

"Nice story," said Tina sarcastically, "that really makes things look good."

"I know it's dumb," said Kat, "but it's true. Just wait like a half an hour before you come over, and try to make your story sound good, alright?"

"Alright, got it," said Tina. "I always have to play the game for you."

"That's right," said Kat, "because you're the better liar between the two of us."

Kat got dressed and had breakfast with her mother. They talked about

summer vacation, and all the fun times they could have. Kat did not let her feelings of guilt show, although she knew her summer was going to end all too soon. It would be the end of her current life and the beginning of an unknown life.

"Tina's coming over," she said softly.

"Oh, good," said Tamera, "are you girls going somewhere?"

"Yeah, probably the park," said Kat.

"That should be nice."

"Yeah," muttered Kat, knowing it wouldn't be. She felt even more guilty now, looking into her mother's face. Would she ever understand? Was Tina going to understand?

"So let's hear the story," said Tina, as soon as she arrived at Kat's house and they had gone upstairs.

Kat sighed, closing her bedroom door. "Let's go down to the park, okay?"

"Sure, but why not just stay here?"

"I want to see if you can see something."

Tina gave Kat a puzzled frown, but Kat offered her friend no further explanation. Kat and Tina walked to the park in silence. When they arrived Tina asked, "Is this where you went last night?"

"I went around the back to the hideout," answered Kat.

"Is there really a house there?"

"I'll show you," replied Kat.

They walked around the park fence to the back where the circle of trees grew at the edge of the pond. Kat and Tina had not been there together in a very long time.

Tina looked around, "same old hideout," she said.

"Come here, look at the advanced hideout," said Kat, beckoning her over to the grove of trees.

Tina walked over, and peeked between the trees. "Wow," she said, "it's pretty overgrown in there now, isn't it?"

Kat stared at the old wooden house in front of her. "You're blind," she said.

"What are you talking about?"

"I'm talking about the house you can't see," said Kat.

"What?"

"Exactly," said Kat, "never mind, let's go."

Tina looked completely nonplussed as they made their way back to the main part of the park. Kat sat down under a large willow tree near the pond. Tina sat opposite her, still looking puzzled.

"Listen, Tina," said Kat. "I really want to tell you what happened last night and I'm going to, but I just want you to know that I don't expect you to really understand."

Tina looked at her uncertainly. "All right," she said finally, "but I'll try to understand."

"Okay then," said Kat. She couldn't help wondering if this was the last day of their friendship. She would hate to lose Tina, but she really didn't expect Tina to accept what she was about to tell her. Kat took a deep breath to steady herself, and began her story.

She told Tina that she had seen the house, and that she had gone inside to the room at the end of the hall on the second floor and waited for the person who had written the note to arrive. Then she told Tina how she had felt when the person had entered the room.

"Who," began Tina, "was it –?"

"Talson, yeah it was," said Kat.

Tina stared at Kat, her eyes wide. "What was he like?" she asked quietly.

Kat tried to think of a way to describe Talson, but she found no words for him.

"Was he really evil and scary?" asked Tina.

"No, not really. He was incredible though, he could tell what I was thinking and answer my questions before I asked them."

"You mean he could read your mind?"

"He said it's not mind reading, he said he can experience other people's minds."

"What's the difference?"

"I have no idea."

"So, he wasn't cruel to you? He didn't try to hurt you or kill you?"

"No, he wanted to talk to me."

"About what?"

"He told me about the power. It was just like you said, I can do what he does."

Kat recounted some of what Talson had said to her the previous night.

"So, you and him are the only ones who have this power?" asked Tina when Kat had finished.

"Pretty much," replied Kat.

"Well, that means I was right," said Tina speaking very quickly now, "when you did that thing to Candace, I told you that was like what he did. That explains what your dad said, 'maybe she's got…maybe that's why he didn't…' he was talking about the power. If you had it then Lord Talson wouldn't want to kill you." Tina paused, taking a breath. "It still doesn't explain why he would sacrifice himself to save you though, does it?"

"Well, it was his fault that I needed to be saved in the first place," said Kat somewhat bitterly.

"But, why did he care about you?"

"I think it was because he never met anyone like him before," said Kat softly. Kat knew that being like Talson was nothing to celebrate, yet she couldn't help feeling proud of it.

"But why did he try to kill you in the first place?"

"He wouldn't tell me," said Kat, "he said he had his own reasons."

"Wow," said Tina, "this is insane, I guess I really shouldn't be surprised, I knew

all along that you had some sort of ability that no one else has."

"He asked me to join him," said Kat suddenly. Tina stared at her. "He said that he's the leader of a group called the Silver Shadows, they gather information about people and places, and stuff."

"That's what your dad was talking about," said Tina. "He said that Lord Talson had followers that passed information to him that he used to kill people, remember?"

"Yeah," said Kat, "I remember."

"Did he say what he used the information for?"

"He said he uses it in many different ways."

"And he wants you to join _"

"Join the Silver Shadows, yeah he does," interrupted Kat. "He said he will teach me how to use my power if I join. He said I should come back to that house in a month if I want to join, and he will start teaching me how to control my mind."

A long silence followed Kat's explanation. Tina merely looked at her. Finally she said, "Are you gonna go?"

This was the moment Kat had been dreading. She had known that Tina would eventually ask this, but she had hoped that Tina would not ask so directly. "Yes, I am," she replied, forcing herself to look into Tina's eyes.

"I thought you would say that," was Tina's casual reply. "I mean I know you have to because you have this power, and what good is it if you don't know how to use it? The only thing is," she continued, "what if it's a trap of some sort, do you think it could be?"

"No, I don't think it is."

"I trust you in that case, you would know."

"Are you surprised that it was Talson?" Kat could not think of anything else to say. She was the one who was surprised at Tina's understanding.

"Not really," answered Tina, "I think I always knew, ever since we got that letter. I mean, I am surprised in a way, of course, but in another way, I'm not surprised at all, are you?"

"No," said Kat, it was only half true. "But I am surprised that you understand my position in the whole thing, though."

"Now I'm surprised," said Tina, "of course I understand, I'm not stupid."

"I'm making a choice, and I don't expect you to support it, even though you understand it," said Kat. "I know he killed your father."

"Yeah, he did, but I'll still be there for you. I never turned my back on you before, and I won't now. If I had wanted to turn against you I would have already done it. You know me Kat, I'm not a traitor."

"Yeah, I know you're not," muttered Kat, "but I am. I am a traitor now."

"Hey," said Tina, "you know what your dad says; there comes a time when loyalty becomes impossible."

"Yeah, along with tact and politeness. We really know what that means now, don't we?" muttered Kat.

"I'll say we do."

Kat said nothing, Tina's support meant more to her than she could say. "Thanks, Tina, you don't even know how much it means to me," she said finally.

"I really think I do," replied Tina, "I've got something of yours," she added, and slowly she pulled Kat's silver necklace out of her pocket.

Kat took it, staring at the silver diamond shape outlined in gold that hung from the silver chain. "That's his sign, it was on his light," she whispered.

"You think he gave it to you?"

"I do now."

Tina hesitated for a moment, "are you going to tell your parents everything you told me?" she asked finally.

"Well," began Kat. "I want to, but I don't think they'll understand, my father hates Talson."

"You didn't think I would understand either," Tina reminded her.

"Yeah, well, I probably should have realized that you…well —"

"—That my loyalties will always lie with you, yeah, you probably should have realized that."

Kat smiled slightly.

"Tell your parents, Kat. If they don't understand that's their problem, you tried."

"Alright, I'll try, but I doubt they will get it."

"Don't worry about how they're going to react, just tell it how it is, don't lie to them."

"You're awesome, Tina, you know that?" said Kat, smiling. "Yeah, I pretty much know that," replied Tina, laughing.

*   *   *

"I made the decision already, and nothing you say will change that," Kat said angrily.

She was sitting at the kitchen table with her mother and father. She had just finished telling them the story of the previous night.

Surprisingly, both had listened to her story without interruption until she told them about the agreement she had made with Talson. That was when her father, as she had expected, spoke up in outrage.

"Listen, Katerina," he said, managing to speak somewhat calmly, "Lord Talson is a cruel man. He will use you to kill people and perform other acts of evil. I cannot believe you would consider joining him. You do not realize what he is and what he is capable of doing. You have never seen what he has done. He has killed innocent people. Do you realize that he killed Tina's father?"

"I do realize that," said Kat stiffly.

"Barty and I had been together for years, it was horrible to see him die that way. You have never seen what happens to the people he kills, you have no idea what he will make you do. He destroys people, his enemies and his followers."

"He is going to teach me how to use my power," replied Kat.

"Yes, and by doing so he will be teaching you how to do what he does, how to destroy people. He tried to kill me, Katerina, and he will try again, except this time he will use you to kill your own family. He will use you to kill everyone you have ever cared about."

"I think you're wrong," said Kat coldly, "he won't be able to make me hurt my friends. I have to learn how to control my power so I won't do cruel things to my friends without meaning to."

"Katerina, I cannot believe this," said John Carl in a soft defeated voice. "I feared that you might have the power when you told me some of the things you heard, but I never thought Talson would come back for you. He would never do that, and even if he did, no one could have told me that you would fall for him. You cannot join this evil," John Carl's voice rose, "you cannot let your thirst for information and power blind you. You must not join Lord Talson," he finished emphatically.

"But –," began Kat.

"No, I will not let this happen," yelled John Carl, "I will not allow my daughter to join a man who has destroyed the lives of my friends! I cannot accept that."

Kat glared at him, she was angry now. "I'm going, and there's nothing you can do about it," she said in a low and angry voice.

"No you're not," said her father defiantly, "I will stop you."

"I would like to see you try," said Kat coldly. "I didn't think you would understand, but I tried anyway," she continued in a voice full of resentment. "I'm not surprised that you never had the guts to tell me the truth. Instead I had to hear it from Talson. The only reason I went last night was because I wanted to find out what happened the night when Talson tried to kill us. If you had told me before I wouldn't have gone last night, and Talson wouldn't have had the chance to ask me to join him. If you have a problem with my decision you will have to live with it, because it's your fault.

"It's your fault that I'm so thirsty for information because you never gave me that information. Talson is willing to tell me what he knows and you're not. I waited for years for you guys to tell me what if… what? Yeah," she added, "I was there, I heard you. You could have told me, but no, I would be too frightened and I was too young to handle it.

"Talson obviously doesn't think I'm too young, and he's willing to answer questions you would never answer. That's why I'm joining him. When you think about it, you guys shouldn't be so surprised."

The silence that followed Kat's outburst was broken only by the rhythmic drip of the kitchen drain. It was one of those sounds that no one ever notices except in the most uncomfortable situations of wounded silence.

Kat stared at her father with eyes full of cold resentment. She spoke again, this time in a soft anger filled voice. "I told you everything tonight, even though it was difficult. That is something you have never done for me. You didn't even deserve to know."

She stared into her father's hard face. This time she knew what she was about to do, it was not an accident like before. Kat heard her father's yell of pain, although he had not opened his mouth. John Carl staggered backward toward the wall, his face contorted. Kat, surprised by the fact that he had not collapsed to the floor the way Candace had, released him. At the moment when her mind left his Kat felt pain, she remembered too late what Talson had told her about releasing someone too quickly. She closed her eyes for a moment, letting the pain pass.

John Carl was leaning against the wall staring at her. He did not look scared and he did not look angry anymore. He now looked very sad. He said nothing and merely continued to stare at Kat.

"You deserved that," she said, and turning her back on her father, she walked out of the kitchen and disappeared up the stairs.

Kat lay on her bed, fuming. Everything she had wanted to say to her father had finally come out tonight. She had kept her feelings inside for far too long, and they had grown each time her questions were left unanswered. Now, as she lay on the bed in her dark bedroom, her feeling of resentment for her father seemed to boil inside her. He had not told her what he knew about Lord Talson or about his suspicions that she might share his power. He had known all that time, and never told her.

She knew that he knew about the necklace and still would not tell her. Did he think she would rather hear it from Talson? She would much rather have her father tell her than someone who had tried to kill him. Even though Talson knew more, Kat would still prefer to hear it from her father. But no, thought Kat, he never told me so I had to ask Talson. Now I have to join him to get my questions answered. Kat knew that if her father had told her about the power she would not have felt so obligated to go and wait for the anonymous author of the note she had found in her mailbox. Talson had known she would come. He had said, 'your thirst for knowledge is the reason you came here tonight.' If her father had not made her so thirsty for information she would not have gone.

Despite her anger toward her father, Kat did not regret having met Talson. His power had amazed her, and given her a strong desire to develop her own. However, the fact that her father did not accept her decision, though it was not a surprise, made Kat feel rejected, alone, and even guilty. It's times like these when we really need our family and friends, thought Kat. At least Tina was there, she understood. Kat remembered how her mother had remained silent throughout the conversation that night, which meant she might have reacted differently from John Carl, however, Kat was not hopeful. She felt a great loss.

There's nothing I can do about it, thought Kat. I tried. All she could do now was wait and go to Talson in a month. Kat saw Talson's face with his huge yellow eyes. She thought about the way he had smiled because she had asked so many questions, and how he had risked his life to save her when he had realized she had the power. He had spent his life trying to discover the truth behind the workings of the mind and had waited so long for another of his kind. Kat remembered how he had thanked her so casually for oiling the door and asked her to sit down in a voice that was half request, half command. He had answered her questions before she asked them, and understood Kat better than she understood herself. Kat remembered the feeling she had felt when the little man with the silver light had first entered the room at the end of the hall. Slowly Kat closed her eyes, there was no longer any doubt in her mind about what she should do.

CHAPTER 5

THE LAST DAYS

The hot summer sun shone down brightly, reflecting off the calm blue sea. Birds circled in the cloudless sky, their calls echoing through the clear air. On the deck of the Royal Mast the crew was working as fast as they could. The fishing wasn't great, but the crew was short a man.

Sono Silven was driving the boat instead of working on deck. Normally Captain John Carl Thomason would be driving, but today the Captain had stayed below deck and told Sono to take charge. Sono was not complaining. He was enjoying being captain for a day, and he was very pleased that John Carl trusted him with the responsibilities. However, he could not help but wonder why his captain was not working today. John Carl had said he was not feeling well, but Sono could not remember a day when his captain had been too sick to work. He always worked no matter how bad he was feeling or how rough the conditions were. Sono could only remember one day in all his time with John Carl that they had come in early because of bad weather, and that was many years ago.

Sono's thoughts were interrupted by his brother, Browen, who had come up to stand next to him at the wheel. "What do you think is up with Cap?" he asked in a low voice.

"No idea," muttered Sono.

"It's not like him to miss a day of work, even if he is sick."

"I know."

"Is he just sitting down there, or what?" asked Browen.

"I guess."

"He doesn't seem himself lately, does he? It seems like something is bothering him."

"Yeah," said Sono, "maybe it's his wife or something. Maybe they're disagreeing a lot now, that happens to people when they're in their forties. You know, midlife crisis and all that."

Browen laughed, "Maybe, but it's still not like Cap, he never misses a day for anything. Normally, he wouldn't care if it was blowing a hurricane out here."

"I'm over this," said Sono, "I'm gonna go down there and see what the hell is going on. Will you drive for a couple minutes?"

"Sure, no problem."

Sono descended below deck and headed to the door of the Captain's room. The door was ajar. Sono silently peered through the crack. Captain John Carl was standing with his back to the door, looking out at the sea through the porthole. He was bent over slightly, his hands gripping the bottom of the porthole. John Carl raised his head slightly and Sono caught sight of his face reflected in the cloudy glass. It took Sono a moment before he realized that his captain had been crying. His face was actually stained with tears and his eyes were somewhat red. Sono was frozen in shock.

Suddenly John Carl's face in the glass frowned. Sono withdrew from the door quickly, hoping the Captain had not caught sight of him. He felt guilty as though he had intruded on something private. He turned and walked quickly up the steps to the deck.

"What was he doing down there?" Browen asked as soon as Sono returned.

Sono stood staring over the rail at the calm water for a moment, unsure of whether to tell Browen what he had just seen. "Browen," he said quietly, "he was standing down there in his room crying."

Browen stared at Sono, his hands on the wheel went slightly limp. He seemed just as shocked as Sono had been.

"I don't think he saw me," muttered Sono, "he might have, though, I'm not sure. He had his back turned and I left in a hurry."

"I don't know what to say," said Browen. "You mean he was actually crying? Are you sure?"

"Oh yeah, I'm positive, I saw his face."

"I just can't imagine Cap crying. He's got to be the toughest person I've ever met. He never gets upset about anything."

"I know, he's really insensitive most of the time. Not the type to start crying, even if his wife is ditching him or something."

"Maybe someone in his family died," said Browen. "He still doesn't seem like the type that would cry. I just can't imagine him crying."

"Neither could I until about five minutes ago."

"Whatever it is, it must be really serious if he's crying about it. Are you going to talk to him about it?"

"I don't want to admit I saw him crying," said Sono. "Do you think I should?"

"You could always be more subtle about it and just ask him if he's okay."

"I doubt he'll want to talk about it, but I could try," said Sono reluctantly.

"You're the one who doesn't want to talk about it," said Browen, "maybe we should stop trying to be so macho about it and go down there and ask him what the hell is going on."

"He'll be mad," muttered Sono.

"So what? It's for his own good."

"Yeah, but I really don't want to see a forty-year-old dude crying again."

"Get over it, being loyal isn't always convenient."

"He told us to leave him alone, though," protested Sono.

"Sometimes loyalty is not about obeying orders…"

"…Sometimes it's about knowing when to disobey orders for someone's own good," finished Sono. "I know, you're right."

"Hey, Sono," said a voice behind them. Browen and Sono turned to see Tido, one of Captain John Carl's deck hands. "Cap said we're going in today, he wants us back at the dock by dark."

"By dark?" repeated Sono.

"That's what he just told me to tell you," said Tido defensively.

"I believe you, mate," said Sono. "Did he say why we're cutting the trip short?"

"He said he thinks we got enough and the price should be good."

"Okay," said Sono. "We'd better move fast if we're gonna get to the dock by dark." He turned and shouted orders to the crew on deck.

"That's not like Cap," said Browen as soon as Tido had gone back to work on deck. "We didn't even do that good today, who does he think he's kidding?"

"When's the last time Cap cut a trip short because he thought we'd caught enough?"

"Never," said Browen. "This is insane. Something really weird must be going on, some reason why Cap has to be home by tonight."

"I've got to go talk to him tonight as soon as we get in."

"I'll be with you, mate," said Browen quietly.

Sono and Browen planned to approach their captain while the rest of the crew was unloading the catch onto the dock, however, as soon as John Carl got off the boat he told Sono to take charge and hurried away. Sono and Browen watched him heading down the street until he disappeared into a small wooden building across from the dock called The Sharktooth Bar.

It was evening, and the strong June sun was sinking below the horizon, leaving it streaked with a reddish hue. Sono was reluctant to leave the rest of the crew when he was supposed to be in charge. Browen reminded him that this might be the only chance they got to speak to their captain.

"I guess we leave Tido in charge then?" muttered Sono.

His brother frowned, "Tido?" he repeated.

"Better him than Remi rat face."

"Yeah, you've got a point there."

"Hey Tido," called Sono. "We need to go talk to Cap for a second, keep stuff under control, alright?"

"Can do, sir," said Tido.

Tiden Offerman was a tall, somewhat handsome, twenty year-old man with blonde hair. He was a hard working fisherman who seemed determined to prove himself. Captain John Carl had had many different people in Tiden's place over the years, and none of them had lasted very long. John Carl was a hard man to work for without a doubt, but Sono and Brown had been there thirteen years, and Remi Nelson had been there even longer. Tido had only been with John Carl for six months, but he seemed to take orders well, and was reliable and willing to work.

"You don't think it was a mistake to leave Tido in charge do you?" Sono asked his brother as they set off down the waterfront street toward the bar.

"No," answered Browen, "he seems like a really cool guy so far, he listens and he works pretty hard, I think he'll be fine. Besides, what's really gonna happen while we're gone?"

"You never know," said Sono, "Remi might slip on a banana peel and fall flat on his face again."

Browen grinned, "yeah, that could be inconvenient for Tido, he'll handle it though."

"I sort of feel sorry for him having to be in charge of that idiot."

"Yeah, sometimes I wonder why Cap keeps him, can't he get someone better?"

"He's had Remi forever, even longer than us, I guess he likes him."

"I don't really think he does, I mean, he's always yelling at him."

"But then again, he's always yelling at us too, and he likes us, so who knows?"

"You know what they say, you can never really know Captain J.C."

"I guess we really know what that means now, don't we?" said Sono darkly.

Sono and Browen reached The Sharktooth Bar and let themselves inside. The place was not crowded. There were only about a half a dozen fishermen sitting at the bar. The crowd would no doubt come later that night. Sono and Browen spotted their captain sitting alone at the end of the counter far from the other customers. The brothers headed straight across the barroom toward him. John Carl looked up as they approached. His face was pale and he looked very strained.

"What the hell are you two doing here?" he snapped. "You're supposed to be in charge, Sono. What the hell do you think you're doing?"

Sono was somewhat annoyed at this, and he decided to be straightforward from here on. "Wondering what the hell you're doing," he retorted. "What the hell is going on?" he continued, taking a seat on John Carl's left.

Browen sat on the captain's other side.

"What the hell are you talking about?" said John Carl coldly.

"I'm talking about you, genius," retorted Sono. "We're wondering what the hell is going on with you. Why are you sitting in your room on your ass when you should be working?"

At this point it was clear that Sono had won. John Carl did not seem to be able to think of an answer to his question. He merely sat there staring into his drink, looking tired and defeated.

"Listen Cap," said Sono, dropping his voice so it was barely above a whisper. "We're worried about you, mate. We know something is going on, and we want to know what."

"It's nothing," muttered John Carl without looking at Sono.

"Don't lie," said Sono, "we want to help you out, mate."

There was a pause then John Carl said, in a barely audible voice, "I'm scared."

"Scared of what?" said Sono and Browen in unison.

"He did it, he's back to his old ways."

"Who's back to what old ways?"

"Talson," whispered John Carl. "Son-of-a_" He turned away, taking a large

gulp of his drink.

Sono and Browen stared at each other over their captain for a moment. "*Lord* Talson?" Sono whispered finally, "are you serious? I thought he died years ago."

"No," said John Carl. "He didn't die, that traitor saved his neck."

"How do you know that?" said Sono, his voice faltered slightly.

"I've been told that he is back," said John Carl quickly.

"How do you know it's the truth?" asked Browen.

There was a long silence. John Carl stared at the blank wall behind the bar. "I just can't stand it," he said finally, his voice shook slightly as he spoke. "It's all my fault. I thought he wouldn't." John Carl slumped forward onto the counter and put his head in his hands.

Sono and Browen looked at each other over their captain's head in shocked silence. Neither one could think of anything to say.

*   *   *

Kat awoke very early on July thirteenth. She stared at the ceiling above her bed without really seeing it. She had been having the same recurring dream ever since she could remember, but only now did she understand what it meant. Kat reached up and touched the silver necklace around her neck and stared at the silver diamond shape that hung from the chain. That cold feeling on her neck in the dream had been Talson hanging this necklace around her neck the night he had planned to kill her. Kat finally understood what her father had always known but refused to tell her.

Kat rolled over and got slowly out of bed. The clock on her bedside table read 6:00 am. Outside the window the sun was coming over the horizon, promising another spectacular summer day. Kat had no idea what she was going to do with herself until ten o'clock that night. She thought about just staying in her room so she wouldn't have to talk to anyone. Then she thought better of it. Today is my last day, she thought, I might as well make the most of it.

Kat dressed and walked slowly downstairs, watching her feet stepping down one stair at a time. She felt like she was walking in a dream where time was running at half its normal speed. When she entered the kitchen, she stopped short in surprise. Her father was sitting at the kitchen table sipping a cup of coffee and pretending to read the newspaper. Kat knew for a fact that her father never really *read* the paper he just looked at the pages to make himself look occupied.

Kat was thoroughly shocked to see him. She knew that he was not scheduled to come home for another four days. "Good morning," she said softly as she entered.

John Carl did not look up, he merely grunted stiffly.

"I didn't know you were coming home today, I thought you were going to be gone until at least Tuesday or something."

John Carl merely shrugged without looking at her, "Something like that," he muttered.

Kat sat down opposite her father. He was still determined not to make eye contact with her, and continued to stare at the newspaper, pretending to concentrate on the news.

"Did you have a good trip? Were the fish biting?" asked Kat, determined to make conversation.

John Carl nodded, then said in a somewhat cold voice, "Yeah, they were biting, but no, I didn't have a very good trip. Why are you so interested?"

Kat stared at her father, who still refused to return her gaze. "I'm always interested in how many fish you guys get and how the trip goes," she said defensively. It was true that ever since she was a little girl Kat had always loved to listen to her father tell stories about his fishing trips. And, up until very recently, John Carl had always told her everything that happened on the trips right down to how many fathoms deep the water was and how hard it was to pull in the fish. Kat had always been interested in her father's job.

John Carl said nothing. He merely sat there staring at the newspaper with an angry expression on his face.

"Listen," said Kat quietly, "I don't want you to be angry with me. I'm sorry about what I did a few weeks ago. I didn't really mean to hurt you, sometimes I just lose control."

"Of course you meant to, or else you wouldn't have done what you did," said John Carl, finally looking at Kat. "I assume you're still going tonight, then?"

Kat look directly back into her father's face, "Yes, I'm going."

"Right," said John Carl, "then we're still enemies."

"Only if you want to look at it like that," said Kat.

"Well, I do look at it like that whether I want to or not," said her father coldly. "If you're going with Talson then we're enemies, that's the deal."

"Okay," said Kat just as coldly, "I'm glad we cleared that up, then." She refrained from attacking her father's mind again, remembering how odd it had been the last time. Kat found, for the first time in her life, she had no idea what her father was thinking. His mind seemed completely blank. Kat realized quite suddenly that she had always relied on what people were thinking to guide her actions. Her father's mind seemed blank and Kat was lost for words.

*　　*　　*

Kat and Tina sat under a large tree in the park under the afternoon sun, discussing Kat's meeting with her father that morning.

"Personally, I think he's being ridiculous," said Tina, after Kat had told her the story. "I mean it's one thing to hate Talson and not want you to join him, but to actually call you his enemy, that's crazy. I could see it if this was someone he just hired and then found out who they worked for, but you're his daughter, he can't just turn against you like that."

"Apparently he can," said Kat coolly. "He decided he hates me now, and he's okay with it."

"He doesn't hate you," said Tina, "and I'll bet you he's not okay with it."

"Yeah, well if he doesn't, he's doing a pretty good impression of it," said Kat angrily.

"In the end he won't hate you though," said Tina. "Deep down he still cares about you because he's your dad."

"Yeah, well, in the end he is going to regret deciding to be my enemy. He'll wish he thought it over a little before he went against the person who saved his life."

Tina looked at Kat without reply. She was thinking that John Carl *would* no doubt regret what he'd said to his daughter that morning whether he had meant it or not. Kat believed in meaning what you say and saying what you mean. She would act as though you meant every word you said, even if she knew you didn't. 'If you didn't mean it, then, why the hell did you say it?' Tina had never understood why Kat was like that, especially since she could tell what other people were thinking. Words shouldn't matter to her, thought Tina. *Maybe Talson knows something that John Carl forgot about.* "So it's ten tonight, right," said Tina finally.

"Yeah," said Kat.

"Well I'm coming down to your place at like nine or something, then."

"No," said Kat, "don't."

"Don't be stupid, say what you mean," said Tina, smiling inwardly.

"Fine, come if you really want to," said Kat.

"You know you want me to," said Tina.

Kat smiled. The fact that Tina wanted to be there for her before she left that night meant more to her than she could even explain.

"You're just lucky you have a father, Kat," said Tina suddenly. "Talson killed my dad before I ever knew him. I still want revenge for that."

"I know," said Kat, "we definitely need revenge for that. I don't want to be with Talson forever, eventually we'll have to do something about him." *I don't think there's much we can do about him.*

"Words matter Tina, they make your thoughts real," said Kat looking directly at Tina now. "There's always something we can do, come on, it's us, we can do anything."

Tina looked up at Kat and smiled slightly. She wouldn't put it past her friend to someday figure out a way to do something about Talson.

Kat's father was not at home when Kat returned to the house late that afternoon. Kat was not surprised, considering that they had already said their goodbyes that morning. Kat's mother acted as if nothing out of the ordinary was happening, which again was not a surprise. Kat's life at home had become depressing over the past few weeks. Although each of her parents had acted very differently toward the situation, neither of them seemed able to face it.

"Tina is coming down here tonight," Kat told her mother after they had eaten dinner. She wasn't sure whether it was wise to tell her mother this, but she felt that she had to say something just to make sure her mother hadn't forgotten what she was doing.

"That's very loyal of her," replied Tamera. "What time are you leaving?"

Kat was so surprised by her mother's reaction that she did not reply immediately. "I'm leaving around 9:30," she muttered finally.

Just before nine that night Tamera said that she was going to bed. Kat looked at her for a moment, then said, "Goodnight, thanks for... you know…everything."

Her mother smiled, "You're welcome. Will I see you in the morning?"

"Yes," said Kat, "I think so."

"Well, good luck," said Tamera. She turned, crossed the livingroom and disappeared up the stairs.

Kat sat in the livingroom, staring into the empty fireplace. She heard a soft rhythmic knock on the front door.

"Why'd you knock?" asked Kat as she opened the front door.

"I don't know," said Tina, "I guess I just have good manners tonight."

"Wow, that's a first," said Kat grinning.

"Shut up," said Tina laughing.

"I told my mom you were coming tonight."

"Well, what do you know?" said Tina sarcastically, "I'm not the only one who remembered my manners tonight." She dropped her sarcastic tone, "what did she say when you told her?" she asked.

"She said it was very loyal of you, and then she asked me what time I was leaving," said Kat.

"Wow," said Tina, "she's reacting a little different than your dad, isn't she?"

"I'll say she is," said Kat. "She was acting like I was going to a party or something."

"I wonder if she and your dad have been fighting about it?" said Tina.

"I don't know, he's never here, and she never mentions him when we talk now. I'll bet you're right, they probably are arguing about it."

"It seems like your mom totally accepts your decision."

"I don't know, she never talks about it. It's like it doesn't matter to her."

"It probably doesn't," said Tina. "She'll still love you no matter who you work for. Moms are cool like that."

Kat grinned, "Yeah, they are. My mom asked me if she'll see me in the morning."

"Nice question," said Tina.

"I said I thought she would," said Kat.

"Nice answer."

"I'd better go," said Kat, looking up at the clock.

Kat took her flashlight and she and Tina walked outside together to the sidewalk. They looked at each other for a moment without speaking.

"I know you'll come back, so I'm not gonna say goodbye," said Tina, "you okay with that?"

"Yep, I'm good with it," said Kat, "I always come back."

Kat turned left and Tina turned right. Above them, Tamera watched from her bedroom window. The two girls walked in opposite directions down the silent street. Tina paused at the corner then looked back for a moment. Kat paused at the corner too, then she turned down the dark side street and disappeared from view.

CHAPTER 6

PAIN

As Kat walked through the warm summer night following the beam of her flashlight, she wondered whether she was being tricked by Talson. Kat had confidence in herself to judge people's intentions and she knew she was not easily fooled, but Talson was different. He could fool anyone; make them think anything he wanted whenever he wanted. Kat knew that Talson understood her personality very well, possibly even better than she herself did. Kat could not help wondering and fearing that he would eventually try to kill her again.

Tina's words came back to Kat. 'Trust yourself, you always know people. Just go with your feeling.' Kat always had gone with her feeling, but would her feeling be enough with Talson? Kat's mother had always told her that she had the gift of understanding people, and told her never to let anything make her doubt her feeling about something. Now, Kat had the feeling that Talson was telling the truth, but someone with his power was no doubt capable of completely fooling her into trusting him. As impressed as Kat was with Talson, she did not fully trust him, especially not after everything she had heard about him. Kat took a deep breath as she walked through the still night. It was a long hard road that now lay before her. Kat made her way around the edge of the park where the trees grew in a circle. There, in the middle of the trees, was the house that only she, Talson, and the other Silver Shadows could see. As she looked up at the house, Kat wondered how Talson could make the place invisible to everyone other than his followers. Kat stepped up to the front door of the old house and pushed it open. It swung smoothly on its newly oiled hinges. Kat remembered how shocked she had been when Talson had thanked her for oiling the door. She had been so scared at the time, yet even then it was funny to think that a man like Lord Talson would say something like that. Talson was so unusual; Kat could not help but wonder how he had come to be what he was. She realized that she really had no idea how old Talson was, where he came from, or anything else about him.

Kat walked up the narrow staircase, taking care to jump the second step from the top. She walked slowly down the hall to the last room and paused for a moment. She thought she heard voices coming from downstairs. Kat stood still for a moment, then pushed the door open.

A fire was already burning in the fireplace. This time, Lord Talson was sitting in a chair in front of the fire waiting for Kat, his yellow eyes gleaming in the firelight. Talson had looked rather tall to Kat when she had seen him standing in the doorway the previous month, but now she realized that he was a very small man.

"Funny how that doorway makes people look taller, isn't it?"

Kat was startled, "I guess," she said, not knowing how to reply.

"Let me tell you something," said Talson with a faint smile, "anything that makes me look tall is probably an optical illusion. Please sit down," he added, gesturing to the chair opposite him.

Kat sat down, still speechless.

"I didn't hear the stairs creak when you came up," continued Talson. "Just out of curiosity, how did you know that the second step from the top is the one that creaks?"

Just out of curiosity, how did you know I knew that. "The second step from the top always creaks," said Kat simply, "and don't ask how I know that," she added, thinking that that was likely to be Talson's next question.

Talson smiled. "See, knowing what other people are thinking isn't always as hard as most people imagine. Many times all it takes is simple human experience."

"How come I can see this house and other people can't?" asked Kat.

"Because their minds are blind," answered Talson. There was a hint of bitterness in his voice, almost as if Talson envied normal people. "Someday you will have enough knowledge of the power for me to explain how it works, but I certainly hope I won't have to. It's rather complicated."

Kat nodded though she did not really understand. "How old are you?" she asked.

"Old," replied Talson, he sounded somewhat bored. "Older than you, anyway," he added.

"Did you have a name before you were Lord Talson?" asked Kat. Now that she knew Talson was tolerant of her questions, Kat wanted to ask as many things as she could. Talson did not reply. Kat looked into his yellow eyes, but his expression was impossible to read.

"I cannot tell you everything, Katerina," said Talson quietly. "If you are always given the information you seek then you will not gain knowledge. You must find some things out for yourself, because this is the only way to challenge your mind. You cannot expect me to tell you everything I know about the power or about you. I undoubtedly know many things about you that you do not, but I will not tell you all of those things. You must find the way in your own life and learn to see your life in your own way. You cannot expect to find the answers to your questions if you are not working to find them. No one is going to give you answers, you must find the answers by other means."

"But if you know things that I don't know, why not tell me?" asked Kat.

"Have I not made myself clear? I just told you exactly why not."

Kat looked at Talson. He did not look angry, but Kat knew that the subject was now closed.

"May I make a suggestion to you?" asked Talson.

Kat looked up somewhat surprised.

"I suggest that you do something to repair your current relationship with your father. Accounting him as your enemy is only going to make you weaker."

"How do you know about that?"

"Sela," said Talson simply. "She is one of the Silver Shadows, and she has been watching you since you were a baby." Talson smiled at the expression on Kat's face. "Not all the time," he added still smiling, "just every few years. You'll have a chance to meet her later. She'll like that, after all these years of seeing you."

Kat could think of nothing to say to this. The idea that there was someone who had been spying on her without her knowledge for her entire life was too much for words. It made Kat angry. *How come I never saw her?*

"You probably did see her. You just didn't know who she was or what she was doing."

"Is that how you knew I used to come here, she told you?"

"No," said Talson with a faint smile, "I saw you out my window."

"Why?" Kat demanded angrily. "Why did you care about watching me since I was a baby?"

"I thought we discussed this last time we met," said Talson quietly.

Kat felt slightly ashamed of herself. She knew they had talked about that. Kat realized that Talson did not appreciate having to repeat himself.

"I'm sorry," muttered Kat, looking away from Talson's face.

Talson nodded, "We all make mistakes," he said. "The important thing is recognizing them and not repeating them."

Kat could tell by the tone in which Talson said the word *repeat* that he disliked repeating his words or his mistakes.

"Yes, it does rather bother me, I must admit," said Talson, breaking the silence.

Kat was startled slightly, she wasn't completely used to Talson responding to her unspoken thoughts.

"So, on a more businesslike note," said Talson, "there are some things I need to make sure you and I understand. Firstly, I assume that you followed my suggestion and thought about the offer I made to you before coming to your decision, and," he continued, "since you have returned here tonight, I further assume that you have made the decision to accept the offer."

"Yes," said Kat. "And you are prepared to do your part of the exchange too, right?"

"Yes," replied Talson. "I am very much prepared and I confess that I have been looking forward to doing that particular aspect of, as you called it, the exchange. Perhaps I should know better than to ask you this, but do you have any questions?"

"Yes," said Kat, she tried not to think. She did not want Talson to know her thoughts at that moment. "I will still live my life the same way that I do now, right?"

"Doubtfully," replied Talson, but he offered no further explanation.

"Are any of your other followers my age?" asked Kat.

"No," said Talson. "You are the youngest by quite a bit. In fact, you will be the youngest Silver Shadow we've ever had."

"Can I tell other people about the things we talk about?" asked Kat, knowing the answer.

"No, I would advise you not to discuss anything you do for me with anyone that is not one of us. Doing that is very risky, but use your good judgment with people that aren't just *anybody*, you understand?"

"Yes," said Kat, "I understand."

"Very well then," said Talson. "Now I believe we should discuss what we are going to do so that you can learn how to use your power. We will meet here, I think. When do you want our sessions to be?"

Kat thought for a moment. She thought that she would want the classes to be at night. "Maybe at eight or nine at night," she suggested.

"Sounds good," said Talson, "let's do nine. You need to work at least three, probably four times per week. What days do you want?"

"The weekend, probably," said Kat. "Maybe Friday and Saturday."

"How about Tuesday, Friday, Saturday, Sunday?" said Talson. "We could add Mondays when I'm available. We don't have to stick to that schedule, just whenever you need it. The more we work on it the better you'll get."

Kat nodded. She knew that this schedule would be fine during the summer, but once school started it was going to be a much different story. I guess I'll worry about that when the time comes, she thought.

"Very well," said Talson, "I think we have discussed everything. If this is your final decision, then we can make it official."

Kat paused for a moment, thinking things over. She was somewhat afraid of what 'making it official' might mean, but she was equally aware of the fact that she could be making a big mistake if she walked away from Talson. Finally she nodded slowly, "I'm in," she said softly.

Talson nodded expressionlessly. "We shake lefty," he said, extending his hand.

As soon as she touched his hand a hot pain shot through Kat's hand. Kat had to try very hard not to scream. Talson let go slowly, opening his hand as if nothing out of the ordinary had occurred. Kat looked at her hand, but there was no mark.

"What was that?" whispered Kat finally.

"Pain," replied Talson simply.

"But why? Did you just create that pain with your mind?"

"Sadly, yes. It's the same thing you did to that girl at school. It's the scream you heard, pain in the mind. It's not real pain, but it seems real to the person experiencing it. Pain is relative to experience, Kat. If you can see someone's thoughts you will know what pain is to them, and therefore you will know how to hurt them."

"But my hand, why did you do that?" asked Kat, still somewhat shocked.

"It is always interesting to see how different people react," Talson said casually.

"You didn't scream, which suggests that you have a fairly high pain tolerance, which you will need once you begin working with the power."

Kat was not thrilled by Talson's fascination with how different people reacted to pain. It was, in her opinion, a very cruel thing to find interesting.

"Pain is a strange thing," said Talson, "amazingly powerful. How different people react to pain tells more about who they are as a person than anything else."

Kat looked away from Talson. This last statement had scared her. She remembered when her father had said that death at the hands of Lord Talson was slow and painful, by far the cruelest and most painful way to die. Kat looked back into Talson's yellow eyes. "That's how you do it, isn't it?" she said quietly. "That's what you have to find out, that's why you need spies. Pain, that's how you do it."

Talson looked at Kat for a long time. He looked slightly pleased, surprised, and amused at the same time. "Yes," he said finally. "It does not completely cover

everything, but to put it in very plain, straightforward terms: yes that is how I do what I do. It's how minds are created and how they are destroyed."

"It is a shame," added Talson. "All these people who have worked for me for so long still haven't noticed that. You figured it out within the first ten minutes of becoming a Silver Shadow. The range of human abilities, there's another fascinating phenomenon."

Kat descended the stairs of the house but this time she did not try to prevent them from creaking. Her hand was still somewhat painful. Talson had told her to go down to the main room because there would be several other Silver Shadows there who she should meet. Kat crossed the hall and opened the first door on the left with her right hand.

It was a fairly large room with a high ceiling, but it was furnished like a livingroom. There was a fireplace at the far end of the room with many armchairs around it. Two people were playing cards at a table nearby, while two others were lounging in armchairs, watching television.

Everyone looked up as Kat entered. "Hey Kat," said a casual woman's voice from the card table. Kat turned, surprised anyone would know her name. A young woman with brown eyes and light hair had stood up at the table. Kat thought that she looked somewhat familiar. "I'm Sela," said the woman coming toward Kat and extending her hand.

"I've heard about you," said Kat shaking her hand.

Sela smiled, "Yeah, I've heard about you too."

"Usually we shake hands lefty," said a young black man at the card table. "But not on your first day, because, well, you know what I mean."

"Yeah," said Kat, moving her left hand uncomfortably.

"Yeah, it'll heal though," said the man. "I'm Milro by the way." He shook Kat's right hand. "My name's Milton Roberts, but everyone calls me Milro for short 'cause that's what he calls me, you know what I mean?"

"Yeah," said Kat, "My real name is Katerina but everyone calls me Kat."

"Well, at least until he starts calling you something else," said Sela. "He comes up with names for everyone."

"Why is he obsessed with nicknames?" asked Kat.

"Who knows?" said Milro with a shrug.

"You got that right," said Kat quietly.

"The boss is a little crazy, but he's cool, you'll see," said a young man with light hair who had been watching television. "I'm Mevsin," he added to Kat, "Melvin Seedan, but don't ever call me Melvin."

"What's wrong with Melvin?" asked Kat.

"Don't worry about it, just don't call me that."

"What's your last name, Kat?" Milro asked.

"Thomason," said Kat, "Why?"

"'Cause I wanna guess what he's gonna call you," replied Milro. "It's gonna be like Katmas or Katson or Komra, somethin' like that."

"Weirdo," muttered Sela, smiling slightly. "Milro is a crazy one, you'll get used to it," she told Kat. "Mevsin's a nutty dude too."

"Yeah," said Mevsin coolly, "you're not exactly sane either."

Kat laughed, "None of you guys are as crazy as me, so it's alright."

"You're scaring me now, man," said Milro, "nobody is crazier than Sela except for maybe Remnel. He's a crazy fool."

Remnel, thought Kat, could that be Remi Nelson? Impossible. "Remnel and Romez should be here in a little while," said Sela.

"I was hoping Dead Paw was gonna get his butt down here too," said Milro.

"Yeah, he'll probably be here too," said Sela.

"Who's Dead Paw?" asked Kat, wondering what sort of person would have a name like Dead Paw.

"He's my big brother," said Milro.

"What's his real name?"

"Tiden Roberts, also known as Tiro, also known as Dead Paw."

"Why do you call him Dead Paw?" asked Kat.

"He messed up his hand really bad a few years ago, and so now he has this silver chain thing covering it."

"Talson calls him Tiro, but we call him Dead Paw behind his back a lot, and sometimes to his face," said Sela. "He's pretty much cool with being called Dead Paw now, he's proud of that injury."

Kat looked around the room and noticed that a dark haired woman was sitting in an armchair watching the television. She was the only one who had not gotten up to greet Kat. She was ignoring the conversation and acting as if she could not hear them.

"Janice," said Sela quietly, noticing where Kat was looking. "She's not a friendly one."

Kat wondered why Janice apparently didn't have a nickname, as it seemed that everyone else did. Just then the door opened and three people entered the room. It was all Kat could do not to gasp in shock. Remi Nelson, fat, short and balding had entered the room, followed by a young man who looked a lot like Milro. He had a black glove and a glove made of silver chain covering his right hand. The chain made it look like he had just broken out of handcuffs. Behind him was a small man with dark hair and shifty brown eyes. He looked directly at Kat as he closed the door behind him. No way, thought Kat, it can't be.

"I'm Tiro," said the man with the chained hand. Tiro looked almost exactly like Milro. Kat shook hands with him, feeling the cold chain against her hand. Tiro couldn't close his hand all the way. "You can't shake lefty, I can't shake righty," he said with a smile.

Remi Nelson did not meet Kat's eyes as he made his way over to a chair. The third man held out his hand. "Roco Ramirez," he said, "call me Romez."

Kat did not let her surprise or dismay show on her face. Roco Ramirez, she thought, what is he doing here.

"Katerina Thomason," she said, "call me Kat."

Roco was not as adept at hiding his reaction as Kat had been. His eyes widened as Kat said her name and his face tightened. "Thomason, you say?"

"Yeah, that's right," said Kat somewhat coldly.

Remi got up and walked over to stand next to Roco. "This is Remnel," said Romez, jerking his head at Remi.

"Yeah, that's right," said Kat somewhat coldly.

"You," said Kat coldly, staring at Remi.

"Yeah me," wheezed Remi. "You gonna tell him? You can, I don't care."

Kat laughed, "Yeah you do," she said, "unless you don't care about losing your job."

"Shut up," said Roco. "You tell him, you're dead, is that clear?"

"Don't try to sound like Talson," said Kat, "you're not good at it."

Roco sneered, "Yeah, well you will be dead, kid, if you don't keep your mouth shut."

"Hey Romez," said Kat as Roco turned to leave, "you missed the card game." She pointed to the table where Milro and Sela had been playing.

Roco's face went pale, "You don't know what the hell you're talking about," he said coldly. He turned and left, shutting the door sharply behind him.

"Wow," said Tiro looking at Kat, "people don't usually stand up to Romez on their first day. What's he got against you?"

"Old grudge against my father," said Kat quietly.

"Oh yeah," said Sela, "your dad's the one who busted Romez's illegal gambling operation."

"Yeah," said Kat, amazed. "How did you know that?"

"I've been here thirteen years now," replied Sela. "Watched a lot of people come and go, picked up a lot of stories."

"So you know Remnel too?" said Tiro.

"Yeah," said Kat, "he works for my dad."

"He's had that job as a cover for a long time," said Sela. "Of course he's been here a long time, definitely longer than me."

"So are you gonna tell your dad then, Kat?" asked Milro.

"My dad would kill Remi if he knew he was here," said Kat quietly.

"Well it depends on whether you want to screw up Remi's life or not," said Milro.

"He's an idiot," said Sela, "I wouldn't complain if anything happened to him. Talson might care, though."

Kat shrugged, she could figure out what to do about Remi later. At the moment she was more concerned with Roco Ramirez. She knew that he would probably stop at nothing to get revenge on her father. The fact that Roco was with Talson was trouble for Kat. She knew that he would try to discredit her, and he might possibly try to hurt her, or even kill her, she thought. Kat could see no way around the problem of Roco. The solution came to her before she realized it. She could kill him. But no, I couldn't do that, thought Kat. She stared at the wall, trying to shake the thought. Sometimes outrageous ideas come into our heads, she thought. I wouldn't really kill him. There has to be another way.

Kat looked at the other Silver Shadows. "I should go," she said. "I'll see you guys later."

"Alright," said Milro, sitting back down at the card table, "take it easy on the hand."

"See you," said Tiro, "don't mess with Romez too much."

"Yeah, later," said Mevsin, "don't bust Remi."

"Bye, punk," said Sela, "watch your back."

Kat tried to smile, "See you guys," she said. She walked out into the hall and then out the front door. The summer night air was still and eerie as she started down the empty street. Kat looked down at her left hand, wondering if the pain was really just in her mind.

CHAPTER 7

THE PERFECT COINCIDENCE

Kat stared at her bedroom ceiling. It was dawn, and the sky outside her window

was streaked with red as the sun prepared to rise. Kat could not sleep. Her mind was racing, and her left hand lay painfully by her side under the blankets. She did not know what to do next. Should she tell Tina? Kat wanted to tell her, but Talson had made it clear that she could not discuss things with anyone outside the Silver Shadows. But this was not a job or task and Kat could not bear the thought of keeping everything to herself. She could tell her father about Roco Ramirez and Remi Nelson, but what if her father really did try to kill Remi when he found out. By telling him, Kat could ruin John Carl's life along with Remi's. Kat did not want her father in prison for murder, but then again, she thought, the way he's been acting lately he probably wouldn't believe her even if she told him.

Roco Ramirez was a bigger problem, Kat thought. Perhaps her father would kill Roco too if he found out that Roco was with Talson. That might solve the problem of Roco, but Kat really didn't want her father to become a murderer. And, Kat thought with a jolt of fear, she didn't want to become a murderer either, if she could help it.

Kat could hardly believe that anything that had happened to her the previous night was real. The only proof she had was the burning pain in her left hand, which kept reminding her that this was no dream. Talson had said 'use your good judgment.' Kat wasn't sure she had good judgment anymore.

*   *   *

"So these guys are just being totally cool to you?" said Tina. She and Kat were sitting in Tina's bedroom, speaking quietly so they would not wake Tina's mother. It was just before eight in the morning. Kat had called Tina and asked if she wanted to hear about Kat's adventures the previous night.

"Yeah," said Kat, "these guys, Milro, Tiro and Mevsin were really cool to me."

"And you're saying that this chick Sela has been spying on you since you were a baby?" said Tina incredulously.

"According to Talson, she was really looking forward to finally meeting me after seeing me for all these years."

"That's so weird," said Tina.

"Yeah, it was weird, but not as weird as seeing someone in my dad's crew and seeing the guy who my dad busted for illegal gambling," said Kat.

"You're talking about that guy Roco, right?" asked Tina.

"Yep," said Kat, "him and that bald loser, Remi Nelson. He's been working for my dad since before I was born, and apparently he's been working for Talson for just as long."

"Are you gonna tell your dad you saw Roco and Remi?" asked Tina.

"I don't know," said Kat. "My dad will probably kill Remi if he finds out. Do you think I should tell him?"

"I think your dad would want to know that, don't you?" said Tina.

"Yeah, he'll want to know," said Kat, "but I don't think he'll want to hear it from me."

"I know," said Tina, "but that's too bad, he's going to have to hear it from you. He's being stupid about this whole thing, anyway, he needs to just get over it. Maybe he'll stop freaking out about you joining Talson when he realizes that Remi and Roco are there too."

"He'll probably just freak out more, knowing my dad," said Kat, "but I'll try."

"So what if he freaks out," said Tina, "it's for his own good."

"So what?" said Kat raising her eyebrows, "I don't want my dad to become a murderer."

"You don't think he would literally kill Remi, do you?"

"Actually, I do," said Kat.

"No way," said Tina,"he wouldn't actually *kill* him just because he works for Talson."

"My dad's psycho," said Kat. "If he's willing to start calling me his enemy just because I joined Talson, he'd kill Remi for it, and probably Romez too if he has the chance."

"Romez?" said Tina questioningly.

"That's short for Roco Ramirez," said Kat, "everyone with Talson has a nickname."

Tina laughed, "what do you think they're gonna start calling you? Kalmas or something?"

"Shut up," muttered Kat, "this is serious, alright?"

"Okay," said Tina, "but what can you do about it? All you can do is just tell your dad what you found out and let him deal with it."

"The first part of that sounds fine," said Kat, "it's the part about letting him deal with it that sounds scary. Roco Ramirez is crazier than my dad. He wants my dad dead for ruining his casino gambling thing all those years ago."

"What casino thing?"

"At the bar by the harbor, it was illegal to have gambling there but Roco did it anyway, my dad told the cops and now Roco wants revenge."

"Well you could just not tell your dad and hope he doesn't find out," said Tina. "The problem with that plan is that if he does find out things are gonna be a lot worse."

"It's a lose-lose situation no matter what," said Kat, "and Romez is a worse problem for me. He's going to do anything and everything possible to make things harder for me, because he hates my father. If he's close with Talson and decides to tell Talson things about my father and about me, I'm gonna be in trouble. I'll never get respect from anyone who listens to Roco."

"What can you do about that?" asked Tina.

"Nothing," lied Kat.

"You're better than that crook anyway," said Tina, "people will side with you before they side with him, if that's what you're worried about."

"Yeah," said Kat, "maybe once I start learning how to control my power I'll be able to take care of this problem."

Tina said nothing. She realized that she did not see the situation the same way Kat saw it. Tina wasn't sure if she wanted to know what Kat meant by 'take care of this.' "Look Kat," Tina said finally, "how Lord Talson feels about his followers is not your problem, what goes on between him and Roco is not your problem, and who the other Silver Shadows decide to listen to is not your problem. I bet a lot of people would listen to Roco before they would listen to you, just because you're a thirteen year-old and he's an adult. You can't expect Talson's followers to treat you like you are their equal because they won't. You are way younger than them, and talking to them is not going to be like talking to me. Gaining their respect is not going to be easy."

"You know what," said Kat, feeling angry now, "it is my problem because I care what Romez says to the other Silver Shadows about me and I don't want to have to deal with him being mean to me every time I see him."

"Kat, why do you think you should get whatever you want? You just have to deal with it just like your dad and if you don't want to deal with it then you shouldn't have joined Talson. You knew you were going to have to deal with a lot of things, and you chose to join."

"I joined so I could learn to control the power, not so I could deal with idiots like Remi Nelson and crooks like Roco Ramirez," said Kat shortly.

"Your dad has to deal with Roco and Remi, so does Talson and so do all the other Silver Shadows," said Tina. "You're no different."

"Yeah, actually I am," said Kat. "Once I learn to control the power I won't have to deal with Roco. If he starts messing with me I'll be able to stop him."

"I don't know, Kat," said Tina. "I think you're overreacting. Things are going to be okay, just do your thing with Talson and don't worry about everyone else, especially if most of them are being cool to you. It's seriously not your problem. Your dad is the one who screwed Roco, not you. Remi works for your dad, not you. Just tell your dad and stop worrying about it. If you try to be cool with Romez and don't give him any reason to hate you, he probably won't bother you."

"He's going to hate me no matter what I do or don't do," said Kat, still angry. "Stop telling me everything I should and shouldn't do. I know people and I know what they are thinking. I'm gonna do whatever I want with my power once I can control it."

Tina felt like hitting Kat, but restrained herself. "Why do you have to be so egotistical all the time," said Tina coldly, "you're not that freaking good. You just admitted that you had this ability about a month ago, and now you think it means you're special?"

"Shut the hell up," said Kat, "I could have you flat on your face like Candace if I wanted to."

"If you didn't want to hear what I had to say, then why did you bother to confide in me? If you think my opinion is beneath you, then get out of my room."

Kat sat motionless on Tina's bed. Tina had taken her completely by surprise. Kat could not remember the last time she and Tina had had an argument. "Tina, it's not that I don't care what you have to say, it's just…" Kat's voice trailed off. She didn't know what to say.

"It's just what?" said Tina glaring at Kat.

Kat paused, "How about this plan?" she said. "When I get home, I'll try to talk to my dad. How's that?"

"Well now that it's your plan, it's a good plan right?" said Tina bitterly.

"I'm not going to be able to tell you what I'm doing for Talson, said Kat coolly, "I'm not even supposed to tell you anything."

"Well that's okay," said Tina, "you don't have to break any rules for me."

"I want Talson to teach me to control my power, I'm not going to break his rules."

"And you don't care what he might make you do as long as you learn to control the power," said Tina.

"Well yeah, pretty much," said Kat. "I'll do what he wants so I get what I want."

Tina looked away from Kat. She honestly didn't agree with Kat's philosophy, but Tina couldn't bring herself to tell Kat this. She had already disagreed with her enough during the course of their conversation. "So if you don't do everything he says he'll kill you, right?"

"No," said Kat, "he didn't say that. I'm allowed to step away from him if I want to."

"Yeah, but you won't because then he won't teach you to control the power and that'll screw up your life."

"Okay," said Kat, "I get the picture. He'll probably screw up my life anyway, but I have to do this. It's not like I really trust Talson or anything."

"Good," said Tina, "you shouldn't."

"Wow, I'm glad we finally agreed on something today," said Kat. "I guess I'll go home now and see if my dad is going to be home tonight. I just hope he isn't a complete bear when I try to talk to him."

There were a lot of things Tina wanted to say to Kat at that moment, but she chose not to say any of them. "I'll see you later then," she said.

"Yeah okay, I'll see you later," said Kat. She walked outside into the front yard. She saw Tina's mom, Tracy working in the garden. "Hi Tracy," she said. "We thought you were still sleeping."

"No," said Tracy, "just getting a little gardening done. How are you?"

"I'm fine thanks," said Kat, "I'll see you later." She walked on down the block toward her house.

Kat's mother was out getting the mail when Kat arrived. "Hey Mom," said Kat trying to sound cheerful, "is Dad coming home tonight?"

"Yes I think he is, why?" replied Tamera.

Kat thought it was sad that her mother would ask her such a question. Kat didn't think there needed to be a reason for a question like this. "Because—," began Kat, "I was just wondering," she finished.

"Oh well, I was just surprised when you asked that's all," said Tamera, "I know I probably shouldn't have been, but—"

"Sad," remarked Kat, before her mother could finish. Kat began to walk away from her house, not wanting to continue the conversation. The fact that her mother was surprised by Kat's inquiry about her father really hurt Kat. Kat knew that her mother hadn't really meant to upset her, she was just expressing how she felt. Kat knew her mother hadn't meant to come across the way she had, but she wasn't feeling very sympathetic to her mother's feelings at the moment.

Kat walked down the street, her mother calling after her. "Where do you think you're going?"

"I just want to go to the park to take a walk," Kat called without looking back.

"Why?" Tamera called back.

Kat looked back at her mother over her shoulder, she was really annoyed now. "For the same reason I wanted to know if my father was coming home tonight," she said coolly. "Or maybe I just want to go because it's a beautiful day and I don't want to miss it." Kat turned without waiting for her mother to reply and continued quickly down the street toward the park.

When Kat reached the park she began a slow walk around the pond at the center of the park, barely feeling the warmth of the sun on her back. There was a path that made a large loop around the pond. Kat and Tina had walked this path, which they called the circle, many times. Kat met no one until she came to a small grove of trees at the edge of the park. Behind these trees was the house where Kat had met Talson the previous night, but the scene looked quite different in the daylight. Kat wondered if the house was even still there, but she did not venture behind the trees to investigate.

"What's up, Kat," said a soft voice from behind Kat.

Kat turned around quickly in surprise, and saw Sela standing by the trees smiling at her. "Sela," said Kat, "how did you sneak up behind me like that?"

"It's my job," replied Sela simply.

"How long have you been—?" Kat began to ask.

"Since I was nineteen," Sela interrupted, "but don't say stuff like that when we're outside, you never know when someone might be listening."

"Oh," said Kat, catching on, "I'm sorry."

"Don't worry about it."

"Sela," said Kat quietly, "do you know how old he is?"

"No," replied Sela, understanding Kat's question immediately. "Forty, forty-five, I'm just guessing. I really have no idea."

"He looks younger than that," said Kat.

"I know," said Sela, "but I'm thirty-two, and I know he's older than me."

"Why do you work for him?" asked Kat.

Sela shrugged, "I like him, in a way," she said. "I mean he's a genius."

"Yeah he is," said Kat, "but how did you find out about him? Did he send you a letter like he did with me?"

"No," said Sela, "and just for the record, I dropped that letter in your mailbox."

"Oh," said Kat.

Sela smiled, "I don't really see any reason to tell you how I learned about Talson."

"I'll tell you why he wanted me if you tell me why he wanted you," offered Kat.

"I already know why he wants you," said Sela, "and I'm pretty sure I know some things about you that you don't even know, so you can't bargain with me on that."

"You know that I can—," began Kat, "did he tell you?"

"No," said Sela, "I overheard your father talking about it. That's when I realized why he was interested in you joining us."

"You know way too much about me, Sela," said Kat.

"I know," said Sela, smiling. "Ever wonder why I work for him?" She laughed. "He doesn't tell me anything but he gives me the opportunity to find out everything."

"What do you mean?" asked Kat.

"We'll see how long it is before you start bending orders and trying to figure things out," said Sela with a smile, "you're smart, so it probably won't be very long."

Kat smiled, 'bending orders' certainly did sound like something she would probably end up doing.

"Listen," said Sela, "you wanna come with me tonight? I'm on duty at Headquarters."

"Where are Headquarters?" asked Kat.

"Down by the water," said Sela. "You have to see the place, it's so awesome."

"Will it be okay with Talson if I come with you?"

"Oh yeah, he won't mind."

"Will he be there?"

"No, I don't think so. I don't know where he is right now."

"How can we have Headquarters without anyone seeing them?" asked Kat.

"Well it's like here at the circle, other people can't see it, they just see the trees."

"Yeah," said Kat, "I used to come here all the time when I was younger and I never saw the house. I think it's just that we don't notice it, not that it's not here."

"I don't know," said Sela, "I don't know how he does what he does, not that anyone else knows."

Kat kept her face expressionless, "No, I guess no one knows," she said, smiling inwardly. This was what Talson meant by followers who had been with him for many years and still hadn't noticed. *Noticed* was the key word, thought Kat. The house was always there and it wasn't that people couldn't see it. People just never noticed it. It wasn't that Talson didn't tell his followers how he did what he did, they just never noticed when he did. Kat had realized in two meetings with Talson what some of the Silver Shadows never understood in a lifetime.

"You never know with Talson," Sela interrupted Kat's thoughts. "He doesn't really tell you anything. You just have to do your job without knowing why he needs you. It's hard sometimes because you feel like you're going through life in the dark, but if you find a way to do it through all of that, you will find something you never knew existed."

"I think Talson gives you all the answers to your questions," said Kat, "you just have to take notice when he gives his answers." Kat felt somewhat superior to Sela now, all those years of trying to 'figure things out' and she still didn't have a clue.

There was a silence between them for a moment, then Kat said, "what time are we leaving for Headquarters tonight?"

"I'm on duty at nine, so let's leave at like 8:30. I'll see you tonight." She turned to leave then turned back and looked Kat straight in the eyes for the first time. "My next job is to wipe that smirk off your face. You know, just because you have the power doesn't mean you have everyone figured out." She laughed at the shocked expression on Kat's face, as she disappeared among the trees.

Instead of going home, Kat continued her walk around the pond at the park, wondering what she should tell her parents about tonight and whether she should really go with Sela or not. She had planned to talk to her father that night, but he probably wouldn't be home until at least eight o'clock. She would not be able to talk to him if she was meeting

Sela at 8:30. She could go with Sela and talk to her father tomorrow, which was probably a better plan. Kat still had the problem of what she would tell her parents. She could say that she was going out with a friend, but she couldn't say Tina because her mother would be sure to mention it to Tracy.

Kat supposed she could just tell the truth, since it would be much easier than coming up with a complicated story. It wasn't as though this was going to be the only time that Kat went out at night, she was going to have lessons with Talson four nights a week. She couldn't just keep making up stories every time she needed one, eventually she would have to be truthful. Tonight, however, Kat foresaw a problem with being truthful. Her father was likely to become even more angry with her than he already was, and would then be even harder to deal with when Kat had a chance to talk to him the next day. Telling John Carl about what she was doing that night might erase any possibility that John Carl would take Kat's information about Roco and Remi reasonably.

Kat walked home slowly, still trying to figure out what to do about her present situation. When she arrived home, she saw that her father was not yet home. Her mother's car was also gone from the driveway. Surprised, Kat went inside. Her mother had left a note on the table.

Kat, I went to dinner with Tracy, and we're going to a show afterwards. I should be home by midnight. Dad will be home tomorrow. Sorry I forgot to mention this when I saw you earlier, but tonight's plans were a little last minute. Love, Mom.

"Nice," said Kat aloud. "That was easy." It was funny how things just work out sometimes, thought Kat. I guess that's just life. She couldn't help thinking, however, that it was a little odd. Kat thought it seemed too perfect to be a pure coincidence.

Kat's thoughts were interrupted by the telephone ringing. "Hello," said Kat.

"Hey," said Tina's voice.

"No," said Kat, knowing what Tina was about to ask. "We can't hang out tonight because I'm leaving at 8:30."

"Right," said Tina, sounding annoyed.

"Sorry," said Kat, "My mom left me a note saying she was going out to dinner and stuff with your mom."

"Right," said Tina again. "So where are you going?"

"Come over here and I'll tell you," said Kat.

"Okay," Tina still sounded angry, "I'll be there in a second."

"Did your mom tell you she was going out to dinner with my mom earlier?" Kat asked Tina when she arrived at Kat's house a few minutes later.

"Well not really earlier," said Tina, "she just told me right before she left, but it doesn't really matter. Where are you going tonight?"

"It's weird," said Kat, not answering Tina's question.

"What's weird?" asked Tina.

"It's weird that on the night when I couldn't come up with a story to tell my parents, they conveniently aren't home."

"Well I guess you got lucky," said Tina somewhat bitterly.

"Yeah, it's real convenient," said Kat, "but also really weird. I mean, about an hour or two ago I was talking to my mom, and she told me that my dad was coming home tonight and she never mentioned that she was going out." Kat left out the fact that she really hadn't given her mother a chance to tell her. "Then I get home and there is a note saying my dad's not gonna be here until tomorrow and she's not gonna be home until midnight. That's weird because midnight is when I'm probably gonna get home, and because my mom never stays out that late anymore."

"Where the heck are *you* going until midnight?" asked Tina.

Kat told her about how she met Sela at the park that day and how Sela had invited her to come to Headquarters that night.

"Sounds interesting," said Tina although she didn't sound at all interested.

"Yeah, pretty crazy, I know," said Kat. "Here I am wondering what I'm gonna tell my parents and thinking how my dad is going to flip and I'm going to lose any chance I had of talking with him, but then I get home and they're gone and everything is cool. It's crazy to think that's a coincidence."

"What's even crazier," said Tina, "is that you're gonna go."

"How is that crazy?"

"Well I don't know," said Tina, "this whole thing is crazy."

"I know," said Kat, "I mean I know sometimes things just work out well, but this seems way beyond that, I think something really weird is going on. What did your mom say when she left?"

Tina looked at Kat for a moment, "Why does that matter? All she said was 'I'm going out to dinner with Tamera, I'll be back later tonight,' I didn't think it was that big of a deal."

"Did she tell you to come over here?" asked Kat.

"No, she actually told me to stay at home. What? You think I shouldn't be breaking my mommy's rules or something?"

"How did she act when she told you?" asked Kat, ignoring Tina's taunt.

"Why the hell does it matter how she acted?" asked Tina shortly.

"Because," said Kat, "there is something weird going on here and I want to know what it is."

"How does any of this information help you?" asked Tina exasperated.

"I don't know," said Kat, "I just think it's worth knowing." She was having trouble believing that Tina was so out of touch with her reasoning. "It's not that hard, you know," she said, "come on, you know how I think."

"No, actually I can't tell what people are thinking like you can, so clearly you're

better than me, happy now?" said Tina coldly.

"Come on, how long have you known me? All these years and you still haven't figured out how I think? It just takes some experience with a person most of the time, not any special power."

Tina sighed, looking disgusted. "My mom acted totally casual. She just told me she was going out and that I should stay home, that's it."

"But does she usually go out at night?"

"No, but so what?"

"So what," said Kat exasperatedly, "don't you think it's weird?"

"For the billionth time, no I don't think it's that weird, okay?"

"Yeah, okay," said Kat, "but I do. I mean, do you think this could have anything to do with Sela or Talson?"

"No, I don't," said Tina wearily. "I think it has something to do with our moms wanting to hang out, and your dad taking an extra day on his trip."

"You're missing the point by about a mile," said Kat, annoyed.

Tina said nothing. She wanted to walk out of Kat's house, but she forced herself to remain, defiantly standing in the middle of Kat's livingroom.

"Do you want to help me to figure out what's going on or not? Because if you don't you *should* leave," said Kat.

"Do I or will I," asked Tina, sounding tired.

Kat considered for a moment. "If you don't care about finding stuff out then you don't have to," she said. "I just thought you might be interested because it concerns your mom. When she gets home will you just ask her how her night was and where she went?"

"Yeah, I will," said Tina, "if it really matters to you that much, I will. If you really want to have a mystery like we used to pretend when we were little, I'll play with you."

"This is not a pretend game," said Kat.

"I'll try to figure something out," said Tina, "for you I'll try."

"Thanks," said Kat, "it really does seem weird to me."

"Really, does it now?" said Tina sarcastically, but she was smiling now. "So what do you think you are going to do with Sela tonight?"

"I don't know," said Kat, "I guess we're just going to go to Headquarters and she'll show me some stuff. She said she's on duty there tonight, whatever that means."

"Talson's not going to be there?"

"No, he's somewhere else right now, I don't know where."

"So do you trust this woman, Sela?"

"I don't know, I mean she seems cool, but no I don't really trust her. I don't trust any of Talson's followers or Talson right now."

"Do you think anyone really trusts Talson?" asked Tina.

"I don't know, I don't think anyone really understands him."

"Yeah," said Tina, "all that stuff your dad was saying about how no one knows how he does what he does, is that true, do you think?"

"No, I don't think it's true," said Kat. "I think there are people who know, they just don't realize that they know." Kat checked the clock above the kitchen counter, it was fifteen minutes past eight. "Wow, I gotta go," she said. "I told Sela I'd meet her at the circle at 8:30. You know that Talson's followers call that place the circle just like we do, isn't that weird?"

"Not that again," said Tina with a smile, "what isn't weird to you? Don't you have to leave, already?"

Kat smiled, "Yeah I do, and you better leave too."

"Yeah, my mom will be mad if she finds out I left the house."

Before they left, Kat ran upstairs to her bedroom and drew the blinds. Then she took a wad of blankets and stuffed them under her bedspread to make it look like someone was lying in the bed. She left her bedroom door open a crack as she often did at night, and turned out the light in the hall. She then went downstairs and put the light on outside the front door. Kat was fairly sure that her mother would arrive home before she did.

"What were you doing up there?" asked Tina.

"Fooling my mom," said Kat.

"I'll bet you're gonna be a pro at that by the time you get done working for Talson."

Kat laughed, "Yeah, no kidding."

C H A P T E R 8

652-302

Tracy and Tamera drove through the warm night with front windows rolled down,

letting the breeze hit their faces. They had just left Tracy's house and were heading toward the freeway.

"I don't completely understand what we are doing," Tracy was saying from the passenger's seat. "I just told Tina I was going out tonight like you told me to tell her, but I know she probably thought it was weird. She knows I never go out late anymore."

"I got lucky," said Tamera, "Kat wasn't home, so I just left her a note. I know she wouldn't have believed my story if I'd told her. You know Katerina, always questions everything. Anyway I don't know why we're going so late, John Carl just told me that this was the best time to go."

"What is it he wants to talk about anyway?" asked Tracy, as they pulled out onto the freeway.

"Well, a few things actually," said Tamera.

"Well alright, is he coming home with us tonight?"

"I'm not sure, I don't think he's planning to, but Kat was asking for him today, I don't know why. He might come home just to see what she has to say to him."

"What's going on? Is there a problem?" asked Tracy, sounding concerned now.

"Well, yes there is a problem, that's why John Carl wants to talk to you tonight."

They drove on in silence until they were on a busy road that ran along the ocean. Since it was just past 8:30, most of the restaurants and bars along the harbor were very busy. The two women made their

100

way down the street to a small, shabbier looking place. A sign over the large wooden door had a large shark on it. The shark's mouth was open, enclosing the words *The Sharktooth Bar* in curving letters. A sign in the window said *Fishermen Welcome.*

"Not exactly the glamorous night out, is it?" said Tracy.

"No, not at all," said Tamera, "but the good news is that the fishermen who come here will all be too drunk to eavesdrop on us."

"Eavesdrop?" said Tracy in surprise, "is this that important and secret that no one should hear us?"

"Yes," said Tamera, "absolutely."

*   *   *

Kat had just made her way into the trees behind the park when she saw Sela standing in front of the house, leaning against the wall. Kat blinked, the house was still there.

"What's up, fool?" said Sela when she saw Kat.

"Are we ready to go?" asked Kat.

"Well, yeah we are, but we've had a slight change in plans."

"What happened?" asked Kat, wondering what other strange things might have happened.

"Well I just got a call from Talson, and he told me that he just talked to Remi Nelson. Remi just got in from a fishing trip and he said that the Captain has plans to meet his wife and Tracy Louis at The Sharktooth Bar tonight. It's this old place down at the harbor that Romez used to run before he got busted. Anyway, Talson asked me to go down there and see what's going on, because he thinks something weird is going on. I told him I was going to have you with me tonight, and he wanted me to ask you if you know anything about this little meeting your parents are having with Tracy."

"No, I have no idea what they're doing down there."

"Well it's just kind of weird that John Carl would go down there, he's always avoided the place ever since he busted Romez. Not to mention the fact that the Sharktooth is just about the worst place to have a private conversation."

"Well we don't know that it is going to be that private of a conversation, do we?" said Kat, still trying to cling to the rapidly fading possibility that there had been at least some truth in the note her mother had written. Although she suspected something was up, she now hoped she was wrong. "I mean, they could just be going there to hang out and have drinks," continued Kat.

"Not likely," said Sela. "Apparently Remi overheard John Carl talking to his wife on the phone. Apparently he said that they should meet at the Sharktooth, so they wouldn't be overheard."

"But if they don't want to be overheard then why would they go there? You just said it was a really bad place to have a private conversation."

"Yeah," said Sela, "but a lot of people don't realize what that place is really like. If you have your conversation at The Sharktooth Bar, everyone you don't want to hear it will hear it."

"Let's go," Sela added, "we can talk about it more on the way there. We have to catch up to them. Follow me."

Sela led Kat around to the front of the park to the parking lot. There were no cars parked there at this late hour except for a small black sports car that was partially blocked from view by the trees.

"Is that your car?" asked Kat."

"Yes it is," said Sela.

"Pretty slick," said Kat.

Sela smiled, "thanks."

They pulled out of the parking lot onto the silent road. "Wow, what's that?" asked Kat, pointing to a small screen below the dashboard.

"Oh, thanks for reminding me," said Sela, "I need to turn that on." Sela pressed a button on the dash and the screen came on, showing a road map with little red dots scattered in various areas.

"What are those red dots?" asked Kat, as Sela pulled out onto the freeway.

In answer Sela touched one of the dots on the screen. A number appeared below the dot, 652-300. "Zoom in," said Sela. The screen zoomed closer to show only the area around the red dot. Kat could now see individual street names and boxes that represented buildings. The dot labeled 652-300 was in one of the small buildings on Harbor Drive.

"Damn it, he's already there," said Sela, as they merged onto the freeway. "It doesn't look like Tamera and Tracy are there yet, though. Locate," said Sela to the machine.

An automated woman's voice spoke, "Please say a number."

"652-301," said Sela.

"Searching," said the voice.

"Wow," said Kat, "is that some kind of GPS system?"

"It's sort of an advanced GPS, Mevsin made all our tech systems." The screen had now shifted to show a different area. Two red dots were visible. Unlike dot number 652-300 both of these dots were traveling very fast. Under the dot on the left was the number 652-301. Sela touched the dot on the right to display the number 657-301. "They're not too far from us," said Sela. "If I step on it a little bit I think we can catch up."

"Locate," Sela said to the GPS.

"Please say a number."

"652-302," said Sela. The screen moved over slightly, continuing to show the same freeway to show two more dots, which were moving very quickly. "Zoom in," said Sela and the screen magnified to show the freeway sign and exit numbers.

The dot labeled 652-302 was just past exit number 62. Kat looked up and saw exit 62. "That's us," she said incredulously.

"Yep," said Sela, "that's us. Move left." The screen scrolled left along the freeway and dot number 652-301 came back into view. "Exit number 67," said Sela, "we're nearly there, if I speed up a little we can catch up to them."

Kat looked at Sela's speedometer. She was already going eighty miles an hour. "Are you sure you wanna go any faster, we might get a ticket," said Kat.

"Nah, we won't get a ticket," said Sela.

Suddenly a black box next to Sela's rear view mirror buzzed loudly and a red light flashed.

"What's that?" asked Kat, startled.

Sela took her foot of the gas and slowed to sixty-eight miles per hour, just as a police car entered the freeway in front of them. "That," said Sela, "is a fuzz buster. It picks up on police radar and buzzes to let me know that a cop is nearby. That's why I know we won't get a ticket."

The police car got off at exit number 63, and Sela immediately sped up, merging into the far left lane. The GPS tracker was showing that 652-301 was now at exit 67. "Speed," Sela commanded the GPS.

"Please say a number."

"652-301," said Sela.

"Current speed is, sixty-two miles per hour," said the woman's voice.

"We can catch those slow pokes no problem."

Kat watched the screen. They were rapidly gaining on 625-301. They were only

two exits away now.

"We're catching up," said Sela. "Ah ha, there they are."

Kat could see now on the map that 652-302 was directly behind 652-301 and 627-301. She looked up and saw her mother's car two cars in front of them. "What if my mom sees me?" said Kat.

"She won't," said Sela, "she doesn't recognize this car, and besides I have tinted windows and it's dark outside."

"So, my dad is 652-300, my mom is 652-301, and I'm 652-302?" asked Kat.

"That's right," said Sela.

"So if Tracy is 657-301, then Tina would be 657-302?"

"303 actually," said Sela.

"Why 303?" asked Kat frowning.

"Well she's the younger child, so her older sister would be 302."

"Tina doesn't have a sister," said Kat.

"Yeah, she did, you mean she never told you that?"

"No," said Kat, "I always thought she was an only child."

"She's not, as far as I know," said Sela.

"Is her sister dead?" asked Kat.

"I don't know," said Sela, "you should ask her."

"I don't think she knows she has a sister," said Kat.

"Her mother must have told her."

"That's weird," said Kat, "maybe she just never told me about it. I thought she told me pretty much everything."

"Just a bit of advice," said Sela. "Never assume that anyone tells you everything, no matter how close you think you are to them."

"Yeah, but even if she didn't tell me I think I'd know," said Kat.

"You're right, I almost forgot, it's different for you."

They drove on, keeping Tamera's car in their sights but never getting too close to it. Kat's mind was racing. She was wondering why in the world her mother and Tracy were meeting her father secretly at a bar.

As though she knew exactly what Kat was thinking, Sela said, "So, you don't know what this whole meeting between your parents and Tracy is all about?"

"I—," began Kat, wondering how much to tell Sela. "I have a hunch," said Kat slowly, "I just really hope I'm wrong."

"A hunch?"

"Well," began Kat, not sure what she was going to say. "I don't really want to talk about it," she finished quickly.

Sela took a hard right at exit 76, and headed toward the harbor. She stayed two cars behind Tamera and Tracy, so they would not suspect that they were being followed. Kat had expected Sela to press her about her hunch, but she didn't.

"That's okay," Sela said, "I have a hunch too, and I really hope I'm wrong too. And as a matter of fact I don't really want to talk about it either," she added, smiling slightly.

"I just have the feeling that we're gonna hear some stuff we don't want to hear," said Kat.

"Yeah, so do I," said Sela, "but hearing stuff I don't want to hear is part of my job and it is now part of your job, so we just have to deal with it."

Kat was not quite sure that Sela understood the kinds of things Kat was worried about hearing from her parents. Obviously it was going to be something they didn't want her to hear them say, and even worse things that Tracy didn't want Tina to hear.

"If you really don't want to hear it we can turn back now and come up with a story to tell Talson," said Sela.

"Are you kidding me?" said Kat.

"Yeah, I am," said Sela turning onto Harbor Drive. "Besides, the more you think you don't want to hear something, the more you have to find out what's being said. Even when I hate listening to a conversation, I can't turn away because I have to know what they're gonna say next. I'll do anything to find out what's going on in any situation."

Kat looked sideways at Sela. She somehow felt as if she had known Sela for a long time even though she had only known her for two days. "I thought it was weird that my mom said she was going out to dinner tonight with Tracy," said Kat.

"Why?" asked Sela. "They're friends, it's not weird that they wanted to go out together. I mean, in reality what they're doing is weird, but I wouldn't have thought it was weird that they said they were going to dinner together. I think that was a pretty good story. But since you didn't buy it," continued Sela, "I guess it wasn't that good of a story after all."

"It was an okay story, I guess," said Kat. "I guess I just don't go for stuff like that very easily, I always think something suspicious must be going on."

"I go for way too much stuff way too easily," said Sela.

Kat laughed, "Tina does that. We were ready to brawl earlier over whether this whole thing was weird or not."

"Well, I guess you get the last laugh, now that we see how weird this whole thing actually is."

Tamera and Tracy pulled into the parking spot in the street in front of The Sharktooth Bar. Sela kept driving, went around the block and parked in back of the bar behind an overfull dumpster.

"Let's wait about two minutes so they have a chance to get inside," said Sela.

"Okay," said Kat. "Hey Sela," she added, "where do you live?"

"I live at the circle most of the time," said Sela. "I have an apartment downtown, where I live sometimes. Other times, I stay at Headquarters."

"So do you live with Talson then?"

"Well, yeah, in the same building," said Sela. "There are two sides at Headquarters. One side is his, the other is ours. So basically, I live with the other Silver Shadows most of the time."

"Do you like that?" asked Kat.

"Yeah," said Sela, "I actually do like it. It's fun a lot of times, more fun than living alone. Let's go now."

"Yeah okay," said Kat, "but I can't let them see me."

"I can't let them see me either," said Sela.

"At least it's not your parents," muttered Kat.

"Let's go in the back door."

For a moment Kat thought Sela looked slightly angry or upset, but the expression was fleeting. By the time Kat got a better look at Sela's face the expression had vanished and Kat wasn't sure if she had really seen it at all. Sela was very hard to read. Her expression always seemed the same, and her thoughts were absent from Kat's mind.

Kat and Sela walked around the dumpster, wrinkling their noses at the smell of rotting garbage. A large rat scurried from behind the dumpster and down the drainage pipe.

"Gross," said Kat.

"Yeah," said Sela, "not exactly a romantic night out for your parents."

Sela and Kat entered through the back door of the bar. They were standing in a fairly large room filled with old card tables. There was a black fireplace in the corner, above which hung what looked like a real human skull. The room was filthy, and the paint had almost completely peeled off the walls. The room smelled like tobacco and liquor mixed with garbage. Some of the tables and chairs had broken legs, and everything seemed to be covered with a layer of dust.

"Wow, nice place," said Kat sarcastically.

"Not what it used to be, that's for sure," said Sela. "This room was by far Roco Ramirez's greatest achievement."

"Some achievement," sneered Kat.

"It wasn't always like this," said Sela. "Roco was very shrewd. He should not be underestimated. He ran this place for years without getting caught. I think his was the most popular illegal card room on the planet, it packed every night of the week. I used to come and gamble here all the time when I was younger. It wasn't legal anyway, so it didn't really matter if you were under twenty-one. I started coming here when I was fourteen. When I was nineteen, I got in with Talson because of coming here. Roco was working for him at the time and he thought Talson might like me. I owe Roco a lot when I think about it, but then I broke him out of jail about ten years ago, so we're actually even now."

"It was you who broke Roco out of prison?" said Kat, shocked. "My dad has been talking about that ever since I was little, about how Roco got away, and how someone broke him out of prison and they never found out who that was."

Sela smiled slyly. "That was by far the most insane thing I ever did," she said.

Kat stared at Sela for a moment. She felt a mixture of like and dislike for Sela at the same time. Kat was impressed that Sela had been able to break someone out of prison undetected, but then again it seemed that Roco was a crook that deserved to remain in jail. Sela had also funded Roco's cheating business by gambling at the Sharktooth. "How did you do it, how did you break him out?" asked Kat.

"Let's just put it this way," said Sela, "it took careful planning."

"I bet," said Kat. She was starting to think that there was a lot more to Sela than she was letting on.

"Let's go," said Sela, her hand on the door that led to the main part of the bar.

"Hold on," said Kat, eying the door's rusty hinges. "Don't you think that door is going to squeak?"

"Yeah, it probably will," said Sela.

"Hold on, I'll put some oil on the hinges," said Kat, taking out the little bottle of oil she had used on the door of the house at the circle. Kat rubbed the oil on the hinges and the door swung open effortlessly.

Kat found herself standing behind a long bar that ran the entire length of the room. The bartender had his back to them. He seemed to be a rather small man. Kat followed Sela who had ducked out from behind the bar. The long bar curved slightly at both ends, and there were small tables at the front of the room by the windows. Two men were sitting at one of the tables, they were both very scruffy looking fishermen.

There was a fireplace against the wall closest to Sela and Kat. It was very much like the one in the back room except that there was a large shark head mounted above it instead of a human skull. Fishing net hung all over the walls, along with all manner of other things. It seemed that every inch of usable wall space was covered.

Kat looked down to the other end of the bar and saw three people sitting at the far end. They were almost hidden from view by a large shark that was suspended from the ceiling. Kat could barely make out their faces, but she knew immediately who they were.

Sela nodded her head toward the three people at the end of the bar, indicating that she should follow her. Kat moved down the bar past a sign that read, *No one under the age of 21 allowed at the bar,* and another that said, *We card if you look under 30 please have I.D. ready to show the bartender.* Yeah right, thought Kat, Sela had just told her that she had come to the Sharktooth when she was fourteen. There were a number of signs along the bar including one that read, *If you're too drunk to read this you won't know what it says,* and another that said *Please try to remember the name on your phony I.D.* Kat almost laughed out loud. She looked up and saw a large black banner above the bar with white letters. It said: *Your life isn't the only one at risk if you drive drunk.*

Sela stopped two tables away from where Tamera, Tracy, and John Carl were sitting at the bar. Sela pointed to a table in the corner within earshot of the bar. There was a large stack of boxes next to the table. Sela pushed the table behind that stack of boxes so it was hidden from the view of those sitting at the bar. The bartender did not appear to have noticed them.

"You think he knows we're here?" whispered Kat, indicating the bartender.

"Nah, probably not," said Sela. "He wouldn't notice his own reflection if it started talking to him," she indicated the mirror that ran the entire length of the bar behind the bartender. "He never seems to notice anything."

Kat smiled slightly, thinking of what Talson had said about people never noticing things.

Sela smiled, "what are you smiling at?"

"Oh nothing," said Kat, "what are you smiling at?"

"Oh nothing," said Sela, smirking. A moment later they heard voices coming from the bar and Kat and Sela fell silent, listening.

"But why are we really here, John Carl?" Tracy was saying.

"Because, Tamera and I feel that there are some things happening right now that you should be aware of. First, you should know that the reason I brought you here is that I want us to be able to speak openly without the risk of being overheard."

Sela raised her eyebrows at Kat across the table. "Told you," she mouthed.

"But surely," Tracy was saying, "if we were at home we would not be overheard."

"Then we run the risk of our children gaining access to this conversation. You never know when they might be listening."

"Oh, I understand that," said Tracy, "the children are always spying on us."

Sela smiled and pointed across the table at Kat, "You eavesdropper," she mouthed.

"What I wanted to say to you," John Carl continued, "concerns Lord Talson."

Kat and Sela exchanged glances across the table. Kat shifted uncomfortably, no wonder Talson had wanted Sela to listen in on this conversation. Now Kat knew that the hunch she had been hoping would be wrong was right.

"Lord Talson?" Tracy's voice sounded shocked and scared.

"Apparently he's been laying low all this time working toward one goal," John Carl's voice contained a hint of a sneer.

Sela leaned toward Kat across the table, "this could get ugly," she whispered.

"What goal," asked Tracy, stricken, "who's he killing now?"

"Not killing," replied John Carl, "he wanted a certain supporter. Everything he has been doing has been directed at getting this particular person on his side, and now he has that person, and we have another enemy. It's a very dangerous enemy at that."

"Who," whispered Tracy, sounding nervous.

There was a pause, then John Carl said, "Katerina Thomason."

There was an uncomfortable silence between the parents at the bar that seemed to stretch on and on. Kat and Sela stared at each other in silence. Kat's chest rose and fell rapidly; her heart was racing.

"No," whispered Tracy finally breaking the silence. "Not another, not again," Tracy seemed close to tears now.

Sela dropped her eyes from Kat's face. Kat had no idea what Tracy meant by 'again'. "What's she talking about?" mouthed Kat.

Sela shook her head without looking up.

"How could she?" continued Tracy, her voice shaking. "She knows what he's done," Tracy seemed somewhat hysterical now.

"Yes," said John Carl, "she's heard about it, but she's never seen it."

"She killed him, John Carl," said Tracy wildly. "When she left, that's what she did, she killed Barton."

Sela looked up at Kat now, her expression completely blank. "I told you this was gonna get ugly," she whispered.

"What's Tracy talking about?" whispered Kat. Kat could see that Sela's chest

was rising and falling more rapidly now. Sela again seemed somewhat agitated. Kat could not help thinking that Sela understood more of this conversation than she did.

"But what if it's, you know, the same way with you," said Tracy.

"I don't think Kat would kill me," said John Carl.

"You think Barton thought she would kill him?"

"No," said John Carl, "but this is different."

"I never thought my daughter would help kill my husband," said Tracy, her voice shaking again.

"I know you didn't," said John Carl, remaining calm. "However, this situation with Kat is slightly different, you see, the reason Kat has gone to work for Talson is that she shares his powers."

At that moment Kat had to use every particle of self-control she possessed to prevent herself from attacking her father's mind, or just jumping out from behind the boxes and hitting him. She did not want the bartender or anyone else in the bar to hear what her father had just said. She especially resented her father for telling Tracy, since it could cause problems for Tina. Kat looked across the table at Sela. She, too, looked somewhat angry now. Kat and Sela sat hidden by the boxes, fighting to remain calm as the conversation at the bar continued.

"She what?" Tracy dropped her voice in apparent shock.

"You heard me," said John Carl.

"But is that why she's with him?" asked Tracy.

"Yes," replied John Carl, "she wants to learn how to use the power from Talson."

Kat put her head in her hands in an attempt to control her anger. "Hey, chill out, punk," whispered Sela.

"I'm trying to," muttered Kat.

"Try harder," said Sela, "this is our job."

"I know, but this sucks," said Kat.

"Agreed," said Sela.

"Kat is being swayed by Talson's power," said Tamera, speaking for the first time. "She is impressed by him, because he represents a way for Kat to learn how to use her power. From what I can tell, Talson has made a very good first impression. He has not exposed his cruel side to her at all. He has been very open with Kat, and is willing to answer many of her questions. Kat is a person who demands answers; she demands knowledge. Lord Talson is playing right into that weakness."

"Kat told us that the reason she wanted to join him was because he was willing to tell her things John Carl and I never told her. That, in addition to his promise to teach her about the power, was more than enough to convince Kat to join him. Lord Talson knows how to get people on his side, I'm sure it was very well done."

"Yes," said Tracy. Tamera's words seemed to have calmed her. "I suppose it was probably very well done fourteen years ago, too."

"The bottom line of this discussion, regardless of how charming Talson is," John Carl sounded resentful and angry now, "Tracy, you have the right to make your own decision now that you are clear on the situation. Tracy, if you would like to tell your daughter about Kat's affiliation with Lord Talson, that is absolutely fine with us. We completely understand that this is probably the end of Kat's friendship with Tina. We truly do not feel that it is fair to let Tina associate with one of Lord Talson's followers unknowingly."

"Well," said Tracy, "I certainly empathize with what you are going through. Are you planning to allow Kat to continue living with you?"

"Yeah, I guess," said John Carl.

"Well, she's only thirteen," said Tracy, "you can't just kick her out. It's not like she's eighteen."

"Well, she will continue to live at home, since Tamera wants it that way," said John Carl.

"Kat is thirteen years old," said Tamera, "and regardless of what she has decided to do in her life, she is still my daughter and I will allow her to live at home as long as she wants to."

"I suppose," said John Carl in a grudging tone, "I'm not home very much anyway."

"Well," said Tracy, "I'm sure this is going to come as a shock to Tina. She will be devastated, I'm sure, but once she knows the truth, I'm sure she will distance herself from Kat."

"Yes," said John Carl, "I hope so."

"Well thank you for telling me all of this," said Tracy. "I'm truly sorry to hear it, but I understand what you are going through."

"Yes," said John Carl, "you deserved to know the truth. We better get going," he added, "it's after eleven."

The three stood up to leave. John Carl left a tip for the bartender and they exited through the front door.

For a moment Kat and Sela sat motionless, staring at each other. "Let's get out of here," said Sela after a moment. They rose and pulled the table out from behind the boxes, back to its original position. The bar was busier now. Fishermen and other scruffy looking people were sitting all along the long bar.

"Hey, Larry," Sela said, catching the bartender's attention. She flipped a twenty dollar bill onto the bar.

The bartender nodded, "thanks," he said quietly. The expression on his face was odd. Kat could not tell whether he understood what had just happened in his bar or not.

Sela went quickly through the door into the back room, and Kat followed closely behind her. They got into Sela's car and were soon back on the freeway heading home. Sela turned up the radio and they drove in silence.

Twenty minutes later Sela pulled into the parking lot in front of the park. She and

Kat looked at each other. "Well," said Sela, "that officially qualified as something we didn't want to hear."

"Yeah, no kidding," said Kat, "unfortunately my hunch was right."

"Yeah, mine too," said Sela. "That conversation is right up there with all the most unpleasant conversation I've ever listened to. Tonight was supposed to be way better than this. Now I have to drive down to Headquarters and tell Talson what happened. He is not gonna be thrilled about this."

"I'm so mad," said Kat. "I can't believe my parents. How could my dad just sell me out like that?"

"That's what people do," said Sela with a hint of resentment, "I've been there. I didn't have any fun tonight, either."

"At least the conversation wasn't about you," said Kat.

"Put it this way," said Sela. "All in all this wasn't one of the most enjoyable jobs I've had in my fourteen years with Talson."

Kat frowned. She felt strongly that Sela was trying to tell her something, something important without saying it directly. It bothered Kat that she could not figure out what it was. Kat almost wished she had the nerve to ask Sela what the conversation had meant to her, but she knew she couldn't. Kat reminded herself that she couldn't afford to trust someone like Sela.

"Listen Kat," said Sela, "you'd better get going before your mom gets home. And I better go so I can get this report over with."

"Yeah," said Kat. "Thanks for taking me tonight even though it wasn't as good as I thought it was going to be."

"Yeah, no problem," said Sela, "I'll take you to Headquarters in a few days, and this time we'll actually go there."

Kat smiled, "Well, have fun telling Talson what happened," she said sarcastically.

"Oh yeah," said Sela smiling, "I will."

Kat got out of Sela's car and began to walk down the street toward home. She saw Sela's black car pass her heading back toward the freeway entrance. She watched until Sela rounded the corner and disappeared from view.

CHAPTER 9

CONFESSIONS AND CONTROL

This is not possible, thought Kat as she lay on her bed in the darkness. But it had

to be right. That was what Sela had been hinting at all night, and it explained Tracy's behavior as well. Sela was thirty-two and has been with Talson for nearly fourteen years. The subtle expression of sadness that had appeared on Sela's face when Tracy had spoken about her daughter who had joined Talson made sense now. Sela had said that Tina had an older sister. The reason Tina never knew this was because Sela had left nearly a year before Tina was born.

Kat now understood why she sometimes felt as if she had known Sela for a long time, instead of just a few days. Sela was Tina's sister. It had to be true, Kat could see no way of denying it. Kat could not fathom the fact that Tracy had never told Tina about her sister. What was wrong with telling her? Tracy probably thought it would frighten her, Kat thought angrily, remembering how her own mother had thought the truth about Kat's past would be too frightening. Kat felt a rush of resentment toward her parents and Tracy, who had kept the truth from their children. It was no wonder she and Sela had chosen to oppose their parents' views. Their parents had never given them reason to do anything different.

Kat awoke with a start. The sun had just come up over the horizon and was shining through the blinds. It was 6:30 in the morning and the house was silent. Kat hurried downstairs and grabbed the phone, praying Tina would answer instead of Tracy.

"Hello?" Tina's sleepy voice answered.

"Hey, good thing it's you," said Kat.

"Why the hell do you have to call so flipping early?" Tina interrupted. "Look, I

didn't get a chance to quiz my mom about last night but I will when she gets up."

"No, don't," said Kat. "That's why I called so early. I wanted to make sure you didn't mention it."

"Why? I thought you wanted me to—"

"Hold on," said Kat, hearing footsteps upstairs, "I think I hear someone awake upstairs, I gotta go."

"Why, what the heck is going on?" Tina sounded confused.

"Listen," Kat said dropping her voice, "just play it cool with your mom this morning and meet me down at the park at like nine, and what ever you do don't tell your mom you're meeting me. Just don't mention me, okay?"

"Okay." Tina still sounded confused.

Kat hung up quickly and hurried back up the stairs into her bedroom.

"So, what's going on?" said Tina, as soon as she arrived at the park where Kat was waiting for her by the pond. "What's the deal with not mentioning you to my mom and all that."

Kat sighed and sat down under a large tree near the pond. Tina sat opposite her. "The deal is that your mom is gonna freak out if she thinks you're hanging out with me."

Tina raised her eyebrows, "Why?"

"Well," said Kat, "because I'm the enemy."

"Come on, Kat, seriously?"

"No seriously, my dad was a complete jerk last night," said Kat. "He told your mom that I'm with Talson and that I have the power, and that she should tell you not to hang out with me anymore."

"What the hell?" said Tina, "that is so messed up, I mean—"

"You wanna hear something even more messed that I found out last night?" said Kat.

"What's more screwed up than that?"

"Well, you know Sela?"

"The chick you went with last night, yeah," said Tina.

"She's your sister. Hold up, you— your mom never told you, because, uh, I don't know why, but_"

"How do you know she's my sister?" asked Tina.

"Well check this out," said Kat. She told Tina the whole story of the previous night at The Sharktooth Bar, including everything that John Carl, Tracy and Sela had said and the connections she had made to lead to the conclusion about Sela.

Tina stared at Kat, apparently at a loss for words when Kat had finished her story.

"Do you believe me?" asked Kat quietly.

"Definitely," said Tina, "the only thing I don't believe is that my mother never told me about Sela."

"I know," said Kat, "me neither."

"She better not try to tell me I can't hang out with you now," said Tina coolly.

"Oh, she will."

"She can get screwed," said Tina, "she never told me I had a sister, and now she expects me to listen to anything she says? No way."

"Well," said Kat, "you'll have to meet Sela now."

"Yeah, definitely," said Tina. "Where does she live?"

"At the house here behind the park," said Kat.

"You said my mom kicked her out of our house when she was eighteen?"

"Yeah, I think that's what Tracy implied, anyway," said Kat. "I can't be sure because I didn't really put it together 'till this morning."

"Well, at least your mom's not throwing you out," said Tina.

"My dad would like to," said Kat, "the way he was talking last night it looks like my mom is the only reason I'm still allowed to live home."

"This is so messed up, I swear."

Kat sighed and looked up to the flawless sky. "You know what I'm doing tonight?" she said.

"Oh, right," said Tina, "your thing with Talson."

"Yeah."

"What do you think he's gonna do with you?"

"I don't know," said Kat, "I'm a little scared, but I'm ready to learn how to control this stuff."

"I still can't believe I have a sister," said Tina after a while. "That's awesome."

"Yeah," said Kat, "Sela is really cool, too."

"You think my mom is gonna give me a lecture as soon as I get home?" asked Tina.

"Probably."

"Well, I'll tell her what I think of her if she does," said Tina aggressively.

"Knock yourself out," said Kat, "I'm ready to brawl with my dad too, if he ever comes home."

"I thought you were going to tell him about Remi and Roco Ramirez."

"Yeah, I *was*," said Kat, "but why should I do that now? If he had come home last night instead of going to the bar and selling me out, I would have told him. I hope Remi sells him out now, he would deserve it."

"What are you going to tell your parents tonight when you leave?" asked Tina.

"Nothing," said Kat, "unless they ask, in which case I'll tell them the truth. It isn't worth it to lie. I'm not ashamed of what I'm doing."

"You shouldn't be," said Tina. "Do you think you'll see Sela tonight?"

"I might," said Kat.

"Well tell her I want to meet her, will you?"

"Yeah," said Kat, "and if you hang out here enough you'll probably run into her. I saw her here yesterday."

"Do you know what her real name is?" asked Tina.

"No."

"Sela can't be her real name," said Tina.

"Why not?" said a casual voice behind them.

"Oh hey, Sela," said Kat, she was used to Sela sneaking up behind her now. "We were just talking about you."

"How could I tell?" said Sela sarcastically.

Kat laughed. "So, how did it go last night?"

"Well, not bad, considering," said Sela. "Talson told me to tell you not to worry about it."

"Right," said Kat.

"He said, don't get mad, get even," said Sela.

Kat laughed, "I'm down with that style."

"What's up Tina, how's it going?" said Sela, turning to look at Tina.

"Um, well, it's going alright at the moment," said Tina, "Kat just told me that…um—"

"So you didn't know then?" said Sela.

"No, I didn't."

"I can't believe our mom never told you," said Sela, "but, then again, I think she likes to pretend I don't exist."

"Why?" asked Tina.

Sela shrugged, "She hates me. I'm the enemy."

"She could have told me that," said Tina.

"Yeah, but that would have taken some guts. It would be easier not to say anything, since it was unlikely that you would ever find out about me. I mean, I changed my name after she threw me out."

"That's what I wanted to ask you," said Kat, "what's your real name?"

"My given name was Selena Louis," said Sela. "When I joined Talson he started calling me Sela. Then my parents kicked me out and I wanted to drop the family name. I took the name Sithe, as my last name. Everyone with Talson calls me Sela. I haven't been called Selena in so long I don't think I'd answer to it right away if someone did."

Kat looked from Tina to Sela. "You guys don't really look alike at all," said Kat. Sela had brown eyes and Tina had blue. Sela's hair was lighter, Tina's skin was somewhat darker and Tina's face was rounder. Sela's eyes were narrower and deeper set.

"We used to look more alike," said Sela. "Everyone sort of looks different after they've been with Talson for a while. I used to have blue eyes, of course, but I had the color changed. My hair is naturally about the same color as Tina's but I lighten it."

"Did you try to change your appearance so no one would recognize you?" asked Tina.

"Well, I thought about getting plastic surgery to completely change my appearance, but it's way too expensive," said Sela. "No one recognizes me as it is, anyway. I walk past people who I used to hang out with and they don't recognize me. I even cross paths with my old best friend sometimes, and he doesn't even recognize me."

"Who was your best friend?" asked Tina.

"This guy named Sono Silven," said Sela. "He and his brother went to the same school as me. I loved those guys, they always made me laugh."

"Those guys work for my dad," said Kat.

"Yeah, my dad used to work with them." There was a strange look on Sela's face as she said this. Kat could not tell what emotion it expressed. It was not quite sadness, but it was not happiness. It was an expression somewhere between guilt, loss, and triumph at the same time.

"Did you hate him?" asked Tina quietly.

"Well no, not exactly," said Sela after a pause. "I guess I did, but I don't think hate is the right word."

"Tracy said you helped Talson to kill him, didn't she?" said Kat cautiously. She wasn't sure it was a good idea to bring this up.

"Yeah, she did say that," said Sela.

"Is that true?" asked Tina.

Sela turned and looked into Kat's face for a long moment. Kat could not read her expression. Then she turned to look at Tina. "Talson killed him," she said quietly, "but I passed information that allowed him to do it."

"Did you know what Talson was doing at the time?" asked Kat.

"Not at first," said Sela, "but then Roco Ramirez told me one night. That was a little while after I broke him out of prison. He told me that Talson didn't want me to know. I was scared because I knew that if Talson found out Roco had told me against orders, he might kill Roco too. I could have backed out of the whole thing right then, but I couldn't leave Roco to face Talson if I did. Roco told me that Talson had really good reasons to do what he was doing, but he wouldn't tell me what those reasons were. I believed Roco though, and I didn't back out. I kept passing the information to Talson and following his orders as if nothing had happened. If I could go back and do it all over I don't know what I would do, but I can't change the past. I don't know why I did it, I don't even know how I did it, I just did it."

There was a long silence. A light breeze rustled the leaves of the trees and sent ripples over the surface of the pond.

"Do you feel guilty about it?" asked Kat, after a while.

"Again, I'm not sure that guilty is the right word, but yes, I guess I do. I was so shocked when Roco told me. I felt so bad. It was like I couldn't believe it, but yet I knew it was true. I guess I just decided that I didn't care, even though I did care. I was so afraid for Roco because he risked everything to tell me just because he thought I had the right to know. It was like I had to choose between my father and Roco. I chose Roco, and I've never really regretted that decision. I guess I just felt closer to him than I did to my father at that time, so—" Sela broke off. "I think I'd feel worse if Roco had died because he told me the truth."

"Why did Roco tell you?"

"He said he just thought I had the right to know what I was doing. He felt he owed me the truth because I got him out of jail. I'm really grateful to him for that. It would have been a lot worse if I hadn't known what I was doing. As it is, I'm just about to take full responsibility for it. I never really forgave Talson for not telling me, though. I would still like to get even with him for that one. Roco tells me he regrets it now, but I still think I'd like revenge for that."

"They say revenge is a confession of pain," said Kat, remembering something her mother had told her.

"Well, yeah, it is," said Sela, "but I just told you guys about the hardest thing I ever had to do in my life. That was my confession of pain."

"Wow," said Tina, "that is some story."

"Yeah, it is," said Sela, "I have a few stories that might even be crazier than that one, but I've got to get going. I'll probably see you tonight, Kat."

"Yeah, later," said Kat.

"I'll see you around, Tina," said Sela. "Take it easy on Tracy tonight, okay? Try not to mention me if you can help it."

"Okay," said Tina, "I'll try not to."

"Look, thanks a million for listening to me and not freaking out," said Sela, "it means a lot, you guys are awesome." Sela turned and headed around the pond and disappeared behind the trees.

Kat and Tina looked at each other for a moment. "This sure is getting complicated," said Kat.

"I'll say it is," said Tina, "but we wouldn't have it any other way, would we?"

"Nope," said Kat. "Our lives were meant to be crazy like this."

CHAPTER 10

SHOULD AND WOULD

Kat walked slowly up the street as the sun sank behind the houses. The warmth

of the day lingered in the still air. Kat could hear every sound. She continued walking, thinking that she was very lucky that her mother had not asked her where she was going. She really didn't want an argument with her. Kat doubted that Tina had been as lucky with Tracy. It seemed that one day very soon both she and Tina would face a confrontation with their parents.

Kat felt lucky that her mother kept things to herself most of the time. Tracy was not like that. Kat knew that if anything came down in her house it would be because of her father, not her mother. Kat would be willing to bet almost anything that things were going to get ugly between Tina and Tracy. Knowing Tracy, Kat expected that it had been ugly with Sela fourteen years ago, and it might be even worse this time.

Kat stopped in front of the house, wondering if she should knock before entering. After a moment she decided against knocking and pushed the door open.

The house was dim and eerie. Two doors stood on Kat's left, and two to her right. The staircase stood straight ahead at the end of the hall. Kat ascended the stairs. She could hear footsteps above her. When she reached the top she saw none other than Roco Ramirez standing at the end of the hall.

Roco looked at Kat for a moment, as if he were trying to decide what to say or do. "Good evening," he said finally, in a somewhat cold tone.

"Hi, Romez," said Kat much more enthusiastically.

Roco continued to stare directly at Kat. "So, how's your father then?" he asked, with a hint of a sneer.

"The usual," said Kat scowling. "He was in your old place, did you hear about that?"

"Sela told me as much," said Roco.

"I thought that was pretty low of him to go in there," said Kat.

"Well, it's not really unexpected," said Roco less coldly. "John Carl, is—" Roco paused, "low at times, if you know what I mean," he finished.

"Unfortunately, I know exactly what you mean," said Kat.

"Well, I'll see you around, good luck with the boss," said Roco.

"Yeah, I'm glad we could, you know, clear a few things up."

"Oh definitely," said Roco, "I shouldn't have judged you by your father. It's not your problem." Roco turned and disappeared down the staircase.

Kat smiled to herself. It was such a relief to be on good terms with Roco Ramirez.

Kat knocked on the door at the end of the hall. "Enter," said Talson's voice. Kat opened the door. Talson was sitting in his large armchair in front of the fireplace. There was no fire burning tonight, since it was so hot outside. Talson turned to face Kat, his yellow eyes shone in the dimly lit room. "Good evening," he said. "Warm outside tonight, isn't it?"

Kat thought it was odd to hear Talson talk about the weather. "Yes, it's quite warm," she said.

"Could you open that window for me?" Talson asked, indicating the window behind him.

Kat crossed the room and pushed open the window with some difficulty. A soft breeze blew across the room.

"I like summer," remarked Talson. "I get so tired of the cold and the rain in the winter."

"Yeah, me too," said Kat, still surprised to be talking about the weather with Talson.

"When I was young I used to go to the arcade and play all those games in the summer," said Talson.

"How old are you?" asked Kat.

Talson smiled. "Since you opened that window for me, I guess I'll tell you. I'm thirty-nine, nearly forty now."

Kat was somewhat surprised. She had thought Talson was much older than thirty-nine, yet looking at him now she thought he looked younger.

"No one can ever guess my age," said Talson with a faint smile. "You are actually the second person who has asked my age today. Sela asked me this morning. She thought I was older. As a matter of fact, she thought I was around fifty. Can you believe that?"

"Well it's really kind of impossible to tell," said Kat.

"People always thought I was younger than I was when I was young. Now I'm old and everyone thinks I'm older. I guess that's just how life is. I got carded at The Sharktooth Bar when I was twenty-five by Milton Roberts, of all people. He thought I was about seventeen. Maybe that's why I like him."

Kat laughed, "I thought they don't care how old you are at the Sharktooth. Sela told me she used to gamble at the Sharktooth when she was fourteen."

"Well, that's Sela," said Talson. "Everyone has always thought Sela was older than she is. Milro was a little more on the job about carding people than Romez because Milro was new to working there at that time. He didn't want to get in trouble. Milro is always the careful one."

"On the subject of the Sharktooth," continued Talson, "I was hoping to hear your side of what happened last night."

"Well, I'm sure Sela told you everything that happened," said Kat, not sure what more Talson wanted to know.

"Yes, I know what happened," said Talson, "but I want to know how you feel about what happened."

"It made me angry," said Kat without hesitation.

"Yes, I know it did," said Talson, "and that is what I want to talk to you about tonight. I want to talk to you about dealing with anger, because I think we both know that you could use some work in that area."

"Yeah," said Kat, knowing that Talson was right.

"Before I tell you what anger is to me, I want you to tell me what anger is to you. Is anger power to you? Does it help you?"

"Well, yes," said Kat, "I can use my power when I'm angry."

"Do you like that?" asked Talson.

"Not really," said Kat.

"What is your initial reaction to anger?" asked Talson. "Does it make you violent? Does it make you want to hurt the person who made you angry?"

"Yes, usually," admitted Kat.

"Why?" asked Talson.

Kat paused. "I don't know, it's just my reaction."

"Don't tell me you don't know when you do," said Talson without a hint of anger. "You already told me. You told me you don't like your anger even though it gives you power. You don't like it because even though anger gives you power, it gives you power that you don't feel you can control. When you are not in control, violence results. That's when you can hurt people. You understand?"

"Yes, I think so," said Kat quietly.

"I would hope so," said Talson, "considering that you're the one who said that."

"I guess I must understand it, then," began Kat.

"Most people understand less than half of what they say even when they think they know what they're talking about," said Talson. "Scary thought, isn't it?" he added.

"Yeah, that is scary."

"Scarier still is the fact that almost no one understands their own thoughts. People aren't even aware of what they are thinking, yet we can understand what they think. We can experience more of people's minds than they experience themselves."

"People are afraid of what they don't understand," said Kat softly.

Talson smiled. "There you go, that's exactly right. You see what happens when you take a moment to talk with your brain rather than only your mouth and your emotions? Did you know you knew what you just said?"

Kat started to say yes, but then realized that the true answer was no. "No, I didn't realize that," she said.

"Do you now?"

"Yes, I think so."

"People don't understand themselves, let alone others, Kat. That is the root of fear and anger, if we understood we wouldn't have to be afraid."

"But wouldn't we still be angry?" asked Kat. "Knowing things doesn't make you less angry."

"Knowing what we know about others probably makes us the two angriest people alive, Kat. But you can change something that angers you into something that will help you. But before you can use anger to your advantage you must feel in complete control of it. I feel that your control last night at the bar was a sign that you have some control in more critical situations, which is a good thing. However, there are other times when control of one's emotions is critical even when it is not immediately obvious. I want you to tell me, Katerina, where do you draw the line between a critical situation, where control of emotions is essential and a situation where it is not. Tell me where you actually draw that line in reality, not where you think that line should be."

"Well," said Kat, thinking hard, "if I need to stay hidden, like I did last night at the bar, I can control it."

"Yes," said Talson, "but the times when your parents would not give you the answers to your questions you did not control your anger. Why was that?"

"Well, that time, I felt I should know so I tried to find out, and—"

"Yes," interjected Talson, "whereas last night you felt that you should stay hidden, correct?"

"Yes," said Kat.

"And how did that affect your behavior?"

"Well, I tried hard to control my anger. It wasn't easy, but I thought I shouldn't

mess things up."

"What two words did you use in describing both situations."

"Umm," said Kat, trying to remember, "I said I tried."

"Yes," said Talson. "Both times you said, 'I tried, because I thought I should.' That means what you feel you should do directly affects what you try to do, regardless of how your actions make you feel afterwards. Do you understand that?"

"I think so," said Kat.

"Controlling one's own emotions is referred to as defensive power. It is about what you think you should do. On the other hand, controlling the emotions of others is offensive power. It is about what you think you would do if you were in that person's situation. Clear?"

"Yes," said Kat.

"Remember that mental power is not about what you think you can do, it's about what you will do. The power is about willingness, not ability. Do not forget that."

Kat nodded.

"Defensive power is what we will focus on first. Only once you discover what you feel can you begin to understand what others are feeling."

"What else besides controlling anger is there in defensive power?" asked Kat.

"Any emotion that you feel," replied Talson. "Love, hate, desire, happiness, sadness, frustration, greed, guilt, and many more. It is important to learn to control as many of them as you can. Of course, to accomplish that one needs several lifetimes worth of experience."

"Can you control them all?" asked Kat.

Talson laughed, "of course not. I have made more mistakes in my life than almost everyone I know, and I'm not even forty yet. I think if someone could control every feeling, they would no longer be considered human. Anyway," he continued, "one must be able to control one's own emotions to an extent before one can hope to control the emotions of others. I have started with what, in my opinion, is your weakest point. I hope that once you gain more control of your anger you will be able to control other emotions more easily. It will take time, of course, but as long as the desired result is achieved, the timeframe is irrelevant. Failure is fast, success is slow in the same way that stupidity takes less time to achieve than intelligence."

"When I ask you a question I do not mind if you take your time in answering as long as you give an intelligent answer. I want to see you use your brain no matter how long it takes. Quiet, slow, and controlled, that is the way our minds are meant to work."

Kat nodded again.

"Before we meet again, I want you to think about everything I have told you tonight, as well as everything that you have told me. I want you to understand it. Every time you feel anger, think of what you should do and then try to do that. Remember that in most every situation, control is what you should do. Don't doubt that. Stay in control at all times."

This was the first time Kat could remember Talson looking directly into her face, giving her unmoving eye contact. Kat felt like his eyes were inside her mind. Then Talson lowered his gaze.

"I will see you on Wednesday then, same time, same place."

"Yes," said Kat, she stood up to leave. "Goodnight."

"Yes, goodnight," said Talson holding out his left hand.

They shook hands. "Thank you," said Kat. She turned, left the room, and headed down the staircase and out into the night. She walked across the park slowly toward the street, lost in thought about everything Talson had told her.

Kat stopped at the front of the park and sat down on one of the swings in the playground area. She turned on her flashlight and shined it upward at nothing in particular. She rotated it, watching the shadow of the swings in the light.

"Kat, is that you?" a soft voice spoke in the darkness.

Kat froze, stopping the swing abruptly. She shined the flashlight at the bushes to her left. The light fell upon someone lying on the ground by the bushes. Kat shined the light on the person's face. It was Tina.

"Tina, what the—" said Kat in shock. "What are you doing out here." The words were barely out of Kat's mouth when she realized, looking at Tina's face, that she had been crying. "Tina, what happened?" said Kat, standing up and walking over to her.

When Tina spoke, there was a cold anger in her voice. "My mother," she said simply.

"You wanna talk about it?" asked Kat, sitting down beside her.

Tina shrugged. "You told me it would happen, but I just had no idea it would be this bad. I've never been so angry in my life. It ended up getting physical. I tried to avoid a fight, but I ended up hitting her, even though I knew I shouldn't."

"Why?" asked Kat, thinking of what Talson had said.

"I don't know why," said Tina, "I mean, I was angry, I lost control."

"You were probably just mad because she wasn't acting the way you thought she should act, so you tried to make her act differently, if that makes any sense."

"Well, it sort of does make sense, I guess," said Tina, "but it doesn't matter. I was mad, so I got in a fight, that's it."

"Tell me what happened, what did she say?"

"I lot of crap I didn't want to hear," said Tina.

"Like what?" prompted Kat.

"I got home after I talked with you and my mom was still at work. She came home at like 5:30 and I acted totally normal, like there wasn't anything weird going on. Everything was cool until after we ate dinner. Then she was like, 'Tina, I need to talk to you, there are some things you need to know.' I'm thinking oh no, here we go, but I played it like I had no idea what was about to come down."

"That's when she starts telling me about last night," continued Tina. "I was ticked off from the beginning, because she said 'I really feel bad about this, but I lied to you about where I was going last night.' Then she tells me where she actually was. I just acted like I didn't know anything, but the whole thing just pissed me off. Anyway, she was all laying it on thick about how sorry she was and how she hates keeping the truth from me."

"I bet you were ready to blow," said Kat.

"Yeah I was," said Tina, "at that point I was still keeping it cool, because—"

"Because you didn't think you should blow up and let your mom know that you heard about the conversation already."

"Right," said Tina. "But then my mom says, 'I know that what I'm going to tell you is going to be hard for you to accept, but I must tell you that John Carl has informed me that Kat has begun working for Lord Talson. She has been completely blinded by his power and is not making well thought out, mature decisions. She does not really understand what she is doing, but nevertheless, she is working for Lord Talson.' She said that all in one breath," continued Tina. "I just looked at her for a moment and then she says, 'I know it's a shock, but you must accept it.'

"I played it cool and said, 'Well, Kat already told me about working for Talson about a month ago. It was a little crazy, but we worked things out.' That's when she freaked out. I don't know why that bothered her so much, but it did. She just started going off about how she couldn't believe I was still hanging out with you and how if I had known my father I would never have done that. She said she thought I would be horrified by this news, not embrace it. I said I understood why you made the decision you made, and that I thought it was a mature decision. Then I said that I probably would have done the same thing in your position."

"I bet she didn't like that," said Kat.

"No, I don't think she did. That's when she really started screaming at me. She said she thought I was 'better than this,' whatever the hell that means. I told her that I thought she was 'better than this' too. I said, 'I'm loyal to Kat because I know she would be loyal to me if I was in her position. I know she has it hard enough right now without me making things harder.' I thought I was being reasonable, but my mom just started going off about how a real friend would try to stop you from going over to Talson instead of supporting it. I just said 'I never told Kat it was a great thing to do. We both knew it was crazy, but I understand where she's coming from.' But she just kept yelling at me and insulting me. Finally she told me that you were dangerous and unstable and that I was being naïve and foolish."

"That pretty much pushed me over the edge." Tina took a deep breath and looked at Kat.

Kat shook her head slightly. "Wow," she said, "I would have been ready to kill her at that point."

"Yeah, I was ready to kill," said Tina. "She was just ranting and raging and then she kind of grabbed me and pushed me. I was shocked at first because my mom has never gotten physical with me before. I just tried to push her away, but she was out of control. She hit me and I hit her back. She was just going crazy, so I left and came down here. I started to feel really bad after a while. I just wish it hadn't come to this with her. It's so messed up."

Kat looked into Tina's pale blue eyes. She felt extremely guilty because she considered herself responsible for the hardship Tina was enduring. "I'm sorry," said Kat quietly, "thanks for staying with me. You don't even know how much it means. People just aren't like that usually. Most people wouldn't take all that stuff from their mother like you did."

"Yeah," said Tina, "but you've always stayed with me. You tell me what's going on, and you found out about Sela."

"Your mom never mentioned Sela in all her ranting, did she?" asked Kat.

"No," said Tina resentfully, "she didn't have the guts. I wanted to mention it, just to really give it to her, but I know I didn't want to make things hard for Sela."

"Yeah, good move," said Kat, "it's not worth Sela having trouble with her mom again."

"I don't even want to talk about this anymore," said Tina, "how'd it go with Talson?"

"It was pretty incredible," said Kat, "I really learned a lot, I think, and I know he said a lot more that I missed."

"So he wasn't cruel or anything?" asked Tina.

"No," said Kat, "I'm really starting to wonder if all the things we hear our parents say about him are even true. I mean, I just don't see this cruelty that everyone keeps talking about."

Tina sighed. "At this point I wouldn't be surprised."

"Talson told me that he's thirty-nine," said Kat.

"Really?" said Tina, "I would have thought he'd be really old. I mean people who talk about Yellow Eyes say he's like a century old."

"I know," said Kat. "He actually looks young in a way, I think. I don't know why."

"Do you think he was telling the truth? asked Tina.

"Yes."

"Are you sure?"

"Yeah, I'm pretty sure. Somehow I don't see Talson as the type who lies. I could be totally wrong about that, but he just seems to either tell the truth or nothing at all."

"Wow," said Tina. "He's really young when you think about it."

"I know. When I see how much he knows and I think how he has probably taught himself everything, it's just incredible."

"I know this is a weird question," said Tina, "but do you like him?"

Kat paused. "In a way. I mean I definitely admire him, but I'm still a little scared of him."

"Are you scared because of how he is, or just because of what you've heard about him?" asked Tina.

"Just because of what I've heard and because of what I know he has done. I'm not really afraid of his intelligence, just amazed. He always asks seemingly irrelevant questions that turn out to be great questions."

"Sounds a little like you," said Tina. "You always ask weird stuff."

Kat smiled, "He talks about stuff that you just wouldn't expect him to talk about. I mean it seems like there are some little sort of unimportant things that are really important to him. Sometimes I think it's weird when Talson says something that's sort of normal, because we all seem to think of him as inhuman. People don't seem to think that he lives and thinks and feels like a human being, but he does. He's totally human, he's just above and beyond the people we see everyday."

"So where am I gonna go tonight?" asked Tina after a while. "I'm kind of afraid to go home. My mom might not even let me in."

"I'd say you could come to my place," said Kat, "but I don't think that's going to be cool either. Maybe I should go back to the house and ask Sela if you can stay there."

"You think I'd be allowed to stay even though I'm not one of Talson's?"

"Well, it's worth a try," said Kat, "I think Sela's the only one there, because Romez left and Talson was leaving too."

"But I can't see the house," said Tina.

"Yeah you can," said Kat, "you've just never noticed it before. You stay here I'll go ask Sela, alright?"

"Alright, thanks," said Tina.

Kat walked off into the night, toward the trees. When she reached the house she found that the door was locked. Damn it, thought Kat, shining the flashlight at the door. She saw a small, elongated diamond shape carved on the door in silver right above the doorknob. Kat extended her left hand and pressed it against the symbol on the door. There was a soft click as the door unlocked. Kat pushed it open and entered.

Kat went through the second door on the right side of the hall, into the common room where she had first met many of the Silver Shadows a few days before. Sela was sitting alone in a large, comfortable looking armchair watching television.

"Hey," said Sela, looking surprised to see Kat, "what's going on, punk?"

Kat closed the door and sat down next to Sela. "Tina just got in a big battle with her mom about me being with Talson," Kat explained.

"We saw that one coming," said Sela wearily.

"Yeah," said Kat, "but apparently Tracy really flipped out and got physical."

"Again, I saw that coming."

"Tina's afraid to go home tonight because she thinks her mom might go crazy again."

Sela scowled, muttering several obscenities directed at Tracy.

"I'd let her stay at my place," continued Kat, "but I can't since my parents will tell Tracy right away. I was wondering if she could come here just for tonight."

Sela nodded. "Yeah, she probably can. I mean, it's cool with me, of course, but you should check with Talson just to make sure. I mean I'm sure he'll be fine, but we have to just make sure."

"Is he still here?" asked Kat.

"No, he left for Headquarters. You can call there."

"Thanks," said Kat, "I feel really bad about this whole thing because Tina stuck up for me. That's why her mom went crazy."

"I feel bad too," said Sela, "Tracy wouldn't be freaking out so badly about this whole deal if it wasn't for the things she went through with me."

Sela pulled her cell phone out of her pocket. "Hey, Milro, what's up man?" said Sela into the phone. "Yeah, give me the boss for a second will you? Thanks."

"Hello, Talson," Sela said changing her tone. "Yes, I'm at the circle and Kat just came in and told me that Tracy flew off the handle at my sister, Tina, about Kat being with us and all of that. It was about the conversation Kat and I overheard at the Sharktooth. Tina is afraid to go home and Kat and I were wondering if she can stay here tonight."

Sela put the phone on speaker so Kat could hear Talson's reply. "That's interesting," he remarked, "but I think we saw this one coming. Anyway," he continued, "of course she can stay. I pity anyone who has to be on the receiving end of that woman's anger. Do you know the details of the argument?"

"No," replied Sela, "but Kat does."

"Let me speak to Kat quickly then," said Talson.

Sela handed the phone to Kat.

"Kat," said Talson, "please tell me what happened between Tina and Tracy if you would be so kind. Did you witness this?"

"No," said Kat, "Tina told me about it. It happened while I was with you."

"Convenient," said Talson, "please continue."

Kat told Talson everything Tina had told her about the argument with Tracy.

"That's interesting, in a way," Talson said when Kat had finished. "Of course we've seen this sort of behavior from Tracy before. She's becoming somewhat of a problem these days, you agree?"

Kat was surprised at Talson's casual remark. "Well yes, definitely," she said. She was beginning to doubt if Talson was being serious.

"Well, Tina is welcome to stay at the circle for a few days if she wants to," said Talson.

"Thank you so much," said Kat, "I really feel like it's my fault that Tina has to deal with this."

"Well, actually," said Talson, "it's probably more of Sela's fault, and technically that means it's mostly my fault. So don't feel alone with the blame. You're very welcome, I'll see you Wednesday."

"Goodnight," said Kat. She handed Sela back her phone.

"Wow," said Sela, taking the phone. "Sounds like Tracy went pretty crazy. I always hoped she got all her anger out with me and wouldn't have any left for Tina."

"I'm gonna go get Tina and come back," said Kat.

A few minutes later Kat and Tina were standing at the front door of the house. "Wow," said Tina, "how did we miss this thing all those times we came here?"

"No idea," said Kat, "let's go."

"Hey Tina," said Sela, when they entered the room on the right side of the hall.

"Hi, Sela," said Tina.

"How are you?" asked Sela, "you okay?"

"Yeah," said Tina, "I'm alive."

"I heard Kat telling Talson about the argument, it sounded pretty rough, I've been there."

"Yeah, it was. Was she that bad with you?"

"I think she was worse, but I wasn't trying to play it cool like you were."

"I think if I was eighteen she would have told me to get out," said Tina.

"Yeah," said Sela, "she probably would have. She might have anyway if you hadn't left before she got the chance. Tracy is a maniac sometimes. I don't even have appropriate words to describe her."

"Yeah, I know what you mean," said Tina, "I had never seen her like that, though. I just didn't think my mom could get like that."

"Yeah, Tracy does a pretty good job of coming off like a really nice lady," said Sela. "Tracy is quite the actress, just remember that."

"I guess she is," said Tina, "did you used to call her mom?"

"Well, yeah, until she threw me out," said Sela.

"Are we the only ones who know she's your mom?" asked Kat.

"Well, Talson and most of the Silver Shadows know, so does John Carl and his crowd, but they don't know I'm still alive."

"Do you think Tracy would recognize you if she saw you?" asked Kat.

"I don't know," said Sela. "I hope I never have to find that out. She doesn't even know I'm alive."

"She thinks you're dead?"

"I'm sure she hopes I'm dead."

"It must be weird," said Kat.

"I'm used to it. It's hard sometimes, but everything in life is hard."

There was a pause. "Have you ever killed someone?" asked Tina quietly.

Sela frowned. "What kind of a questions is that?"

"And you say I ask weird questions," said Kat, looking at Tina.

"I told you the answer to that the other day, remember?" said Sela.

"But you said Talson killed him, you were only indirectly responsible. I meant have you ever directly—"

"When you kill someone no one really cares how directly or indirectly responsible you are," interjected Sela. "Why did you want to know that anyway?"

"I was just wondering," said Tina.

Sela laughed. "Is she always asking weird stuff like that?"

"Yeah, pretty much," said Kat with a small smile. "Talson openly admitted to being a murderer, so why not just tell the truth."

"Well, that's Talson," said Sela, "he doesn't really lie. He either tells you the truth or he tells you to get lost."

"Can you believe he's only thirty-nine," asked Kat, suddenly changing the subject.

"Yeah," said Sela, "he's only seven years older than me. I thought he had to be older than that."

"What did he look like when you first met him?"

"A lot different than he does now. He looked a lot younger then, but I still thought he was older since so many people have heard of him."

"Yeah, that's incredible," said Kat. "I mean he was only twenty-five when you joined him, right?"

"Yeah, how old is your dad, Kat?"

"Forty-five."

"Wow, I would have thought Talson was older than John Carl."

"Me too," said Kat. "Talson said he was nearly forty, when's his birthday?"

"You know, I've never asked him, all these years," said Sela. "I honestly don't really know Talson at all, I have no idea who he really is."

There was an awkward silence between them. Kat intentionally avoided Tina's

eyes, but it didn't stop her from knowing exactly what Tina was thinking.

I shouldn't be here. These people killed my father, and now I'm betraying him just because I don't want to face my mother. Maybe my mom is right, maybe Kat is making the wrong choices... Maybe I am better off without her now...

Kat felt angry and betrayed by Tina's unspoken doubts, but she didn't let her emotions show.

"Thanks so much for this, you guys," said Tina looking from Kat to Sela. Her eyes were open and honest, and her tone was earnest. There was nothing to suggest that her words were anything but sincere.

Kat nodded, taking a deep breath to steady herself. Kat wanted to leave the situation as quickly as possible. "No problem, you deserve it for sticking up for me." Kat hoped she sounded as genuine as Tina had. "Listen, I have to get home, I'll see you both tomorrow."

Sela gave Kat a knowing look. "See ya, punk."

"Bye, Kat."

As Kat walked down the deserted sidewalk she gazed at the deformed shadows of the trees made by the dim street lamps. 'People say what they mean, and think what they don't mean.' Those were the only words that had ever truly mattered to Kat, but they were not words, they were thoughts. Kat wasn't sure whose thoughts they were, but she had always known they had to be true. Now she feared the day would come when the statement that had guided her mind wouldn't be true, and thoughts would begin to speak louder than words.

C H A P T E R   1 1

BEEN THERE HEARD THAT

"She'll have to come back, Tracy," Tamera was saying in a consoling tone.

"She didn't come home at all last night. Are you sure she didn't come here to stay with Kat?" Tracy sounded more angry than worried.

"I'm sure," said Tamera. "Kat came home very late and she was alone. I asked her this morning if she had seen Tina last night, and she said she hadn't."

Tamera and Tracy were sitting on the back deck of Tamera's house. It was late morning but the sun was not very warm. Tracy looked tired and stressed. "I didn't want her to leave." She sounded more upset now.

"If she didn't take her things that means she'll be back," said Tamera in an attempt to calm Tracy.

"If she didn't sleep here, then where was she? Where could she have gone?"

"I don't know," said Tamera, "I would think that if she tried to stay with a friend their parents would call you to see what was going on."

"Exactly," said Tracy, "I don't see how she could have been at someone else's house without me finding out where she was."

There was a pause. Tamera seemed to be trying to decide what to say. "There is another possibility," she said slowly.

"What's that?"

"I would hate to think that this could be the case," continued Tamera. She seemed to be choosing her words very carefully. "I suppose this would be very unlikely, but do you think it is possible that Tina could be with someone who Kat knows from… you know," Tamera broke off awkwardly.

"Who on that side would do a favor for Tina?" asked Tracy. "She's not one of them, they have no reason to help her."

"Tracy," said Tamera, "I know this sounds crazy, but there might be someone on that side who would help Tina—"

"No," Tracy cut in, "I doubt that. She's not around here anymore, if she's even alive."

Tamera frowned. She looked sad. "How long has it been since you saw Selena?"

"Oh, it's been a long time," said Tracy coldly. "Twelve years, I think, since I last saw her guilty face. I hope it stays that way. I have no desire to see her."

"Don't you ever miss her? I mean, I know you had problems and fights, but I would think that a mother could always find a way to accept her daughter no matter what happens."

"I can accept her for the murderer that she is," said Tracy coldly. "I can't think of her as anything else. You didn't know Selena."

"I did know her," said Tamera. "She wasn't a bad girl."

"Not when she was a kid, no she wasn't bad. Things changed when she got a little older. She had a cruel side that no one ever saw. She made that cruel side her only side. I don't miss that girl."

"What if you found out she really was dead, then how would you feel?" asked Tamera.

"I'd feel relieved that she finally got what she deserved. I've been assuming she was dead for years now. Let's hope I don't find out anything different."

"Well, I guess I'm just different from you, Tracy," said Tamera. "I believe in giving people a second chance."

"That girl deserves no second chance."

"Maybe that's your crueler side coming out," said Tamera.

"Don't you tell me that," said Tracy angrily, "I would never do anything like what Selena did. You never knew the real Selena, Tamera. You don't know what she was really like."

Neither do you, thought Kat. She lay with her back against the tree in her back yard below the deck, listening to her mother and Tracy.

She was becoming very angry with the conversation, however she was glad that her mother wasn't agreeing with Tracy's views on how to treat Sela. Kat wanted to do something to hurt Tracy very badly, but she stopped herself.

Kat remembered what Talson had told her. I'm angry because I think Tracy is wrong about Sela. I know she's wrong, so I think I should try to do something to make her understand. But hurting her won't make her understand even though I think it will. Kat sighed, she still felt angry, but she had less desire to act on that anger now.

Kat wondered why everyone seemed to think that Talson and his followers were so cruel. So far Talson had helped Kat to prevent herself from doing something cruel, even if it was not intentional cruelty. Was it because there truly was another side to Talson, or was it because no one understood his true intentions?

"I still think that Selena could be a clue to where Tina might be right now," Tamera was saying.

"If that's the case, where would they be?"

"You tell me," said Tamera, "she's your daughter."

"No, she's not anymore," said Tracy coolly, "Tina's my only daughter now."

"Did you report Tina missing?" asked Tamera.

"Yes."

"Did you tell the police that you and she had had an argument?"

"No, what's the point of telling them that. I just told them she ran away."

"You might want to tell them about Selena."

"Tina better not be with her right now. She'll be lucky if I let her back into my house as it is, after what she said to me."

"What exactly did she say?" asked Tamera.

Kat sat up straight behind the tree. She was not sure she could handle hearing the details of the argument from Tracy. This is what Talson was trying to help her with. She needed to avoid this kind of situation until she knew she had the control to handle it.

Kat rose and quietly snuck around to the front of the house. She went through the front door, through the house and out onto the back deck. "Hi mom, hi Tracy," she said casually.

Tracy jumped, and Tamera turned around very quickly. Kat smiled inwardly. Kat always enjoyed walking up to people who she knew were talking about her and seeing the expressions on their faces.

"Is Tina home?" Kat asked Tracy, who still looked too shocked to speak.

"Tina's missing, she ran away from home," said Tamera, giving Kat a very significant look.

"She what?" said Kat, with the perfect expression of surprise.

"She left last night and never came home," explained Tamera.

"Where did she go when she left?"

"We don't know," said Tamera. "She and Tracy got in an argument."

"So she just what? Walked out?" said Kat.

"Yes."

"Wow," said Kat. "Where would she go?"

"We don't know," said Tamera. "Maybe you could help."

"Are the police looking for her?" asked Kat with concern in her voice.

"Yes they are."

"Did she take her stuff with her when she left?" asked Kat.

"No, which means she'll probably be back soon."

"I hope so," said Kat. "She has to come back, I mean, why would she run away just because of a silly argument?"

"It wasn't exactly a silly argument," said Tracy, speaking for the first time.

"I didn't mean that it was," said Kat, "I just don't think that's a good reason to leave home. What happened?"

"Well, I see Tina hasn't filled you in then," said Tracy sneering.

"What are you talking about?" asked Kat, "I haven't seen her since she had the argument."

"Well it was serious," said Tracy. "I suppose you had a good time last night," she added coldly.

All this time Kat had been trying to avoid a situation where she might lose control and now Tracy was pushing her. Oh yeah, thought Kat, and I bet you had fun two nights ago at the bar. Kat knew she needed to get out of this situation as fast as possible.

"So," continued Tracy, her voice dripping with sarcasm, "what's he like?"

"Get lost," said Kat, coldly turning away. She looked back at Tracy. "Why are

you worrying about my life while your daughter is missing? Worry about your own problems, not mine."

Kat walked back into the house, closing the door sharply behind her. She made a rude hand gesture at the closed door. Kat supposed Sela would say this was typical of Tracy. Kat was starting to understand exactly what kind of person Tracy was, but it didn't make her any easier to deal with.

Kat went upstairs to her bedroom and yanked her closet door open angrily. She took out a sweatshirt and pulled it forcefully over her head. Today was the coldest day Kat could ever remember in June. Kat walked downstairs, out the front door, and began to jog along the sidewalk.

Kat always found that running allowed her to clear her mind. It seemed to relax her anger. Kat wondered as she ran whether Sela might get in trouble if Tracy told the police that she might be the one hiding Tina. Perhaps Tina should just go home, thought Kat. That would probably be easier on everyone except Tina.

Kat sighed and looked at the sky. The clouds were lumpy and shapeless. The cold air that was so unlike summer seemed to make everything appear dull and colorless. Kat felt down, but she could not blame that on the weather. She was more inclined to blame her poor mood on the conversation she had overheard and Tracy's unreasonable rudeness. She wished she could talk to Talson about what had happened, or about anything for that matter, but she had no idea where he was. Kat dropped her gaze from the sky, back to the monotonous gray cement sidewalk. It seemed to stretch on endlessly without change and without end. Tina's thoughts still ran through her mind, and try as she might she could not get rid of them. *Maybe I'm better off without her.* Kat wished more than anything that she didn't know Tina had thought that. Kat tried to tell herself there was no reason to be upset, she was used to hearing the cruelest, most insensitive, and offensive and downright scary things in the thoughts of many people around her, including Tina. For the first time, however, Kat truly realized that no one else, apart from Talson, had ever experienced other people like that.

Kat reached the park and decided to go to the house to see how Tina was doing. The door was again locked and Kat pressed her left hand against the door to open it. She noticed that her left hand was no longer sore. There was absolutely no visible mark or scar on her palm whatsoever.

Upon entering the house, Kat looked at all six doors that lined the hall. There were three doors on each side and she had only been through one of them. There were also three doors upstairs besides the door where Kat met with Talson. Kat wondered if Talson allowed his agents into any of those rooms.

Kat pushed open the familiar door into the lounge area. There was a fire in the fireplace today, and the sound of crackling sparks met Kat's ears. Sela and Tina were sitting on the floor in front of the fire playing cards.

"What are you two slackers doing?" asked Kat.

"Chilling out, having some fun," replied Sela. "What do you expect?"

"It's not unexpected," said Kat. Normally she probably would have laughed at Sela's casual statement, but she was not in a laughing mood at the moment. "Are you guys the only ones here?" she asked.

"Yep," said Sela, "how's it going?"

"Not awesome," said Kat.

"What's the problem?" asked Tina.

"Did I say there was a problem?" asked Kat.

"No," said Tina, "but you might as well have. What happened? What are you mad about?"

"I'm mad about the conversation I just overheard."

"A conversation between who?" asked Sela.

"My mom and your mom," said Kat. "They were at my house talking and I was listening."

"What were they talking about?" asked Tina.

"What do you think they were talking about?" asked Kat.

"Well, I know," said Tina, "but what did they say?"

"I don't wanna talk about it."

"Oh okay," said Sela sarcastically, "you can just come in here all mad, and tell us you overheard a conversation and then not tell us anything about it. You can just wait and tell Talson about it tomorrow. Just because it's about Tracy doesn't mean you have to tell us."

Kat felt guilty. "Sorry," she said, "it's just hard to repeat what Tracy said. It was about you," added Kat, looking at Sela.

"She can't hurt me," said Sela, "I can handle whatever it is, I've heard it all."

Kat hesitated. Sela was now looking her straight in the eyes. "Will you tell me?" she asked quietly.

Kat took a deep breath and began. She told Sela and Tina everything that had happened between Tamera and Tracy, and how she had entered the situation pretending to be unaware that Tina was missing. She told them how Tracy had treated her, and how she had said Tina would be lucky to be allowed back in her house.

"Nice," muttered Sela sarcastically, when Kat had finished. "Same old Tracy, same old story. I've heard her say all that same crap before."

"This is so screwed up," said Tina in outrage, "I can't believe she said that stuff about you and Sela."

"I believe it," said Sela, "I been there, heard that before."

"She's sick in the head as far as I'm concerned," said Tina. "I can't believe any mom would say that about their daughter, especially not my mother."

"Yeah, it made me sick too," said Kat.

"It's not unlike her, believe me," said Sela. "I'm not surprised. I know she hates me. I know she wouldn't care if she found out I had been murdered. She would just say I deserved it." Sela's tone was indifferent, but Kat remembered the momentary expression on Sela's face when they were listening to Tracy at the bar. Kat knew Tracy's words had to hurt Sela deep down.

"She wouldn't," gasped Tina.

Sela raised her eyebrows. "You want to bet?" She laughed. "She can't think of enough cruel things she would like to see happen to me. She thinks the slower and more painful my death is the better, because that's how her husband died."

"So she thinks you would deserve to die slowly at Talson's hands then?" said Kat quietly.

"Sure," said Sela. "She'd like that, since that's how her husband died. I'm sure she thinks that's exactly what I deserve."

"How bad is it?" asked Kat. "Do you think anyone actually deserves to die like that?"

"Well, people like Tracy think I would deserve that because they believe in an eye for an eye, a life for a life. I don't really know whether anyone deserves to die at all. I mean everyone dies, regardless of what they deserve, anyway."

"But," said Kat, "Talson believes that some people deserve it."

"No," said Sela, "I don't actually think he does."

"Then why does he kill people?"

"Because he has to," said Sela. "It's complicated. I don't think anyone fully understands it. It's odd because killing is the only cruel thing anyone has ever seen Talson do. No one really knows why that is, or how he does it. For all his control, I don't think he can control that."

"I think I might know how he does it," said Kat, "but I definitely don't understand why."

CHAPTER 12

US AND THE OTHERS

"So what are you working on with Talson?" asked Sela. She and Kat were in Sela's car on the way to Headquarters. It was Tuesday night and Sela had offered to bring Kat there so Talson wouldn't have to come to the circle.

Sela merged into the left lane and took the exit onto the expressway to bypass downtown. Kat had rarely been on the bypass because her mother disliked how everyone tended to drive aggressively. With the speed limit posted at seventy, people usually drove at ninety miles an hour or more.

"We talked about controlling anger last time," said Kat, "I was hoping we could talk about depression or feeling down this time."

"You feeling down lately?" asked Sela.

"The last couple days, yeah," said Kat, "I don't know why, it's just hard..."

"Yeah, I know," said Sela, "the first month is the hardest. That's what Roco always told me, but it's never easy. Life's never easy, and as lives go, this is a hard one to have."

"Yeah," said Kat, "it's really hard."

"Yes, but sometimes you will find that the hardest things you do in life are also the greatest things you'll ever do."

"I want to ask Talson about killing," said Kat.

"Ask him, but don't expect a straight answer."

"No, I wasn't," said Kat, "I just want to hear what he says."

Suddenly a small car cut into Sela's lane, narrowly missing her front bumper. Sela honked her horn. "What the hell was that?" she said. "What does that idiot think he's doing?"

"No idea," said Kat, watching the car. The car swerved, almost hitting a car in the lane beside it. "Looks like that guy has been drinking or something."

Sela merged one lane to the right and came almost level with the car. "It's not a guy," she said, craning to see the driver. "I think it's a woman." Sela backed off as the car merged into her lane missing the car in front of Sela by inches.

"Display map," said Sela. The GPS unit responded immediately, producing a map of the area. There were no exits on the expressway so Kat could not tell where they were. "Locate," said Sela.

"Please give a landmark," said the voice.

"What does that mile marker say?" Sela asked Kat.

Kat squinted to see the mile marker as they passed. "5.18, I think," said Kat.

"5.18 on express 920," said Sela to the machine. The map moved to display a red dot labeled 657-301 moving along the road now labeled 920 express.

Sela frowned. "Show exact location of 657-302."

Sela merged into the left lane and sped up to keep the car in sight. The driver was still swerving badly. A dot labeled 357-302 had now appeared on the map. It was right behind 357-301. "Tracy," murmured Sela. "What the hell is up with her?"

"That's Tracy," said Kat in shock. "Why is she driving like that, is she crazy?"

"Definitely crazy," said Sela darkly. They were now directly behind Tracy.

Kat leaned toward Sela so she could see the left side mirror of the car. Kat caught a glimpse of the side of the driver's face reflected in the mirror. "It really is her," muttered Kat.

"Yeah," said Sela, "this little machine never lies. I think we need to get off this road as soon as we can. She is endangering everyone on this freeway. Hand me my cell phone in the glove compartment," she added to Kat. They had just passed a sign saying: *dial 780 to report aggressive diving.*

Kat got Sela's phone out and handed it to her. "What's her license plate number?" asked Sela. "There is paper and a pen in the glove compartment, write it down for me so I can report her."

Kat took out a piece of paper and a pen. They were now two cars behind Tracy, but Kat could still make out the license plate number.

"Hello," said Sela into the phone, "I am calling to report unsafe driving on expressway 920. It's a white Honda civic, license plate number 5XQR385. The vehicle is swerving in and out of traffic, speeding at about ninety to ninety-five miles per hour. Thank you, sir."

"I'd love to see Tracy get busted," said Sela, putting down the phone.

"I wonder where she's going in such a hurry?" said Kat.

Sela looked sideways at Kat for a second. "You want to find out?"

"Well," said Kat uncertainly, "yeah, I do want to find out, but—"

Kat broke off as the device above Sela's mirror buzzed suddenly. "Cops coming," said Sela, slowing down slightly.

"I hope he saw how Tracy was driving," said Kat.

"I'll bet you anything it will be a DUI if she's pulled over," said Sela, "I'd be willing to bet that's she's been drinking."

A police car had just pulled up behind them. Sela looked in the rear view mirror and frowned. The police car's lights were flashing and the siren sounded.

"I think he wants me to pull over," muttered Sela.

"Yeah he does," said Kat nervously.

Sela merged across two lanes and pulled onto the shoulder of the road. She looked at Kat. "Was I speeding?"

"I don't think so," said Kat, "you weren't going any faster than anyone else on this road."

"Power down," said Sela and the display on the GPS went blank. The police officer came up to Sela's window and shined a flashlight into the car. "License and vehicle registration please, ma'am."

Sela reached over and pulled the registration papers from the glove compartment. She handed them to the officer along with her driver's license. Kat sat very still, she felt scared. She had never been in a car that was pulled over before.

The policeman looked at the picture on the license, then at Sela. He then checked the registration papers.

"If you don't mind me asking," Sela said softly, "was I driving too fast? I thought I was going at the speed limit."

"This isn't about your driving," said the officer. He held out a photograph for Sela to see. "This is the photograph of a girl who has been reported missing."

Sela didn't move or show any sort of recognition.

"Do you know this girl?" asked the officer.

"No," said Sela, "I'm sorry, sir."

"This is a photograph of Kristina Louis, daughter of Tracy Louis. Look familiar to you now?"

"Of course," said Sela, "I haven't seen her since she was very young, that is why I didn't recognize her immediately."

"Kristina Louis is your sister, am I right?" said the officer.

"Yes, sir," said Sela.

"Were you aware that she was missing?"

"No sir," said Sela.

"You have no information for us on where she might be?"

"No sir," said Sela again. "I have never had contact with her."

"I have a warrant to search this vehicle."

Sela frowned, "Am I being accused of something?"

"Please get out of the vehicle."

Sela nodded. She and Kat got out of Sela's car and stood a few paces away. A second police officer got out of the police car and joined the other. "Open the trunk," the second officer said to Sela. Sela pressed a button on her key to release the trunk. The policemen shined their flashlights into the trunk. Satisfied that Sela was not hiding anyone or anything, the policeman turned to Kat. "What is your name?"

Kat paused. She knew that they were caught now. Tracy had heeded Tamera's advice and told the police that Sela might be hiding Tina. Obviously the police had been able to locate Sela and were now searching her car and would likely search her house. Once they knew that Kat was with Sela they would have even more reason to suspect her. Worse yet, when the police reported it to Tracy, she and Kat's parents would know that Kat had lied about not knowing where Tina was. Kat could see no way around it.

"Katerina Thomason," said Kat quietly.

The officer nodded, "Alright, Ms. Sithe, both you and Ms. Thomason will be contacted and you will report to our station for questioning. I would urge you to reveal any information you may have regarding Kristina Louis at that time. Have a good night."

Sela closed the trunk and got into her car. Kat followed quickly. "Goodnight

officers," said Sela, and she rolled up the window and pulled back onto the expressway.

Sela looked sideways at Kat after a few minutes. "They searched my car, so my apartment is probably next on the list, maybe your place too."

"I should have known they would be onto this. I overheard my mom telling Tracy yesterday that she should tell the police that you might have some information about Tina. Tracy didn't think it could have been you, but I think my mom talked her into it. I should have realized how serious this was."

Sela sighed. "God damn Tracy," said Sela quietly. "That was an act that she put on for your mom. She wasn't doubting that it was me. She probably jumped on the idea that I might be behind this. She would love to see me busted, of course. She was probably surprised that I was still around, but I'm sure she'll be glad to find that I am." Sela muttered a few more obscenities directed toward Tracy.

"We're in big trouble now," said Kat. "The police know I was with you, so now my parents and Tracy will find out. Plus, we have to go for questioning, and your house is going to be searched. This is really bad."

"Don't sweat it too much," said Sela. "I've got nothing to hide and neither do you."

"I'm just afraid we'll get caught," said Kat, "I'm afraid we've already been

caught."

"Caught with what? There is no proof whatsoever. I wasn't hiding anything in this car, and I have nothing to hide in my apartment."

"Is it illegal?" began Kat, "I mean, is what we did with Tina illegal?"

Sela shrugged, "Nothing is really illegal unless you get caught." Sela went off the expressway and took the exit for The Sea District. "Just remember that," she said, "it's very important."

"Okay," said Kat, smiling slightly, "I'll remember that."

They were now driving along a frontage road that ran along the sea. Kat looked out the window. The cliffs were high, and below them she could see large waves crashing against the rocks.

"Where do you think Tracy went?" asked Kat.

In answer Sela pressed the power button for the GPS system. " Damn cops," she added, "there they are pulling me over and letting a dangerous driver go. I guess they never thought that the woman who is so worried about her missing daughter would be breaking laws too. She's such an act, and everyone seems to fall for her."

"Look," said Kat pointing to the map. It was still showing number 657-301. "She's on Harbor Drive."

"We're on Harbor Drive too," said Sela, "just at the other end."

"She's down by the Sharktooth," said Kat.

Sela cursed Tracy, "Give me my phone again, Kat."

"Hello, Larry," said Sela. "I have a favor to ask. A woman is going to come into the bar in a moment. Could you please keep an eye on her? Thank you. Just let me know what she does. He'll appreciate it as much as I. Thanks, Larry."

"Who did you call?" asked Kat.

"Larry, the bartender at the Sharktooth." replied Sela. "He can be quite useful when he wants to be. That is, when he knows there is something in it for him. I'll probably have to pay him, but that's alright."

"Do you work?" asked Kat.

"Yeah," said Sela, "I'm a dealer at a card club downtown."

"That's cool," said Kat.

"I don't need the money that badly anymore," said Sela. "Talson gives me money for some jobs, so that covers most everything like the rent on my place. I have to have a legal address, and the extra money does come in handy."

"Will I get paid to do jobs for Talson someday?" asked Kat.

"I don't know," said Sela. "Eventually you might, but I think Talson wants you for other things. None of us are entirely sure what his plans are for you. Maybe you know more than me, but I doubt it," she added with a sly smile.

"I doubt that too," said Kat.

Kat had never been on this end of Harbor Drive before. It was still on the outer edge of the city, but it was much darker now. Kat could still see waves crashing against the rocks in the moonlight.

"Looks rough down there," said Kat.

"Yeah, it's crazy down there," said Sela. "The way the beach is with all the

rocks, it makes the water go up the cliffs."

Sela turned up a dark, narrow side street. The buildings were dilapidated and large, bulging bags of trash littered the sidewalk. A few of the houses had dim lights on inside, but most seemed to be abandoned.

They drove for several blocks before Sela pulled into the driveway of a crumbling house with peeling paint. A rusty gate stood in front of the door which hung slightly crooked on it's hinges. A single light shone in the tiny upper window.

Kat felt very apprehensive. She had been in this part of the city only once in her life and she had not gotten out of her father's car. She knew that before she was born, the area had been a well populated ghetto, home to gangs and high crime. Now it was abandoned, but it was said that it was still home to gangs and even organized crime.

"Are you sure we should go outside here?" said Kat, looking at Sela. "Isn't this

place supposed to have some bad gangs and crime and stuff?"

"Yeah," said Sela smirking, "us."

Kat stared at her. "Are you serious?"

"Yeah," said Sela. "The most dangerous people out here right now are you and me. Let's go."

Sela's statement didn't make Kat feel any more comfortable, but she got out of Sela's car and stood on the cracked and filthy sidewalk. "Who lives here?" She asked quietly, pointing to the crumbling house before them.

"Officially, Milro," answered Sela.

"He doesn't really live here though, does he?" said Kat.

"No, he used to. When we say he lives here we mean it in terms of how it is for the others, that is, those who are not with us. There are many differences between how it is for us, the Silver Shadows, and how it is for the others."

"Right," said Kat, not really understanding what Sela meant.

"Come on," said Sela, starting down the sidewalk. "We're already late."

"Does Talson get mad if you're late?" asked Kat, jogging to catch up to Sela.

"No, not really, there is a sort of line that you shouldn't cross with that, though. It's a pretty fine line at that, so you kind of have to feel things out. Figure out when you have to apologize and when you don't. I used to take his time schedule thing really seriously when I first started, but he doesn't like that. He said I was just keeping my life at the level at which it was given to me. I realized then that he doesn't want us to take the rules really seriously. He wants us to take them somewhat seriously, if that makes any sense. You have to just feel it out. You'll be good at that though, Kat, because you understand this stuff."

"I do?"

"Well, you can get a good feeling about what a person is thinking," said Sela.

"Yeah, but I need to learn how to figure out Talson," said Kat.

"Good luck with that," said a strange voice to Kat's right.

Kat turned so quickly that her feet almost left the sidewalk. A woman was standing in an alley between two dilapidated houses. She was the oddest-looking woman Kat had ever seen. She was small, with straight black hair that was streaked with gray. She was dressed in a long black skirt and had an orange scarf draped over her shoulders. Large golden hoops hung from her ears and many gold rings covered her fingers.

The most notable thing about her appearance was her eyes. They were very dark and striking. Kat felt that as the woman looked at her, those dark eyes were inside her.

"Good evening, Marissa," said Sela.

"Ah, Sithe," said the woman looking at Sela. "How are you this fine evening?" The woman had an exotic sound to her voice.

"I'm surviving at the moment, thank you," said Sela with a small smile.

The woman smiled, "Always the fight for survival," she said.

"Always," agreed Sela. "This is Kat, by the way," she added, nodding to Kat. "She's our newest shadow."

"Ah yes," said the woman, smiling. She had a gold tooth that glinted in the dim light of the lone street lamp. "I've heard many things about you," she said, extending her left hand. "I am Marissa."

Kat shook her hand, feeling the many rings on her fingers. "Katerina Thomason," said Kat.

Marissa looked directly into Kat's face with her huge dark eyes. "I have waited a long time for this," she said, "it is an honor, Katerina."

"Thank you," said Kat, wondering how Marissa could have known her, and why Marissa was honored to meet her.

"We have to run," said Sela. "We're a little late."

"Ah yes," said Marissa with a smile. "The young ones are always pushing the limits. You always have to push it, don't you, Sithe?"

"Pretty much," said Sela smiling. "See you later."

"Goodnight," said Marissa, "good luck tonight, and always, Katerina," she added.

"Thank you," said Kat, as they walked on.

"Who was that?" asked Kat, after she and Sela had walked about a block.

"Marissa," said Sela.

"Oh really?" said Kat sarcastically.

Sela chuckled, "she's been with us a long time, ever since I've been here anyway. She's a gypsy who begs money to tell people's fortunes."

"To the others, you mean?"

Sela smiled. "You catch on quickly. Marissa is more like a mother figure to all of us. She's the closest thing to a mom I've had since I was about ten years old. I think she's known Talson a long time. She knows more about him than anyone, I think. I really don't know much about her history, but she's a great person."

"How did she know me?"

"I was surprised that she did," said Sela. "She not only knew you, she was honored to meet you and said she had waited a long time for it."

"I know," said Kat. "I don't understand it."

"Neither do I," said Sela. "I can only guess that she and Talson have talked. I never really understood her place among us. I mean, technically she's not a Silver Shadow, but she is one of us. Regardless of that, though, I trust Marissa."

"She knows me," said Kat, still perplexed. "What am I to her?"

"I don't know," said Sela. "She seemed truly honored to meet you. I know there are things about you that you don't know, Kat, and I know there are things about you that I don't know either. Maybe Marissa knows more than both of us."

"Probably," said Kat. "Most people seem to know more about my history than I do."

"That's alright," said Sela. "I feel the same way a lot of times. Marissa is way older than us too, so she probably knows things about all the Shadows."

They had now reached the road that ran parallel to the ocean. "How old is she?" asked Kat.

"I don't know," said Sela. "I would guess her to be in her fifties or early sixties, but I'm not very good at guessing age, as you well know."

They crossed the road and stood in the darkness on the bluff top. Kat could see the lights of the city behind them. The wind blew straight at them off the sea, but it was surprisingly warm. The clouds swirled above their heads in the night sky. Kat automatically looked out to the horizon. Suddenly she gasped in surprise. Out in the sea a large circular building stood on a huge rock island. It had a ring of gold light all the way the around it and silver light shone through its windows. "Wow," said Kat, "that's incredible."

"Yes, it is," said Sela. "Welcome to our headquarters."

"How do we get there?" asked Kat.

"Come," said Sela, "I'll show you."

Sela started climbing down the cliff. "Are you crazy, we can't climb down that," said Kat.

"It's not very steep," said Sela, "it's easier than it looks."

Kat followed Sela. There were many rock ledges, and the cliff was not as steep as Kat had thought it would be. There was no sand beach; below them the sea came right up to the rocks. When they reached the beach, Sela began climbing over the rocks, heading down the beach. Kat followed, scrambling over the sharp edged boulders.

They reached the far side of the cove and Sela stopped in front of a huge rock with a pointed top that stood nearly fifty feet high. "See that?" she said, pointing to the rock.

Kat saw the shape of a large diamond with an elongated corner etched into the rock.

"You know how this works?" asked Sela.

"We touch it," said Kat.

"Let's do it," said Sela.

Kat and Sela touched the rock with their left hands. Kat looked down at her hand. The outline of the diamond shape had appeared upon it for a second. It faded quickly, as if it were being absorbed back into the skin. A crack suddenly appeared in the rock before them. Kat took a step back as the crack opened wide, splitting the giant rock to reveal the arching entrance to a dark tunnel.

Kat gaped in shock at the rock tunnel. "Wow," she whispered, "how does that work?"

"How does it work?" repeated Sela, "it doesn't, let's go."

Kat followed Sela into the tunnel. "It's so dark in here," remarked Kat.

"It's about to get a lot darker," said Sela.

Just then the rock behind them shifted back into its original position, closing off the entrance. The tunnel was plunged into complete darkness. Kat closed her eyes then opened them. Having her eyes open did not improve her vision.

Kat blinked, waiting for her eyes to adjust. She wished she had brought her flashlight. "How can you see?" she asked. Her voice echoed eerily in the tunnel. "Do your eyes just adjust after a while?"

"No, I can't see, I just know the way," replied Sela. "No one can see in this. There is no light; your eyes won't adjust. There's nothing to adjust to."

"Why can't there be light in here?" asked Kat. She did not like this deep and utter darkness.

"I don't know," said Sela, "there just isn't. Let's go, follow me."

Kat followed Sela down the tunnel, although she could not see her. Kat could hear the roar of the ocean coming from above them. "This is insane," whispered Kat.

"Insane, insane, insane…" echoed the tunnel.

"I really don't like this," said Kat. "Are we really under the sea?"

"Yes," said Sela.

"Yes, yes, yes…" replied the tunnel.

"How is that possible?" whispered Kat.

"Let me rephrase what I said before," said Sela. "Yes we are under the sea. Are we really under the sea? I don't know."

"The water out there is really rough," said Kat. "You can't just tunnel under it. How does that work?"

"I told you already," said Sela, "it doesn't work."

"For the others you mean?"

"Does this work for you?"

"No, not at all."

"There you go, then."

Kat closed her eyes again. She had never in all her life been in a place as disorienting as this tunnel. It was the strangest and scariest place she could imagine. All this craziness, she thought, and we haven't even gotten to Headquarters yet. Kat opened her eyes. In the distance she could see a faint sliver of silver light now.

"The light at the end of the tunnel," said Sela. She turned and looked at Kat, smiling at Kat's expression. "Weird isn't it?" she said.

"Beyond weird," said Kat.

When they reached the source of the light, a large stretch of rock wall stood before them. Kat blinked, not sure if anything she was seeing was real after the complete darkness of the tunnel. As she looked at it, the rock wall split open to reveal a wide and steep staircase, at the top of which was a pair of large double doors. Kat supposed they had to be on the rock island now, but she knew better than to ask how *that* worked.

"Rocks don't just split open like automatic doors, that's impossible," said Kat. "Are we on the island?"

"Yeah," said Sela with a smile. "I asked Roco all the same questions when he brought me here for the first time. He gave me the same answers as I gave you, except I said a little bit more. Someday you'll probably be answering the same questions, and I'm sure you'll know a little more than I told you."

"Is that how it works?" asked Kat.

"Yeah," said Sela smiling, "assuming that anything around here actually works."

Sela and Kat climbed the staircase to the large doors. Sela and Kat touched their left hands to the door handles and the doors opened silently. They were in a wide hallway with a high ceiling. A little way in front of them stood two large doors, one leading to the left, the other to the right.

"Talson's office is to the right," said Sela, "The Silver Shadows' office is on the left side. Do you want to come with me and see the left side first?"

"Yes," said Kat. She was eager to see where most of the Silver Shadows lived.

Kat followed Sela through the left door. They entered a hall much like the one they had just left, only much longer. Sela indicated the first door on the left side of the hall. "That's the lounge. It's a lot like the one at the circle only a little bigger. Down the hall are the offices and surveillance room, and the game room."

"You have a game room?"

"Of course," said Sela, "as long as Romez is around you can guarantee that there will be games. We have pinball, foosball, darts, poker, and slots, just to name a few. It's like a mini arcade and casino in one. We even have a basketball court."

"Wow," said Kat, "do you guys even have time to play?"

"Oh yeah," said Sela, "Talson loves all those arcade games. Pinball and all those wheels that you spin to win prizes, he's great at that stuff. He always wins."

"I won a prize the first and only time I ever played one of those wheels," said Kat.

"I'm not surprised," said Sela. "It's going to be fun to see you and Talson playing each other. We'll have to play later, when you and Talson are done and I'm off duty. I played poker with Tina the other day," continued Sela, "she's good."

"I know," said Kat. "Tina has a really good poker face."

"I realized that," said Sela, "she was killing me. Anyway, we'll hit the game

room later, ok?"

"Definitely," said Kat. She thought it was very interesting that a group like the Silver Shadows would play games and have fun, but nevertheless she was looking forward to it. Seeing Headquarters had made Kat momentarily forget about her encounter with the police.

They entered the lounge. It was a large circular room, furnished with armchairs that formed a semi-circle around the fireplace. Kat noticed that some of the chairs looked bigger and more comfortable than others.

There was a man sitting in one of the more comfortable looking chairs, reading a magazine. It was Tiro. "What's up?" he said, looking up at Kat and Sela.

"How's it going, Tiro?" said Sela.

"Alright," he replied. "Everyone is kicking it in the game room right now, except Romez. He's still in the office, ticked off that you're late to relieve him."

"Whatever," said Sela, "problems arose."

"Hey, don't look at me," said Tiro. "You know how Romez gets."

Just then, the door of the room opened. "Sithe, you're late," said Roco when he saw Sela. "Why the hell are you so late?"

"I'm not illegal, that's why," said Sela casually.

"Shut up," said Roco.

Sela smiled. "Yeah, I'll shut up and get in the office. See you Tiro."

She and Kat left the lounge and headed down the hall. "This place is amazing," remarked Kat.

"Yeah, It's pretty cool," agreed Sela.

"Where's Talson's office?"

"Go through the door on the right and it's the last door at the end of the hall. Just knock. I've got to cover in the office right now or Roco is going to flip, so just tell him what happened on the way here, alright?"

"Okay," said Kat, "I'll see you later."

"Later," said Sela, heading down the hall toward the office.

Kat went back through the door at the beginning of the hall and opened the door on the right. She was in a hallway very similar to the one on the left, except that the doors were on the right side of the hall rather than the left. The hall curved in a small semicircle. As Kat rounded the curve she could see a small door at the end of the hall.

"Enter," said Talson's voice when Kat knocked. His voice sounded casual, even bored.

Kat pushed the door open. Talson's office was a medium sized circular room. There was a fire burning in the fireplace and Talson was seated in a large armchair in front of it. The room was softly lit by lamps that cast a silver light, making a subtle but sharp contrast to the golden glow of the fire. Out the small window, Kat could see waves being thrown against the rocks in the moonlight.

"Good evening," said Talson, "sit down." He indicated the armchair that stood opposite him.

"Good evening," said Kat, sitting down.

"What do you think of our headquarters so far?" asked Talson. He seemed to have more energy in his voice than a few minutes before. His eyes looked almost orange in the firelight.

"It's amazing," said Kat.

"Thank you, I have always thought that too."

There was a short silence between them. "I'm sorry I was late tonight," said Kat, thinking that Talson might have been waiting for her to say this.

"No apology necessary," said Talson. "Undoubtedly you have valid reasons."

"Well yes," said Kat. "Sela brought me here and she wanted me to tell you what happened to us on the way. Also I wanted to tell you about a conversation I overheard yesterday morning, since it had a lot to do with what happened tonight."

Talson sat up a little straighter. "Sounds interesting," he said, "by all means, tell me."

Kat took a deep breath and began. She recounted the conversation that had taken place between her mother and Tracy the previous morning. Then she told Talson about her and Sela's encounter with Tracy on their way to Headquarters, followed by their encounter with the police. She finished by telling Talson that Tracy had gone into The Sharktooth Bar although she and Sela were not sure why.

"I trust Sela did address her going into the bar," said Talson when Kat had finished.

"Yes, she—"

"It is not necessary to reveal her sources," interrupted Talson. "I know Sela will handle that correctly. The rest of this, however, is a very complicated situation."

"Yeah," said Kat, "I'm really afraid that Sela and I are going to get in big trouble. I mean, I think we already are in trouble."

"Oh yes," said Talson, "without question, you are in trouble, however, we must find a way out of trouble."

"It's my fault," said Kat desperately, "if it wasn't for me Tracy wouldn't be acting like this, and Tina wouldn't have run away, and none of this would be happening."

"True," said Talson softly. "But it is not fair to say that you are the problem. Tracy Louis is a vengeful person, and that is her fault, not yours."

"My dad too," said Kat. "He sold me out."

Kat thought Talson looked sad now. He merely looked at Kat, saying nothing. "Don't forget whose fault it is that Tracy wants revenge," he said finally in a soft voice.

Kat frowned. She felt sorry for Talson in a way, but angry with him in another. "Why did you do that?" she asked, knowing she shouldn't.

"If you know you shouldn't ask, why ask?" said Talson softly.

"I'm sorry," muttered Kat.

"Don't be," said Talson, "just know that there was a reason and I didn't enjoy it."

"Why should I believe that?" asked Kat. "I mean, not that I'm saying you're lying, but I don't have any reason to believe you."

"Do you have reason not to?"

"Not really," said Kat, shaking her head.

"When it comes to believing a person we always have a choice. Often we have no reason to believe a person or not to believe them. In that situation we must choose whether to trust the person or not. That is one of the most important choices in the world."

"You want me to trust you?" asked Kat.

"Well, I want to you to make the choice as to who to trust and who not to trust."

"And you want me to choose to trust you."

"Well, of course, everyone wants to be trusted. People tend to be stingy with their trust, I have found. Most of the time people only trust someone who seems to be a good person, a person who they consider noble or honest or good hearted. Those who have gained the reputation of being low, dishonest and cold are rarely trusted even when they should be."

"You think no one trusts you?"

"I won't say no one," said Talson, "but most people don't. They always think I lie."

"Sela said you hardly ever lie, but people lie when they think, everyone does."

"She's right," said Talson, "I only lie in the most extreme situations, usually only

if someone's life is on the line. Many people assume that if they knew what others were thinking they would know the truth, but you are right, thoughts lie just as often as words."

"People always seem to trust Tracy, and think she's a good person," said Kat.

"Those people are fooled by her words. Tracy Louis is neither honest nor good hearted, but if you only listened to her words and believed they were true, there would be no reason to doubt her good intentions."

"People think my dad is a good person, too. People trust him, and look what he did."

"Yes," said Talson sadly, "but sometimes being a supposedly good person isn't the best thing to be. John Carl understands that much, anyway."

"I can't believe what Tracy is doing," interrupted Kat, "I mean having Sela searched by the police..."

"Neither can I," said Talson, "I was under the impression that she distrusted the police."

"Because Sela wasn't caught when Tracy's husband died?"

"Exactly," said Talson, "that is really the reason for all of this."

"What do we do about it?" asked Kat.

"Well, we can either take a risk or we can not take a risk. First we have to know what it is that Tina wants. If she returns home we can eliminate part of the problem."

"So, if she goes back home then Sela and I won't have to go in for questioning, and Sela's house won't be searched, right?" said Kat.

"Right," said Talson. "As long as Tina's story about where she was doesn't include you or Sela and you do some good acting, Tracy probably won't be able to accuse you. However, with that problem out of the way, I foresee another problem emerging. This is a much bigger problem."

"What problem?" asked Kat.

"I could be entirely wrong about this," said Talson, "but I believe that Tracy may not feel satisfied with Tina being back home, especially now that she knows that Sela is still around. Not to mention the fact that she will also find out that you were seen with Sela. I could be wrong but I think this might be the moment Tracy has been waiting for."

"What do you think she is going to do?" asked Kat, confused.

"I don't know," said Talson, "it would be a lie if I told you that I did. All I know is that Tracy never got past the things that happened fourteen years ago. She may act like she's over it, but now she is being given a chance to do something about it. She probably doesn't have the courage to do anything herself, but there are others who might."

"So what do we do?" asked Kat, "do we tell Tina to go home, or do we keep hiding her?"

"Well I don't think we can hide her now. Like I said before, I didn't think that Tracy would contact the police."

"Sela was surprised too," said Kat.

"The greatest mistake one can make is to underestimate others," said Talson. "We all have the tendency to believe that other people will not act in a given situation and that we ourselves will act. But in reality we often fail to act, while others carry out their plans. By the time we realize what our enemies are doing it is often too late to act."

Kat looked at Talson. "Has something like this happened before?"

"Oh yes," said Talson, "and this time it will be worse if we do not act. That is to say, if I am right about Tracy. As I said, I could be entirely wrong."

"I doubt that," said Kat softly.

"Unfortunately so do I," said Talson, "but let's talk about something else, shall we? I'm sure you can think of a question to ask me," he added with a smile.

Kat was nowhere near ready to change the subject, but she knew that as soon as anything else crossed her mind, Talson would force the conversation to follow her thoughts. "I wanted to ask you about Marissa, I met her today."

Talson merely nodded with a small smile.

"She knew me," continued Kat. "She said that she had waited a long time to meet me, and that it was an honor. How does she know me? Is she a Silver Shadow?"

"She is not a Silver Shadow, but she is our friend. She is under the protection of our headquarters and is considered one of us. She knew you because I told her you were our newest shadow. She is very interested to meet all of the Silver Shadows. She has been a supporter of ours for a very long time. She has a unique arrangement with me, actually, because she is useful."

Kat looked into Talson's face. She knew he was telling her the same thing he told all the Silver Shadows, and although it was not a lie, she knew there was more to Marissa than Talson was saying.

So is that what you tell us?

"Yes it is," said Talson smiling now. "I can see that another distinction would be of use to us at the moment. Perhaps we should have how it is for the others, how it is for us, and how it is for you and I. How is that?"

"That works," said Kat.

"It works, which is interesting, considering how few things there are in the world that actually work," said Talson, picking up on the entire conversation Kat had had with Sela the moment it crossed her mind.

"For the others you mean?"

"No," said Talson, "even for us, even for you and I."

"So why does Marissa know me, really?" asked Kat, fighting to keep her mind focused on the subject of Marissa.

"She knows the stories of many of the Silver Shadows, including you. And just between you and I, she knows more than most about me as well. I have known her a long time, and I would not be sitting here right now if it were not for Marissa."

"Sela said she thinks Marissa knows things about me that she and I don't know."

"That sounds like something Sela would say," said Talson. "It's always interesting to see the things Sela figures out. She has a way of being one with the truth, yet she can always lie with a straight face."

Kat smiled. The description seemed to fit Sela. "Sela also said that Marissa is a very good person," said Kat.

"Sela is right, Marissa is good even in her thoughts, which is truly remarkable. I'm not sure I have ever qualified as a good person, but she is very loyal to me despite that."

"I don't think you're a bad person," said Kat quietly.

"Thank you for that, Katerina," said Talson. "Unfortunately most of the others only judge us by what we do, not by what we think."

"Can I ask you something that's kind of off topic?" asked Kat, thinking of something she really wanted to ask Talson.

"Yes, by all means," said Talson.

"I hear people like my dad and Tracy always call you Lord Talson, but all the Silver Shadows just call you Talson. Shouldn't it be the other way around? Do you want to be addressed that way."

"I have never asked to be called Lord anything, but for some reason they do. I never want to be thought of as a lord. Lords are men who sit around and give orders. Their followers do all the work and they take the credit. They take credit for the great ideas, plans, and actions of others, while blaming their own failures on others. Also the image of a lord is that of someone who is conceited and thinks that he is indestructible. Perhaps I was once that, but I am no longer. I give you and Sela a lot of credit for that.

"A lord might feel lost without his supporters, but he will be the same man. I would not be lost without my supporters, but I would be a different person. I would be less of a person. For a lord, those who support him are a faceless group, a mob. They cannot stand alone and act without their leader. My supporters are individuals, each with their own talents, personality and power. I am not what makes them great. I may have made them better, but they are all great people by themselves.

"And just between you and I," continued Talson, "a person who considers himself a lord would never care for his followers the way I do. To me the Silver Shadows are not just my followers, they are my friends, they are my family. I would not be who I am without any one of them in my life."

Kat looked at Talson. He was gazing into the fire now. He looked as though he were sad, yet very happy at the same time. Kat could think of nothing to say to express any part of what she was feeling. Kat could see less and less truth in the legend of Lord Talson, the cruel killer. *Was it possible that there was no truth in it at all?*

"There is always truth," said Talson softly. "Now I want to ask you a question," he continued. "Have you found the things we talked about last time useful?"

"Yes," said Kat immediately.

"I thought it might have come in handy during the conversation you overheard between your mother and Tracy. I could imagine hearing that would invoke some anger."

"Yeah, I was pretty angry," said Kat. "I controlled it for a while but then I knew I had to get out of there."

"Good," said Talson, "I'm glad you could make use of the things we talked about. That is my goal in all of this. We can talk about anything you want tonight, I didn't really plan anything. Forgive me for that," he added.

"I wondered," began Kat somewhat tentatively, "if we could talk about killing."

"Yes, we could," said Talson casually. "I think it makes sense after our discussion about anger to discuss the ultimate result of anger. The three things that most people have trouble understanding are anger, pain, and killing. I suppose that is because they are the three most complicated things in human existence.

"Anger and pain are often the two things that inspire one to kill," continued Talson. "Of course, anger often causes one to kill another, and depression causes one to kill himself. I am always surprised how many people have attempted one or both of those things. I personally have attempted both."

"Me too," said Kat quietly. "I mean in a way."

"My point exactly," said Talson casually. "Failed on both accounts I suppose?"

"Well, kind of, I guess," said Kat. "I didn't really try to kill anyone, but I guess I came up with the plan but I didn't think it was real. It's complicated. I guess we succeeded in a way, I don't know. It wasn't really me. The other failed."

"Obviously," said Talson, "since you're alive. As far as the other situation goes,

indirect murder is not nearly as serious as direct. Basically if you're not sure whether you did it or not, then you didn't do it. Killing is much harder than people expect. Killing is very difficult, in fact, it is the most difficult thing I've ever done."

"It is very lucky," Talson continued, "that we both failed in our attempts to destroy ourselves."

"Yes," said Kat. She was beginning to wish she had not brought up the topic of killing. "I'll never try again," muttered Kat.

"Neither will I," said Talson. "Life is too fleeting to be destroyed at one's own hands. Just out of curiosity, how old were you when you tried?"

Kat looked away from Talson. She was ashamed of the memory. "I was ten," she said without looking up.

"What happened?" asked Talson

"I don't want to talk about it."

"I am not sure why you would come here with hopes of talking about killing if you are not willing to tell your own story."

"You don't need me to tell you, it's in my mind."

"That's true, but I think *you* need to tell me."

Kat continued to stare at the floor, avoiding Talson's eyes. She had never told anyone this story, not even Tina. She felt even more ashamed now that Talson had expressed something that resembled annoyance. Kat knew she would have to tell him now, but still she did not speak or look at Talson.

"Shame," said Talson. "It is sometimes difficult to overcome. I, too, am ashamed of my attempt to destroy myself. I tried when I was three."

Kat raised her head. "Are you serious?" said Kat incredulously, "when you were three years old?"

"Yes," said Talson, "I was going to jump off a fourth floor balcony. Someone grabbed me right as I was going to jump."

"Why?" whispered Kat.

"I don't want to talk about it," said Talson in an almost challenging tone.

"Who saved you?" asked Kat.

A darkness seemed to come over Talson's face; it was something cold, hard and even cruel. Kat felt scared. "Did I push you before?" asked Talson. His voice was soft and cold now.

Kat felt as though a giant hand was clenching her mind, threatening to close its fist completely. *No, Talson, I'm sorry. You didn't push me, and I was grateful for that. I'm sorry, it's my weakness, I always push people for answers even when I don't deserve them.*

It is not that you do not deserve the answers, only that you have not given me a reason to give those answers. I too have a weakness, Katerina. The words seemed to float through Kat's paralyzed mind.

I have a greater weakness than you. You gain knowledge through questions. Your so-called weakness is your power, and that in itself is power. There is no reason for this, except for shame. Shame causes cruelty.

Kat felt like her mind had been released from a crushing grasp, and it was as if she had been thrown backward, but she had not moved. Pain seemed to fill her head. It was unlike any pain she had felt before, this pain was inside her mind, it was inside her thoughts. Kat closed her eyes, trying to relax. Slowly the pain faded away.

"You have high pain tolerance," said Talson casually.

Kat opened her eyes and looked at him. The cold expression in his eyes had vanished. "That was really painful," said Kat softly, "that was insane."

"Yes, the release always hurts," said Talson. "If the connection has been held for long enough and the release is done quickly, it can kill one or both of the people involved. That connection was not held very long, so I knew it would do no harm to release you quickly. I just wanted to see how you would respond. It was not a punishment," he added, before Kat could speak. "I am not angry with you. You in fact were the one who created that connection between us. It was cruel of me to take advantage of that. Like I said, shame causes cruelty."

"Unfortunately," continued Talson, "anger is what ultimately causes this pain. Anger is the root of pain. Vengeance is a direct result of pain. Shame, guilt, and anger are in my opinion, the three components of human weakness. We kill in anger, which results in guilt. Our guilt becomes shame. The pain of this causes anger again which is what makes us kill. The cycle of human weakness repeats. It is a circle and each component of that circle has its own components. Breaking free of that cycle of continued destruction is very difficult. The thing you and I have to be most careful of is that it is quite easy to kill someone when you can experience their thoughts. We have a gift that lets us see beyond what's in front of us, but seeing that makes us angry, it makes us hurt people."

"But you said killing was difficult," said Kat.

"It is," said Talson, "but the part that is difficult is not doing it. The difficult part is making the choice to do it. For example, anyone can point a gun and pull the trigger, but they could never do that if it meant they would kill someone. For us it is not difficult to use the mind to kill, what is difficult is deciding that we want to use our power to kill. This, I believe, is fortunate, because otherwise we would have very little control over who we killed."

"So you are saying that if a person with the power doesn't learn to control it then they can kill people without meaning to?"

"Yes," said Talson, "it is not that they don't mean to, so much as they have no control."

"So if I can't control my power then I could kill someone without trying to?"

"Well, you could kill someone without consciously being aware of what you were doing," said Talson. "I doubt, however, that you personally would have that problem. You have the self control to prevent that."

"That's scary," said Kat. "I mean, I know people go crazy when they realize you can tell what they're thinking. I was going to do that to this boy I hated, but I decided not to. He had horrible thoughts, but they had no effect on his words, so it didn't really matter, they didn't mean anything."

"Not to you, but to him they had meaning. That's why people go crazy. Take away the privacy of thought, take away it's meaning. Take away the meaning of higher thought, and you are left with someone who is no longer truly a person."

"Do you think killing is cruel?" asked Kat.

"A cruel expression of weakness perhaps," said Talson, "but we humans cannot answer such questions, because each of us has his or her own opinion. One person may answer that particular question and say, 'yes, killing is cruel.' Some would agree with him and others would not. There are no absolute truths or absolute right answers. There is only how it is for each individual, that is, what a person chooses to believe and how that person chooses to judge those who cross his or her path in life.

"But," continued Talson, "you asked me what I thought, not how it is for the rest of the world. I cannot answer the question without knowing the specifics of the situation. Without knowing who or what we are killing, I cannot possibly make judgments as to how cruel it might be."

"Are you saying that some people deserve to die and others don't?" asked Kat. "So if someone deserved to die then it would be less cruel?"

"I don't personally believe that anyone truly deserves to die. Some certainly do not deserve to live, but that is completely different."

Kat frowned. She didn't see the difference at all. "I don't think I understand what you mean."

"That is because you are not a killer," said Talson. "Perhaps if we think of an example you will understand. Think of someone in your life who you dislike to a minor extent. Don't make it Tracy," he added with a slight smile.

Kat smiled slightly, "I won't," she said. She thought of Candace Peterson. She disliked her, but it was over minor things.

"Do you believe that this person deserves to die?" asked Talson.

"No," said Kat.

"Does this person appreciate what she has been given in life? Is this person grateful for her life?"

"No, not at all," said Kat.

"Now do you understand?"

"Yes, I think so," said Kat. "You are saying that it is not about what a person deserves it's about what they don't deserve."

"I am tired of that word *deserve*," said Talson, "but considering that I can't think of a better word, yes you are exactly right. Let me put this in terms of what I personally believe. You may agree with me or you may not. I believe that killing is only as cruel as the person that is killed. It is not necessarily a matter of what the person has done, but rather, a matter of what they have not done, that in my mind determines the cruelty of killing. To me, killing someone for what they have done is just a way to get revenge. To me that is low. Not cruel necessarily, but classless. On the other hand killing someone for what they have failed to do does not seem low to me. It is, however, very cruel."

"Is that why Tracy and my dad and the others say you are the cruelest of all killers?"

"Yes," said Talson, "I never said they were wrong, I just said they were low."

Kat could think of nothing to say to this. She felt like her brain was going to explode from all the things she was trying to understand. A few minutes before, Kat had thought that she was closer to understanding Talson, but now she was just as confused about him as ever. There seemed to be two sides to Talson's statements. He seemed to keep everything universal, never being specific about his own experiences, yet Kat knew that behind his words were his own thoughts, his stories, and his life. Behind all of his statements there seemed to be a message about life in general, as well as a clue to his personal life. Talson's powers, strengths, weaknesses, thoughts, and wishes were all hidden in the depths of those yellow eyes.

His eyes, like Sela's, seemed to hold many secrets that Kat could not see. Kat wondered if that was why Sela had changed her eye color. That was what Talson must have done to hide himself. But why? Kat wondered what had been behind Talson's sudden cold expression. It was as if a dark shadow had covered his face for a moment but then it vanished, replaced by the same relaxed, emotionless expression that Talson always wore.

Kat realized that Talson probably knew exactly what she was thinking as she sat opposite him. She looked at him, half hoping he would offer her an answer to some part of her thoughts. She could tell that he was wondering about her as well. Kat knew that her refusal to tell Talson about the time she had tried to kill herself was bothering him. She knew he was very curious to know. Kat would not tell him. The only person who did know was John Carl. He had stopped her. Kat could remember his anger at the time. She had never understood it. The memory of his anger haunted her, and she would never share it with Talson. She knew he could use it against her, if he knew. Kat was not about to open the door like that for Talson to use his power against her, no matter how many times he said he did not want to kill her. Talson thought Kat trusted him, but she did not.

Talson's thoughts suddenly crossed Kat's mind. Kat knew Talson had not meant to show her what he was thinking, but he had not blocked her. Kat decided to answer Talson's unspoken question this time.

"No," she said, speaking somewhat defiantly to Talson for the first time. "Why should I tell you? There are many things about yourself that I know you will never talk about. Why should I tell you a story about my past? Now we are even. I have no reason to share that with you. You cannot expect me to trust you if I have no reason to."

Kat stopped, fearing that she might have gone too far. Talson's expression was unreadable. "Trust," he said calmly. "It seems that we should talk more about that someday soon, since it keeps surfacing in our conversations. Aside from that," he continued, "I see that your control of your power has improved greatly. You have learned a lot in a short time. I did not mean for you to reach my thoughts, yet you reached them without forcing me. Tell me why that happened."

Kat looked at him. She was not sure how to respond. "I don't know," she said, "it just happened."

"Yes, that much is obvious," said Talson, "but why did it happen?"

"Because you weren't blocking me," said Kat quietly.

"And why not?"

"Because you didn't think I could reach your thoughts."

"No," said Talson, "I knew you could do that. I know that you do that very often to people with no mental shield. I was, in some regards, expecting you to do exactly what you did. However, even expecting that, I did not stop you. I did not stop you even when I obviously could have. So why would I do that?"

"Because you didn't care if I knew what you were thinking," said Kat, feeling slightly disappointed that Talson had let her into his mind.

"Yes," said Talson, "and why didn't I care?"

Kat shrugged, "you tell me," she said somewhat coldly.

"It is because of the thing that you just mentioned," said Talson. "The thing I said we needed to talk about."

"Are you saying you trust me?" asked Kat.

"Of course," said Talson. "I trust all of the Silver Shadows. Without that trust I would be completely alone. As a matter of fact, I trust you more than most of the other Silver Shadows, because you have the power. Believe me, if I didn't trust you, you wouldn't be here."

"You say I give you no reason to trust me," Talson continued. "Why do you say that?"

"I'm sorry," muttered Kat, "I shouldn't have—"

"We are all entitled to a moment of defiance now and again," said Talson casually. "Just tell me the truth. You can't hurt me, if that's what you're worried about."

"Well," Kat began slowly, "I just meant that you never tell us about your life and your secrets. You never show anyone who you are." Kat stopped.

"Finish that statement," said Talson. "Say what you want to say."

"I think you are hiding yourself from everyone," said Kat slowly. "Like there is something you don't want the world to see."

Talson looked at her for a long time without speaking. "I have, for some reason, gained the reputation of not trusting my followers and not telling them anything about what they do," said Talson finally. "It is often said that I leave everyone in the dark, never letting them know what I want or why I want it. I have that reputation because most people do not notice when I tell them things. I never make things obvious, because analyzing the obscure trains the mind. The answers in life will not come to you with all the pieces put together. To understand, you have to work to put the pieces together yourself, then you will understand things in your own way. That is what a talented, genius mind can do."

"What do you mean, a talented genius mind?" asked Kat.

"They say talent does what it can, and genius does what it must," said Talson. "I believe that talented genius does both. The goal is for the mind to work on two different levels."

"Your mind does that," interjected Kat.

Talson shrugged slightly. "I'm not sure if I have ever achieved that distinction, but I certainly try."

"You're modest," said Kat.

"Yes, I have been told that many times before," said Talson softly. "Many people are born with talent. Some of them develop that talent into genius. Most of those

people leave their talent behind at that point, feeling that they are beyond it. Very few people have the ability and the desire to keep both. We are never beyond the ability that we are given and we can always find better ways to use that which we are given."

"Does that mean there are people who have the power but don't use it?"

"Yes," said Talson. "There are some people who have the mental ability to do everything that we can do, but they do not have the desire. Sometimes it is because no one trains their mind, other times it is because they are afraid of it. Talent is everywhere, the desire to use that talent is what's rare. The power has two distinct components; the ability to connect with the mind of another and the desire to do so."

Kat and Talson sat in silence listening to the crackle of the fire and the soft tick of the clock on the wall above Talson's desk. They had talked about so many things, yet Kat still felt so far from understanding any of it. Kat could hardly believe that just that morning she been listening to her mother and Tracy, and just a few hours ago she and Sela had been searched by the police. It was as if talking with Talson had made everything else seem unreal. Kat had so many more things she wanted to ask Talson, but she didn't think her brain could absorb any more answers at the moment. Her mind felt tired. It was like no other feeling Kat had experienced, and it was surprisingly pleasant.

"Feels good to think sometimes, doesn't it," said Talson with a small smile.

"Yeah, it does," said Kat, "it feels like I just ran a mile, only it's not physical, it's mental."

"It helps the mind very much to connect to another. Sometimes it is possible to

share memories and experiences with another person through the mind, which increases knowledge and broadens one's perspective. It leaves you with a certain feeling, like no other feeling in the world. Once you experience it you will want to feel it again.

"But, enough work," said Talson, standing up. "We are missing a lot of fun in the game room, I expect. You are welcome to stay here and strain your mind a little more, or you can come to the game room. Poker night tonight," he added.

Kat got up. "No, I think my brain has had enough of this," she said.

"As has mine," said Talson.

Kat followed Talson out of the room, down the hall, and through the left door. As they approached the third door on the left side of Headquarters, Kat could hear music playing and people laughing.

"Sounds like a party," said Kat.

"It's always a party in that room," said Talson. "If there is one person in there it's a party."

Kat laughed. "I guess you guys have a lot of fun."

"Oh definitely," said Talson. "We have a lot of good times together, and a lot of bad times together."

The talk quieted as Talson and Kat entered the game room. Kat looked around the large room. It looked like a cross between an arcade and a casino. In the middle of the room a large table was set up, around which eight people were sitting. Roco, Mevsin, Tiro, Milro, Sela, Remi Nelson, Janice, and Marissa were all seated at the table playing poker. There were two empty seats.

"Hey boss, you in?" asked Roco, looking at Talson.

"Yeah, I am," said Talson, sitting down. "Playing cards while on duty, I see," he added, looking at Sela.

Sela cocked her head to one side and smiled.

"Nice work today," Talson said to her.

"Thanks," said Sela, "but we're really in a mess now."

"So I've heard," said Talson. "I didn't think that would happen, with the police and all."

"Neither did I," said Sela. "Damn Tracy. You in, punk?" she added to Kat.

Kat was somewhat intimidated by the idea of playing cards with Talson and his agents, but Kat didn't see refusal as an option. "Yeah, I'm in," said Kat, sitting down between Talson and Tiro. Sela was sitting across from Kat, between Marissa and Janice, the woman who had been sitting alone in the corner the night Kat had met Sela and the other Silver Shadows. "We've got a full table now," said Milro, shuffling the cards.

"Since when do we let kids in here?" asked Janice, surveying Kat with disdain.

"Shut up, Janice," said Sela coldly.

"There is no need to be rude, Sela," said Janice.

"Yeah, my point exactly," muttered Sela.

Janice had very short, dark hair and piercing dark eyes. She would have been very pretty, Kat thought, if it were not for her scornful expression and cold eyes. She looked to be about the same age as Sela.

Kat decided to act as if Janice had not just been rude to her. "I'm Kat," she said, extending her left hand. "Katerina Thomason."

Janice sneered slightly, shaking Kat's hand. "Janice Carlson," she said coolly.

Carlson, thought Kat. Austin Carlson was the name of her father's new deck hand. If Janice really were Austin Carlson's wife it would make yet another Silver Shadow who had a connection to Kat's father. Kat could not understand why all the people who worked for her dad seemed to have some connection to Talson or the Silver Shadows.

"How old are you? You know how to play this game?" asked Janice, as if to challenge Kat.

"I'm thirteen," said Kat, "and yeah, I know how to play. It's Texas Hold 'em, isn't it?"

"Yep," said Roco. "Costs ten bucks to play."

"I got you covered boss," said Milro to Talson, adding a ten-dollar bill to the stack of money at the end of the table.

"Thanks Mil," said Talson.

Kat reached into her pocket for money. "I got you covered, punk," said Sela, adding another ten dollars to the pile.

"Thanks," said Kat. "I'll pay you back at the end of the night if I win anything."

"You don't have to," said Sela. "Unless, of course, I don't win anything and you do," she added with a smile.

Milro passed poker chips to Kat and Talson. "Here Kat," said Milro, handing her the cards. "Youngest one deals the first hand, so shuffle up and deal."

*　　*　　*

The sun sank slowly behind the dilapidated buildings in the most run down section of the city. A rat snuck around the side of a dumpster, sniffing hopefully. The rat was unaware of the scraggly gray cat that sat crouched a few feet away, waiting.

The rat moved closer to the dumpster. Seeing his opportunity, the cat pounced. The rat felt the cat's full weight on his back. The last thing he saw before the cat's jaws crushed his neck was two huge gray paws and two pointed white teeth.

The cat dragged its kill away from the dumpster and through a hole in the fence. On the other side of the fence was a small junkyard. There were scraps of metal and old rusty cars. The cat dragged the rat into an old rusty truck that lay on its side.

The cat was gray with a few darker stripes. It was very thin and its fur was scruffy and sparse. Under the truck, the cat stopped, holding the rat in his jaws as if to display it.

On the ground at the back of the truck a small boy sat up, looking at the cat. The boy's clothes were torn and dirty, his black hair matted and uneven. He had very dark green eyes. The boy was ragged, skinny and very young. He could not have been more than five years old.

The boy crawled forward and patted the cat on the head. "Good catch, Gray Paws," he said. "The rat dies so the cat lives," he added softly. He sounded older than he looked.

The cat stared at the boy, it's green eyes huge in the dim light. The boy looked back at the cat. Their eye colors seemed to match perfectly. "One thing always has to die for another thing to live, doesn't it Gray Paws?" said the boy.

The cat meowed softly as if to agree with the statement.

"It's hard isn't it?" said the boy. "Yeah, it is," he answered his own question.

CHAPTER 13

FIVE AND TWENTY-FIVE

"Raise to twenty-five," said Sela.

Kat looked at her. "Do you think Larry found out what Tracy was up to?" she asked.

"I hope so," said Sela.

"What's up with Larry?" asked Roco, overhearing them.

"Oh, well, it's a long story," said Sela. "The bottom line is that Kat and I saw Tracy Louis driving like a maniac on our way here. She stopped at the bar and I called Larry and asked him to keep an eye on her. We were wondering what he might have found out."

"What do you think she's up to?" asked Milro. "This is Barty's wife we're talking about, right?" he added.

"Yeah," said Sela. "We're not sure, but we know she's looking for me. Her younger daughter ran away from home and she suspects that I'm responsible, or that I'm the one who's hiding her."

"So she has the police on you?" said Roco, sounding shocked. "I thought she hated the police for their failure and all that."

"I guess she's giving them another chance or something, I don't know," said Sela. "Kat and I got pulled over on our way here and the cops searched my car. I think they are gonna search my house soon, and we have to go for questioning."

"What the hell is Tracy playing at?"

"I'm hoping Larry can figure that out," said Sela.

"Well if anyone can figure this out, Larry is the one to do it," said Roco. "That man doesn't miss a trick."

*   *   *

178

Larry James leaned against the bar, thinking about the call he had received from Sela. Tonight promised to be a slow night at the bar.

Larry was a medium sized man who looked older than his age of sixty-six. He had light hair that was curly and somewhat sparse. His light brown eyes seemed vacant, as if the person behind them was no longer present. Larry's voice and movements always resembled that of someone who had had a few drinks even though Larry was sober now.

Larry now spent his whole life at the Sharktooth, living in a small room above the bar. He was an expert bartender. Twenty-five years behind the bar had taught him every trick in the business. He had the innate ability to watch everything that happened between any particular group of people that came into the bar while never making the customers aware of the fact that he was watching them. Many people came to The Sharktooth Bar simply because they liked how the bartender didn't always stare at every move they made, or try to listen in on their private conversations. Larry always found it funny when he heard people say he was the most oblivious bartender they had ever seen and that you could probably jump right over the bar and steal a drink without him noticing. He also thought it was funny when he heard people say that a ten-year-old could probably get served because he never carded anyone. What Larry didn't find funny was when people joked that he would never notice if a man was shot right at his bar.

The truth was that Larry might let a guy jump over the bar and steal a drink, but he would be sure to charge him double for it at the end of the night. It was true that Larry carded very few people. He preferred to card older people just to watch their reaction. Larry thought that the sign in front of the bar that read "We card if you look under 30, please have I.D. ready to show the bartender", should have said over thirty. Larry loved to card people who were obviously well over twenty-one, especially women over forty just to flatter them.

Larry chose not to notice things sometimes, but he never let the truly important things go unnoticed. Larry was often disgusted by how people focused so much of their energy on insignificant things that they failed to notice much more important matters. The best example of this, in Larry's mind, was the infamous night when the bar was busted and police officers were so busy trying to arrest Roco Ramirez that they failed to notice a man who pulled out a gun and shot a woman at one of the poker tables. Larry felt that it was inexcusable that he was the only witness to a murder that took place in a room full of people, including at least six policemen.

Roco Ramirez was the only reason that Larry continued to tend The Sharktooth Bar. He did it out of respect for Roco, because, in Larry's mind, Roco was a good man despite his crimes, and Larry liked to think that he could be the same. Larry had respect for all the Silver Shadows. He knew the names of all nine of them, and he could name the nine Silver Shadows from previous years as well. There were always nine. Larry knew their rank order, and sometimes he even knew what jobs Talson was counting on each of them to do. Larry knew who was in, who was out, who was loyal and who wasn't. He knew more about the secret organization than some of the Silver Shadows themselves. When asked how he knew the things he did, Larry always replied by saying, "If you want to learn something, stop talking and start listening."

Larry heard the door of the bar open. He did not turn around to see who had entered, he just listened. It's a woman, thought Larry, and she's already drunk. Larry turned slowly to look at the person who had seated herself at the bar. The woman looked to be in her fifties and had medium brown hair and glassy blue eyes that were somewhat out of focus.

"Can I help you, ma'am?" asked Larry, guessing that politeness could be very important in this situation. Larry could always adapt his manners, depending on what he needed to accomplish.

The woman ordered a drink. As Larry filled her glass she said, "I need to talk to you."

"Go right ahead ma'am, what do you want to talk about?" replied Larry, wondering what this woman could possibly want from him. Struck with a sudden idea, Larry asked the woman for I.D.

"Wow," said the woman, "I must look good tonight."

Larry smiled inwardly. He knew this woman was probably over fifty, but he thought that carding her could accomplish two things in one shot. First, of course she would be flattered by it and second and more importantly, Larry could see who she was. He was very curious about the woman because she looked very familiar and he knew he had seen her before, but he could not recall when.

Larry looked at the woman's driver's license. Tracy Louis, 5'5", brown hair, blue eyes, born May 24, age fifty-one. "Thanks ma'am," said Larry, "we are supposed to card everyone in here. Can I get you anything else?"

"Have a drink yourself," Tracy said.

"I don't drink," said Larry, thinking that whatever this woman wanted from him was probably something he would only do if he had a few drinks. Nice try lady, he thought to himself.

"You work at a bar, you can't not drink."

"I go to AA," replied Larry simply.

"Oh, I'm sorry, I didn't mean to tempt you," said Tracy. "By the way, I'm Tracy Louis."

"Larry James, pleasure to meet you," said Larry, extending his hand across the bar. He noticed that Tracy's hand was somewhat sweaty, indicating that she was nervous.

"I was wondering," she began hesitantly, "if you have ever met or heard of someone named Selena Sithe?"

Larry did not move. "No, I'm sorry ma'am," he said, "I can't say I have."

"Are you sure?"

"Sorry, the name doesn't ring a bell."

"Have you seen a woman of about thirty-two with brown hair and blue eyes come in here?" asked Tracy.

"There are a lot of thirty-two year old women with brown hair and blue eyes who come through here, but they aren't my regular customers," said Larry.

"It is important that I find her. I thought you might know her, she works for…she works for *him*."

Larry kept thinking that this woman looked familiar and now it hit him. Tracy Louis, she had come into the bar with Captain John Carl and his wife. It had been very strange considering that John Carl never came to the Sharktooth since he had busted the place. But that night they had come in and sat at the end of the bar, deep in conversation. Sela had come in the back with another Silver Shadow. They had hidden themselves from view by moving some boxes in the corner near the fireplace. Larry had heard part of the conversation between Tracy and

Captain John Carl. Of course he knew the name Louis. Barton Louis, John Carl's first mate, Larry felt a hint of disdain. This could only be Barton's wife. But why would she be looking for Sela?

"You say she works for—"

"Yes," said Tracy, "you know who I mean."

"Don't you think this might be a job for the police, ma'am?"

"I want to find her first," said Tracy.

"Listen ma'am," said Larry, "I'm just the bartender. I really don't know what you want me to do."

"Can I trust you?"

Larry forced himself to keep a straight face. "Of course," he replied.

"I want you to keep a lookout for a woman that fits Selena Sithe's description and I want you to tell me if you see her in here. I'll come to confirm that it's the right person."

"And if we confirm that it's her, then what?" asked Larry, guessing the answer. He could tell by Tracy's body language that she was very nervous now. He suspected that she was fighting herself about something.

"Did you know Barton Louis?" she asked.

Larry had expected the question. "Yes," he replied without a hint of surprise or coldness. "I'm guessing you are his wife."

"Yes," said Tracy, her voice wavering slightly. "My husband was murdered."

He deserved it, thought Larry, never letting his bitterness show on his face. "I'm sorry ma'am," he said sincerely, "I didn't know that was how he died."

"Very few people know that," replied Tracy. "The murderer is still out there. No act of justice was taken and the main person behind the killing was never punished. That is why I do not put this in the hands of the authorities. They have already failed to catch the killer, so I must now avenge the death myself."

"And what does that have to do with the woman you want me to look for?" asked Larry, again knowing the answer.

"She passed information about Barton to him, Lord Talson, I mean. She was the reason my husband died, she is his killer."

"Why are you telling me this, ma'am?" asked Larry.

"Because you know what you are doing and you can help me," she whispered in a shaking voice. "I'll pay you to help me avenge my husband. I'll pay you to find a way to kill Selena, you can serve her final drink."

Larry looked at Tracy, his face expressionless. This woman has been drinking, Larry reminded himself, she's not thinking clearly. "Have another drink while I think about this," he said, refilling her glass. "It's on the house."

*   *   *

The telephone at Headquarters was ringing. "I got it," said Tiro, getting up from the poker table where he Roco, Sela, Milro, Kat, Tiro and Talson were still playing.

"I always thought we shouldn't have a phone in the game room," said Milro. "No business while gaming."

"Just put all Tiro's chips in while he's gone," said Sela.

"That would be funny, he'd probably have the worst hand he's had all night."

"That's just wrong," laughed Roco.

"I know," said Milro, "he'd be ready to kill me if I did that. I'd have to pay him all the money I owe at the end of the night, and it would come out of my pocket if I didn't win anything."

"Sounds like you're speaking from experience," said Kat, smiling.

"Yeah," laughed Milro, "it's a brother thing. That's what little brothers are for, you know what I'm saying?"

"Tiro's a good poker player, though," said Kat.

"Oh yeah, he's better than me when he's catching good hands. Tiro just doesn't have very good luck, but he's great at playing with junk hands. If he had any luck he'd probably never lose."

Just then Tiro came back to the table. "Sela," he said, "it's for you."

"Who is it?" asked Sela.

"Larry," said Tiro frowning, "he didn't sound like himself, he sounded pretty pissed off, actually."

"Oh," said Sela, glancing at Kat. She left the game room to pick up the phone in the office.

"Now we can put all Sela's chips in," said Roco with a smile.

"Nah," said Kat, "she paid for me."

"Oh yeah," said Milro laughing, "you know what that means."

"Yeah," said Kat. "If I get a phone call she can do whatever she wants with my cards because she paid for them in the first place."

Roco laughed, "You bet she can. I wonder what Larry has to say," he added.

"It's good he called," said Talson. "It means that he must have news for us."

"He sounded really mad or scared when I talked to him, I couldn't really tell which," said Tiro, "far from the usual vacant Larry."

"Sela's really serious about following Tracy, isn't she?" said Milro.

"Well I'm not surprised that Sela is suspicious about Tracy's activities," said Roco. "That woman is crazy as far as I'm concerned, and with what Sela has gone through she has every right to be a little paranoid about Tracy."

At that moment, Sela reentered the room. Kat had never seen Sela look scared or angry but she certainly looked that way now.

Talson immediately picked up on Sela's worried expression. "What happened?" he asked.

Sela stood next to the table, gripping the edge. "Well, according to Larry, Tracy came into the bar and said she needed to talk to him," began Sela. "Tracy proceeded to tell him that she was looking for me. Apparently, Tracy asked Larry if he had ever seen me in the bar or if he knew my name. Larry said he hadn't. Then Tracy said that I work here, and Larry suggested that she take the case to the police. Tracy then told him that the police had already failed to avenge her husband's death because they never caught the murderer. She told Larry that I was behind the murder and that she wants to get revenge for it. She doesn't have the guts to kill me herself so she wants Larry to help her. So basically she went into the bar and offered to pay Larry to do her dirty work."

A long silence followed Sela's explanation. Everyone was looking at Sela, whose eyes were fixed downward.

"Wow," whispered Roco, finally breaking the icy silence. "She wants to pay him? How much money is she talking?"

"I don't know," said Sela still not looking up.

"Any money is good money for a guy like Larry," said Milro. "He's not making too much at the bar anymore."

"I don't see Larry wanting to kill Sela," said Talson.

"Tracy was talking about Larry poisoning my drink if I came into the bar," said Sela.

"Is she serious?" said Tiro. "A guy with a record like Larry can't do that. If someone died a month after they had a drink at his bar he'd be under investigation."

"What kind of request is that, anyway?" said Kat. "I mean imagine asking someone to serve a poisoned drink in their own bar."

"I bet you Larry wasn't going for that idea," said Milro.

"Yeah, well Tracy was half plastered when she came into the bar," said Sela. "She was driving like a maniac earlier and Larry said she was slurring when she was talking to him."

"I doubt she was serious about the poisoned drink," said Talson. "She probably meant something else and just said that to make Larry think she was stupid. If Tracy really wants to make this happen I bet she'll find a way to do it."

"What do you think she really wants then, boss?" asked Roco.

"I don't know," replied Talson. "I have a hunch, but I could be entirely wrong."

"So where is she now?" asked Roco.

"Apparently she's still there, Larry served her a couple more drinks and she passed out."

"Nice," said Milro sarcastically.

"Larry knows what he's doing, he'll make sure she stays there until she's sober," said Talson. "The most admirable thing about Larry is that he never forgets the mistakes he has made and he never lets others repeat his mistakes."

Kat wasn't sure exactly what Talson was talking about. She realized that what Sela had said about the bartender being oblivious was the way he was seen by the others. It was just an act, he obviously did notice quite a lot.

"He's a good man," said Roco. "The question is how loyal is he? What is he willing to do for money?"

"I think this is a major problem," said Talson in a tone that did not indicate any sort of problem. He turned to Sela. "This is your life that's on the line, not to mention the fact that your mother is the main person involved, you make the call."

"She's not my mother," said Sela.

"Yes she is," said Talson calmly. "The way I see it, this is your mother, your life,

and your decision."

Looking around the table, Kat noticed that Talson's statement to Sela had taken everyone present by surprise. Apparently it was not customary for Talson to give someone the opportunity to take a matter such as this one entirely into his or her own hands.

"Thank you," murmured Sela.

"Of course, Sela," said Talson. "You have more than earned that right."

"I honestly don't want to deal with Tracy if I can help it," said Sela in a more businesslike tone. "I have nothing to say to her, and unlike her, I do not want revenge for anything. The past is behind me. She needs to put it behind her because killing me won't bring her husband back. I can't change the past."

"No, you can't," said Talson, "but you can always change the future."

"What would you do?" asked Sela.

"I'm afraid that I am not sure what I would do in your situation. I unfortunately know very little about the mother to child relationship, since I hardly experienced it."

A very slight hint of sadness flashed in Talson's yellow eyes for a moment. Kat looked at him, trying to touch his mind, but he was blocking her. "I can only advise you as to what I believe is the most effective and risk free course of action."

"What's that?"

"Well, before Tracy does anything to you or anyone else, it would be a very opportune time to eliminate her. That, of course, would be a way to play things safe."

"I thought you might say that," said Sela. "I don't really care if she lives or dies, honestly."

"You don't think you care now," said Talson, "but you do, and when the time comes you'll come to see just how much. It is more now a question of how much risk you want to take. I really don't want you to have to live here to hide from Tracy, because as you know, I need you to be able to live and work with the others. The way I see it we have two options. Either we eliminate the problem before it becomes a problem, or we face the problem and hope we have some luck on our side."

"You're saying that killing Tracy would be the easiest way to deal with this," said Sela.

"It is the safest, not the easiest," corrected Talson. "Killing is never easy but it will probably be even harder to dodge the bullet in this situation. It really will depend on whether Tracy is planning on dealing solely with Larry or if she is planning on working with others as well. It's one thing if you know the person who is trying to kill you, it's quite another if you don't know who your enemy is. It will be very difficult to come out of this alive if Tracy puts her mind to getting you killed, Sela."

"I know she is going to put her mind to killing me, she already has."

"Well, then only one question remains," said Talson. "Have we?"

"Wait," said Kat, looking from Sela to Talson, "you would kill Tracy over this? We don't even know what she's doing."

"We find out what she's doing and who she's using to do it, then we act," said Talson.

"What's our next move?" Sela asked Talson

"Talk to your sister," said Talson. "I know she is not one of us, but Tracy is her mother too, and it is important that you consider her as well. As I told Kat before, I think it would not be a bad time for Tina to return home, however, if she is unwilling to do that, I am willing to let her live here for the time being. If it comes to that, I'm sure I can make use of her talents if nothing else, after all, we do have a spot open."

"How many spots are there?" asked Kat, after a short silence.

"Nine Silver Shadows," said Sela. "There is a rank order and the top three are the captains. That's Roco, Tiro and me right now. Then there are two people who are to be considered if a spot opened up, they are number ten and eleven."

"When do spots open up?"

"If someone gets hurt or sick, or if someone dies," said Sela. "Sometimes people leave or get thrown in jail, any number of reasons."

"So something happened to the person who used to have my spot?" asked Kat.

Sela looked at Talson. "That person died," said Talson quietly. "Not too long ago we were two short of nine. Technically we still only have eight, but I count Marissa in the nine now, until someone comes along to fill the spot."

"Why is it nine?" asked Kat.

"Well, nine is the highest number. I always wanted nine and then myself, the one with the power. I think that was exceedingly arrogant of me now, but I cannot change the past. I realize now that I am not the only one with the power and I never was. We all have a small part of the power, some of us just have more than others and some are more willing to use it than others. The ability is anything you want it to be, the power is anything you need it to be."

*   *   *

An orange cage of light hung over the city. A tall man with dark hair staggered, drunk, out of his car. Feet away from him a ragged looking woman stood in a grimy doorway clutching two children.

"Get in the car, we're leaving," yelled the man.

"No, you're drunk," the woman protested.

"I SAID GET IN," roared the man, advancing toward the woman and raising his hand as if to strike her.

The woman looked terrified and she hurried toward the car, pulling her children with her. The smaller of the two boys, who looked scarcely four years old, pulled away from his mother as the older boy quickly climbed into the back seat of the car without argument. "Come here," the woman called desperately to her younger child.

"No," said the boy in a voice of soft defiance. He stood a distance from the car with his arms folded across his chest.

The drunken man advanced toward the boy. "Did you just say no to me?" he demanded.

The boy said nothing, but continued to stare defiantly at his father. *Get in, Larry.*

"Shut up," the man yelled at the other boy, even though the boy hadn't said anything. He grabbed the boy by the front of his shirt and threw him headlong into the back seat of the car. He slammed the door and staggered into the driver's seat. The younger boy landed sprawled across the older boy's lap. He sat up immediately, staring at the back of his father's head with cold green eyes.

The older boy, who looked no more than eight years of age, grabbed the younger boy by the shoulder.

Calm down, man.

I'm gonna run.

Are you crazy?

Maybe.

The man pulled out onto a highway that ran along the sea, driving fast and swerving slightly. Below the tall cliffs, the stormy sea roared in the darkness. The woman in the front seat screamed in terror as the car almost went off the road.

"Shut up," the man snapped at his wife, who sat in terrified silence.

"Don't talk to her like that," the younger boy said coldly.

The man turned around in his seat, taking both his hands off the steering wheel. He raised his hand and made to hit the boy, but the small boy ducked. The car swerved across the median. The man quickly turned around, cursing as he tried to pull the car straight. The car spun out of control and hit the guardrail on the right, then flipped across the road and over the bluff top.

Rain began to fall on the empty road. The stormy sea slammed water against the rocks.

"Mom, Mom," the older boy called, as he struggled to sit up. There was blood on his hands and down his shirt. The car had landed upside down on a rock ledge. Amazingly it had not tumbled down the face of the cliff. "Mom?" the boy called again. There was silence except for the storm. "Larry?" the boy whispered.

"Get out of there." The younger boy was standing on the rocks outside the car. He was cut on his right arm and across his chest.

"How did you get out?"

"The window is broken on my side."

The older boy could not get his door open, so he climbed out the broken window. His body ached all over. The younger did not offer his hand to help him out through the window. He stood next to the car watching him struggle.

The car's windshield was shattered but the headlights were still shining, illuminating the rocks below. Feet below the car a broken body lay sprawled across the rocks.

"Mom," cried the older boy, catching sight of the body on the rocks below. He tried to scramble down the rocks, but the younger boy grabbed his brother by the back of his jacket.

"Don't go," he said, his voice shook slightly, "it's over."

"No," said the older desperately.

It was my fault, I made Dad turn around, that's why we crashed and that's why she…

No it's not, it was Dad's fault for making us get in the car with him.

The two boys stood together in the darkness, looking at the body of their mother below them. Tears fell silently down the older boy's face. The younger boy frowned, holding back tears.

Inside the car their father grunted and moved slightly. The boys turned, both staring at him in disgust.

"Murderer," said the older boy.

He'll wake up soon, and when he does, I'll be gone. I'm running.

Are you crazy?

Not crazy enough to stay here with him.

You are going to leave me with him?

I'm not leaving you with anything. Did I say you couldn't run too?

No, but you know I won't.

That's your problem.

You'll die. You won't be able to survive out there, you're too young.

You wanna bet?

Yeah.

"You're on, five bucks," said the younger pulling the money from his pocket and handing it to his brother. He held out his hand. The older boy looked slightly surprised as they shook hands.

The younger boy gave his brother a sort of half hug with one arm before turning away and began to climb the cliff. He never looked back as he crossed the road, heading toward the lights of the city. His brother watched him until he disappeared from view in the rain and the darkness. He turned again to face the sea, hearing police sirens in the distance. "I hope I lose that bet," he murmured softly.

CHAPTER 14

THE FOURTH SHADOW

John Carl was trying to untangle a large coil of rope as he prepared to leave the dock. Normally untangling rope was not part of John Carl's job description as captain, but today he was missing two deck hands. Remi Nelson had simply not shown up for work. John Carl's other deck hand, Austin Carlson had called to say there had been an emergency in his family and he could not make the trip.

John Carl had decided to go out anyway with only two deck hands, Sono and

Browen. This meant that all three of them would have to work much harder than usual, and John Carl had to do some jobs he hadn't done since his days as a deck hand twenty years ago.

"The one day when Austin can't come, that idiot Remi doesn't show up," muttered John Carl.

"Yeah, I know," said Sono, "but we can do it ourselves. We'll be fine."

"It could be worse, Cap," said Browen.

That's Sono and Browen, thought John Carl, always optimistic. The captain was feeling anything but optimistic at the moment. He had been very depressed lately, even more than his usually gloomy attitude.

Ever since the day when Sono had seen the captain crying in his quarters, he and Browen had been trying to keep a close eye on John Carl. They noticed that he talked less than usual, and kept to himself more. He gave the crew less orders and more freedom to run things their way. These days, he often left Sono in charge and went below deck for long periods of time.

191

Although Sono and Browen were still very curious about their captain's behavior, neither of them tried to spy on him in his cabin again. They hoped that on this trip, since they would be the only two deck hands, John Carl would have to remain on deck or at the wheel at all times. This might give them the opportunity to ask John Carl what was going on.

"Listen, mates," said John Carl. "If the fishing is good this is going to be hard, but we'll stop fishing and rest when we can. It's gonna be two men on deck and one man driving. When the fishing is slow we can have one man sleeping, got it?"

"Got it, Cap," said Sono.

"We're in," said Browen.

"We can do this, Cap," said Sono, "you know the old mate, Barty will be out there with us. We're never really alone, right Cap?"

"Yeah," said John Carl, not meeting Sono's eyes. "Life's hard."

"Yeah, but it's worth it, man," said Sono.

"I wonder why Remi didn't show," said Browen as they left the harbor.

"He probably had a job he couldn't get out of," said John Carl sounding slightly annoyed.

"What kind of job?" asked Browen, frowning.

"Who knows," said John Carl. "I expect that Remi is on the edge and can't afford to miss a job."

Sono and Browen looked at each other with identical confused expressions. Neither of them had any idea what John Carl was talking about.

"So are you going to fire him?" asked Sono. He really didn't think he needed to ask, considering how many deck hands John Carl had fired for not showing up to work.

"Nah," said John Carl. "Not unless this trip goes really bad, in which case I might be mad enough to fire him."

"Where else does Remi have a job?" asked Browen.

"Talson," replied John Carl simply.

"No way," said Sono and Browen in unison.

"How long has he been doing that?" asked Sono in a shocked voice.

"Years and years," said John Carl, still very casually. "He's been working with me for fifteen years now, and I'm pretty sure he's been on the other side for at least that long, if not longer."

"So you don't care that one of your deck hands works for Lord Talson?"

"Well, it's not that I don't care," said John Carl, "it's just that there is very little I can do about it. I would care a lot more if it was someone important, but not Remi. It's actually kind of useful in a way. I can sometimes get him to tell me stuff, so I know who's in with Talson and who's not. Roco is still there, now that he's out of jail of course."

"How did he get out?" asked Sono, "that was insane."

"No clue," said John Carl. "I'm sure Talson helped him, I just don't have any idea how. Milro is still there too," he added.

"Milton Roberts?" said Browen in surprise. "I haven't seen him since the old days at the Sharktooth."

"Yeah, I can't believe he never got caught," said John Carl bitterly.

"That's crazy," said Sono. "I mean, how do we know whose side Remi's really on. Aren't you afraid that he'll pass information about you to Talson?"

At this John Carl actually laughed. "No," he said still laughing. "This is Remi Nelson we're talking about. I seriously doubt Talson would learn anything about me that he doesn't already know from listening to Remi."

"What about information about us?" asked Browen.

"Believe me," said John Carl, "if Talson wants to know stuff about you two, Remi won't be the one he'll ask."

"Who will he ask then?"

"Selena Louis," said John Carl simply.

"What?" whispered Sono, "is she still there?"

"Of course Remi said she wasn't. Tracy and I know that was a lie."

"So where is she?" asked Sono.

"I don't know," said John Carl. "But she's been seen by the police. They stopped her on express 920 last night. We don't know where she is now, but Tracy is determined to find her."

"That's insane," said Browen. "What does Tracy want with her?"

"Tracy wants to find her because she's the one who sold us out," said John Carl angrily.

"I can't believe she's still around and I've never seen her," said Sono. "I miss Selena."

"Yeah, well she's the biggest traitor on the planet," said John Carl coldly.

"I never understood that whole thing," said Browen.

"None of us did," said John Carl.

"So what's Tracy going to do if she finds her?" asked Sono.

"She wants to get revenge for her husband," said John Carl simply.

"Yeah, but Selena is her daughter," said Sono.

"Yeah, the daughter that killed her husband," said John Carl coldly.

"What do you mean, she wants revenge?" asked Browen. "What does that mean?"

John Carl sighed. "Can I trust you guys?"

"Of course," said Sono, wondering if anyone had ever answered that question any other way.

"Well, just between us," said John Carl, "Tracy is hoping to find a way to eliminate Selena, if possible. Tracy believes that only then will she feel like justice has been served for her husband's death. She is very angry that those responsible were not punished when he died."

"But there isn't any real proof that Selena was responsible, is there?" asked Browen.

"We know it was her, there is no question," said John Carl.

"I mean real hard evidence," said Browen.

"Well, that was the problem. There is no evidence that can be used in court to try to convict anyone. There never seems to be any true evidence with Talson, because there's always more than one person behind a murder. It's easy to tell who the guilty ones are, but we cannot prove it in the sense of the law."

"But you guys are sure beyond a doubt that it was her, right?"

"Yes, we are sure it was her," said John Carl. "I was close to Barty and I saw what he went through. I saw what she did."

"But Selena might not have known what she was doing," said Sono.

"How was she supposed to know what Talson was doing?"

"She knew," said John Carl coldly. "Roco Ramirez knew and he told her. I overheard the conversation in The Sharktooth Bar. Roco told her that Talson was trying to kill Barty. She asked him why and Roco said he couldn't tell her that. She may not have known why Talson wanted to kill Barty, but she did know that Talson was using her to do it. She knew, and she did it anyway."

"But—" began Sono.

"Selena is a traitor and a murderer," said John Carl in a deadly voice. "Stop defending her."

"Sorry," muttered Sono, not meeting his captain's eyes. "It's just hard to accept, I mean, she was the best friend I ever had, and…" Sono's voice trailed off.

"I know," said John Carl softly, "I've been there, mate."

"I just can't believe she would do that," said Browen. "I mean Selena was so cool. I just can't imagine her doing something like that. She was so smart, and funny, and such a good person. She had no cruel intentions."

"Well, no obvious cruel intentions," said John Carl. "Some people are just good actors. You would be surprised at the kind of people who go to Talson."

"Like who else besides Selena?" asked Sono. "I mean, I can see it with someone like Remi, it's not that shocking."

"I wasn't talking about Remi," said John Carl. "You want an example that will really be shocking?"

"Go for it," said Sono.

"How about Katerina Thomason."

Browen and Sono stopped working and stood speechless on deck, staring at John Carl. "Are you serious?" whispered Sono.

"That's what I said," said John Carl. "Man, I freaked out when Kat told me. So did my wife, of course. We told Tracy and she was hysterical. First Selena, now Kat, it's just too much, you know? And of course, it's even scarier with Kat."

"How is it scarier?" asked Browen.

"Because Kat has ability which she does not hesitate to use."

"What?" said Sono, "are you talking about the stuff Lord Talson does?"

"Yeah, I am," said John Carl. "She's used it on me, or at least she tried to, when I made her angry."

"No wonder you freaked out," said Sono.

"Yeah, I was so angry when I first found out," said John Carl, "then I started to feel really upset, now I'm just scared."

"No kidding," said Sono, "of course you're scared. God, I remember Kat. Born on Friday the thirteenth and all that. She changed our luck. She used to come out with us and every time she did we had great luck."

"Yeah," said Browen, "she was great. She always made me laugh, too. Her and Tina."

"What about Tina?" asked Sono. "How is she taking all this? Is she going that way too?"

"Well, she ran away from home after she got in an argument with her mother. Tracy told her about Kat joining Talson, and was just trying to explain to Tina that her friendship with Kat had to end. Apparently, Kat had already told Tina, and Tina supported Kat's decision. When Tina told Tracy that, Tracy lost control, as you could imagine."

"And what did Tina do?" asked Browen.

"She walked out without any of her stuff and never came back," replied John Carl.

"Wow," said Sono, "what about Kat, have you asked her if she knows where Tina is? Or is she gone too?"

"No, Kat's still home, but she claims she hasn't seen Tina since she ran away," said John Carl. "We all think she's lying, but she might not be. It's hard to tell with Kat. She can lie with a straight face, plus Talson's working with her now."

"Kind of like Selena," muttered Sono. "She could always lie without getting caught in it." He paused. "I guess that's how she—"

"Fooled us and betrayed us," finished John Carl.

"Selena never let her feelings show unless she wanted to," said Browen. "I guess it was easy for her to fool all of us who liked her so much."

"Does Tina know about Selena?" asked Sono.

"She didn't, but we think she does now. Kat was in the car when the police pulled her over last night. We're almost sure that they are hiding Tina, we just don't know where."

"Kat was with Selena?" said Sono, in shock.

"Yep," said John Carl.

"Where were they?" asked Browen.

"On the 920 expressway at about nine last night," replied John Carl. "Tracy told

the police on Monday that she suspected Selena Louis was hiding Tina. They couldn't find Selena at first because she changed her name, but eventually they found her. Apparently she has an apartment in the downtown area and she has a registered vehicle. The police found her on the expressway last night and pulled her over. They didn't find anything in her car, but Kat was with her."

"That's insane."

"What's even more insane is that Tracy told me that she was on that same road in the same area that Selena was pulled over at that time last night. She was on her way to The Sharktooth Bar."

"Why was she going there?"

"Well, Tracy wasn't ready to sit back and let the police do their job," said John Carl. "You know Tracy, she has to get into things herself. She went to the bar to ask Larry James if he knew anything."

"What did Larry say?" asked Browen. "Isn't he supposed to know a lot about Talson's followers?"

"Supposedly," said John Carl off handedly, "but he didn't tell Tracy much. I don't know the details, I only saw Tracy very briefly this morning. She was pretty hung over at that. She didn't remember much. I bet that bartender, Larry, spiked her drink because she passed out at the bar."

"So did the police call you?" asked Sono.

"Yeah, last night," said John Carl.

"What did you tell them?"

"Well, they asked me if Kat had permission to be with Selena," said John Carl, "and I said no. They said they would follow the vehicle, but apparently they never found it again, and Kat never came home."

"Where do you think they went?" asked Sono.

"No clue," said John Carl.

"So I guess this means that Kat really does know where Tina is. She and Selena are probably hiding her somewhere," said Browen.

"But how?" asked Sono. "How did they just disappear? How could the cops not have found them again?"

"Figuring out what Talson is doing is a lot easier than figuring out how he's doing it," said John Carl. "Kat probably was the one who met Selena and figured out that she was Tina's sister. The reason Tracy never told Tina about her sister is that she was afraid that Talson would use it against her. It is for the same reason that my wife and I never told Kat a lot of things. It has come back to hurt us now that Kat has taken it upon herself to find out everything she possibly can, even if it means working for Talson. It's been a huge blow to me, especially now that she seems to have taken Tina with her," finished John Carl.

"Well it sounds like Kat kind of sold you out too, if that's what you want to call it," said Sono.

"I'll say she did, she and I had a big argument which ended with me up against the wall. A lot of things came out in that, but she stayed at home. I'm just letting her live there," he added in a resentful tone. "I can't kick her out, so I have to just sit here and let her sell me out."

"Now I see why the thing with Remi isn't a big deal," said Sono.

"Are you afraid that Kat is going to, you know, do what Selena did?" asked Browen softly.

"She might," said John Carl, "but I doubt she will be able to tell Talson anything he doesn't already know, either."

"Is that because Kat doesn't know you very well, or because Talson knows you very well?" asked Browen.

"Unfortunately, or perhaps in some ways fortunately, the second one," said John Carl. He felt a slight twinge of fear as he said this. How much did he actually know? Without a doubt it was enough, but yet he had not tried again. It was ridiculous to think that he cared or even remembered. It was wishful thinking to imagine that this was a gesture of apology or even peace. That was impossible now. It's all gone, thought John Carl. All lost behind the yellow eyes of murder.

John Carl's hand clenched something in his pocket. He wanted to throw it over the side of the boat into the sea. He wanted to end it, but he could not. "You've taken everything now, Talson," he said softly. "My life is all that's left for you."

*   *   *

Kat walked slowly down the street. The air shimmered above the road in the extreme heat. Kat could not remember a day hotter than this one in a long time. The sun beat down on her, and the air seemed to hang stagnant. The distance to the end of the block seemed endless.

Kat paused at the corner. The houses along the street were all closed up and there was no one in sight. The only sound that could be heard was the rhythmic hum of air conditioners and the squeal of the power lines overhead, the sound of the city's power supply being pushed to the maximum.

Kat turned her head to the left and saw a figure walking toward her down the sidewalk. Kat squinted through the haze as the person came closer and realized that it was Tracy.

Tracy looked at Kat. "Where is she, I know you know."

"Hello Tracy," said Kat pleasantly. "Crazy how hot it is today, isn't it?"

Don't talk to me like that. "Yes, it's terrible," said Tracy, being perfectly friendly as well.

"You still haven't seen Tina, have you?" asked Kat, with concern.

"No, we haven't," said Tracy, *but I bet you have.*

"I can't believe she did that," said Kat, "it's unbelievable."

Easier to believe what Tina did than what you did. "Yes, I know," said Tracy, "it's really terrible."

"So what brings you outside on a day like this?" asked Kat.

Maybe I should just ask her. "Well, I was actually looking for someone, not that I expect to find them out here on a day like this… But I wonder, maybe you've met someone named Selena Sithe," her voice gave no hint of anger or hatred.

"I'm sorry," said Kat, "I haven't, why do you ask?"

Liar "Well, I thought you might know her. She and I go way back, and I was hoping to, you know, catch up on things."

It was very well done, Kat thought. Both she and Tracy knew full well that the other was lying, but yet Tracy kept acting. Kat supposed that Tina and Sela had to get their lying abilities from somewhere.

If only I could get her to tell me the truth, thought Kat.

Tell me the truth, why don't you? It can't hurt.

Selena is my oldest daughter and she killed my husband.

Why would she do that?

You know full well why.

I mean, why did she want to kill your husband?

I don't know, I guess it was because of John Carl.

What does he have to do with this?

I don't know, I guess there is more to John Carl than he says. He knows things, and that's why Lord Talson tried to kill him and my husband. I think Barton was trying to help John Carl or prevent him from being hurt, so Talson just killed him, using Selena.

So now what? Do you want revenge?

Of course I want revenge, and I will get it.

How?

I have allies. My husband had friends who will help me. We will succeed.

Yes I'm sure you will. "Have a good day, Tracy. Stay out of the heat."

"Oh yes," said Tracy vacantly. "Thank you for your concern about Tina. It means a lot, you were always her greatest friend."

"Of course," said Kat.

Kat stood completely still as Tracy walked past her down the street. Once Tracy was out of sight, Kat crossed the road and headed to the park. She sat down under a tree, staring at the swarms of midges in front of her without really seeing them.

"Wow," whispered Kat aloud after a moment. She had no idea what had just happened. Whatever it was, it seemed impossible that a conversation had just taken place entirely inside her mind. Kat knew what people were thinking, but she couldn't change it or affect their train of thought. Was Tracy weaker than most? If Kat could make Tracy reveal her thoughts the way she just had, Kat wondered if that meant she had the power to hurt her. Talson had said it wasn't difficult. This thought scared Kat, she wasn't sure she wanted to discover her power anymore.

Kat got up, and headed to the back of the park. She entered the old house, and was met by a rush of cool air. Happy to be out of the heat, Kat entered the common room on the right side of the hall.

"Hey punk," said Sela when Kat entered. She was lying on the floor watching baseball on the television. Kat thought she was acting exceedingly casually, considering the circumstances.

"Where's Tina?" Kat asked.

"Upstairs in the shower," replied Sela.

"Did you tell her what's going on?"

"No."

"Why not?"

"Because there is something you're supposed to be telling her as well," said Sela.

"How do you know that?" asked Kat.

"Talson and I talk too, you know," said Sela sitting up. "He told me to make sure you are with me when I tell Tina the story."

"When did you talk to him?" asked Kat.

"After I took you home from Headquarters last night I met Talson at The Sharktooth Bar. We wanted to talk to Larry in person about this whole thing just to make sure he's telling the truth. Not that we don't trust him, but it is Larry, after all."

"How can Talson just walk into a bar?" asked Kat. "Isn't he illegal?"

"Well no, technically he's dead," said Sela. "I mean most people don't know he actually exists. They think he's just a myth, but Larry at the bar knows him, he knows all of us."

"Is Larry a Silver Shadow?" asked Kat.

"No, I really don't know why Talson never let him in after all these years with open spots. Anyway, Talson usually doesn't go anywhere other than here and Headquarters because he doesn't want to be discovered, but it was safe to go to the Sharktooth late last night after it closed."

"How did he get there?" asked Kat.

"He drove," said Sela simply.

"He has a car?"

"Well, technically it's Milro's," said Sela.

"What would happen if he got pulled over?"

"He'd just mess with the cop's mind so he didn't remember what he was doing," said Sela. "Kind of erase that part of the officer's memory and fill it with something else."

"You can erase a person's memory?" said Kat.

"Talson can," said Sela, "or at least he used to be able to."

"Why wouldn't he still be able to?" asked Kat.

"Well he's not as powerful as he used to be, I mean mentally. At least that's what he says. But then again, he's always been more powerful than he would give himself credit for. I know he's not what he was, but it doesn't matter. There was a time when he couldn't even raise his arm, it's amazing he's here at all."

"What happened to him?" asked Kat. She momentarily forgot the situation with Tracy and Larry as her curiosity about Talson took over.

"What happened is that you almost killed him. He always says he should have died that night. I must admit that I thought he was gone a few times after that. It's incredible that he didn't die. He always found the strength to keep living somehow. That's Talson, though," added Sela, "he always says he doesn't deserve to live, but he always fought for his life. In the end I think that's why I'm still here," continued Sela. "If only we could all appreciate our lives the way he does."

Kat stared at Sela. "He told me that I damaged his mind," she said quietly, "but he never told me that he almost died."

"I think he doesn't want you to feel guilty about it," said Sela, shrugging. "He

doesn't want anyone to feel sorry for him, either. Roco always told me that if any of us knew the half of Talson's story we'd know that it was impossible not to feel sorry for him."

"He's really modest, isn't he?" said Kat.

"Yes, extremely. He is also extremely hard on himself. The only person who thinks Talson isn't good enough, powerful enough, strong enough, and intelligent enough is himself. Talson has never been good enough for Talson."

"I didn't realize that," muttered Kat.

"It took me a long time to figure that out," said Sela. "I thought that Talson had unreasonable expectations of me and that I was never good enough for him. Then I realized that I wasn't the one he was disappointed in. By the time I realized that it was almost too late."

"Were you going to leave him?" asked Kat.

"Yeah, I was. But then he got hurt, and I didn't want to leave him to die after everything that we had gone through. Even though I was angry and I thought I hated him, I helped him and in the process I saw a completely different side to him. I realized something I had never known about him before, and I realized something about myself as well. I hope that someday, Kat, you will have the chance to realize the same thing."

Kat looked into Sela's face, but still could not read her expression. Kat wanted to ask Sela what it was she had realized about Talson and how she, Kat, had almost killed him, but she didn't think Sela was going to tell her.

"Hey Kat," said Tina's voice at the door. "I was hoping you'd show up soon so I could find out what the heck is going on."

"Hi Tina," said Kat, turning around slowly, "How are you?"

"I'm okay," said Tina, sitting down. "I'm surviving. So what happened yesterday?"

Sela looked at Kat. "This is going to take both of us to explain," she said. She turned to Tina. "I'm warning you now, this is going to get complicated."

Sela and Kat told Tina everything that had happened from the time they left for Headquarters the night before. Kat told Tina how Talson had said it would be a good time for her to return home, and Sela explained the situation with Tracy.

"So it is up to us to make the decision," Sela finished.

"Talson wants her dead doesn't he?" said Tina when Sela had finished.

"No, he thinks it would be safer to kill her," said Sela, "but that's not the point."

"The point is that you want her dead because she wants you dead," said Tina, sounding annoyed

"No," said Sela, "I don't want Tracy dead, I just don't want to make it easier for her to kill me."

"You already killed our father, and now you are going to kill our mother," said Tina, there was anger in her voice now. "How can you live with that?"

"You don't know why your father died, Tina," said Sela, "and you don't know why your mother might die, either."

"Yeah I do," said Tina forcefully. "He's dead because Talson killed him, because Talson's a killer."

"You don't know why Talson killed him," said Sela.

"Yeah I do," argued Tina. "He killed him because he wanted to and he could."

"No, you're wrong," said Sela calmly.

"Then why?" asked Tina aggressively.

"I can't tell you that," said Sela. "You are not one of us."

"You're afraid he'll punish you if you tell me, aren't you?" challenged Tina. "You're afraid of him, that's why you let him kill your father and now you're going to let him kill our mother. You're scared. You're scared of him and scared to die."

There was an uncomfortable silence. Sela's expression was blank. She did not make eye contact with Tina or Kat. Kat could think of absolutely nothing to say. She did not want to be part of this challenge that Tina had given Sela.

"Talson does not punish people for what they do," said Sela finally, "he only punishes people for what they don't do. It is not so much a punishment as a lesson. That much information about Talson is more than any person outside the Silver Shadows deserves to know. I told you something that you do not deserve to know because I trust you. I trust you because Kat trusts you. She has told you more about Talson than I have, and anything I don't say, she will. Just remember that we don't have to tell you anything and he doesn't have to help you."

"I think you're lying," said Tina. She looked at Kat.

"Leave me out of this."

Tina glared at Kat. "Whose side are you on?"

"There aren't any sides to take," said Kat. "We're on the same side. We have to work together, not against each other."

"You don't have to believe me," said Sela, "but as I said before, that is not the point. You have to go home. That's the bottom line."

"I'm not going back home," said Tina. "Just because I don't want my mom dead doesn't mean I want to live with her."

"If you don't go back, you'll be illegal. You'll always be on the run," said Kat.

"I don't want to go back," repeated Tina.

"What you want is irrelevant at this point, Tina," said Sela. "What any of us wants is irrelevant. All that matters is what we have to do."

"Sela," said Kat, "you don't think he might, I mean if she goes back, and we decide—" Kat broke off.

"No," said Sela, "he won't." Kat saw a tiny flicker in Sela's expression and knew that she was lying, but Tina was staring at them suspiciously, so she didn't press the matter.

"Listen Tina," said Sela seriously. "Kat and I got caught last night. The police searched my car and they are going to search my apartment. Tracy reported me as the top suspect in this case and now Kat is a top suspect since she was seen with me. We both have to go for questioning now. This is a serious crime we are being accused of, and because we are actually guilty we will be in serious trouble if there is evidence against us."

"But they won't have evidence," said Tina shortly, "they can't find me. They can't prove anything."

"I know," said Sela. "It's not the police that I'm the most worried about. The problem is that Tracy is on to me now. She's back on the warpath. She doesn't care if the police can't prove I'm guilty. She knows I am."

"What is she gonna do?" asked Tina coldly.

"Try to kill me," said Sela simply.

"How?" scoffed Tina, "she can't kill you."

"But she is going to get people to help her," said Kat.

"Exactly," said Sela. She took a step toward Tina. "You have to choose now, Tina," she said. "The day will come when you will have to choose who to side with. You can go home now and save Kat and I from having to go into hiding. Once you do that you will have another chance to save us. It is going to be up to you."

"Why me?" asked Tina, her anger seemed to have melted away, "I didn't ask for this."

"Technically you did," said Kat with a slight smile. "You asked for it when you stuck up for me."

"I guess so," said Tina. "When do I have to go back home?"

"Go now," said Kat. "Your mom isn't home, I just saw her outside heading away from your house."

"What do I say when she gets back?"

"Hey mom, how's it going?" said Kat sarcastically.

"Shut up, this is serious," said Tina.

"You have to come up with a story," said Sela.

"Like what?" asked Tina.

"Come on you know how to make stuff up," said Sela. "Just stick as close to the truth as possible without actually telling the truth."

Tina sighed. "This is going to be hard."

"Life is hard," said Sela. "But you can lie, it's in your blood to be a good liar."

"This is cruel," said Tina.

"Life is cruel," said Sela. "Good luck."

Kat looked at Tina. She felt far away from her, yet close to her at the same time. "You can do it, Tina, go now. I know you can do the right thing."

Tina left the room with her face set. She walked out the front door into the stifling heat and headed home. Sela had told her she had a choice, but Tina could not see where she had any choice at all.

Sela sighed and looked at Kat. "Tina is definitely going to get used now if we go through with this whole thing."

"But then why did you tell her to go home if you know he'll use her?" asked Kat.

"Because, obviously I want to avoid any more trouble with the police," said Sela.

"Yeah, but Tina could be in a lot more trouble than us, now."

"As I told Tina before," said Sela, "she will be able to choose. She knows what is at stake now. It is all going to come down to her now, whether she wants it that way or not. She may not have asked for it, but she is going to get it anyway. We're far from being out of this mess, Kat."

"What else can happen now?" asked Kat. "The police can't catch us."

"I was never worried about the police, Kat. Tracy is the problem, not the cops."

"And she is going to get Larry to help her, isn't she?" said Kat.

"Larry's not the one I'm worried about either," said Sela. "I know Larry, he and I are cool. No, Larry is not the one I'm afraid of at this point."

"Who are you worried about then?"

"I'm not sure I'm the right person to tell you that, Kat," said Sela.

"What about your dad, are you not the right person to tell Tina about that?"

"I didn't tell Tina because she is not a Silver Shadow, no matter how much Talson would like her to be one."

Kat's eyes widened. "He wants Tina? Did he tell you that?"

"He never said it, but I know he has a thing about siblings. If he finds out that one of his followers had a brother or sister he'll try to get them to join us. When Milro first joined, for example, he told Talson that he had an older brother who was in jail. Talson got Tiro out of jail and gave him the open spot. That's the only reason a guy like Remi could ever become a Silver Shadow. Remi has virtually no talent but his older brother did, still does."

"Remi's has a brother that's a Silver Shadow?" said Kat in surprise.

"He used to," said Sela. "Remi's older brother, Conner Nelson, was a Silver Shadow when I first joined. His nickname was Nelco and he was one of the high ranked Shadows, one of the Captains."

"What happened to him?" asked Kat.

"He left," said Sela. "Apparently he and Talson got in a fight about something one night at Headquarters. I wasn't there, so I have no idea what it was about, but apparently Nelco just took all his stuff and walked out on Talson. He never came back."

"Wow," said Kat. "Does anyone know what happened?"

"Roco probably does. He and Nelco were pretty close, I think. Anyway, back to this thing with Tina," continued Sela, "not only is she my sister, she is your best friend. The reason Talson let us hide Tina here is because he's hoping that he can get her to join us. That's the only reason I was willing to even mention Talson in front of her. Normally I would never do that, but I know Talson would take her. Even considering all that, I still probably told Tina too much."

"You're allowed to tell me, aren't you?" said Kat.

"Yeah, I can tell you."

Kat felt slightly disappointed in herself that she was unable to see any part of Sela's thoughts. She was sure that Sela continually didn't tell her the whole truth, and it bothered her that there was nothing she could do about it. She had no choice but to be content with Sela's explanations. "So why did Talson kill Tina's dad, then?" asked Kat.

Sela sighed. "It's complicated. I didn't know any of this at the time when it happened, but I found out afterward. I don't know if anyone actually knew what Talson was doing when I first joined. Maybe Roco and the other captains knew, but I had no idea.

"I kind of knew that something weird was going on because there seemed to be a lot of anger and sadness among the other Silver Shadows. I thought maybe it was just how they always were. Everyone was very distant with me, especially Talson. It was nothing like it is now with us joking around and playing poker together.

"I met Talson at The Sharktooth Bar when I was seventeen," continued Sela.

"Roco was the one who told me about the Silver Shadows. He told me that Talson liked me. A few months later the bar got busted and Roco went to jail. One day I went down to the bar, it was closed but Talson was there. It was like he was waiting for me. I remember he looked different than I had remembered him. He looked older. He said, 'I need you to do something for me, Sela.' He told me he wanted me to join him.

"I said I would, but that I wanted to know what he needed me to do first. He told me that he wanted me to help him get Roco out of jail. I liked Roco so I went for it. I didn't read anything into it, I just thought that was why Talson wanted me, to help Roco."

"And that's not what he really wanted?" asked Kat.

"No, I mean he did want that, but he didn't need me to do that. There I was thinking that he needed me to get Roco out. I was stupid. It wasn't like I could do anything to get Roco out that anyone else couldn't do, but I didn't know that."

"So we got Roco out, and that's when Talson asked me for information about my father. Again, I went for it. I just told him. Then one day Roco came to me and told me that Talson was using the information I was giving him to kill my father."

"Did you ask him why?" asked Kat quietly.

"Yeah, I did," said Sela, "but Roco said that Talson didn't want me to know, and that he would be angry if he knew that Roco had told me. Roco told me that he was scared that Talson would kill him too. I didn't know anything about Talson's power. I guess I just didn't believe it. I wanted to ask Talson what was going on, but I was afraid. I may not be afraid of Talson now, but I was then. I just kept doing everything he asked me to do. I think the only reason I did it was that I was afraid to get Roco killed."

"For a long time I didn't really see a change in my father. I wasn't living home, obviously, because my parents threw me out, but I still saw him down at the docks with the fishermen. He seemed fine, and I didn't really think there was a problem. After a while I started to notice that his expression seemed vacant, like he didn't know what was going on. I started spying on him more closely and I noticed more and more that he seemed out of it. It was like he wasn't thinking clearly or something. He didn't know where he was or who he was. I started to really get scared at that point. I remember that I went to Roco and told him. He just said, 'I warned you.' I told Roco that we had to do something before it was too late, and Roco just looked at me. I remember he looked sad, and he said, 'no, it's all over now.'

"A day later I found out that my father died," continued Sela, her voice quieter now. "I was really devastated. I felt responsible for the death and I didn't want to live anymore. I tried to end my life and failed. After that I just decided to leave Talson. I came here and packed up all my stuff.

Talson was at Headquarters at the time, so I just left him a note in his office upstairs and left. I went out and put my stuff in my car. I was just going to drive to my apartment, take the rest of my things and go somewhere far away from here. That was my plan, but when I drove past the parking lot down the road from here at the end of the park, I saw Talson's car parked behind some trees. I was wondering what his car was doing there since he was not at the circle. I thought about just giving it some gas and ramming into the back of his car, but I was smart enough not to do that. Instead I just pulled up next to his car and sat there.

"It was the first time that I had ever really sat back and thought about what Talson was trying to do. I started thinking about all the things he had said to me and all the things we had done together. It really hit me then, that despite everything we had done I still had no idea who he was. It dawned on me that I had trusted him blindly and that I had been stupid.

"I started thinking about the other things I had been doing for Talson. The main one of those things being spying on your family, Kat. All of a sudden I realized that it could not be a coincidence that Talson wanted information on your family. My father had been working with John Carl for years and they had been friends since they were teenagers. I realized that Talson was probably planning to kill John Carl as well, and I felt like I had to do something to stop him.

"I decided to go to John Carl's house and try to talk to him. I left my car and walked down the road to your house. I knocked on the door and no one answered. I remember having this feeling that something was wrong. I was about to leave when I heard this voice in my mind calling me. It was like, *Sela, Sela, help me, Sela I need you.* I just stood there at the door for a minute trying to figure out what was going on. Then I decided to go inside.

"I remember that I walked into the hall and the door to the livingroom was closed. I could hear a baby crying inside. I went in, and John Carl was lying unconscious on the floor by the wall. There was a baby wrapped in a blanket lying on the sofa. I remember I looked at you and you stopped crying. I turned around and I saw someone lying curled up on the rug in front of the fireplace and I heard the voice again. *Sela help me, please Sela, I need you.*

"After a second, I realized that it was Talson laying there. I guess I never really thought twice about helping him at that point. I couldn't just leave him there, but I didn't know enough about the power to know what had happened. I tried to wake him but he didn't respond.

"Then John Carl woke up," Sela continued in an even, unwavering tone. "He said, 'whose side are you on, Selena?' I told him there was only one side. He asked me if I was going to help Talson, and I told him I was, and he called me a traitor. I asked him what had happened, but he wouldn't tell me." Sela paused, blinking slowly.

"How did you get Talson out?" asked Kat quietly.

"I carried him," said Sela.

"How?" asked Kat. She couldn't imagine Sela being able to carry a full-grown man.

"I really don't know," said Sela. "I think sometimes we find the strength to do what is required of us. Maybe it's just that Talson is not a very big guy," she added.

"Did my dad do anything?" asked Kat.

"No, he just stood there staring at me and at Talson. He looked shocked or scared or upset, I'm not sure which. I really thought he would try to stop me, but he didn't.

"So I brought Talson here," continued Sela. "I really have no idea how I carried him that far, but I did. When I got here I called Headquarters. We didn't have many Silver Shadows at that time, and Marissa was the only one at Headquarters when I called. She came here right away. I don't know, but I think Marissa knew exactly what had happened. I feel like there's a lot between her and Talson, I feel like they just know what the other is thinking all the time."

"Yeah, I know what you mean," said Kat. "I felt like that when we were playing poker at Headquarters. I felt like Marissa knew exactly what Talson had."

"Yeah, I know," said Sela. "Anyway Marissa and I lived here for months, just taking care of Talson. The day after it happened, Roco came here. Talson was still unconscious, but as soon as Roco got here, he woke up. I remember he looked at Roco, then at me and Marissa, and he said, 'that was painful'."

"He told me that it was more painful than anything he ever felt," said Kat.

"Yes, he told me that too, but he didn't really tell me what happened. One day, about a week after it happened, I was alone with Talson and he said 'Sela, there is something I need to tell you. I know you don't want to hear it, but I have to tell you why I killed your father.'

"I remember that Talson looked me straight in the eyes when he told me. I never remember him looking at me like that. He looked at me like we were just two people talking, like we were equals. I remember every word he said. 'Killing Barton Louis was the hardest thing I ever had to do, because Barton was one of the greatest friends I ever had.' Then he said, 'you never knew this Sela, but Barton Louis was a Silver Shadow'."

Kat stared at Sela, speechless.

"Not only was he a Silver Shadow," said Sela, "he was a captain. Roco, Nelco, and Barton were the three captains back then. My father was a Silver Shadow all while I was growing up, but I never knew. Talson was very weak when he was telling me this, but he told me that Barton had been in the third spot, which is the last captain's position. Talson said that Barton was worried that Julie Operman was going to become a captain and he was going to lose his powerful position.

"Roco lied when he told me that he didn't know why Talson was killing my father. Roco did know. He told me when I first joined that the person who had my spot was a woman named Julie Operman, and that she had died. Romez said that Julie was very intelligent and very beautiful. Apparently she rose quickly through the ranks of the Silver Shadows, and was in the fourth spot when she died. That is one spot away from being a captain. Roco didn't tell me anything else, about Julie or about how she died.

"Talson told me that one night Julie went to The Sharktooth Bar to gamble. This was before the place was busted, and Roco was still running the gaming. Apparently the night before Julie came in, John Carl had come into the game room. Barton went to Roco, and said they should play a joke on John Carl. Roco thought it would be funny and the two of them cheated John Carl out of a bunch of money as a joke. Apparently Roco had no idea that Barton was really planning something.

"The next day Barton went to John Carl and told him that Roco had cheated him. John Carl was furious and wanted to find a way to get back at Roco. Barton suggested that they tell the police about the gambling, since technically it was an illegal business. That would be the ultimate way to fix Roco."

"I bet my dad went for that," said Kat.

"Yeah, he did," said Sela. "Of course, John Carl had no idea that Barty was a Silver Shadow, and that the whole thing had been his idea."

"So that means the bust was a set up?" asked Kat, her eyes wide with surprise.

"Yes," said Sela. "The night after John Carl got cheated out of his winnings was the night when Julie went to the bar. Barty went with her, knowing that the place was going to be busted. Barty and Julie sat at the same table to play poker. Then the police came and chaos broke out. Roco and some of the other people who ran the gambling tried to resist arrest. The place was packed with people and they were all trying to run for the exits so they wouldn't be seen there. In all the confusion, Barton pulled out a gun and shot Julie."

"No way," whispered Kat.

"No one saw him do it. Everyone was running out of the place and Barty just ran with them. Roco was trying to hold off the police so he didn't see it. The police didn't realize what had happened right away, and by the time anyone realized that Julie had been shot, Barty was long gone.

"Julie was still alive and was rushed to the hospital, but she died in the ambulance on the way."

"Didn't she see who shot her?" asked Kat.

"Yes, she saw," said Sela. "Of course they tried to get her to say who had shot her, but she wouldn't tell them. The only witness to the crime was the bartender of the Sharktooth, Larry James, but he was ruled incompetent as a witness."

"What did Talson do?" asked Kat.

"I asked Larry about the whole thing, and he told me that Talson was really shocked when he found out what happened. Larry also said that Talson was devastated. Apparently he and Barty hadn't been getting along that well before it happened, and Talson was just really upset about the whole thing.

"Barty got away with the crime, or at least he thought he did. He made the mistake of thinking that the police were the only thing he had to worry about. He didn't think any of the Silver Shadows knew what he had done. He came back to Headquarters, acting like nothing had happened. Talson had a little memorial service at Headquarters for Julie, and Barty pretended to be all sad about it."

"I bet Talson didn't like that," said Kat.

"No, I don't think he did," said Sela. "Talson told me that he told Barty to get out of his Headquarters and get out of his life. He didn't take Talson seriously. He and Talson had a huge fight, and finally Barton just left. He went home to his wife and me, and lived his life the same way he always had. He worked with John Carl, so he still had a job.

"It was right after Barty left Talson, that Talson asked me to join. As you know, my parents freaked out when I told them. Of course my dad was acting. He screamed and called me a traitor, and Tracy told me to get the hell out of her house. So I left and got a job dealing cards at that casino downtown. I used the money to rent my apartment. Talson let me stay at Headquarters most of the time. We broke Roco out of jail and then the whole thing with my dad happened. I was mad at my dad for how he reacted, so I just went and did it. Six months later, my dad was dead, Talson had killed him, I had killed him." Sela paused and took a long breath.

"After Talson finished telling me, he said, 'That, Sela, was my confession of the hardest thing I ever had to do. I killed a Silver Shadow, I killed a great friend of mine, I killed a person I had once loved. It was the cruelest of all crimes.' Then Talson apologized to me for making me help him, and he thanked me for helping him. He said he never expected me to forgive him, he just wanted me to know the truth."

The silence in the room was endless. Sela turned the volume up on the television. Kat looked at the TV without really seeing it. There were so many things she wanted to say to Sela, but she could find no words to say them. She hadn't expected Sela to tell her anything, let alone a full account and confession.

"You remember everything, don't you?" said Kat.

"Everything about what?" asked Sela.

"Everything Talson said to you."

"I have a good memory for important things."

"Do you think Talson was really devastated about Julie?" asked Kat.

"Well, I believe Larry," said Sela. "I wouldn't know, since I wasn't there. Roco could give you a better answer to that."

"They must have been close if Talson was willing to kill Barton over it, especially since he says Barton was one of his best friends."

"Yeah, I guess so," said Sela. "It's definitely against Talson's rules to kill another Silver Shadow. Besides, Talson told me that he had had no intentions of giving Julie the captain spot."

"So why didn't Julie tell anyone who had killed her?"

"Because all the Silver Shadows are together no matter what happens. We never do anything against each other."

"But she was dying," said Kat. "Why would that matter?"
"Honor, Kat."

"So did Barton just take advantage of the opportunity when chaos broke out in the bar, or did he plan the whole thing?"

"I don't think there is any way to prove that he planned the bust as a diversion, but I also don't think there is any way to deny it."

"The whole thing would have been very well done," said Kat. "I mean who would think that the trick Barton wanted to play on my dad was really to set up the bust, or that the bust was only there to set up a murder? No one could have figured that out. He would have had to be a really good actor."

"We know he was a good actor," said Sela. "John Carl never knew he was a Silver Shadow, neither did Tracy, and neither did I. Barton Louis was a cunning man, Kat. He fooled almost everyone."

"I guess so," said Kat, "but how could you kill someone just because you thought they might get a higher position than you, or prevent you from getting the position you want. That's stupid."

The words were barely out of Kat's mouth when she realized that she had considered the same thing when she had first joined Talson. But it wasn't really serious, she told herself. But then again maybe Barty hadn't thought it was that serious, either. At that moment Kat was exceedingly glad that she had worked things out with Roco Ramirez instead of acting on her first impulse.

"It does seem stupid," Sela interrupted Kat's thoughts. "I wish I could have met Julie, I think I would have learned something from her. But if she hadn't died, I might not have met Talson. It's so weird," she continued. "When Talson told me the story it took me a long time to accept the truth about my father. I felt completely different about having been responsible for the death. I felt less guilty, less hurt, less sorry. I felt angry at my father for being such a coward, being afraid to lose his spot with the captains, so afraid that he would kill Julie. Knowing the truth helped me to get over the whole thing, and it helped me to forgive Talson. I believe that he deserved what he got, although Talson told me that no one deserves that, and he tells me not to forgive him. It's hard," Sela finished.

"Everything is hard, Sela," said a soft voice at the door. It was Talson. "What fascinating conversation do I have the pleasure of walking in on this time?"

Sela looked up at Talson. "We were just talking about, well everything, pretty much."

Talson nodded, "That's good."

"Can I ask you something, Talson?" asked Sela quietly.

"Why is it that when Kat is in the room everyone asks more questions?" asked Talson.

Kat smiled slightly.

"Of course, Sela," Talson added smiling, "as always."

"I don't know if you really want to answer this," said Sela.

"Undoubtedly, I don't," replied Talson casually, "but ask anyway."

"Why do you think Barton Louis killed Julie? Was it really about the Captain's position? I mean, I thought that didn't really matter."

"So when you said everything, you really meant *everything,*" said Talson. "It wasn't really about the rank."

"But then what was it about?" asked Kat.

"My mind fails me now," said Talson softly, looking at Sela. "You have no thoughts for me anymore."

"We were talking about that," muttered Kat. "You never told me that you almost died that night when I—"

Talson nodded. "It is Sela's job to tell you things like that, I am too old to deal with explaining things."

"You're thirty-nine," said Sela, "don't tell me you're old. I'm thirty-two, you know. I don't want to think that I'll be old in seven years."

"You won't be," said Talson. "I lost a lot, as we all know."

Kat felt guilty. It was her fault that Talson had lost so much.

"Don't be guilty, Kat," said Talson looking at her. "You are the only reason I'm here at all. I lived through that because of you and Sela and Marissa. I lived through it for you, Kat, because I had to help you learn how to control the power, and I lived through it for Sela because she didn't leave me to die when she could have, and I did it for Marissa because she is the only reason I'm Talson."

"She gave you that name?" said Kat.

"You heard what I said," said Talson softly. "You tell me. I like baseball," Talson added in a more casual tone, looking at the television for the first time.

"Can I ask you about Julie Operman?" asked Kat.

"Yes," said Talson, "as always."

"Will you tell me about her?" asked Kat.

"Well, Julie was a very intelligent and loyal person," said Talson. "Something I never really was."

"Get real," said Sela. "You're a genius, and you just said you lived through that for us, if that isn't loyalty, what is? Come on, give yourself a break."

"She was better than me in those respects, she was special."

"Did she have the power?" asked Kat.

"Not like you and I, but she was a very powerful person as well as a very beautiful person."

"Were you angry when she was killed?" asked Kat although the answer was obvious.

"Yes, I was," said Talson. "I was so angry that I killed Barty. I was angry because I thought that what Barty did was low. I probably shouldn't have killed him. It was too late to make a difference. Barty had already fooled me and he had already won. No one benefited from his death. I hurt Sela more than anyone, I put Romez in a terrible position, I turned Nelco against me, I made Tracy permanently angry, and then I hurt Sela again, now that Tracy is trying to get her killed. Not to mention the fact that I hurt myself by destroying one of the greatest friends I ever had.

"I did a cruel thing when I used Sela to kill her father," Talson's voice was even and unemotional, despite the sadness he clearly felt about the situation.

"Why did you use me?" asked Sela softly.

Talson looked directly at Sela. "Because I hated you then. I hated you because you reminded me of Julie. It hurt so badly when I looked at you. Your voice, your face, your style, it all made me think of Julie. Anger causes pain, pain causes cruelty."

You loved her didn't you? That was the real reason.

I love all my Silver Shadows, Kat, especially now.

But it was different with Julie, wasn't it?

Yes it was different in a way. I didn't mean it to be, but I guess it was. How did you know?

I don't know, I could just tell.

You're smart, Kat

"Why do you guys have to do that?" asked Sela.

"Because we can," said Talson.

"I did it this morning with Tracy," said Kat. "It was like I was hearing her thoughts and I could make her say anything I wanted."

Talson nodded wordlessly.

"How is that possible since she doesn't have the power?" asked Kat.

"You impose your thoughts upon her and she is compelled to answer them."

"So it's possible to make people think anything you want them to?"

"Not anything, and not everybody."

"Pretty much anyone, though," said Sela, "you're just being modest about your own abilities."

"Modesty is a strength," said Talson. "No one is as great as they think they are."

"No one except you," said Sela. "You've always been greater than you think you are."

"I think I understand my place," said Talson, "but perhaps that is, like it is with so many others, a misconception. But again, we digress from the topic of discussion. Kat, what did Tracy say to you when you touched her mind?"

"Well, I knew she was thinking about looking for Sela, and so I just wanted her to tell me why. Tracy said that she thought that the reason her husband died was that he was trying to help someone that you were trying to kill. She thinks that my dad had something to do with it and that there is more to him than he says."

"I suppose she has two out of three right," said Talson. "Barty's death had something to do with John Carl, but Barty was not trying to help someone I was killing. I suppose they thought I was trying to kill Julie, who knows. Of course there is much more to John Carl than he says."

"You knew him, didn't you?" said Kat.

"I still do," said Talson. "I know him all too well."

What is it about my dad that he's not telling me?

What he chooses to tell you, or not to tell you is his business, not mine.

But you've already told me things that he had chosen not to tell me.

Yes, things about you, not about him. "But, back on the subject of Tracy," said Talson aloud, "I think what you did was very wise, Kat. Was it difficult?"

"No, it wasn't hard at all. I don't know how I did it, I could just hear what she was thinking. She was so bitter and angry that her thoughts were easy to hear."

"Yes," said Talson, "yet another reason to control one's anger. When a person is angry or resentful about something it is not difficult to force that person to bring those thoughts to the forefront of their mind, unless that person is able to control those feelings. Only exceptional individuals are able to control their emotions and hide their thoughts when they feel strongly about something. Sela, for example, is one of those exceptional people."

Sela smiled slightly. "I don't know about that," she said softly.

"Don't be so modest," said Talson with a smile.

"Can you learn to hide your thoughts, or is it just an ability that some people have and others don't?"

"It is a gift, but you can also learn it," said Talson. "Some just hide their emotions naturally, while others must work at it. It is not only anger that makes the mind easier to access," continued Talson. "Any emotion that you can feel strongly makes your mind easier to touch. The more a person controls their emotions the harder it is to touch that person's mind."

"I can't always hide my feelings," said Sela.

"No one can always do anything," said Talson. "We all have emotions and we all need to feel those emotions. Without strong feelings we are not human. We need our strong desires, because without them we have no power, and without power we have no life."

There was a silence before Talson spoke again. "Can I ask the two of you a question now?"

"Of course," said Sela.

"Where is Tina Louis?"

"She returned home," replied Sela. "She left just a few minutes ago."

"Her decision or yours?" asked Talson.

"Listen," said Sela seriously, "Tina is not ready to handle being with us."

"But can she handle being with Tracy?" asked Talson.

"I don't know," said Sela. "When the day comes when she has to do something, I hope she will do the right thing."

"I trust your judgment, therefore I trust hers," said Talson.

"Maybe Tina could handle this better if she knew the truth about her father," suggested Kat.

"She's not the only one," said Talson.

"She doesn't understand that there were valid reasons behind her father's death," said Kat.

"That is because there aren't," said Talson.

"But—," began Kat.

Enough with that. "Kat, you have already shown that you have a knack for Tracy's mind, meaning that you have earned the job of dealing with her mind," said Talson.

"Does that mean we're going to—" began Kat. "I mean, that I'm going to—" Kat stopped.

"We are going to do what is required of us," replied Talson calmly.

"What are you fools talking about?" said a voice at the door.

"Hi Romez," said Talson, without looking to see who had entered.

"We're talking about what's going on, what are you doing here?"

"Trying to find out what's going on, but you already knew that."

"Good," said Talson, "so are we."

Sela looked at Kat and shook her head. "They are always like this," she muttered.

Kat smiled.

"Sela," said Talson in a much more serious tone, "I was thinking that you could go check on Tracy and see how she reacts when she gets home and finds that Tina has returned, and more importantly, see how she takes Tina's story. That is to say, see how much of the story she doesn't buy."

"You want me to go back to my old house and spy on Tracy," said Sela, frowning. "Do I have to?"

"Yes," said Talson without a change of expression.

"But—" began Sela.

"But nothing," said Talson sharply. "Do it."

"But Talson," pleaded Sela, "you know how hard it is for me to go back to that house. I really don't want to."

At this Talson smiled the way a child would smile when he knew he could make a most clever reply. "What you want is irrelevant at this point," he said, quoting what Sela had said before he had arrived. "What any of us want is irrelevant."

Sela scowled. "Fine, I get it, you win," she said. "See you guys later." She stood up and left quickly, closing the door sharply behind her.

"Wow, no one ever wants to be anywhere near Tracy, do they?" said Roco, staring at the door through which Sela had just exited.

"One can hardly blame them," said Talson.

"So I take it that Tracy's daughter is back home, then?" said Roco.

"Well, both of them are now," said Talson with a faint smile. "Don't tell Sela I said that, though," he added. "She will not find it very amusing."

"So we're counting on Tracy to believe this kid's story when she says that Sela and Kat had nothing to do with it?" said Roco.

"No," said Talson simply.

"Good," said Roco.

"Why is that good?" asked Kat. She could not see how Tracy not believing Tina could be a good thing.

"It's good we aren't counting on it, because you can bet Tracy isn't gonna buy it," said Roco.

"But Tina is a good liar," said Kat.

"Yeah, but Tracy knows that you and Sela are around," said Roco, "and she's got her mind set on revenge. She's not going to believe anyone who tries to tell her that she doesn't have a chance at the revenge she wants."

"So you're saying that no matter what Tina says to Tracy, it won't make any difference?" said Kat.

"Oh it will make a difference," said Talson. "It will make Tracy want to find Sela even more than she already does."

"Then why did Sela tell Tina to go home?" asked Kat, feeling somewhat confused and annoyed now.

Talson shrugged, and looked somewhat sad. "Because Sela wants to finish what she started with Tracy."

"No way," said Kat. "That's the only reason why she— No way," Kat said again. She could not imagine that Sela would use her and Tina that way.

"Yes way," said Roco. "You don't know Sela, kid. She's Tracy's daughter, she's a master of manipulation."

"That's not fair," protested Kat. "She's using Tina, and Tina has no idea what's going on. Sela can't do that, and besides, I thought Sela said she doesn't care if Tracy lives or dies."

"First of all Kat, life is not fair," said Talson. "Secondly, Tina will figure this out pretty quickly, considering what a reliable information source she has, and as for what Sela said, it's true she doesn't care if Tracy lives or dies. She doesn't care as long as she gets a confrontation and a chance to show Tracy the truth."

"What truth?" asked Kat.

"The truth about Barty Louis," replied Talson, still sounding somewhat unenthusiastic. "Not that Sela knows the whole truth, but she knows more than Tracy," he added.

"Are you saying I should tell Tina about this?" Kat could not think of anyone else who could be the reliable information source that Talson was talking about.

"No," said Talson. "I'm not saying you should, I'm saying you will."

"Do you think I shouldn't tell her?" asked Kat, very confused now.

"I didn't say that either," said Talson. "I just—" Suddenly Talson frowned. "What the—" he muttered.

Kat looked at him, then at Roco who was still standing near the door. He was looking at Talson with a puzzled expression.

"Talson, are you okay?" began Roco, but Talson held up his hand for silence.

"Hold on a second," he muttered. "Something is going on."

"What?" asked Kat. "What's going on?"

"I don't know, something important I think, but I have to concentrate." He put his head in his hands. "I really hate this," he muttered, "but it's so useful."

"Come on Kat," said Roco, beckoning her to follow him out of the room.

"What's going on with him?" asked Kat once they were in the hallway.

"I don't know," said Roco, "but he must be trying to see something or hear something in his mind. I don't know how it works, but last time he did that he saved my neck, so we'll just leave him to it."

"Okay," said Kat. "Where should we go?"

Roco shrugged. "Where do you wanna go?"

"Can we go in there?" asked Kat, pointing to the first door on the left side of the hall.

"Sure," said Roco. "That is kind of like our library room."

"And we are allowed to go in there, right?"

"Yeah, of course," said Roco, "why wouldn't we be?"

"I didn't know if Talson had rules about things like that," said Kat.

"No," said Roco. "Who told you we had rules? Come on, you have to see all the stuff we have in there from the good old days."

CHAPTER 15

MAGIC

Twilight had fallen over the city. In the back of a dilapidated schoolyard, a young boy dribbled a basketball, turned, and laid it into the hoop. He was small, with black hair and wearing a ragged basketball jersey that was too big for him.

It was Saturday, and the school was closed. Children always tried to sneak into the back of the school on weekends to shoot hoops or skateboard, but most of them were unsuccessful. The fences around the school had been raised in attempts to prevent the frequent burglaries. The rise in crime had caused the school to fall into disrepair along with the neighborhood around it.

"Hey, how'd you get in there, kid?" A stocky, tough looking boy of about thirteen was standing on the other side of the fence watching the younger boy.

The boy with the basketball said nothing. He merely glanced at the older boy and continued playing.

"I said, how'd you get in there?" the boy outside the fence said more loudly. "How did you get through the gate without setting off the alarm?"

"I jumped," said the younger.

"Shut up, no one can jump that."

"I know," replied the younger boy. "I just wanted to see if you were stupid enough to believe me."

"You think I'm stupid? You wanna get beat up? Do you?" the older boy challenged.

"No, I know you're not stupid now, but go for it. Try to get in here."

"You better not push it kid," replied the older. "If I break through that gate, the alarm is gonna go off and you're going to get busted."

"No, I'll be gone and you'll be busted," said the younger.

"Who are you? What makes you think you're so good, huh?"

"What makes you think you're better than me?" replied the younger.

"Who are you?" repeated the older. "What's your name?"

The younger boy shrugged. "I'm no one, really, I'm dead. People call me Magic."

"What do you mean you're dead?"

"What do you think I mean?"

"Shut up."

The younger boy turned away and dribbled the ball away from the basket to the three-point line. He was much stronger than he looked. The ball went right through the hoop, barely touching the net.

"How old are you," the older boy asked.

"You didn't think I could do that, did you?" replied the younger. "I'm eight, and yes, I know I look younger than that," he added.

"Yeah, I thought you were like six," said the older. "Anyway, how did you do that? How can a little guy like you make a shot from that far?"

The boy with the ball shrugged. "I practice a lot, I guess."

"Do it again."

"Right hand or left?"

"You can shoot with both hands?"

"Yeah, why not?" replied the younger boy. "I mean we have two hands, you might as well use both." He backed up and shot the ball with his left hand this time.

"Do you ever miss?" asked the older boy as the ball went through the hoop yet again.

"Of course I miss," said the other, "everybody misses."

"Yeah, but you're like three feet tall," said the older.

"I'm actually three feet and nine inches, but yeah, I know I'm short," said the younger.

"Whatever," said the older, "I'm short for my age, too."

"How old are you?"

"Thirteen. Look, little man," he added, "let me in there."

"Why? What am I getting out of it?"

"I won't mess with you," said the older.

"Not like you could anyway," said the younger. He crossed the court to the fence, unlatched the large gate and pulled it open. "You owe me one," he said softly.

"Wait a minute," said the older boy as he entered the schoolyard, "you opened the gate. How come the alarm isn't going off?"

"Because I know what I'm doing," said the younger.

"Don't they have cameras?" said the older.

"They're off too," replied the younger. "I don't want the cops showing up."

"They better not."

The younger boy laughed. "Yeah, you already owe me one. If the cops come you'll owe me two."

"What do you think you're going to do if the cops show up?" asked the older boy, picking up the basketball.

The younger boy shrugged. He reached down and stole the ball out of the older boy's hands, turned around, jumped, and shot over the older boy's head. "Hey, you got any money?" he asked.

"A little," said the older. "Why?"

"Because I'm hungry. If you buy me some food we'll be even."

"Why do I want us to be even?"

"Because right now you owe me one. I let you in here." He paused suddenly, frowning. "And I'm about to get you out of here," he said quietly.

"What are you talking about?" asked the older.

"Someone saw us, and they're coming down here."

"Who? What are you talking about?"

`The boy stood motionless for a moment, staring at the street beyond the fence. There were a few shabby looking apartments across the street from the school, with peeling paint and windows with bars on them.

"What are you looking at?" asked the older boy.

"Shut up," said younger boy. "I need to concentrate, I'm trying to do something." The boy continued to stare at the apartment building across the street. "Come on," he said finally. "We have to get out of here."

"Why? What's going on?"

"Someone saw us."

"Who?"

"The window," muttered the younger boy.

"What? How do you know?"

"Don't doubt me," said the younger. "I know what I'm doing, remember?" He crossed the schoolyard and pulled open a panel on the side of the building. He pressed a few buttons then slammed the panel shut. "Hurry up," he called to the other boy. "We have to get out before the alarm goes off." He turned and ran through the gate, holding it open for the other boy to follow him.

The other didn't move. "Come on man, we are going to get busted if you don't move," said the younger.

"What's the problem?" asked the older. "Just tell me what's going on."

"There isn't time," said the younger. "Trust me."

The older boy looked at the younger for a moment, then he dropped the ball and ran to the gate.

The younger boy slammed it closed. "Run," he said.

Suddenly three figures rounded the corner and came into view. Three grown men emerged from the building across the street, their eyes on the older boy. "There you are, kid," said one in a raspy voice.

The older boy froze.

"Just give up the money and no one gets hurt, kid," said the man.

The younger boy turned and ran down the street away from the men.

"Where do you think you're going?" yelled one of the men.

The younger boy did not turn around. The older boy stood frozen, staring at the three men for a moment, then he turned and followed the younger boy, running as fast as he could.

The two boys ran through the gathering darkness, with the men in close pursuit. It was amazing how fast the younger boy ran. He jumped a low park fence and cut across the field. The older boy followed, trying to keep up. He hoped that the young boy knew where he was going. He had said that he would get them out of it if the police came. The older boy was getting the feeling that his young friend really did know what he was doing.

He followed the younger out of the park and onto the street. The young boy turned down an alleyway. Their pursuers did not see where he had gone by the time they reached the street, and they kept on running past the alleyway. The older boy ran to the other side of the alley and came out on a dark street. He was not immediately sure where the younger boy had gone. Then he saw a broken window in the building next to the alley, and realized that the younger boy had jumped through the broken store window.

The older boy climbed awkwardly through the window, trying not to touch any broken glass. He was standing in the front of an abandoned store. In the dim light he could just make out the younger boy standing a few feet away on the dusty floor. He was smiling slightly.

The older boy bent down and put his hands on his knees, gasping for breath after the long run. "You're really fast," he gasped.

The younger boy shrugged. He was barely breathing hard. "I'm not always fast enough," he said.

"You were fast enough this time."

"I guess so."

"How did you know those guys were coming, anyway?"

"I told you," said the younger. "The window."

"What window?"

"The one that's always open. The guy who lives there across from the school is always watching out that one window. That's the guy that's after you. He was watching me playing hoop, and when you showed up he got way more interested. He's mad at you and so he called a couple of his buddies and they came after you. How good are you at pool, anyway?" he added.

"What the hell?" whispered the older, staring at the younger boy in disbelief.

"Hustling is really risky, you know," said the younger. "I mean, I know it can work really well to get a lot of money, but you can also get burned really easy. It was pool you were playing, wasn't it?" he added. "How much did you win off those fools?"

"How the hell do you know all that?" asked the older boy. "Who the hell are you?"

"How much you win?"

"Two hundred bucks, but that's not the point. How the hell did you know that?"

"I thought you said you had a little money," said the younger.

"Okay, so I lied," said the older. "That is not the point. I wanna know how you knew all that stuff."

"Buy me some food, and I'll tell you," replied the younger. "Deal?"

"Okay, deal," said the older, "but why do they call you Magic? Is it because of basketball or because of," he paused, "you know, what you just did?"

"Both, I guess," said the younger. "Are you going to buy me some food with your two hundred bucks or not?"

"Of course I'm going to buy you food," said the older. "You saved my life, Magic."

"I'll say I did," said Magic. "You really do owe me two now."

*   *   *

There was absolutely nothing remarkable about Conner Nelson. He worked at a telephone company in the downtown area and lived in a fairly nice apartment across town from his work.

Conner Nelson was a fairly tall, thin man in his early forties with fair hair and light brown eyes. He was clean-shaven and had an extremely neat look about him. Today he was dressed in a tan collared shirt, tie, and tan trousers. He grabbed his black briefcase and his car keys and headed out of his second story apartment to his car. Another day, he thought as he drove toward his work, another day like this.

Conner walked out of the parking garage into the stifling heat of the day, heading across the crowded street toward the buildings that scraped the sky. Conner did not stand out from the people around him in any visible way. He was just another head in the massive crowd. Conner watched the people that hurried past him. Every one of them was living a different life, he thought; yet in his eyes they were all living the same life.

Conner rode the elevator up fourteen floors to his office. "Hello Conner, Good morning Mr. Nelson, Hi there Mr. Nelson," Conner heard this over and over as he passed his colleagues.

"Good morning," he replied over and over in an expressionless tone. "Good morning, Barbara," Conner greeted his boss as he met her outside the elevator on the fourteenth floor.

Perhaps the only clue to Conner Nelson's true identity was the fact that, at age forty-one, he lived alone in an apartment, and he had an entry-level position at his company. He did not own a house and he did not have a family.

Conner Nelson usually told people that he was divorced when he was asked about his personal life. He did not want to draw attention to himself by saying that he had never been married. Conner had been working at his current job for only three years. He was a reliable worker, but his past record kept his boss from promoting him to a higher position.

Conner Nelson's supervisor, Barbara Higgins, had been warned by a previous employer about hiring Conner. Barbara had hired him anyway, and was very satisfied with his work. She found him to be a hard worker, who always did exactly what he was asked to do, and did it well. He had never complained about his pay or asked to be promoted. His previous employer had told Barbara that Conner would be a good worker, but he warned her that he had "an odd history."

Barbara Higgins, upon being warned about Conner's past, decided to try to find out exactly how odd her employee's history actually was. She found that Conner had dropped out of school at the age of ten and run away from home. Apparently he was never found, until he went back to school at age eighteen to earn his high school equivalency diploma. Once he received his equivalency, there was nothing to indicate that he had applied to a university, and there were no employment records. There were no more records of Conner Nelson until about ten years previous, when he had finally enrolled in a university, and earned a degree in communications. With that degree he had applied for several jobs. He had had three jobs before the one he had now, having only lasted a year or two at each company.

What baffled Barbara the most was that from the time Conner had allegedly run away from home until he turned eighteen there was no evidence of his existence at all. Then, once he got his high school equivalency there was another gap of nearly ten years, in which there was no record of where he had lived or what he had done. Barbara had never heard Conner speak about any part of his life before he had attended the university. It was as if he was trying to erase everything that had happened in the first thirty years of his life.

Conner placed his briefcase on the floor and sat down at his very neat desk. Conner did not have any pictures of his family in his office like many of his coworkers. There was only one photo in his office, which was framed and hung on the wall behind Conner's desk. This photo was perhaps the one and only clue to the past that Conner tried so hard to hide.

In the photo, two teenage boys stood in front of the entrance to the Flying Fox Arcade. The boy on the left was very handsome with dark brown hair and eyes, while the boy on the right was fair-haired with light brown eyes. The dark haired boy had his arm around the other's shoulders and they both wore grins on their faces.

Conner stared at the picture on the wall, wishing he could smile like that again. Conner pulled the picture off the wall and held it in his hands. It was so cruel, he thought. He didn't care what they said the reason was. Conner knew the real reason. Everyone tried to make it seem so simple, but Conner knew better. And there was Tracy, going on and on about Sela as if she was the one behind it all, and talking about killing Sela, as if that would make any difference. She doesn't have a clue, thought Conner, still staring at the photograph.

Conner turned the picture frame over, pulled open the back, and removed the photo from its frame. *Barlo and Nelco* was written in the far corner of the picture in small letters, along with a date in July twenty-five years previous.

Conner didn't think he could bear to look at the picture any longer. He bent down and slipped it into his briefcase. "I never said I wanted to, I never said I enjoyed it, I never said it was fair. It was cruel, but Nelco, I had to. I just did what I had to do; you of all people should understand that."

Conner could hear those words as clearly as if someone was speaking them at that very moment. "I had to, Nelco, I had to." The words repeated themselves over and over in Conner's head. *Nelco, I had to.* Conner put his head in his hands. The words were inside him, driving him insane. You had to, he thought, and now I have to.

Conner had known for a long time that something had to be done, and now he could finally see an opportunity to do something. There was no way to deny it. Now was the time and Conner knew what he had to do, and he knew there was only one way to do it. The only question was how.

Suddenly Conner sat up straight in his chair. He had been struck with a wild and incredible idea. No, he thought, that's insane. But then again, it might be possible. He might be the only man both willing and able to do the job. Conner knew one man could never do this alone. He turned and caught sight of his reflection in the blank computer screen in front of him. A man in a collared shirt and tie with neat hair looked back at him. Conner Nelson hated that version of himself, but it was all he knew now. Can I still do this? he wondered. Am I a killer?

"You on lunch, Conner?" the man in the office next to Conner asked, four hours later.

Conner stood up. "Yeah, and I might not be back, I think I'm going to work from home this afternoon."

"Alright then, see you tomorrow," said the man.

Conner nodded, picked up his briefcase and hurried toward the elevator. Once Conner was inside the parking garage and sitting in his car, he pulled out his cell phone. He frowned, trying to remember a number he hadn't called in many years.

"Hello," said a sharp voice.

"John Carl," said Conner tentatively.

"Yeah, who's this," said John Carl, sounding annoyed.

"Conner Nelson."

There was a pause at the other end. "Conner Nelson," John Carl exclaimed after a moment. "What a surprise, long time no talk. What's going on?"

"Listen, John Carl," said Conner seriously. "Weird stuff is happening right now."

John Carl laughed sarcastically. "Weird stuff?" he said with a hint of a sneer. "You have no idea."

"Yeah, I do, and I need to talk to you. Are you working today?"

"We just came in from an insane trip, so I could use a break," said

John Carl, losing the sneer. "You can come down here if you really want to talk."

"I'm on my way," said Conner, starting his car and pulling out of the parking garage. "Where should I meet you?"

"How about The Sharktooth Bar?"

"No," said Conner sharply, "I can't go in there."

"Why not?" asked John Carl. "If I can go in there anyone can. It's different now, anyway. It's just old man Larry running the place now."

"I really don't want to be overheard, John Carl," said Conner, "least of all by Larry."

"Fine, in that case just meet me on the fifth dock."

"Alright, I'll be there in a few minutes," said Conner, turning down a side street toward the harbor.

The Sharktooth Bar, he thought as he drove. Why were they all such fools? John Carl was no doubt the greatest fool of them all, but he was also useful and he was the right man for the job.

Conner walked out onto the dock. Even down by the ocean the heat was stifling. Conner looked around and spotted John Carl's boat, the Royal Mast, tied to the dock. Two men were working on deck.

"Hello there," said Conner, coming up alongside the boat. Sono turned off the hose he was using to wash the deck and looked at Browen. They were surprised to see a man dressed like Conner on the dock.

"Nice suit, mate," said Sono with a slight smile.

"How's it going?" asked Browen. It was as if the two had planned their lines for the conversation ahead of time.

"It's going fine, and it's not a suit," said Conner annoyed.

"Collared shirt and a tie, my bad, dude," said Sono.

"What you need?" asked Browen.

"Do you two work for John Carl Thomason?" asked Conner coldly.

"Yep," said Sono and Browen in unison.

"Where is he?"

"Right behind you," said Sono. John Carl had just walked up the dock and was now standing behind Conner.

Conner turned around. "John Carl Thomason," he said extending his hand. "It's been too long."

"Conner Nelson," said John Carl with the slightest hint of disdain, as he shook Conner's hand. "These are my hard working deck hands Sono and Browen Silven," he added, indicating the brothers. He turned to them. "Guys, this is Conner Nelson, an old friend of mine." There was just the slightest hint of coldness in his voice.

"I didn't know you had friends that wore suits," said Sono, "I mean collared shirts and ties," he added, grinning rather cruelly.

"Neither did I," said John Carl with a slight sneer.

Conner looked disgusted. "Nice to meet you, mate," said Browen shaking Conner's limp hand.

"Is that the best handshake you've got?" asked Sono, as he too shook hands with Conner.

"Go easy on him," said John Carl with a real sneer this time. "He's not used to using his right hand for that, are you mate?" He smirked at Conner.

"Shut up," said Conner angrily. "Listen, John Carl, I need to talk to you—"

"Privately, we know," said Sono and Browen together.

"We're out," said Sono, and the two walked away down the dock toward the street.

"Get yourself some better deck hands, will you," said Conner, after Sono and Browen were out of earshot.

"Are you —ing kidding me?" said John Carl, "they are the best ones I've got, and at the moment the only ones I've got. You're not one to talk anyway," he added. "You think your little rat of a brother is any better?"

"Whatever, that's not the point," said Conner.

"Yeah, actually it is, since Remi didn't show up for this trip. We came in because it's too crazy with only three people out there. Where the hell is he?"

"Why do you think I would know?" asked Conner coolly.

"I don't think you know, I know you do," said John Carl.

"Why do you think I know anything about what Remi does now?"

"Because he's not on the other side anymore."

"How do you know that?" asked Conner looking surprised.

"Oh a sea lion jumped on deck and told me," said John Carl sarcastically. "Remi told me that he was telling you stuff he wasn't supposed to tell you, you idiot."

"He did not tell you that," said Conner, obviously furious at Remi.

"Yeah, he did," said John Carl. "You shouldn't have trusted him."

"I know he plays both sides, John Carl."

"He plays three sides now."

"What are you talking about?" demanded Conner, "there is no third side, there never has been."

"Quit playing stupid, Nelson," said John Carl, "you're the one that said weird stuff was going on. I know full well that Remi is keeping you up to date on all that weird stuff at least as well as he's doing it for me. Don't pretend you don't know what's going on with Tracy and Selena and everything else."

"Sela is not the problem, John Carl. Anyone who thinks that killing her will make any difference is a fool."

"Why is it Sela now, and what do you mean it won't make a difference? Besides, this is Tracy's thing, not mine."

"Sela is Selena's name since about fifteen years ago," said Conner coolly, "and it most definitely *is* your thing. Tracy is a fool and you know it. Sela's not the one."

"Actually, she is, considering that she killed Barty, but what does it matter to you anyway, you're one of them."

"I am no longer one of them," said Conner, his voice rising. "Barty meant everything to me. He was the best friend I ever had, and Talson destroyed him. I left him," said Conner, dropping his voice, "and now I'm going to kill him." Conner took a step toward John Carl and grabbed the front of his shirt. His voice was shaking now. "You've got to help me John Carl. This *is* about you, it is *your* thing, it's not Sela that needs to die, it's Talson."

John Carl looked down at Conner's hand on his chest. He looked scared and shocked, "What do you want from me?" he whispered.

"You have to help me, John Carl," said Conner again.

"How? What are you talking about?"

"You have the power," whispered Conner.

John Carl pushed Conner's hand off his shirt and took a step away from him. "What the hell are you talking about?"

"Don't play stupid, Thomason, you know exactly what I'm talking about."

"Tell me what the hell you want," said John Carl, his eyes narrowed.

"You are the man for this job, John Carl," said Conner. "You are the only one who can do this. If any one is going to kill Talson it is going to have to be you, you and I. I can't do it alone, and neither can you. But together we can do it. You have the power and I can get the information."

"You're insane," said John Carl, sounding scared now. "Why do you think I want to do this?"

"Because you hate Talson," said Conner.

"Yeah, I do," muttered John Carl, "but that's not the point."

"What is the point then?"

"The point is that I'm not a killer. Why are you obsessed with killing Talson all of a sudden, anyway?"

"Why? Because he deserves to die for what he did," said Conner.

"But why now? Barty died fourteen years ago, why do you want revenge now?"

"It has taken me all these years to get my life together and to understand what I need to do. I know it has taken me a long time, but I realize what needs to be done now, and you have to realize that as well."

"Why do you think I need to do anything?"

"I said don't play stupid, John Carl," said Conner. "You say I am one of them, you are one of them."

"I am not," said John Carl, clearly offended, "and unlike you, I never was. I have no power to kill Lord Talson and no desire to do so, either. You go do what you want, I won't stop you."

"I can't do this alone," protested Conner, "this is Talson we're talking about. I need you to help me."

"You're going to have to do it alone, mate," said John Carl more calmly. "I am not a killer, and I have no desire to become one."

"Even with Talson?"

"Even with Talson."

"You hate him, and you can't deny that, John Carl."

"I am not denying it," replied John Carl, "but as I told you before, that is not the point. You want to kill him, go do it, but I'm not helping you, I'm not killing."

"Think of how hard this is for me, John Carl," whispered Conner desperately. "For me to kill Talson is insane. Of course it isn't easy, it will be the hardest thing in the world for me to do, but I know I have to. It will be so hard for me, but not so hard for you, think about it, John Carl. Think of how hard it is for me to live with this, without doing anything."

"Hard," sneered John Carl, "you have no idea."

"And you think you do?" said Conner, his voice cold now. He reached into his briefcase and pulled out the picture that had been hanging in his office. He thrust in into John Carl's face. "You think you know what hard is?" he said coldly. "Do you?"

John Carl looked at the photograph. "You think this is hard to live with, do you?" he said softly. "If I trusted you I'd show you the picture of what's harder."

"Show me then," said Conner, clearly challenging John Carl.

"I said if I trusted you," said John Carl coldly.

"You will end up killing him whether you want to or not," said Conner with equal coldness. "You just go on with your life like nothing is wrong."

"I have never lived my life like that, Nelson. I know you think I'm some idiot

you can use to do your dirty work, but under no circumstances will I become a killer."

"You will be a killer, John Carl Thomason," said Conner. "You will help me kill Talson whether you want to or not. You think you know what's coming, you have no idea." Conner Nelson turned sharply, and walked away from John Carl.

John Carl stood motionless on the dock, staring after him as he got in his car and drove away. John Carl looked at the blue and cloudless sky, and then he turned and stared out at the calm ocean. How could Conner Nelson know? *My God, Talson, what more can you do to me?*

*   *   *

The first room on the left side of the hall was small and packed with books, photo albums and the like. Everything was arranged on bookshelves that lined the walls of the circular room. There were several chairs around a small table in the middle of the room.

"What is all this stuff," asked Kat.

Roco turned on the light in the room and closed the door. "All kinds of stuff," he replied. "Feel free to look at anything you like."

Kat stared around the room wondering where to start. She caught sight of a large black photo album by itself on a shelf above all the other books. "What's that?" she asked, pointing to it.

"That's the book of Silver Shadows," said Roco. "Hold on, I'll get it down." He pulled a chair over and stood on it to reach the high shelf. He brought the book down and placed it on the little table.

The book of the greatest people to ever live, the Silver Shadows, was written on the front of the album in curvy silver lettering. "The greatest people to ever live, really?" said Kat, with raised eyebrows.

Roco shrugged, "Why not?"

Kat opened the cover. There was only one picture on the first page. It was a picture of four boys. Below the picture was the caption, *the magic four*. The boy on the far left looked Hispanic, with dark brown hair and dark eyes. He was not very tall, but looked to be in his early teens. He wore a wide smile on his face and had his arm around the shoulders of the boy on his right. This boy was much smaller than all the others and seemed younger. He had black hair and very dark green eyes. He had a look of intensity on his face despite his smile, but it was his eyes that were the most remarkable. They were an extremely dark shade of green, and they seemed very alive, as though there was a fire lit behind them. Kat had never seen anyone with eyes like that.

Kat forced herself to look away from the green-eyed boy after a minute. She looked at the other two boys in the picture, both of which appeared to be around twelve or thirteen. The boy next to the green-eyed boy was tall and very handsome with dark brown hair and brown eyes. The boy on the far right was also tall, but he had fair hair and very light brown eyes. "Who are these boys?" asked Kat finally.

Roco sighed, looking at the picture over Kat's shoulder. "I'm not sure I'm the right person to tell you that," he said.

"Then who is?" asked Kat.

"I don't know," said Roco softly, "I don't know who those boys are, anymore." There was a touch of sadness in his voice now.

Kat looked at the picture, then at Roco. She pointed to the boy on the far left. "Is that you?" she asked quietly, looking up at Roco.

Roco stared at her for a moment, then at the picture. He nodded slowly. "Yeah," he said softly, "that was me."

"Were these the first four Silver Shadows?" Kat asked.

"Yeah," said Roco.

"You were kids," whispered Kat.

"Yeah, I was fourteen in that picture," said Roco, "I was the oldest."

"Where's Talson?" asked Kat, curious to see what he had looked like as a child.

Roco said nothing. He was still staring at the picture.

"Who are the other boys?" asked Kat softly.

Roco pointed to the light haired boy on the far right. "Have you heard of Nelco?" he asked.

"Yeah, Sela mentioned him," said Kat. "Is that him there?"

"Yeah, that was him," said Roco, "Conner Nelson, he's about eleven in that picture."

"Sela said he left Talson."

"Yeah, he did," said Roco.

"Sela said he and Talson had an argument," muttered Kat.

"They had an argument, alright, it was ugly."

"What was it about?"

Roco pointed to the handsome, dark haired boy next to Nelco in the picture.

"Who's that?" asked Kat.

"Barlo," replied Roco, "Barty Louis."

Kat looked at the picture, then at Roco. "Barty," she said softly, "the argument was about him?"

"You know about the whole thing with Barty and Julie Operman, right?" said Roco.

"Yeah.'

"Well, Talson wanted to kill Barty for killing Julie."

"And Nelco didn't?"

"Exactly," said Roco, "Nelco was mad at Talson for even considering giving Barty's captain spot to Julie. He thought that Barty was more important than Julie because he was one of the original four, and that, in his mind, meant that Barty should be forgiven for what he did."

"Sela told me that Talson was never really planning to give Julie the captain's position," said Kat.

"That's true," replied Roco. "Talson told Nelco that, but Nelco didn't believe him. He called Talson a liar and a traitor to his friends. He said that what Barty had done was wrong, but he still shouldn't be removed as a captain. Talson said that if anyone was low and cruel it was Barty for killing Julie. Talson said that anyone who was willing to kill over a captain's position was low and backstabbing.

"That pretty much pushed Nelco over the edge," continued Roco. "He totally lost control of himself. He punched Talson in the face. Nelco tried to hit Talson again and Talson just covered his face. He didn't fight back. I ran over and pulled Nelco off Talson, and then he and I got into it."

"So you definitely sided with Talson?" asked Kat.

"I thought what Barty did was low, cruel and cowardly," said Roco. "I also didn't appreciate how he talked me into messing with John Carl in my own bar, knowing that John Carl would call the cops and bust my place, so that he could kill Julie and I could go to jail. That all came out in my fight with Nelco. A lot of stuff came out over the course of that fight. We beat each other up really badly."

"And you and him were friends before that, right?"

"Yeah, we had been friends since we were kids," said Roco, indicating the picture. "We were friends right up until the day we beat the living hell out of each other."

"Wow," said Kat, "so then Nelco left?"

"Yeah," said Roco, "Talson finally stopped the fight, and Nelco just left. He never came back. I haven't seen or spoken to him since then. By the end, I don't think we were really fighting over Barty or Julie. We were fighting about Talson. We were fighting over the way Talson felt, and what he wanted to do. I lost two of my greatest friends over that whole thing, and I just couldn't bear to lose another one, so, yes, I sided with Talson."

Kat stared down at the photograph. "Have you known Talson as long as Nelco and Barty?" she asked softly.

"Longer, actually," said Roco. "I knew him for about a year before I met those guys."

"So, you've known him a long time," muttered Kat.

"Yeah, like thirty-one years, I think," said Roco.

"So are you older than him?"

"Five years older, yeah."

"What's his real name?"

Roco shrugged. "I know this sounds crazy, but I don't know."

"So you always called him Talson?"

"No, not when I first met him. He would never tell me his name, so I never told him mine. He figured out mine after a while, but I never figured out his."

"What did you call each other?"

"Well he called me Pool, because I got in trouble hustling at a pool table. I called him Magic. Then one day he just called me Roco. I don't know how he found out. I guess he could see it in my mind. He used to see stuff in my mind all the time and ask me about it. I felt like he was spying on me. I hated it. He would usually be really close to the truth about stuff, like with my name and even how I was feeling. I hated him, but maybe that's why I loved him, he understood me."

"Past tense?" asked Kat.

Roco smiled and looked down at the picture. "No," he said, "I still hate him for that sometimes."

"That's not what I meant," said Kat with a small smile.

Roco smiled slightly, "I know."

C H A P T E R   1 6

TRAITORS

"What do you think that guy in a suit wants with Cap?" said Browen as he and Sono walked down the street away from the dock.

"Who knows," said Sono, "it's probably not that important."

"I don't know," muttered Browen, "Conner Nelson, I feel like I should know who he is."

"I guess the name does kind of sound familiar. I guess he's an old friend of the Captain."

"Not so much old friend as old enemy, judging by how John Carl talked to him," said Browen.

"Yeah, there was a sort of sneer in Cap's voice, you know how he talks down to

people he doesn't like."

"I'll say there was," said Browen, "but you weren't exactly nice to the guy either."

"Hey, the guy is a jerk."

"What did he do to make you think that?"

"Nothing, he just rubbed me the wrong way, I don't know why."

"I know what you mean," said Browen, "I wonder if this has anything to do with what's been going on."

"What do you mean?"

"Well," said Browen, "first we see the captain crying, then we find out that his daughter joined Talson, then—" Browen paused.

"Then we find out that Tina ran away after an argument with Tracy, and Selena got pulled over and searched by the cops," said Sono picking up where his brother had stopped.

"And then we find out that Remi has been with Talson for years and Tracy wants to get revenge for her husband," continued Browen.

"And then this weird guy in a suit shows up to talk to Cap," Sono finished.

"Collared shirt and tie," corrected Browen.

The brothers stopped in front of the eighth dock. "This is insane," said Sono, staring out to sea. "The thing that really freaks me out is how all the cool people, all the smart people, all the people who, I don't know—"

"Yeah, they all go with Talson, I know," said Browen. "Kat was one of the smartest people I ever met, and she's just a kid, and Selena—"

"You don't have to say it," said Sono before Browen could say anything else. "I can't even believe it with her. I don't even want to talk about it."

"The biggest traitor on the planet," Browen repeated John Carl's words, "Cap was taking a really hard line about her."

"I wish he wouldn't," muttered Sono. "He knows I don't want to hear it."

"I don't think he gets it," said Browen. "He thinks that when we find out that someone is with Talson we are just going to let them go and not care about them anymore, like he does."

"Yeah, well, I'd like to see him do that with his daughter."

"What about Tina running away, or walking out, or whatever she did?"

"I bet it got ugly between her and Tracy," said Sono.

"It got ugly and she left, just like with Selena," said Browen.

"Selena's parents told her to get the hell out," said Sono. "It was because she joined Talson. She didn't just walk out, there's a difference."

"Well, why did Tina walk out?" said Browen, "not because she joined Talson, but because Kat joined Talson. The only difference is that Tina is underage and Selena was eighteen. You can't throw a kid who is under eighteen out of your house, that's the difference."

"True," said Sono. "Lord Talson has certainly broken up the Louis family. I just don't understand why. What did they do to deserve that?"

"Who knows? No one knows why he does what he does."

"So what do we do?" asked Sono. "We can't just stand here and watch this crap happen all over again. We need to find out what's really going on."

"How is it that Cap knows so much about Lord Talson? I mean, how much has Remi told him?"

Sono frowned. "Do you remember how he said he wasn't afraid of Remi passing information about him to Lord Talson, because he doesn't think Talson would learn anything he didn't already know?"

"Yeah," said Browen, "which means that John Carl thinks that Lord Talson knows a lot about him."

"He seems sure of it," said Sono. "I don't see how that's possible, though. Kat might be the one telling Lord Talson about her father."

"But Cap said that Kat didn't know enough about him to help Talson either, which means she doesn't know anything more than Remi," said Browen.

"I'm sure she knows more than Remi," said Sono, "which means that Talson just knows John Carl really well."

"He pretty much told us that, didn't he?" said Browen.

"Yeah, he did," said Sono. "The thing is that if Selena got pulled over that means that Remi *was* lying when he told Cap that Selena wasn't around anymore."

"Yeah, I guess we can't trust Remi for information. We need someone who can tell us the truth."

"Doesn't that brainless fool Larry at the Sharktooth know every Talson supporter that ever lived?" said Sono.

"Supposedly he does," said Browen, "but I doubt he'll tell us anything."

"Yeah, unless we tell him we're friends with Selena and we pay him. The fool is pretty oblivious, he'll probably be easy to work with."

"I know he seems really stupid," said Browen, "but then again, if he really knows all about Lord Talson and his followers he might not be as stupid as he looks."

"You're giving him way too much credit, dude. Let's go to the Sharktooth right now while we have the time. If he doesn't want to talk, we'll just get him drunk so he will talk. It's as simple as that."

"I don't know," said Browen, shaking his head, "Are you coming with me or not?" asked Sono.

"Of course I'm coming with you," answered Browen, "I just don't think it's going to be that easy."

* * *

Larry sat on a stool behind the bar, leaning his back against the mirror with his eyes half closed. For the first time in a long time he allowed his thoughts to wander into the past. Almost every night, fishermen would come into the bar for a drink after work. Larry would serve them a few drinks and they would go to the back room, where Roco Ramirez would help them gamble away their pay. The games had often been unfair, or as Roco had put it, fair only to those who played for the game instead of the prize. In other words, Roco chose who won.

Those were the days, thought Larry. Those were the good times, but ever since that one night nearly fifteen years ago, The Sharktooth Bar had never been the same. The bar looked the same and the same shark bones hung on the walls, but now the back room was empty and business was slow.

Larry felt angry as he relived the night the bar was busted in his mind. In hindsight, Larry realized that the events of that night had been more unfair and rigged than any game that had taken place in the back room of the Sharktooth.

The front door of the bar opened and Larry looked up, his mind immediately returning to the present. Two young fishermen entered, made their way to the bar and sat down without speaking.

"Good evening, mates," said Larry. "Good to see some fishermen in this old place. Long trip?"

"Yeah," said one, "we went out for two days with only three men counting the Captain. It was a grind. We're about ready for a drink."

"Three men, you say?" said Larry as he made their drinks. "Your captain had to be either a genius or a mad man to go out with only two deck hands in these conditions."

"Yeah, he's probably both."

"Who you guys work for?" asked Larry. "I know most of the captains around here."

"John Carl Thomason."

Larry smiled slightly. "That explains it, he is a mad genius when it comes to fishing."

"Sorry," said one of the fishermen, "I forgot about how he—"

"Don't mention it," said Larry dismissively, before Sono could finish. "The bar's open now, and that's all that matters. Who are you guys anyway?"

"I'm Sono Silven."

"Browen Silven," said the other.

"Larry James," said Larry. "So why were you the only deck hands?"

"One guy had an emergency in his family and the other guy just didn't show," replied Sono.

"A no show, huh?" said Larry. "Is John Carl gonna fire him."

Sono shrugged. "That's what we thought, but apparently the guy has another job, if you know what I mean."

Larry raised his eyebrows slightly. "Who we talking about?"

"Oh just this fool Remi Nelson," said Browen in a forced casual tone. "No great loss if he is fired anyway."

"Another job you say?"

"Do you know Remi?" asked Sono.

"I know 'em all," said Larry.

"Have a drink yourself, Larry," said Sono.

"No thanks, mate, I can't do that anymore."

Sono changed tactics quickly. "So did you work here before the place was busted?" he said in a more direct tone.

"Yeah," said Larry flatly.

"What really happened? Is it true that someone was shot in the back?"

"I can't really talk about that, it's a legal thing, you know."

"What about the people who have 'another job,' can you talk about them?"

"Why should I?" asked Larry.

"We're friends with one of them," said Sono.

"Really, who?"

"Selena Louis."

Larry did not move. "What makes you think she's around anymore?"

"We didn't know she was around, but we heard she got pulled over by the police and Kat was with her," said Sono, throwing caution to the winds.

Larry did not appear surprised by Sono's boldness. "You're talking about that kid, Katerina Thomason?" he said casually, "John Carl's daughter; what a surprise that was. Anyway, what does that matter to you guys?"

"It matters because she's been seen," replied Browen, "plus she's been searched by the police."

"It matters because she was our friend and she works for Talson now," added Sono somewhat emphatically.

"Hold on a minute," said Larry. He stood up and disappeared through the door that lead to the back room.

*   *   *

Somewhere in the house a telephone was ringing. "I'd better get that," said Roco, closing the photo album. Kat followed him out of the library and across the hall. They entered a small office with two desks. Roco picked up the telephone that sat on the desk closest to the door.

"It's Headquarters," he said. "Hello, Romez at the circle," he said into the phone. "Hey Milro, what's up, man?" Roco paused listening for a moment. "Larry?" he said, sounding surprised, "what does he want?" Roco paused, listening again. "No, Sela's not here, she's on a job, why?" Roco listened to Milro for several more minutes without speaking. "Wow," he said finally. "Browen and Sono Silven, damn, that's weird. I'll tell the boss, and see what he wants to do. I'll call you back if we need you." Roco put down the phone and looked at Kat. "This is really weird," he muttered.

"What did Milro say?" asked Kat.

"He said that Larry from the Sharktooth just called Headquarters."

"Why?"

"You know Browen and Sono Silven?"

"Yeah, they work for my dad."

"Well, apparently they both came into the Sharktooth and started asking Larry about Sela and Remi. It sounds like they're trying to get information about us."

"Wow, why are they asking Larry?"

"Larry is a smart man."

"But how does he know about Talson and the Silver Shadows, or why do Browen and Sono think he does? Does he really know anything?"

"Oh yeah, he knows tons of stuff," said Roco. "He's known Talson a long time."

"I didn't know that, I mean, Larry's not a Silver Shadow."

"No, he's not, but he might as well be. He has the reputation of knowing all the Silver Shadows, but this is weird. The only thing Browen and Sono could possibility want from Larry is to know where Sela is. They were her best friends before she joined Talson."

"I know, but what do they want to do if they find Sela?"

"I really have no idea, maybe this has something to do with what Talson was trying to concentrate on before. He probably already knows what's going on."

"But did Larry tell Sono and Browen anything? I mean would it be bad if he did?"

"I don't know, I don't get this whole thing right now. Let's go tell Talson what we know and see if he can figure out what the hell is going on."

Kat and Roco left the office and headed down the hall to the main room. Talson was still sitting where they had left him. He looked from Roco to Kat and back again as they entered. He smiled sarcastically. "Now what happened?"

Roco sighed. "You explain," he said to Kat.

"Can I call you Magic?" Kat said, looking at Talson.

Talson paused, looking at Roco, then he laughed. "No," he said, "I don't think I really deserve that name anymore."

"Sure you do," said Roco.

"I do not," said Talson

"Yeah, you do."

"Do not."

Kat wanted to laugh, but she couldn't tell if Talson and Roco were being serious or not. "Do you guys always argue like that?" she asked, allowing herself a small smile.

"No," said Talson.

"Yes," said Roco.

"Shut up," said Talson.

"I told you we always argue," said Roco.

"I told you shut up," said Talson.

"Larry called," said Roco, changing his tone completely.

"Really? What did he want?" asked Talson seriously. It was as if he and Roco had suddenly returned to the present after a flashback to their childhood days together.

"Apparently Browen and Sono Silven came into the bar and started asking him about Sela. They wanted all sorts of information about us. Milro told me that Larry said he didn't like the way the conversation was going, so he decided to call Headquarters."

"That's interesting," said Talson, "I guess Sono and Browen just got off work and thought they would go have a drink."

"Milro told me that Sono and Browen told Larry that Remnel didn't show up for work yesterday, so Sono and Browen were John Carl's only deck hands."

"That's interesting," said Talson again. "I expect John Carl didn't really appreciate that."

"Apparently Sono and Browen got the whole conversation with Larry started by telling him that John Carl wasn't mad about Remnel not coming to work because he 'has another job'."

"That is all the more reason for John Carl to be angry about it, though. He could never accept people missing work because they work for me, you know that, Romez. Besides," continued Talson, "Remi isn't doing anything for me at the moment."

"Then what the heck is he doing?" asked Roco.

"I have no idea," said Talson, although he didn't sound confused. Talson sighed, and rubbed his brow. "My head hurts so bad right now," he muttered more to himself than to Kat or Roco.

"What do you think the Silven boys are on to?" asked Roco.

"I think Sono and Browen are on to—," Talson pointed at Kat. "I'm guessing that everything they know they have heard from John Carl. I have no idea what would make John Carl tell Sono and Browen anything, but I think he has. He must have told them that you, Kat, are with us now. He may have told them about Sela getting pulled over, and about Tracy wanting revenge."

"What does that mean?" asked Roco, frowning.

"It means that Sono and Browen can see a repeat of events on the horizon and they want to stop it from happening," said Talson. "In that case, they will be looking for Sela, who everyone so foolishly thinks is the one responsible for everything. Larry is the logical information source for that, considering how much time Sela has spent at the Sharktooth. Sono and Browen Silven think that by finding Sela they can make a difference somehow, but they have no idea."

Roco and Kat looked at each other when Talson had finished, trying to understand what he had just told them.

"I understand why your head hurts now," said Roco. "So you think Sela is in trouble?"

"Yes, I know she is in trouble," said Talson, "but I don't think Sono and Browen are the ones she has to worry about. Right now the problem comes from Tracy, Remnel, Janice, and more importantly, Nelco."

"I thought Remi and Janice are with us," said Kat.

"Nelco?" whispered Roco, "he's in on this?"

"Remi and Janice were with us up until quite recently," said Talson. "The problem starts with Remi Nelson. Remi told John Carl and Nelco that we are looking to eliminate Tracy."

"He sold us out to Nelco and John Carl?" Roco exclaimed in outrage. "Remi hasn't spoken to Nelco in years, why now?"

"Why, I don't know," replied Talson, "but Nelco, has always sided with the Louis family, and now he has decided to take action on their behalf."

"So he told Tracy that we are going to kill her?" asked Roco.

"Yes, he did. Tracy automatically assumed that I would use Sela to do the job, because that would be my expected course of action. Tracy thinks that if she gets Sela killed she won't have to worry anymore."

"What makes her think that?" asked Roco. "Like I said before, everyone is under the misconception that Sela is the one

behind Barty Louis' death. Everyone, that is, except Mr. Conner Nelson."

"So what does Nelco think?" asked Kat.

"He thinks I need to die," said Talson simply.

"What?" said Kat and Roco together.

"Nelco met with John Carl a few minutes ago and whatever he said, it scared John Carl."

"What does that have to do with you?" asked Kat. "What did he say?"

"I'm not sure," said Talson. "My power has its limits, especially when John Carl is involved, but there are very few things that John Carl truly fears, so I can guess."

"You used the power to figure all this out?" asked Kat.

"Yes," said Talson listlessly.

"Is that how you knew that Remi and Janice sold us out?" asked Kat.

"Yes," said Talson again, expressionlessly.

"Is that how you knew that Nelco told Tracy that she might be killed?"

"Yes again."

"That's how you figured this whole thing out?" asked Kat.

"Most of it, yes," replied Talson. "I see bits and pieces of what is going on in my mind and then I put it together to see what it really means."

"So this really means that—" began Roco.

"That Nelco wants to kill me, yes it does," Talson finished Roco's sentence.

There was a silence.

"How is he going to do it?" Roco asked finally.

"He seems to be trying to get people on his side at the moment," said Talson, "and except for John Carl, they all seem to be going for it."

"Well I'm surely not going for it," said Roco. He turned away, muttering obscenities directed at Conner Nelson.

Kat looked at Talson. He did not look worried or scared. "Do you think Nelco would really try to kill you?" she asked.

"Yes," said Talson without a change of expression.

"But do you think he can?" asked Kat.

"Yes," said Talson again.

"You think he'll succeed?" asked Kat in surprise.

"No, I do not think he will succeed, at least as long as he doesn't get all the Silver Shadows to side with him."

"He won't," said Kat immediately.

"He definitely won't," said Roco.

Talson smiled. "I have always found, among all the traitors, those people who are loyal."

"What about Larry?" said Roco, "is he with us? He's the one who can really help Nelco and Tracy if he wanted to."

"Yes, he could," said Talson, seemingly unconcerned. "We shall see where his loyalties lie very soon."

"So what do we do now?" asked Roco. "Do we tell Sela about Sono and Browen?"

"Yes, most definitely," said Talson. "Someone has to go find Sela and tell her what is going on. That person is going to be you, Kat," he added.

"Me?" said Kat in surprise.

"Yes, and don't get caught by Tracy. That will complicate things. Also," continued Talson, "someone has to find Nelco and figure out what he's really doing."

Roco scowled, "and it's gonna be me."

"Exactly," said Talson. "Find him, figure out his game, don't get caught, and don't get in a fight with him."

"Right," said Roco, not sounding too enthusiastic.

"You guys have a choice, you don't have to help me and you don't have to help Sela. I'm staying here until I know what Sela is going to do," he continued. "I'll call Larry and tell him to keep Browen and Sono at the bar, just in case Sela wants to go and see them. If she decides to do that I'll probably go down there too, so I can talk to Larry. We need all the support we can get at this point. Are we all agreed on this?"

"Yup, I'm in boss," said Roco.

Kat nodded, "agreed."

"Good," said Talson. "Just remember, don't hurt anyone, don't get in any fights, and DO NOT GET CAUGHT," Talson strongly emphasized the last four words. "I'll be upstairs in my office. Good luck." Talson got up and left the room, closing the door softly behind him.

"Wow," muttered Kat after Talson left. "You think Nelco would really kill Talson?"

"He's going to try," said Roco, "but if he wants to kill Talson he is going to have to kill me too."

"Do you think that the other Silver Shadows will side with Nelco? I mean like Milro, Tiro and Mevsin."

"No way. Talson has always had loyal friends, even though there have always been traitors. You're doing the right thing supporting him, Kat."

"I hope so," said Kat uncertainly.

"You're going to find something out about him when this is over," said Roco. "You'll find out why he deserves our loyalty."

Kat looked at Roco. She could think of nothing to say.

"Welcome to the crazy life, kid," said Roco in a much lighter tone. "Good luck," he added with a small smile as he turned to leave.

"Yeah, good luck," said Kat, following him outside. "Where will you find Nelco?"

"At his apartment, I hope. Where will you find Sela?"

"At her old house, I hope."

Roco smiled. "There are good reasons to side with Talson, believe me."

"Better him than Nelco, I suppose," said Kat.

"I like the way you think, kid," said Roco. He turned and disappeared among the trees behind the house on his way to the parking lot.

Kat walked away from the house in the opposite direction. She paused on the sidewalk at the edge of the park. She kept picturing the fair-haired, eleven year-old boy in the far right of the photograph in the library. Kat wondered what he looked like now. She couldn't imagine anyone being able to kill Talson, yet Talson seemed to think that Conner Nelson could do it.

Kat wondered for a moment if maybe Conner Nelson was right, maybe Talson did need to die. Then she remembered what Roco had just said. 'You'll find that he deserves our loyalty.' Sela had told her the same thing. Kat turned right and headed down the street toward Tina's house.

CHAPTER 17

BARTY'S LIE

On the edge of the city brightly colored tents had been erected. The traveling circus was in town. Two men strolled down the street past shabby looking houses and dumpsters.

"See that?" said one man, pointing to the tents. "The gypsies are back."

"What are you talking about," said the other, "there are no gypsies here."

"Yeah, there are."

"Shut up," said the second man. "Gypsies aren't even real."

"What the hell do you mean gypsies aren't real?"

"I just mean that isn't a real circus, it's some group of mind reading freaks."

"You're full of it, it's called fortune telling."

From across the street a young boy watched the two men with interest. He wondered whether the first man was right. Maybe there was more to this circus than it appeared. He looked at the tents flapping slightly in the breeze. Even if they were mind readers he didn't see how they could help him, but it was his only chance. The boy listened as the voices of the men faded away down the street. He crossed the road to the field where the tents stood. He walked between the tents, not sure if he wanted to meet someone or not.

"Who's there?" The sudden voice from behind a tent made the boy jump.

The boy peered around the edge of a tent to see who had spoken. A small woman stood between two tents. The boy stood staring at her for a moment. She was the oddest looking woman he had ever seen.

She had flowing black hair and was wearing an orange scarf draped over her shoulders and a gold band in her hair. Her skirt was purple and she wore many pieces of gold jewelry. The boy looked at her face and felt as though her dark eyes were looking right through him.

"Who are you, little one?"

"It doesn't matter," replied the boy, "I'm no one."

"What do you want, then?" asked the woman.

"I want a job in your circus." said the boy.

"Do you? What do you really want?"

"Can I trust you?" asked the boy.

"No, most likely not," replied the woman. "I don't advise that you ask that question, anyway. It is really pointless considering that almost everyone will lie and tell you you can trust them. If I tell that you can't trust me, you won't, but chances are it's the honest person who you would do well to trust. You understand?"

The boy frowned, but said nothing.

"You want to find something out, don't you," said the woman. "Why don't you just ask me your question."

"It's true then," said the boy. "There are really people who can read other people's minds."

You have a name little one? No.

Well, in that case neither do I.

This is real isn't it?

"I'll tell you something, little one," said the woman, "If you want answers you have to ask the right questions, and if you want true answers you have to ask them the right way."

"But you can do it too, can't you."

"Did you not hear what I just said, or did you not understand it?"

"I'm sorry," said the boy, looking slightly ashamed for the first time. "I do understand, no one ever asks the right questions. I can never think of the right questions when there is anyone around to answer them. I always remember them later when there is no one."

"You'll get better," said the woman, "and you'll learn how to control it. I can't help you with it though, I could only help if I knew your name."

"What does my name have to do with this?"

"If you won't tell me your name I know you don't trust me, and therefore I can't trust you. I can't help you if I don't trust you."

"You're a gypsy," said the boy. "Gypsies are dishonest, it shouldn't matter."

"I'm a lot more than just a gypsy," said the woman. "I'm not a gypsy for you."

"But then what are you? People said you can see into the future."

"For them I see the future, but for you, I doubt it."

"Why not?"

"Because you're not one of them, you're not one of the others."

"What do you mean by 'the others'?"

"I mean the ones who don't see the way we do. They see only what is on the outside."

"I need a job to earn money," said the boy, "that's why I came here."

"You want to tell people their fortunes?"

"Could I?"

"Of course, I can teach you how. Then if you decide to tell me your name someday, I'll teach you how to really control it."

The boy gazed at her. "Would you really do that?"

"Of course."

"But, I don't want to—"

"You can't hurt me, little one," interrupted the woman. "Why won't you tell me your name?"

"Because I'm dead," the boy replied.

The woman laughed lightly. "Interesting, so am I. In that case, what do you go by, what do the others call you?"

"They call me a lot of different things," said the boy.

"What should I call you?"

"Magic," replied the boy.

*   *   *

Kat slowed down as she neared Tina's house. She was not sure where Sela would be or how she could possibly find her without anyone noticing her. Kat saw Tracy's car parked in the driveway, but since she had seen Tracy out walking a few hours previously, she was not sure if Tracy was home. She walked around to the back yard and climbed onto the back deck, trying to be as quiet as possible. The sliding glass door was open and only the screen door was closed. Kat could see that no one was in the kitchen, but she could hear voices that seemed to be coming from the front of the house.

"You think I'm stupid, do you?" Kat recognized Tracy's angry voice immediately.

"No," Kat had to strain to hear Tina, who was not speaking nearly as loudly. "I'm sorry, I know I shouldn't have left, that's why I came back, okay?"

"No, not okay," replied Tracy coldly. "You can't tell me that you never saw Kat all that time you were gone."

"Well I'm telling you that I didn't," said Tina, "I didn't see her. You should be happy about that."

"You should be happy I'm still letting you live here," snapped Tracy. "Go upstairs to your room now and stay there." Kat heard the door slam and Tina's footsteps on the stairs.

"Well, that could have been a lot worse," said a voice from below the deck. Kat jumped, turning around to see Sela leaning on the railing of the deck. "What are you doing sneaking around here, punk?" she asked.

"What are you doing here?" whispered Kat.

Sela shrugged, "same thing as you I guess."

"Sela," said Kat, "I gotta tell you something."

"Okay, well come under here so Tracy doesn't see us," she said gesturing to the space under the deck.

Kat jumped off the deck and crawled underneath it, following Sela into the musty darkness. "It's really dirty under here," she muttered.

"Yeah, well, eavesdropping is a dirty job," said Sela. "Anyway, what's going on?"

"Sono and Browen went into The Sharktooth Bar a little while ago."

Sela raised her eyebrows. "Why?"

"Apparently they wanted to ask Larry about you. I guess my dad told them that you and I got pulled over and that I'm a Silver Shadow. So now they're trying to find you."

"Does Talson know?"

"Yeah, he sent me to tell you."

"What made you think I'd be here?"

"I didn't think you would be, but I thought I might find some clues here."

"Well, nice move. What do Sono and Browen want with me?"

"I don't know. Talson said he thinks they are trying to avoid a repeat of past events or something like that. I'm not sure what he meant."

"Yeah, I guess they are," said Sela, "but things are a lot different this time."

"Yeah, it's really different," said Kat. "Talson just found out that Remi and Janice sold us out to Nelco."

"Wait, Nelco is working against us now?" Sela sounded surprised.

"Yeah," said Kat, struggling to find a more comfortable position in the cramped space under the deck. "Talson said Nelco is trying to kill him."

There was a pause. "No way," whispered Sela softly after a moment. "Kill him?"

"That's what Talson said.".

"He's sure?"

"He sounded pretty sure."

"Wow," muttered Sela, "that's insane."

"Apparently Nelco met with my dad today and told him that he wants to kill Talson."

"How does Talson know about that?" asked Sela.

"He saw it in Nelco's mind."

"What's Nelco doing telling John Carl? How did John Carl react?"

"Talson doesn't know, he just said my dad was scared. He sent Roco to go find Nelco and see what he's really up to."

"Damn," said Sela, "a lot of stuff came down while I was waiting for Tracy to get here. I had better go down to The Sharktooth Bar and see what is really going on with Sono and Browen. You don't think they are somehow connected to Nelco, do you?"

"I don't know," said Kat. "Talson said you would probably want to go down to the Sharktooth. He said that if you go he is going to go down there too, and talk to Larry."

"How did Talson react when he found out about Nelco?" asked Sela.

Kat shrugged, "pretty casual, considering."

"Typical Talson," said Sela. "Let's get out of here, my car is back at the park."

Sela and Kat quietly moved through the yard to the front of the house. Kat caught a glimpse of Tracy through the livingroom window. She was standing in profile with her hands on the edge of a table. As Kat looked at her she felt as if her mind was suddenly working much faster. She could see the side of the house and Tracy through the window, but for a moment she could also see the table in front of Tracy and felt as if her own hands were resting on its edge. *Tina was lying. She saw Kat and Selena.*

No, she's telling the truth. She doesn't know anything. Kat forced the thoughts into Tracy's mind.

She's lying.

No she's not.

She saw Selena and she can tell me where to find her.

No she won't, she doesn't know anything. Leave Tina alone.

"Move, Kat, we need to go," Sela pulled Kat back to reality.

"Sorry," muttered Kat, following Sela down the street away from the house. "That was weird, I didn't mean it to happen."

"Apparently you never do with that stuff," said Sela. "Imagine what Talson is going through with his mind right now."

"Yeah," said Kat, "he said his head hurt."

"That means it really hurts, and things are really bothering him. When he admits that something hurts, you know it hurts like hell."

"Why did that just happen with me and Tracy?" asked Kat.

"I have no idea," said Sela. "Ask Talson."

*   *   *

When Kat returned to the house she found the common room deserted. She headed upstairs and found Talson sitting in his office, looking tired.

"Sela went to the Sharktooth," said Kat, standing back in the doorway.

Talson motioned for Kat to sit down. "Tracy didn't see you, did she?" he asked.

"No," said Kat, taking a seat in front of Talson's desk. "But a weird thing happened when I saw her through the window."

"What sort of weird thing?" asked Talson, although Kat had the feeling he knew exactly what she was about to tell him.

"Well, I was looking at Tracy from outside her house, but then I felt like I was standing where she was standing, and her thoughts were in my head. Tracy was thinking about how Tina was lying to her about not seeing Sela and me when she left home. I told Tracy that she was wrong, and Tina was telling the truth. At least that's what I think I did. I could hear what I was thinking and what she was thinking at the same time and it was like I couldn't tell which thoughts were mine and which were hers."

Talson nodded, slowly. "That's because for that moment her thoughts were your thoughts and vice versa. That's just how the power works sometimes," he added. Kat thought Talson sounded tired and bored at the same time, but it was impossible to tell how he was truly feeling.

"But I don't understand what's going on," said Kat. "I mean what did I do with Tracy? I just saw her and it happened."

"I'll explain it on our way to the bar," said Talson.

"I'm going with you?" said Kat, surprised.

"You might as well," said Talson, "unless you don't want to."

"No, I'll go," said Kat immediately.

"Then let's get out of here," said Talson. "We'll borrow Milro's car, since he left it here."

Talson opened a drawer of the desk and took out a pair of black sunglasses and put them on. "I can't have anyone see my eyes," he muttered.

"Why are your eyes yellow anyway?" asked Kat.

"That is something I never really understood," replied Talson. "Let's go."

Kat followed Talson out of the house and through the trees to the parking lot at the back of the park. She could hardly believe that she was going to The Sharktooth Bar again, and this time she was going with Talson.

"Odd, isn't it?" said Talson as they reached the parking lot. There was a small black car with tinted windows half hidden behind some trees. It was the same car that had been parked in the driveway of the run-down house near Headquarters. "This whole day has been weird, and I have the feeling we haven't seen the worst of it."

"This whole thing with Tracy is really weird," muttered Kat. "And Nelco—"

"Yes it is," said Talson, as they got into the car and Talson pulled out onto the street. It was afternoon now, but it was still very hot. Talson took a deep breath. "What I have been talking to you about in terms of the power is what I call defensive power. The thing between you and Tracy right now is offensive power. It requires not only that you work to control your own mind, but also that you work to control Tracy's mind. Offensive power is, for lack of better words, the cold side of the power, the darker side. Controlling another person's mind requires knowledge and control of one's own mind. As we gain self control, the ability to control others develops."

"So you're saying that I was controlling Tracy's mind?" Kat asked quietly. She felt scared now.

Talson merged onto the freeway. "You are in the early stages of control, yes," he replied slowly.

"Why?" asked Kat, "I didn't mean to."

"Controlling your own mind is one of the most difficult things you will ever have to do, Kat. It is never easy to understand why our minds do what they do, and it is even harder to prevent our minds from doing things we don't want to do."

"So if I can control Tracy's mind, what does that mean?" asked Kat.

"It means, quite simply, that you have the power to do anything you want with her."

"Can I stop controlling her?"

"Right now the connection between your mind and hers is not very strong, but it will continue to get stronger unless you intentionally destroy the connection."

"And if I destroyed it?"

"Tracy would lose all the areas of her mind that were under your control at the time when the connection was broken."

"So if the connection was really strong when I broke it, would she lose everything?"

"If enough of the mind is being controlled the destruction of the connection can kill. In that case the mind has become dependent on the connection with the controller in order to function. Without that connection everything is lost, leaving the person with nothing. They lose all their knowledge, memories, and feelings and eventually they die."

"Where does everything go when the person dies," asked Kat. "Is it just lost?"

"No, it stays in the mind of the controller."

"So if you are controlling someone's mind and then you stop controlling them, the person dies and you are left with all their memories and thoughts and everything?"

"Yes," said Talson.

Kat and Talson were silent as they drove. Kat was shocked and scared by what she had just heard. She did not know what to think, now. As Talson pulled into the parking lot behind the Sharktooth, he turned and looked at Kat. "Just be thankful your mind is the only one you have to deal with. It's not easy living with dead people's minds inside your head, believe me."

He turned off the car. "Now here's the plan," he changed to a more businesslike tone. "We go into the bar and we listen. We will listen and nothing else, understood?"

Kat nodded. "Understood," she said softly.

*   *   *

Larry was standing behind the bar facing Sono and Browen. His expression said this is my bar, and you have to follow my rules. Larry did not enjoy being pushed for information, and Sono and Browen had gone too far.

"Listen," said Larry, looking at Sono and Browen in the mirror behind the bar. "Why would you come in here to ask me to rat someone out? Go find someone else to bother about it."

"Someone else like who?" asked Sono.

"Don't ask me. I don't know anything about it," snapped Larry.

"I think you're lying," said Browen.

"Well, I'm sorry you think that," said Larry coldly, "but I have no reason not to lie to you right now. This is my bar and we play by my rules, you get it?"

"It's not a big deal," said Sono, "just tell us about Selena. She's our friend, we just need to find her right now."

"Screw you," said Larry looking away from Sono and Browen in the mirror.

"Why won't you just tell us?"

Larry turned around to face Sono and Browen. "Because I don't feel like it kid, and this is my damn bar, I do what I feel like doing. Do you get it?"

"Look_"began Sono.

"I said DO YOU GET IT?"yelled Larry. It had been a long time since Larry had raised his voice like that. Larry hated to raise his voice. It reminded him of things he wanted very badly to forget. Larry felt that it was not only drinking that returned him to his old ways, but also any behavior that he associated with his days as a drunk. By losing his temper Larry felt like he was repeating his old mistakes. As much as Larry hated being aggressive, there were some situations as a bartender when it was unavoidable. Larry did not do whatever he *wanted* to in his bar like he had told Sono and Browen. Larry always did whatever he *had* to do, no matter what.

"We get it mate," said Browen quietly. He and Sono looked somewhat intimidated by Larry now.

"Good," said Larry. "You need to get it because you ain't gonna be able to change my mind unless you decide to play by my rules."

"What are your rules?"

"My number one rule is that nothing comes free. No free drinks, no free games, no free information."

"So what do you want from us?" asked Sono.

"Simple," replied Larry. "You tell me what you're trying to do and why you want to know this stuff and then you tell me how much you already know. Then I'll tell you what I know. Deal?" Larry turned away to clean the counter. He didn't always use the same procedure in these kinds of situations, but this time he knew he had to be careful. He liked this exchange because it put him in the position of power. He could choose how much he wanted to tell Sono and Browen and they would not be able to push him.

Larry glanced in the mirror to check on Sono and Browen. The brothers were looking at each other as if they were trying to come to an agreement on what to do without actually speaking to each other. Finally Sono spoke.

"No," he said. "No deal."

The moment Sela entered The Sharktooth Bar a flood of memories came back to her, the many days she had come to the bar to play cards in the back room, and the many hours she had spent working off her debts behind the bar. Sela accounted herself lucky that she had always been a fairly conservative player, otherwise she might have lost a lot more money gambling at the Sharktooth. Sela remembered when she had first met Talson at the Sharktooth. "I hear you like to gamble," he had said.

"Yeah, but I'm kind of conservative," she had replied. "I'm poor, so, you know, I have to be."

"Yeah, I know," Talson had said. "I'm conservative too."

Sela felt almost at home in the back of the Sharktooth. Perhaps it was because she hadn't been there the night when the bar was busted and Julie Operman was killed. Sela stood in the now dusty back room, her hand on the door that lead to the bar. This was not the same as the day she had come with Kat. Sono and Browen had not been there that day. Sela could feel the flood of memories at the edges of her mind and she knew she would be hit with them as soon as she opened the door and saw her old friends.

It was not as though Sela had not seen the Silven brothers since their days together. She had, upon occasion, seen them on the docks, but usually only at a distance. It was always sad when she saw them and she thought about how it had once been, how it could have been, and how it actually had turned out. It had been years since the days when Sela had gone to the arcade to play games with Sono and Browen. It felt like a previous life to her now. She had different eyes, a different name and a different life. Sono and Browen didn't even recognize her anymore.

Sela opened the door slowly at first, then more quickly. There they were, sitting at the bar. Sono and Browen, Selena's best friends in the world. Sela stared at them for a moment feeling somewhat numb. She wanted to cry and laugh at the same time. She knew she had to pull herself together. She had to let go of the past and focus on what she needed to do in the present.

She turned her attention to Larry. He was standing a distance down the bar from Sono and Browen, cleaning glasses. Sela could tell he was angry. He was stacking the glasses much more forcefully than was necessary and he kept slamming them down on the counter.

She turned her attention back to Browen and Sono, and made her way quietly across the room and came up to stand behind them.

"Are you sure we shouldn't tell him what we know just to hear what he has to say?" Browen was saying in a low voice.

"Well, the guy may be useless, but he definitely knows something," said Sono. "I guess telling him a few things couldn't hurt. He'll probably forget what we said by tomorrow, anyway."

"Yeah, and who knows, he could be the only one who can tell us anything about Selena."

"No, I don't think he's the only one," said Sela.

Browen and Sono turned around so quickly they almost fell off their stools. They had not seen or heard Sela come up behind them. They both sat frozen, staring at Sela.

"Selena?" said Sono incredulously. "Is it really you?"

"Yeah, it is," said Sela casually.

"I can't believe you're here," muttered Browen. "I mean, we were just trying to get this bartender to tell us where we might find you."

"I know," said Sela casually, "I thought I'd make it easy on him."

"Thanks for that, Sela," said Larry, turning around. It was clear that he had known she was there all the time. "I really need a break from people coming in here asking questions about you."

"Yeah, I'm getting popular for all the wrong reasons these days," replied Sela.

"Oh well, same old story isn't it?" said Larry with a sigh. "Been there before, haven't you?"

"Oh yeah," Sela turned back to Sono and Browen, "what is it that you wanted to know about me?"

The brothers stared at her for a moment without speaking. Finally Sono spoke.

"We wanted to know if it was really you. Did you really kill him?"

"Technically it was Talson," said Sela, showing none of the remorse she had expressed previously to Kat and Tina.

Kat and Talson crouched behind the bar near the door to the back room. Talson looked at Kat. "Technically," he mouthed, "more like absolutely."

"Do you think this is bad?" Kat whispered back. "I mean, Sela being here talking to them."

"Technically, yes, it is bad, but actually it could be useful."

Useful?

Just listen.

Back at the bar Browen and Sono were glaring at Sela. "Technically my ass," Browen said angrily. "You helped him."

"I just realized that I don't think I want to hear this," muttered Talson.

"That seems to happen a lot in this bar," muttered Kat. *Do you want to leave?*

"It does happen a lot here, and I do want to leave," said Talson. "But I'm not going to leave. We need to hear this."

"Okay, so I helped him," there was a sneer in Sela's voice.

"Why would you do that?" asked Sono.

"You have no idea," said Sela coolly. "Why are you guys here?"

"We were here to ask him," Sono indicated Larry, "but now we don't have to since you showed up."

"You knew we were here, didn't you?" muttered Browen. "That's why you came."

"That's right."

"How did you know?" asked Sono, frowning.

"Amazingly, Larry has a cellular telephone," said Sela airily.

"And more amazingly he actually knows how to work it," muttered Talson.

"You called her," spat Sono turning around to glare at Larry.

Larry shrugged. "So what if I did," he said coldly.

"You're a spy," said Sono incredulously. "You tell them everything, you tell them everything that happens here, don't you?"

"Yeah, at times I do." There was no trace of the anger Larry had expressed

earlier.

"You lie and you cheat," said Sono angrily. "It's an act. You act like you haven't got a clue what's going on so it's easy for you to spy on everyone. You're just an act."

"Yeah, a damn good act," muttered Talson.

"As a matter of fact I am somewhat of an act," said Larry calmly. "It is always amazing how long it takes most people to figure that out."

"You're on his side then?" asked Sono.

"Whose side?" asked Larry.

"Lord Talson's side," said Browen coldly.

"What's Talson got to do with anything?" asked Larry coldly.

"Good question," Talson muttered to Kat from behind the bar.

"He has everything to do with this," said Sono. "You heard Sela, he killed Barty Louis and he killed Julie Operman."

"Since when did you kill Julie?" asked Kat looking sideways at Talson.

"Since no one knows who killed her, they just assume it was me."

Someone needs to tell them the truth, show them the truth. Sela knows, why doesn't she tell them?

Sela had made no move to explain anything and neither had Larry.

Why don't they tell them about Tracy and Nelco and everyone? They know, why don't they tell them?

Telling them won't be enough, and they have no way to show them the truth. I'm sure they want to, but Sela and Larry have never been too friendly with the truth.

But someone has to do something.

I agree.

Kat frowned, staring at Sela who was still standing behind Sono and Browen, her expression blank and emotionless. Suddenly the door of the bar opened, and to Kat's shock, her father entered. Kat looked at Talson, but could not touch his mind.

"What the hell are you guys doing here?" said John Carl, angrily approaching Sono and Browen. Suddenly he stopped dead, staring at Sela. John Carl looked as if he had been momentarily paralyzed. Sela seemed slightly amused by this.

"John Carl," she said lightly, "it's been too long."

John Carl's eyes narrowed in anger at Sela's falsely friendly tone.

"You traitor," he said through clenched teeth.

"Hardly more of a traitor than you," replied Sela.

Larry turned around as if he had just noticed John Carl. "John Carl," he said brightly, "can I help you?"

"Yes, actually, you probably can," said John Carl turning his gaze to the bartender. He looked at Sela then back at Larry. "Where is Talson?" he asked quietly.

"What?" For the first time Sela seemed to be caught off guard.

"Fine," said John Carl, "don't tell me where he is, just tell him something for me."

"And what might that be?" asked Sela.

"Tell him Conner Nelson is trying to kill him."

Talson was staring at the dusty floor making no eye contact with John Carl or anyone else in the room. Kat found that his mind was completely closed. She felt for a moment that she was alone in the bar, as if Talson was no longer beside her.

"He already knows that," said Sela.

"How can he?" asked John Carl.

"Why do you care if he knows?" asked Sela. "Why do you even care if he lives or dies?"

"I don't really," began John Carl, "I just_"

"Hate Conner Nelson," Sela finished John Carl's sentence.

"I don't hate him," said John Carl, "I just don't like him very much."

"Whatever," said Sela, "why do you want to warn Talson?"

"I guess I should have known he didn't need me to warn him," said John Carl. There was a hint of resentment in his voice now.

"Are you kidding?" said Larry, looking directly into John Carl's face, "how do you think he found out? He found out from you. He heard what you heard, you fool."

"He couldn't have," said John Carl, he sounded angry, even scared, and was clearly trying to avoid Larry's intense gaze. "There is no connection anymore."

"You fool," said Larry again. "You know that it only ends one way. When will you see the truth, John Carl Thomason?"

"The truth," spat John Carl with contempt in his voice. "You cannot speak the truth, Larry James."

"Obviously neither can you," said Larry with a faint smile now.

The smile seemed to scare John Carl. He turned to Browen and Sono. "You guys have ducked work for long enough, let's go." He turned and marched angrily to the door. He paused in the doorway and turned back to Sono and Browen. "If you two don't want to lose your jobs you had better quit talking to this fool and get to work." He exited, slamming the door behind him.

Sela looked at Sono and Browen. "Do yourselves a favor and try not to get fired," she said.

Sono and Browen looked at her for a moment. It was clear that they both wanted to say something, but for some reason couldn't. Finally they rose, and followed their captain out the front door.

Talson finally moved his eyes from the floor and looked at Kat. His expression was completely unreadable.

 What was that all about?" Kat asked in a whisper.

"It was about seeing the truth," he said softly.

"My father can never seem to do that," muttered Kat.

"I know," said Talson. He stood up from behind the bar. Sela, who had known he was there, looked into his face, her hands clutched the edge of the counter. Her expression was hard to read, but she looked sad. Larry had his back to Talson and did not turn around when he stood up.

"So is Nelson really trying to kill you," Larry asked without a hint of concern in his voice.

"Yeah," said Talson just as casually, turning to look at Larry's back.

"So for once old J.C. is right, huh?"

"Well, not exactly," said Talson.

It was one of the oddest conversations Kat had ever witnessed. Talson and Larry were still not facing each other, and continued to talk in overly casual tones. Kat had the impression that they were trying to hide the fact that either they hated each other very much, or that they were very close friends. What scared Kat was that she could not tell which it was.

"Same old John Carl," continued Talson. "I see nothing has changed. He still can't see the truth."

"Oh, he can see it," said Larry, "he just can't face it."

"Clearly neither can you," said Talson. His casual tone was gone now, and there was something that resembled anger in his voice.

Kat looked between them. She was even more confused now. She felt that there was something between them, but she could not see or feel it. It was as if something was clouding her mind and preventing her from seeing what stood right in front of her. Kat looked at Sela. She too looked somewhat confused. She seemed to be trying very hard to understand the way Talson and Larry were acting.

"Whose side are you on, Larry?" asked Sela, walking over to stand beside Talson. Kat remained crouched on the floor at their feet.

"You're trying to tell me about sides, Sithe?" Larry still did not turn around. "You know I've never been on Nelson's side."

"Prove it," said Sela.

Larry laughed. "There is nothing to prove."

"Yeah there is," said Talson. "Look at me. Look at us." Talson looked down at Kat. *Stand up.* Kat obeyed, getting up and standing on Talson's other side. Larry still made no effort to look at any of them.

"Prove you can face the truth, Larry James," said Talson.

"Prove you can speak the truth, Talson," replied Larry.

"You first."

"And take your word that you will do your part of the deal? I think not."

"You don't trust me?"

"You're a dishonest man, Talson," said Larry. "We both know that."

"As are you," said Talson. "We were both here before, and we both know what happened."

"Yes, and I know that you didn't do anything to make it any different than it was."

"Neither did you," said Talson. "They are going to use you, Larry."

"Let them try."

"Not if I can help it. We can't just repeat our mistakes, Larry. You of all people should understand that."

"It's not me that's in trouble and you know it."

"I owe him nothing, Larry," said Talson.

"He warned you about Nelson, you owe him the same warning."

"He didn't warn me of anything. I have nothing to say to him."

"Well of course you're not going to talk to him. I know your style, Talson. He didn't say it to your face and I know you won't say it to his. You and him are the same, always using others."

"I'm better than him, Larry," said Talson.

"Prove it," said Larry coolly. "I know you, Talson, you'll never face him."

"Don't tell me about not being able to face people, Larry," said Talson. For the first time there was real anger in his voice.

Don't lecture anyone about facing the truth, Larry James.

Kat stood frozen, looking up at Talson. "The truth, Kat, you wanted the truth," he murmured.

He has the power too doesn't he?

Yes.

Why didn't you tell me.

Larry had to tell you that.

Why does he hide it?

It is a truth he could not face, Kat.

Why?

Shame, guilt, pain, loss, grief, fear, those are the things no one can face. This time Talson was not the one in Kat's head, it was Larry. He still did not turn to face Kat and Talson, but rather stood facing the counter, his eyes on the floor.

You never know for sure who's in your head, do you? Talson told you nothing. Kat felt the third voice in her mind. It was not Talson or Larry.

You want to know the truth? I can tell you everything that happened. Everything that Talson is too cowardly to tell you.

Conner Nelson?

That's right.

Talson is not a coward. Get out. Kat felt like her mind had screamed the words. She looked at Talson and suddenly his eyes seemed to change from yellow to a dark shade of brown. Kat's mind exploded with a clear picture of the back room of The Sharktooth Bar.

The room was empty except for a dark haired man who sat alone at a small table in the corner of the room. He seemed to be waiting for someone. A fair-haired man entered the room and approached the other man. "Barlo," he said in a soft voice.

"Nelco," said Barty Louis. "You came."

Nelco laughed softly, "Of course I came." He sat down opposite Barty. "What is it? What's going on?"

"It's about Julie," said Barty.

"What's wrong?" Nelco looked concerned now.

"He's going to kill her, Nelco," whispered Barty.

"No," said Nelco immediately, "he wouldn't."

"He's going to, you know he will." He spoke sincerely, but in his mind the lie was evident. Nelco was so shocked and scared that he did not recognize the lie.

"He can't do that," Nelco whispered, "she's one of us."

"And you are actually naive enough to think he cares?"

"I thought he did."

"You should know better than that, Nelco, he has never really cared."

"I thought he was going to make her captain."

"You actually think he would replace me with her? You're being a fool, Nelco."

"Barlo, I don't understand why he would do this. Are you sure? I mean, I know you don't want to lose your position as captain, but seriously, you have to let it go."

"Conner, are you insane? You don't understand this at all. That's just a cover for his real plan. It's a cover for the murder he is about to commit. You know he wouldn't really replace me as captain. The magic four will always stand at the top. He's just using that to make her trust him. You have to see through these lies."

"But he likes Julie, I can't imagine him killing her."

"Don't be a fool, Nelco," said Barty leaning forward across the table. "Think about it, Conner. Talson can kill anyone no matter how he feels. You know that."

"But why would he? She hasn't done anything."

"She loves you, Nelco," replied Barty simply. The anger burned inside him as he said this, but he didn't let it show.

"Why does that mean he would kill her?" Nelco looked confused now.

"You really don't get it do you?" said Barty. "Talson loves her too."

"I thought you said he doesn't care about anyone. You're the one who keeps saying that. Besides if he does love her why in hell would he kill her?"

"Because she doesn't love him, she loves you and he's jealous."

"If that was the case, why not kill me?"

"Are you crazy? I thought you knew Talson. He wouldn't kill you, that would be too easy, too simple. You have to think about it like Talson does. If he kills you he still won't have Julie, because he knows she won't want to be with anyone other than you. Besides, if you die you don't suffer. On the other hand you will suffer if he kills Julie. In his mind, if he can't have her then neither should you."

"That's the cruelest thing I've ever heard," said Nelco.

"I know it is, but he's a cruel man."

"No, he's not," said Nelco, "you know he's not."

"For God sakes, Conner," said Barty exasperatedly, "why can't you see the truth? You are going to lose the woman you love because you can't face the truth. Face it, Talson doesn't care about you." Barty smiled inwardly as he saw the effect of his words on Nelco. Finally he had succeeded in convincing him.

Nelco put his head in his hands. "He can't kill her," he gasped, his voice shaking

now. "We have to do something, I can't lose her. You have to help me, Barty."

Barty put on an expression of concern, reaching across the table to grasp Nelco's shoulder. "I'm with you, man," he said softly. "You know I want to help Julie as much as you do. Like you said, she's one of us." Barty looked upset, but on the inside he was burning with excitement. His plan had worked, and now the last possible person that could make his plan fail would be helping him.

Cruel man, wasn't he? Kat felt like her mind was being dragged away from the back room with Barty and Nelco and back to the present. She was still standing beside Talson in front of the bar. "Nelco," muttered Kat. "He was in my head."

"I know," said Talson.

"I was in there," muttered Kat, pointing to the back door. "I was in Barty's mind, he lied." She looked into Talson's face, breathing hard, "Barty was lying." Kat realized that she and Talson were alone in the bar now.

"I know," said Talson softly. "It's okay," Talson murmured, "it's only the truth."

"How did that happen?" whispered Kat. "Barty is dead, how could I be in his mind."

"His mind is not dead, Kat," said Talson.

Kat realized that she was shaking slightly. She leaned against the bar for support. "That was horrible, he was saying that you were going to kill Julie. That wasn't true, was it?"

"You know he was lying, don't you? Nelco was his friend."

"Yes," said Kat quietly. "He lied to his best friend. He lied so Nelco wouldn't know that he really wanted to kill Julie. Nelco thinks you were responsible and that's why he wants to kill you now."

"Yes," replied Talson.

"That's horrible. Nelco loved her and Barty used that to his advantage. He was evil, he deserved to die."

"It was even more horrible having to kill him," said Talson, "but I felt that I had to. I suppose you understand why I feel that way."

"Yeah, I do," said Kat. "But because you did it, you have to live with his mind inside you, don't you?"

Talson looked at her for a moment. "Yes, I do," he said finally. "It is like a monster that tries to control me. I try so hard to control it, to control him, but there are times when the monster controls me. I'm sorry I made you see that, I was trying to block Nelco because I thought he was going to try to hurt you. He's stronger than I thought. He made me lose control of Barty's memories."

Kat looked back at Talson. For the first time she felt like she understood him, and she felt so sorry for him. At that moment she felt like she was being crushed by the pain of the truth. Talson was not cruel, he appeared cruel because of the cruel minds that lived within him.

"Don't feel sorry for me, Kat."

"I can't help it," said Kat. "It's not your fault."

"Yes it is, Kat."

Kat felt like Talson had been trying to hide his pain from her, but now it had spilled over. Kat didn't really think about doing it, but she hugged Talson. He looked slightly surprised, but he smiled slightly and returned her embrace. His yellow eyes were no longer bright, they appeared clouded in the dimly lit bar. "I'm sorry, Kat," he said. "I'm sorry I can't always face the truth."

"Don't be," said Kat.

"You're the one who can face it," said Talson, taking a step back from Kat. "You're the one who can show everyone the truth. It's going to have to be you, not me, not Larry, not Sela, but you. That's why I knew I needed you. I know you can see the truth."

Kat felt tears on her face. She didn't want Talson to see her crying, but she couldn't prevent it. "You're the green eyed boy next to Roco in that picture," she muttered.

Talson looked at her without speaking. He looked sad. "Yes," he said softly, "that was me."

"Why are they yellow now, though?" asked Kat.

"I think it's because there are others inside me now. I don't look at the world through one man's eyes."

"But then, can you be killed like one person?"

"Physically, yes, but mentally I think not," replied Talson.

"Does Nelco know that?" asked Kat, pulling herself together.

"No, I believe I am alive as a result of Nelco's ignorance of the power of the mind. If he was content to simply shoot me like Barty shot Julie, his job would be considerably easier."

"He can't kill you, then?" asked Kat somewhat hopefully.

"Oh yes, I think he can," said Talson. "He just can't do it alone."

"He can't kill you, he won't succeed."

"I hope he doesn't, but I know he is going to try to use others to help him."

"He was in my mind. Does that mean he has the power?"

"No, he doesn't."

"Then how did he do that?"

"He is using other people."

"Who?"

"John Carl."

"Does my dad know about this?"

Talson sighed. "No, I have to warn him, just like Larry said."

"But you don't want to, do you?" said Kat.

"No not really, but what I want is not a consideration right now. I have to at least try to talk to him even though I know he won't listen."

"But if Nelco is in John Carl's mind then if you get inside John Carl's head, Nelco will be able to get to you. That might be what he wants. That is probably why he talked to my dad in the first place. For some reason he knew you would have to warn John Carl and he knew that when you did he would have the opportunity to gain control of your mind."

"I think you're exactly right," said Talson. "I suspect that he did plan the whole thing."

"So that's why you can't go talk to John Carl. Nelco might be able to kill you if you do."

"I will have to take that risk, or he'll just use John Carl to kill me and John Carl will end up dead too."

"I'll do it," said Kat. "I'll go find my dad and tell him."

"I don't want to use you to do my dirty work. Larry is right, I'm always using others."

"That's the way Nelco wants you to feel," said Kat. "He wants you to feel guilty and then he'll be able to hurt you. We can't give Nelco that kind of opportunity. You're not using me if I volunteer."

Talson looked at Kat with a slightly surprised expression. "You would really do that for me?"

"Of course," said Kat. "You said it before, I'm the one who can show everyone the truth. It's my job to show them the truth, that's why you need me."

"I don't think I deserve it," muttered Talson

"Deserve what?" asked Kat.

"Your help," said Talson. "You shouldn't take a risk for me, I don't deserve it."

"You do deserve it," said Kat softly. "You would do the same thing for me."

Talson's mouth twitched into a small smile. "Alright," he said quietly.

Kat smiled back. "It won't be hard for me. I'll tell him the truth, trust me."

"I trust you, Kat," said Talson, "even if you don't trust me."

"I trust you," said Kat. "At least I trust part of you, the part that is really you," Kat smiled. "You know, the kid in the picture, Magic."

CHAPTER 18

LUCKY SEVEN

Kat walked down the street away from The Sharktooth Bar, toward the docks. It was twilight now, and the western sky was streaked with red and orange. The sun seemed huge and red as it sank toward the calm ocean.

John Carl sat alone at the end of the dock, staring out at the sea. The anchor lights of the many boats in the harbor gleamed in the dying sunlight.

"Dad?" said a soft voice behind him. "John Carl?" John Carl turned around so quickly he almost slipped off the edge of the dock. "Sorry," said Kat approaching her father at the end of the dock. "I know I probably scared you, but I've gotta tell you something."

"What?" asked John Carl, "I'm listening. Did he send you?"

"No, I volunteered myself, actually," said Kat, knowing exactly what her father was talking about. "Conner Nelson is using you."

"To do what?" asked John Carl.

Kat frowned at him. "You know very well what," she said. "To kill Talson."

"No, he's not, because I told him I'm not helping him."

"That doesn't matter," said Kat. "He'll make you help him. He wants Talson dead badly."

"I know he does, but why?" asked John Carl. "Why does he want that? Nelson is Talson's man."

"Not anymore. Nelco left years ago and now he is back for revenge. He wants Talson and Sela dead. He's working with Tracy. They are definitely going to try to drag you into this, because you might be Nelco's only chance to kill Talson."

"Wait a second," said John Carl. "Are you saying that when Nelson says he wants to kill Talson, he means kill him Talson's way?"

"Yeah."

"Says who?"

"Says Talson."

"Is he sure?"

Kat was somewhat surprised by the question. "Yeah, I think so," she said.

"Why did you come instead of him?" asked John Carl. "He couldn't face me?"

"He was going to, but I thought he had better not because if he came and Nelco was in your mind then if—"

"If Talson got in my head, Nelco could screw him over. Yeah, I get it," John Carl finished Kat's sentence.

"Did you want Talson to come talk to you?" asked Kat.

"Is Talson trying to stop Nelco?" asked John Carl, ignoring Kat's question. "Do you know who else Nelson is using?"

"I think he is," said Kat. She honestly wasn't sure what Talson was trying to do at the moment. "We think Nelco is trying to use Larry, and Janice Carlson and Tracy are working with Nelco now. I think he went for Larry first, but Larry didn't help him, so he went to you."

"Insane," muttered John Carl. "I guess I knew from the beginning that Nelson would want me to do it, but I just—" John Carl broke off, staring out to sea. He had avoided eye contact with Kat for most of their conversation.

"Just what?" asked Kat.

"Just not sure anyone deserved that," he muttered. "How can he—" John Carl paused again. He seemed to be wondering if he should say something or not. Kat sensed that there was a question he wanted very badly to ask, but wasn't sure that she was the one to ask.

"What?" asked Kat. "You can ask me whatever question you want."

"Does Talson think Nelco is trying to transfer power?"

"What does that mean, transfer power?" asked Kat.

John Carl stiffened. "Ask Talson if you don't know," he said roughly. "And tell him he needs to do his job better if he hasn't told you about that." He paused. "So Talson was going to come himself to warn me?" he asked quietly.

"Yeah, he was," said Kat, "but I thought it would be less risky if I did it."

"It's still risky," said John Carl. "It's unbelievable though."

"What's unbelievable?" asked Kat.

"Talson warning me."

"You tried to warn him."

"But he didn't need my warning."

"And you didn't need his. Why is it unbelievable that he would return the favor?"

"Because he hates me," said John Carl looking at Kat now.

"Does he?" asked Kat.

"Isn't that obvious to you?"

"No," said Kat truthfully. "I never really got that impression. I get the impression that you hate him, not the other way around."

"Insane," muttered John Carl again. "Anyway, tell him that I'm not doing it, I'm not helping anyone. I still don't believe him, and he still can't make me."

"Will he understand what that means?" asked Kat.

"Absolutely," said John Carl.

Kat stood up to leave, then stopped. "Why didn't you tell me about Larry?"

"Technically, I did," said John Carl. "I wasn't really talking to you, but you heard so—"

"What are you talking about?" asked Kat. "I thought it was Talson."

"For God sakes tell that man to do his job," said John Carl.

"What do you mean?" asked Kat, more confused than ever.

"Ask Talson. Tell him what I said."

"He won't understand if you don't tell me what the heck you're talking about."

"Oh yes he will," said John Carl with a slight smile. "I've never once had to tell Talson what I was talking about."

Frustrated, Kat headed back toward The Sharktooth Bar. When she arrived, she saw that the closed sign hung above the front door. The door was locked. Kat frowned, she could not understand why Larry had closed while she was gone.

"Everyone is in the back, kid," said a voice from behind her.

Kat turned to see Roco coming around from the back of the bar. "Hey Roco," she said.

"Hi Kat, what are doing skulking around here in the dark?"

"Look who's talking," said Kat. "I had a job."

"Yeah, at Tracy's, not here," said Roco.

"I had another job after that, said Kat with a smile. "What about you, how'd it go with Nelco?"

"Oh great," said Roco sarcastically. "We're having a meeting with everyone in the back. Let's go." They went around to the back of the bar where Milro's car was parked. There were no other cars in sight.

"Where's your car?" she asked Roco.

"Around the block," replied Roco, "We can't have like eight cars park back here, people would notice. I see Talson took Milro's car without telling him," Roco added. "I had to give him a ride here, and he kept worrying that someone stole it. I guess he knows who stole it now."

"We didn't steal it, we borrowed it without permission," said Kat with a sly smile.

"Talson borrows everything without permission," muttered Roco.

"Where's Larry's car?" asked Kat. "Is he still here?"

"He lives above the bar, so he's always here," said Roco, "he doesn't drive."

"I just found out about him today," said Kat.

"How do you mean?" asked Roco.

"He has the power," said Kat. She wasn't entirely sure why she was telling Roco this. For some reason she kept seeing the photo of the magic four in her mind's eye, and thinking how Roco was the only one who had remained loyal to Talson.

Roco stopped outside the door to the bar and looked straight at Kat. He looked shocked. "What the hell? You mean like you and Talson?"

"Yeah."

"I don't believe it," muttered Roco. "Who told you that?"

"I just, I mean, in my mind I just heard it, so I guess Talson told me. I'm really not sure, though."

"I hate when he does stuff like that," muttered Roco.

"Stuff like what?" asked Kat.

"When he makes people talk to you in your mind and stuff," said Roco. "He thinks it's entertaining to do things with people's minds. Don't ever forget that about him."

"I'll remember that," said Kat. "I found out the real truth about Barty and Nelco today too," she added.

"Yeah, it's rough," said Roco. "And just when I thought I knew it all, I found out more."

Kat and Roco entered the back room of the bar. One large circular table had been set in the middle of the room. Sela, Tiro, Milro, Marissa, and Talson were sitting at the table waiting for them. Roco and Kat took two of the four remaining chairs, Roco on Talson's right and Kat two seats to his left, next to Sela.

"Hey punk," said Sela softly, "are you okay?"

"Yeah," said Kat, "I'm okay, are you?"

"Yeah," replied Sela, but her expression was as blank as ever.

"Roco, do you have any news?" asked Talson.

"I'll say I do," said Roco. He glanced around the table. "Does everyone know what's going on with Nelco?"

"No," said Tiro, Milro, and Mevsin together.

"He's trying to kill me," said Talson rather casually. "I sent Romez to figure out what's going on."

"What the hell?" said Milro. "Kill you?"

"Where the hell are Remi and Janice?" asked Tiro, narrowing his eyes.

"They're with Nelco now," said Roco.

"Traitors," muttered Milro. "What's Nelco doing?"

"He's trying to kill the boss," said Roco.

"Can he do that?" asked Mevsin.

"Does he have support?" asked Milro.

"Is he insane?" asked Tiro.

"Yes, yes, and yes," said Talson with a sigh.

"Why now, though?" asked Milro. "He left us years ago and never did anything."

"Well, apparently Nelco," Roco held up his index and middle fingers to indicate quotation marks, "just now realized the magnitude of Talson's crimes and the urgent need for drastic action against him."

"Took him a while, didn't it," said Talson coolly.

"Bastard," said Tiro.

"Oh yeah," said Roco, "he said that Talson's murders were brutally cruel and he lied to all his followers about the reasons behind the killings and only pretended to care about us. Then Nelco said that Talson really accounts all his followers as servants who live only for him to use."

"Is that what he's told Remi and Janice to try to get them on his side?" asked Sela.

"Yeah," said Roco.

"Damn traitor," muttered Sela.

"Yeah, and I had to sit there and listen to that crap," said Roco. He muttered a long stream of obscenities directed at Nelco.

"You listened to the whole thing without doing anything stupid?" asked Talson with a slightly amused expression.

"Always the tone of surprise," said Roco, shaking his head.

"I'm surprised too," said Milro. "I would have killed him."

"You think I didn't want to?" asked Roco. "I wanted to kill him fourteen years ago, and now I want to kill Remnel and Janice too."

"F_ Nelco," said Tiro.

"So I take it Janice and Remi bought Nelco's speech about why Talson needs to die," said Sela with a hint of contempt.

"You know how brainless Remi is," said Roco, bitterly. "Whatever Nelco says he goes with it, and Janice just wants to impress Nelco, if you know what I mean."

"She's married," said Mevsin in disgust.

"Like she'd really care about that if Nelco took an interest in her," said Roco. "She'd leave him for Nelco in a second. You should have seen how she acted around him."

"I would have gagged," said Milro, curling his lip in disgust.

"Janice is a bitch," said Sela.

"We know that," interrupted Talson. "What's Nelco's plan of action apart from the touching story he's using to gain followers?"

"I think he's still hoping to get more Silver Shadows on his side," said Roco.

"Is that something that he is likely to get?" asked Talson. It seemed that for the first time Talson was challenging his supporters.

"No way," said Sela immediately.

"You heard us cussing him out," said Milro, "I would have killed him if I had been there, no joke."

"You think we would leave you for him?" asked Tiro.

"Yeah, give us a break, boss," said Mevsin.

Marissa smiled faintly. "You must know you can trust us by now."

Roco looked straight at Talson. "Just because I didn't do anything stupid doesn't mean I didn't want to." He paused still staring directly at Talson. "Screw you for even asking us that."

Kat remained silent as Roco and Talson continued to glare at each other. Finally Talson looked away. Kat looked at him, knowing that a look could say more than words at the moment. She merely nodded, knowing that Talson already knew she supported him. Anger burned inside her at Nelco for being so weak when it came to Barty and his lies, and now for being so low as to lead others on with the same sort of lies.

"Any other news, Roco?" asked Sela.

"Nothing much, just that John Carl didn't go for it when Nelco tried to get him on his side, and that's the polite version of his reaction. You know how John Carl is."

"Impressive," said Talson. "I guess Nelco didn't lay the brutal, filthy, heartless killer thing on thick enough to convince J.C."

"He probably thought John Carl wouldn't need that much convincing to go against you," said Roco. "I would have thought he would have gone for it, but John Carl has been known to surprise me at times."

"Speaking of John Carl," said Talson, turning to Kat, "any news?"

"Yeah," said Kat. "I told him that we think Nelco is using him, and he said to tell you he's not doing it, he's not helping anyone, he doesn't believe you and you still can't make him. Whatever that was supposed to mean."

Talson sneered slightly at the ceiling, looking bored. "Typical John Carl, did he

say anything else?"

"Well, he seemed to understand why you didn't come and tell him yourself, but I think he wished you had come instead of me. He asked if you thought Nelco was trying to transfer power."

"What did you say?" Talson had abandoned his expression of boredom.

"I don't know," said Kat. "I asked him what it meant."

"And what did he say?" asked Talson, he was smiling slightly now.

"He said to ask you, and told me that if I don't know what that means I should tell you to do your job better."

At this Talson actually laughed. "Who does he think is transferring, then?"

"I don't know, he just asked me that after I told him that Nelco was using him."

"Is he insane?" muttered Talson, more to himself than to anyone else. "What gives him the idea that Nelco can transfer? Who is he supposed to transfer with? I didn't think we were dealing with a high-class enemy."

Kat would have laughed if the situation weren't so serious. High-class enemy, she thought of Candace. Her life at school seemed so far away and insignificant now, almost as if it had been a previous lifetime. "What does he mean by transfer power, then?" asked Kat.

"It means that the power is transferred from a person who posses it to the mind of a person who doesn't. In most cases it is done in order to allow someone who does not normally posses the power to control the mind of someone in order to kill them. In this way the people who posses the power will not be stuck with the consequences of the killing."

There was silence around the table when Talson had finished. Finally Kat spoke. "So that means you don't have to have the power to control someone as if you did?"

"Well technically, the person who gains from the transfer temporarily possesses the power, but it's very difficult."

"So how could that have happened with Nelco?" asked Kat.

"I'm not sure what John Carl was on to. Perhaps he went to John Carl in the hope that John Carl would give him his power. But as you said, Romez, John Carl didn't go for it. He's not going to do it, but yet Nelco told John Carl that he would end up helping him whether he wanted to or not. That suggests to me that if there is a transfer, it will be a forced transfer."

"What do you mean by forced?" asked Kat.

"If the person in possession of the power does not want to give up their power, then a person can force the transfer if he knows how. To do this a person must force his victim to enter his mind. It is possible for the transferor to hold the power and control it, which means that he has stolen a part of the victim's mind. In the case of forced transfer, it is more like stealing power. I guess transferring sounds less brutal than stealing through force, and mental transferor sounds nicer than mind thief."

"So this has been done before?" asked Kat.

"Not by Conner Nelson, that's for sure," said Talson.

"So my dad was talking about someone using your power, or stealing it?"

"No, your dad is paranoid," said Talson. "He painted himself into a corner. He thinks he knows what he's talking about, but he doesn't have a clue." Talson's voice was calm, but Kat could hear anger behind it.

"So you don't think Nelco is using you, then?" Kat asked tentatively.

"What do you think?" said Talson sarcastically. "No, it's not me he's using," he added more seriously, "he is not using me to kill me."

A sudden fear hit Kat. If Nelco wasn't using Talson's power, maybe he was going to try to use hers. That would explain why her father had been worried about it. "Does that mean that he would use _," Kat paused.

"You?" asked Talson raising his eyebrows. "I honestly don't imagine Nelco having the ability to force any sort of transfer, but you were the one who talked to John Carl, so I can't say for sure."

"Well, do you think there is any chance that he is right about Nelco trying to transfer power?" asked Sela. "I mean what would make John Carl think that?"

"There is a chance that he's right," said Talson, "I am unsure. At times I have trouble seeing things from John Carl's perspective."

Why?" asked Kat.

"Don't ask," said Talson. "I hope they do use him." He muttered, the anger in his voice more evident now. "He would deserve it, he would deserve it for everything he never did and all the times he did nothing."

"What do you mean did nothing?" asked Kat.

"Once again, don't ask," said Talson. "It's very complicated."

"How does my dad even know about transferring power?" asked Kat.

"He should tell you that himself," said Talson. "I won't answer that for him."

Kat stared at a large shark head mounted on the wall across the room. She was confused. It seemed that her father knew something that she didn't and so did Talson. He and Talson certainly seemed to know each other much better than anyone knew.

"My dad was surprised that you decided to warn him," said Kat, looking back at Talson.

"Really?" said Talson. "Did he say why?"

"Because he says you hate him," said Kat.

"Well, I do, but that's not the point. He's paranoid enough to think that Nelco will use me and he will be screwed, then, I suppose. What an idiot."

Kat had never heard Talson say anything like that before. "I said I didn't think you hated him," she said quietly.

"Well like I said, that's not the point. Nelco is going to make crazy things happen whether or not this transfer happens. Maybe I should give the old captain some more credit for his transfer theory, but in the event of a forced transfer he will be the victim, not me or even you, Kat."

"What does that mean for us?" asked Sela.

"Wait a second," said Roco looking at Talson. "When you figured out that Nelco had gone to talk to John Carl you were in Nelco's mind weren't you? He could have done it then."

"I was in John Carl's mind, not Nelco's," said Talson. "However, John Carl may have entered Nelco's mind for a brief moment during the conversation. It was accidental if it happened at all. I felt something, but I don't know what."

"You would have known if there was a transfer, though, right?" asked Sela.

"I should have but I was in a lot of pain at that point," said Talson. "I can't connect with John Carl anymore, it hurts."

"So he could have used that to get into both your heads, then," said Roco.

"Maybe Nelco thinks he did, but I know that he is not going to be able to use Talson's power to kill Talson," said Talson with a hint of annoyance in his voice.

"You are underestimating him, Talson," said Roco.

"You think so do you, Ramirez?" asked Talson, this time it was clearly a challenge.

"Yeah, I do, but tell us what you want us to do now."

"Nelco transferred with John Carl," muttered Kat. The truth had hit her just now, even though she felt like she had known it ever since Nelco had entered her mind. Kat looked at Talson. "John Carl was in my head before Nelco was, but then Nelco was there and my dad was angry. That's why he told me about Larry."

"Technically no one told you about Larry," said Talson, "but that's not the point. I think you could be right, Kat. John Carl was in your mind only because Nelco was."

Kat wasn't sure what had triggered Talson's sudden willingness to believe in the transfer, but she didn't really care. A terrible thought had just occurred to her. "Does that mean that Nelco heard everything I said to my dad before, and everything he said to me?"

"He probably heard bits of it," said Talson. "If the transfer really occurred, that is."

"It did," muttered Roco, "I just remembered. Nelco said that he could 'do it Talson's way now'. He didn't elaborate, but you know what that means."

There was a long silence. The bar seemed eerie and cold. "This puts my problems with Tracy in perspective," Sela muttered, finally breaking the silence.

"No, that's still just as much of a problem," said Talson. "As a matter of fact, I think it is the same problem."

"That's right," said Roco. "Nelco is working with Tracy."

"Which means, now that Nelco has the power he can use it against Sela too," said Kat.

"And he will," said Talson. "There is no hiding from the truth now."

"I can't believe they sold us out," said Roco.

"If loyalty was money the world would be very poor," said Talson softly.

"I don't get it," said Roco. "Why does loyalty have to be so rare? Why don't people feel any responsibility to a side when things get tough? Is it so hard to show your loyalty during hard times?"

"Loyalty is a form of love, Roco," said Talson. "Love is harder to come by than anything. Most people don't care who wins as long as they're on that side on the day they win."

"You could have stopped them from leaving, Talson," said Roco. "You could have made them stay loyal to you."

"No, Roco, loyalty cannot be forced. I do not demand loyalty. I know loyalty can get you killed, and I won't demand that anyone does something that could get them killed. I can expect it, but I cannot demand it. Now I expect that we will all do what is required of us."

"I'm in," said Roco. Holding out his left hand over the middle of the table. Sela wordlessly grasped Roco's hand, Marissa followed.

"You know I'm in, man," said Tiro.

Milro and Mevsin nodded, extending their hands. Kat looked at each face around the table, then extended her hand and placed it on top of the others.

Talson smiled faintly, and placed his hand on top of Kat's. "We're down to seven Shadows now," he said. "Lucky seven."

C H A P T E R   1 9

THE WRONG SIDE

She was standing in a well lit kitchen with spotless white counters and a tile floor. She felt satisfied, finally she was in power. Tina would have her chance to tell the truth, but until she was ready to talk this is what she would get. She felt a small twinge of guilt, but she brushed it away, guilt was meaningless now. There was no room for those sorts of feelings at a time like this. Her hand fingered a small key that hung around her neck. It was not really cruel, she thought. It was the easiest and most painless way, really. She had the key and therefore the command. It would be almost easy to get the information now. Conner would be pleased.

The kitchen floor was melting away and the spotless white surfaces were disappearing. Kat sat up and the light purple walls of her bedroom replaced the flowery wallpaper of Tracy's kitchen. She sat motionless in bed, looking down at her hands. "Tracy," she muttered into the silence. She closed her eyes trying to remember exactly what Tracy had been thinking. There was a key. She had locked someone up until they would give her information on someone or something. The picture seemed fuzzy in Kat's mind now, as if it was receding to the edges of her brain as her own thoughts rushed in.

Kat struggled to go back to Tracy's thoughts. Suddenly, the truth hit her. She sat up very straight, breathing hard. Tina was the one Tracy had locked up. She was the reason Tracy had felt guilty. She was locking Tina up until she told her about Sela.

Kat stood up quickly. She knew she had to do something. If Tina really was locked up in her own bedroom for refusing to sell out Sela, Kat felt responsible. Tina had lied to protect Kat. Sela had said that Tina would have to make a choice, and now it was clear which side Tina had chosen.

Kat left her room and tiptoed down the stairs. She knew her father had come home very late the previous night and suspected that he was still asleep.

Sela had driven Kat home after the meeting at the Sharktooth. Sela had been very quiet for the whole drive and Kat was still convinced that there was something more that Sela wasn't saying. Kat was exhausted when she got home and had gone straight to bed. Her dreams had been filled with the memory of Barty lying to Nelco and of Nelco telling Remi and Janice about Talson's brutal murders. Kat had seen Nelco sitting at the table with Remi and Janice. "Talson is a cruel man who sees us all as his servants." Then the dream changed. Roco and Nelco were standing in the main hall at Headquarters. "That's a lie, you weren't there. Talson is a liar, he killed Julie and you know it."

"What I know is that the evidence that Barty killed her is in your face and you refuse to see it because you can't accept the fact that Barty fooled you with his pathetic lies," Roco spat back at Nelco.

"How dare you take Talson's side?"

"He's my best friend, that's how. Ever heard of loyalty? How dare you side with Louis?"

"Because he was *my* best friend," yelled Nelco.

"Yeah, your best friend who sold you out, lied to you, killed the woman you loved, and framed one of your other best friends."

Headquarters had disappeared and was replaced by Tracy's kitchen. That's when Kat had seen Tracy with the key. Kat knew that part wasn't a dream. None of them were, they were all real events, and they were all connected. Kat knew the scene with Roco and Nelco at Headquarters was part of the fight they had had right before Nelco had left the Silver Shadows. She just wasn't sure whose memory it was, Nelco's, Roco's or maybe Talson's. She wasn't even sure if that mattered.

Kat stood on the stairs looking down at the hallway below. She could hear Talson's words in her head now. "I am not one person anymore." She wondered if the same thing was going to happen to her. Was that what Talson wanted or was it what he was trying to prevent? More confused than ever, Kat went downstairs, picked up the phone and dialed Sela's number.

"Hello?" Sela sounded distracted.

"Sela," said Kat.

"Yeah, punk," said Sela. "What's up?"

"Tracy, she has Tina locked up until she tells her about you and me."

"How do you know that?"

"I just know. Tracy won't let Tina out until she gives Tracy information about us. Tracy thinks that it's going to be easy to get the information she wants now, and she thinks Nelco will be pleased. It's my fault this happened to Tina."

"It's just as much my fault as yours, Kat."

"So what do we do? We have to help her, she made her choice and she chose us. I'm going to tell her everything I know about her father now. I know I'm not supposed to, but I'm going to do it anyway."

"Good," said Sela. "You should, she deserves to know exactly why her mother has locked her in her own room."

"Can we get her out?"

"We could, but I don't think we should. I'm afraid that if we do, Nelco will be able to use her."

"But wasn't locking her up Nelco's plan?" asked Kat. "Tracy thought he'd be pleased."

"Yeah, but he may not have told Tracy what he's really trying to accomplish with this. Nelco knows we will go and get Tina out. I think that's what he wants."

"How's that possible? Doesn't he need her for information?"

"Nelco may have told Tracy that he needs information from Tina, but I don't buy it. There's nothing Tina can tell him that he doesn't already know. She knows nothing about Talson, and she barely knows me."

"But she knows about the house at the circle and she knows I have the power, and she knows that you are still around. She even knows that Talson is teaching me to control my mind."

"Those are all things Nelco already knows," said Sela. "He was a Silver Shadow, Kat. He knows all about you, me, Talson, the power, and the house."

"But then if he doesn't want information from Tina, what does he want?"

"Well I am only guessing here, but I suspect that Nelco is lying to Tracy in the hope that we will come and take Tina to stay here with us. Then Nelco will be able to gain access to Talson through her."

"How is that possible?" asked Kat.

"Listen Kat," said Sela, "this transferring stuff is really complicated and dangerous if it goes wrong."

"How is it that you know anything about it?"

Sela sighed. "It's what we did thirteen years ago when we killed Barty. Talson transferred part of his power to me. In the end he didn't want me to get stuck with all my father's thoughts so he took back his power. So when Barty died, Talson was the one who got all his memories. Barty's mind is inside Talson, and now that Nelco has forced a transfer, he can get inside Talson's head and he can try to control Barty's mind. Barty's mind will have a tendency to connect with Tina's, meaning that if Tina comes face to face with Nelco, Nelco can transfer Barty's power to Tina. Then he can use Tina to kill Talson and Tina will get Talson's mind instead of him."

"Why wouldn't he just use you?" asked Kat. "Wouldn't your mind connect to Barty's too?"

"Yeah, it would, but since I transferred with Talson once before it would be hard for Nelco to use me. I know how Talson thinks and I know how his mind works. Tina, on the other hand, will be easy to use because she knows nothing about what is going on. Nelco knows he can't kill Talson alone, he has to use someone or he'll fail."

Kat stood in the empty livingroom, the receiver held limply in her hand. She could hardly believe what Sela had just told her. "You never told me you transferred power with Talson."

"Yeah, well, it's not something I just tell people. Apart from Talson and Roco no one else knows."

"You never told me the real reason why Julie got killed," said Kat. "It wasn't just over a captain spot."

"Listen, Kat," said Sela. "I can't always tell you everything. We need to talk face to face. Meet me at the circle in five minutes."

Kat sprinted up the stairs, dressed and hurried out. As she jogged down the sidewalk toward the park, she could feel her heart hammering against her chest, and it had nothing to do with her running. Kat was scared for Tina, and for Sela.

Kat entered the house and saw that the door to the library was ajar. She knew she needed to talk to Sela as soon as she could, but she wanted to see the picture of the Magic Four, now that she knew who the little green-eyed boy was and what each of the boys had become. She entered the library and climbed onto a chair to reach the large black photo album. She put the book on the table and opened it to the first page. Kat gazed into the four laughing faces of the boys. There was Barty, dark haired and handsome, the man who would later sell them all out. On his right stood Nelco, fair haired and skinny, and evidently easily fooled by his friends. Then there was Roco on the far left, stocky and strong looking, the only one who was still loyal to Talson. And then there was Talson, standing between Roco and Barty. He was small, with blazing green eyes. His facial expression showed intensity and laughter at the same time. Kat thought of the Talson she knew now, with hard yellow eyes and that blank look of sadness and intensity. She thought she had been foolish not to recognize him the first time she had seen the picture. He looked the same, except for the sadness and the yellow eyes. The boy seemed to have a certain darkness behind his laughter that was the same darkness that Kat saw in Talson's eyes now.

Kat flipped the page. There was a picture of Larry and Roco standing behind the bar at the Sharktooth. Kat recognized Larry even though he looked somewhat younger than he did now. His hair was less grey, but his hazel eyes seemed more sunken and vacant than Kat remembered. There was a very haunted look in his eyes, giving him the look of someone who had been through a lot of pain in his life.

"What you doin' in here, punk?" Sela was standing in the doorway, leaning against the wall. Despite the seriousness of the situation, Sela's demeanor was as casual as ever.

"Sela," said Kat, turning around quickly. "You scared me, I didn't hear you coming. I was just looking at this picture," she indicated the picture of the four boys in photo album. "Roco showed it to me last time I was here, and I just wanted to see it again."

Sela walked over and looked at the picture. "Oh yeah," she said. "I like that picture."

"It's kind of sad, though," remarked Kat.

"Yeah, it is," said Sela, but her voice was emotionless. "I used to have a hard time believing that was my father," she pointed to Barty in the picture. "I mean, I look at that picture of him now, and all I think about what he ended up doing to his friends."

"Yeah, I know, me too," said Kat. She pointed to the green-eyed boy. "It's hard to believe that's Talson."

"Yeah, I know. Roco told me it was him after I asked, but it's still kind of unbelievable. I know it's him, but it still doesn't seem real when I look at the picture."

"I feel like there is something about Talson that we don't know, something about his childhood," said Kat. "Has he ever talked to you about when he was a kid?"

"Very little, Roco knows stuff, but he never talks about it. I know Talson's been through hell in his life, and I don't know half the stuff he's been through. Look at this," she added, flipping through the photo album to a page near the end. "This is like eleven years ago."

Kat looked at the picture, and could think of no words to describe what she was seeing. The picture had been taken at the circle, and Kat recognized the room as Talson's office where she had first met with him. Sela, who looked much younger, was standing behind Talson's large black armchair. Her arms hung over the chair and were resting on the shoulders of the man sitting in the chair. He looked weak and frail, his narrow shoulders hunched forward, wrapped in a black blanket. His face was paste white and sunken, with glassy, dead looking eyes. His eyes expressed only pain, loss, and sadness. Kat shifted her gaze to Sela's face. Her expression was not like any expression Kat had ever seen on Sela's face. It was certainly nothing like the blank and overly casual expression she wore now. In the photo her face echoed the pain on Talson's face. Kat could not explain it, but there was something distinctly powerful yet exceedingly sad about the photo. The way Sela's hand lay on Talson's hunched shoulders was soft, even loving, yet harsh at the same time. It was as if she was holding him up, yet pushing him down at the same time. Kat stared into Talson's gaunt, dead looking face. She thought of the green-eyed boy laughing with his friends. A deep feeling of emptiness seemed to invade her chest.

"I know," murmured Sela, as if she knew exactly how Kat was feeling. "I don't pretend to know everything about Talson, but if you know anything about his life it's impossible not to feel his pain. But he doesn't want anyone to feel sorry for him. Most people who have been through a lot of pain and loss crave sympathy, but Talson doesn't. He says you can only keep living and keep going forward. He says there are no excuses in life, no matter what you've been through."

"Did I do that to him?" asked Kat quietly.

"No, Kat," said Sela. "Barty Louis did that to him."

"What about you?" asked Kat.

Sela shrugged. "I don't know."

"Yeah you do. I know there is a part of you that you don't want anyone to see."

Sela looked straight at Kat with a completely blank expression. "We thought this was over when we killed Barty, but it's not. The same things are going to happen all over again unless we figure out how to stop it."

"I just don't get how we can be fighting someone who's dead," muttered Kat. "I know what Talson said, but how can a mind live on after a person is dead, that just doesn't make sense."

"I don't know either," said Sela shaking her head. "Mental connections are immensely powerful and extremely difficult to control. It's amazing Talson even knows who he is, anymore."

"Does he still know?"

"He knows," replied Sela, "but sometimes I think he just doesn't want to remember."

"Do you think Nelco can really kill him?"

"I'm not sure. Talson doesn't seem worried about it, but I think he should be. Honestly, I don't understand why he's not. He keeps pretending that he doesn't really know what Nelco's doing."

Kat didn't say anything for a moment. She didn't really think about asking the question, the thought just fell out of her mouth. "Do you think Talson wants to die?"

Sela looked at Kat. Her face was more lined than the twenty-one year old Sela in the photo. There was that emotionless expression that was always present on Sela's face now. "No," she said slowly, her tone did not suggest any emotion. "I don't think he wants to die."

"Do you think he can control Barty in his mind?"

Sela shook her head. "I don't know. He's already lost control of it twice in the past couple days. I know he's trying really hard but it's not easy, especially now that Nelco is in his head too."

"Wait," said Kat. "I thought Talson said that the transfer was only with my dad. He didn't say Nelco was in his head."

"Like I said, he keeps pretending not to know what is going on," said Sela. "I didn't believe him when he said Nelco wasn't in his head. Talson heard the conversation between John Carl and Nelco when Nelco asked John Carl for help. When I heard about the transfer I knew that Talson would be involved. Talson was in John Carl's head when Nelco took John Carl's power."

"So does that mean Talson was lying?" asked Kat.

"I don't know. All I know is that Nelco is using John Carl's power and he's in Talson's mind. He's trying to make Talson lose control of Barty's mind like he did in the Sharktooth, only permanently."

"And if Talson loses control, then what?"

"Then Nelco can control Barty's mind, and he can do anything he wants with it, including use it to take over Talson. The only thing is that he can't do it alone, because if he does he'll end up with Talson's mind."

"And I'm guessing he doesn't want that."

"Sufficient to say, that would be hell," said Sela.

"So Nelco knows he can't live with Talson's mind, so he's going to make someone else do the dirty work."

"Yes, someone like Tina," answered Sela.

"Do you think he can do that?"

"I don't know, but I'm not going to sit on my ass and wait to see if he can."

"Neither am I," said Kat, "but Talson doesn't seem to think Nelco can do it."

"I know, for some reason Talson seems sure that Nelco can't do it, but like I said, I'm not going to sit here and pray Talson knows what he's doing. That's Roco's style, not mine."

Kat was slightly taken aback. She was not sure if Sela had meant to insult Roco or not. "Did you know that my dad had the power before this whole transfer thing?" asked Kat.

"No I would have told you if I knew. He never used it so far as I saw, but Nelco knew about it so it couldn't have been too big of a secret. It doesn't really matter what John Carl does, Nelco wants his revenge."

"What if we told Nelco the truth?" said Kat. "I mean, told him that Barty lied."

"We'd have to prove it," said Sela. "Prove that Barty killed Julie, not Talson."

"Wasn't Larry the only witness?"

"Yeah, and unfortunately Nelco will never believe anything he hears from Larry, because he knows Larry will always cover for Talson. Besides, Nelco knows that Larry witnessed the murder and he hates Larry for not revealing who the murderer was."

"Larry knows it was Barty, so where is the proof it was Talson? Was he even in the bar that night?"

"No he wasn't, but Barty told Nelco that Talson hired someone to do it. Barty said that was the reason why Julie didn't say who the killer was before she died. If it was a hit, Julie wouldn't have known who actually shot her."

"Julie should have told them it was Barty," said Kat. "I mean, why not?"

Sela shrugged, "I don't know, I can't blame her for not saying, I mean I think I would have, but who the hell knows what you would do if you were about to die and were being asked to incriminate one of your best friends?"

"There has to be a way to tell Nelco the truth," insisted Kat. "If he knew that Barty had lied, he wouldn't want to kill Talson."

"I wish it was that simple," said Sela. "Talson killed Barty. Nelco will still want Talson dead for that regardless of why Talson did it."

"But Nelco doesn't know that Barty lied to him. Nelco loved Julie and Barty killed her."

"Nelco doesn't care. Roco told me it all came out when he and Nelco got in that fight at H.Q. Talson told Nelco that Barty had lied to him and that Barty was the killer. Nelco said he didn't believe Talson, so Talson said he would show him the surveillance tape from the Sharktooth to prove it to him. Apparently, Nelco told Talson he didn't care what Barty had done, and he didn't want to see the tape. Nelco told Talson there was no reason for him to have killed Barty, no matter what happened at the Sharktooth."

"Well, by those rules it shouldn't matter what Talson did either," said Kat.

"Maybe that's why it took Nelco so long," she indicated quotation marks with her fingers, "to realize the magnitude of Talson's crimes."

"It probably took him a while to figure out how to transfer the power," said Kat. "I think this has to be about more than just Julie's murder."

"Just a murder? What makes you think he needs more motive than that?"

"If he wanted to get even with Talson for Julie's death he would have shot Talson. That would have been a lot easier than what he's trying to do now. There is something else, he doesn't just want to get even. Nelco wants to be more than even, he wants to win."

Sela looked directly at Kat now. She nodded. "Maybe that's why Talson's not talking about it. He probably knows a lot more than he's telling us. Who knows, most of the time when I look at Talson he has the same look in his eyes, and I have absolutely no idea what he's thinking."

"Like you," said Kat before she could stop herself.

"Not like me," Sela glanced at the picture of her and Talson, her face expressionless. "I just did what I could to help him."

"We have to know where Tracy is so we can get that key from her," said Kat, deciding not to press Sela any further.

"You're the one who can tell us that," said Sela. "But I still don't think we should take Tina away."

"How?" asked Kat, ignoring Sela's doubts.

"Focus," said Sela. "Look into her mind. Just remember what it was like to be her, standing in her kitchen."

Kat stared hard at the wall without really looking at it. Slowly she felt the memory of being in Tracy's mind coming back to her. Kat let the memory of Tracy's mind fill her, replacing her own thoughts. It was a cold, unpleasant, angry feeling.

"Get down here," she yelled, standing at the foot of a staircase. At the top of the stairs, Tina stood in the doorway of her bedroom.

"No," Tina's voice was cold. "Not unless you tell me where you're taking me."

"You see how no one came to help you?" she sneered.

"I didn't think anyone was gonna come," snapped Tina.

Tracy laughed coldly. "Get in the car."

Tina walked quickly down the stairs, pushed past her mother and headed out the front door. Tracy followed closely behind her.

"Where are we going?"Tina asked angrily, as she got in Tracy's car.

"To see a friend of mine," said Tracy. *Conner's place.*

Kat fought to get back to her own thoughts. She felt stuck halfway between the gloating Tracy who was driving Tina to Nelco's house, and the confused Kat who was standing in Talson's library with Sela.

Need help Kat?

An almost lazy sounding voice became audible in Kat's mind. She easily recognized it as Talson, but found that she could not answer. She had no thoughts, it was as if everything was just passing through her mind but she could not respond to it. Suddenly her thoughts seemed to break through the barrier. She was hit with a momentary feeling of pain as her own thoughts and surroundings rushed back to her.

Be careful. Always make sure you can get out.

Thanks Talson I—

Don't mention it.

Tracy is taking Tina to see Nelco.

Yeah, looks like she is.

What do we do?

Help her.

Talson, are you okay?

Yes.

Are you sure? Kat felt Talson fade from her mind.

"Sela," said Kat, turning away from the wall to look at her. "Tracy took—"

"I know,"interrupted Sela.

"All he said was 'help her'," said Kat. "It's not like him to be so vague. What should we do?"

"Follow Tracy again, I guess," said Sela shrugging. "Let's just hope we can stay away from the cops this time,"she added with a hint of a smile.

"Where does Nelco live?" asked Kat as they drove. They were using Sela's GPS to follow Tracy's car.

"No clue,"said Sela. "Although Tracy seems to be heading toward downtown." Tracy had just taken an exit for a downtown residential area. "There are a lot of apartments in this area. I live near here. I use the same exit that Tracy just took."

"You don't think she's going to your place, do you?" asked Kat.

"No, that wouldn't make any sense, she doesn't know where I live." Sela took the exit and followed Tracy down the narrow streets past identical apartment buildings and houses, all of which were considerably nicer than the houses near Headquarters, but still rather simple and shabby.

"I thought Nelco would live in a nicer place," said Kat. "I mean he just seems like the type who would want a big house in a nice neighborhood."

"Yeah, I'm sure he'd like that," said Sela. "Tracy's definitely not going to my place, we just passed my building."

"Did you know you lived near Nelco?"

"No," replied Sela.

They could see Tracy's car a little way ahead of them now. Sela stayed several cars behind her so she would not catch Tracy's attention. Tracy pulled into an apartment complex about five blocks from Sela's building.

"Damn it," said Sela. "I had no idea I lived this near to Nelco. I don't even know the people who live in my own building because I'm never there. I'm gonna have to hang back and pull into a different parking lot, otherwise Tracy will see us. I just hope we can find Nelco's apartment when we get there."

"218A," said Kat without thinking.

Sela looked sideways at her. "You really are in Tracy's head now, aren't you?"

"I guess," said Kat. "I don't know how I knew that."

"Tracy knew it, that's how," said Sela, as she pulled into a parking space around the block from Nelco's building.

Kat and Sela hurried down the block toward Nelco's apartment. When they reached the parking lot they saw Tracy's car parked in front of the building. The car was empty.

"I guess Tracy took Tina inside," said Kat.

Suddenly Sela grabbed the back of Kat's jacket and pulled her down behind a car. She pointed to the second floor of the building. "218A is right there, they're still outside."

Kat peered around the side of the car so she could see the door of Nelco's apartment. Tracy was standing outside the door holding Tina by the elbow as if she feared that Tina might make a run for it. A tall thin man with light hair, dressed in a collared shirt and tie was standing in the doorway. Kat recognized him immediately as Conner Nelson. His voice carried down to the parking lot where Sela and Kat crouched, hidden from view.

"Tracy," he said warmly, "and you must be Tina. Well, come in, come in." He had a somewhat high-pitched voice and Kat thought he looked nervous. His eyes darted back and forth as if he was paranoid that someone was watching him. He was trying to hide how nervous or even scared he was, but his extreme friendliness and forced smile gave him away.

Nelco let Tracy and Tina into the apartment and closed the door behind them. "What do we do now?" asked Kat.

"Let's go around to the back and see if there is a back door to Nelco's apartment," said Sela. She ducked out from behind the car and headed through the walkway that separated the two sides of the building. Kat hesitated for a brief moment then followed.

Once they were at the back of the building, Kat followed Sela up the stairs to the second floor. Nelco did indeed have a back door. Sela walked up to the door and tried the handle. "It's unlocked, let's go."

"We're going in there?" said Kat in disbelief. "We can't do that, we'll get caught."

Sela shrugged. "I'm going in there," she said casually, "you don't have to."

"But_," protested Kat.

"I told you, I'm not going to just let Nelco try to kill Talson and hope he fails. That's not good enough for me. If it's good enough for you then you can go wait for me in the car."

Kat looked at Sela, not knowing what to say or do. Sela raised her eyebrows, as if to challenge Kat. Then she turned around to face the door and slowly pulled it open. She did not look back at Kat as she entered the apartment but she left the door slightly open as if to invite Kat to follow her. Kat paused for another moment then followed Sela. They were standing in a small laundry room. The door at the opposite side of the room that lead to the main part of the apartment was open a crack.

Sela crossed the room and peeked through the opening. Kat followed her and stood on tiptoe to look over her shoulder. All Kat could see was a small hallway that seemed to lead to the front of the apartment. Voices could be heard coming from the front room. Kat stood motionless at Sela's shoulder, listening.

"So, I'll get right down to business here," Nelco was saying. "I'm going to make this very simple."

"Fine, what do you want?" Tina sounded angry.

"I wanted to ask you a couple of questions," replied Nelco. "Your mother told me you ran away from home, is that correct?"

"Yes," said Tina stiffly.

"Why?" Nelco's voice was casual and non-threatening.

"Because I was being stupid, okay?" said Tina coldly. "Why do you even care?"

"As I told you before, I am a friend of your mother's, so naturally I care."

"Well my mother doesn't care, so that's not a very good answer," said Tina, with a sneer.

"You say you were being stupid," said Nelco ignoring Tina's comment. "I doubt that, you don't seem stupid to me."

"Well thanks, but I meant that in the heat of the moment when you're angry anyone can do stupid stuff."

"But you came home, didn't you," said Nelco.

"Yeah, well, I realized I was being pretty immature," replied Tina. "I didn't plan on running away, I just did it without thinking."

"And where did you go?"

"I went to the park and hid out. Why does it matter?"

"It matters because the park was searched and you were not seen."

"I left the park when I first saw the police searching, and I went to the museum. I hid there after it closed."

"How did you get there?"

"I walked to the bus stop and took the bus downtown. I got lucky and no one recognized me."

"No one helped you?" asked Nelco, still remaining as casual as ever. "No one knew where you were?"

"I don't think so. Like I said, I don't think anyone recognized me on the bus or at the museum and no one saw me when I was in the park." Tina had abandoned her angry tone and seemed to be trying to figure out what Nelco really wanted. "I don't really understand why you want to know all these things from me," continued Tina. "I mean, you don't even know me."

"Your mother and I have talked," said Nelco. "What about your friend Kat, what can you tell me about her?"

"What do you want to know?"

"Specifically I want to know if you saw her after you ran away," said Nelco.

"Yeah, I did."

"Did she see you?" asked Nelco.

Sela shook her head frowning.

"What?" mouthed Kat.

"Nelco is making this conversation go his way so he can get into Tina's head. He's gonna know if she lies to him now."

"No, she didn't," Tina answered.

"Why did you hide from her?" asked Nelco, his voice even and casual.

"I didn't really know what to say to her," said Tina quietly.

"So, you couldn't find a good place in the park to hide from the policemen?" Nelco was speaking almost as if he was talking to a very young child.

"He's good," muttered Sela.

"Of course not," said Tina, a hint of anger had returned to her voice. "It's a park, what makes you think I could hide there?"

"What makes you think you can lie to me?" asked Nelco, his voice lower and colder now.

"I'm not lying," said Tina angrily.

"You must have forgotten who I used to be, Tina Louis," said Nelco. "I know all about the house at the circle and about Mr. Talson's soft spot for runaways and the siblings of his followers."

"What are you talking about?" asked Tina, sounding convincingly confused.

"You know how to play it, I'll give you that," said Nelco. "But the thing is that I've been playing this game a little bit longer. You're good, but I'm better. You're not fooling me, kid. I know him and I know you."

"You don't know anything about me," said Tina, angrily. "My mom hasn't told you everything. You don't even know each other."

"Yes we do."

"Only since recently," argued Tina.

"What makes you think that?" asked Nelco.

"What makes you think you can lie to me?"

"Ouch," whispered Sela, smiling slightly. "She is good."

Nelco was laughing. "Well, well, I suppose I was mistaken. Like I said, you know how to play, the problem is you don't know what game you're playing. You're playing a dangerous game now, and you are in a very dangerous position."

"What do you mean by that?" asked Tina. Now she was truly confused.

"I mean Mr. Talson's game," replied Nelco smoothly. "You don't know what it's like to have to play his game."

"And you do?"

Nelco laughed. "Of course I do. I understand the position you are in, not because anyone told me, I know because I know how Talson thinks. Do you know why he hid you at the circle?"

Tina did not reply.

"Because you ran away. You ran away just like he did once. You were like him, and you have a sister who is one of his. Why do you think Kat told you about Sela?"

"She was talking to her and she just figured it out," said Tina. "What does that have to do with anything?"

"She didn't just figure it out, Tina," said Nelco. "Talson told her, and he told her to tell you. You think Kat came up with the idea that you should stay at the circle? Talson told her to let you stay there, otherwise she never would have suggested it."

"That's not how it went," said Tina resentfully. "Sela and Kat asked his permission." It was evident that Tina resented having to admit that she had been at the circle and that she had met up with Kat and Sela, but she must have realized she no longer had a choice.

"They did that as a formality," said Nelco. "You think they actually care about you? You think Talson was just being a nice guy and letting you stay there?"

"You should be ashamed of yourself," Tracy spoke for the first time. "How could you go do that?" Tracy sounded like she was about to lose her temper.

"Calm down, Tracy," said Nelco. "People make mistakes."

"Talson wants you to join him," Nelco continued to addess Tina. "He wants you to kill your family like your sister did. He wants your mother dead just like he wanted your father dead, and he will let you do the honors this time so you and your sister will be even."

"I'd love to kill that guy," muttered Sela.

"You think Kat doesn't know what Talson is planning?" continued Nelco. "She knows, and she's not doing a thing about it. Talson told her what his plans are and she is not helping you. She doesn't care."

"I already hate him," muttered Kat.

"Talson is going to use you to kill your mother, just like he made your sister kill your father. And what are you going to do? Just sit there and let it happen? Do you know why Kat has the power?"

"No," Tina sounded somewhat defeated.

"Because Talson gave it to her. You thought it was a gift that people are born with, didn't you? You want to know the truth? The power is something that is generally passed through families, but Talson has no family. The power can be forced into someone's mind or transferred from one mind to another. Talson was not born with any special mental power. He stole his supposed gift a long time ago and then used it to kill the person he took it from. Then he transferred some of his power to Sela so she could kill your father. Then he gave part of his power to Kat because she is your best friend. He can make her give her power to you. Then he can force you to use it to kill your mother and anyone else he wants, including me."

"He's good, Kat" whispered Sela. "He's a manipulating, lying, back stabbing jerk, but he's good at it."

"You can't help Sela," Nelco was saying to Tina. "It is too late to help her, but you can save your mother and you can save yourself."

"What about Kat?" asked Tina.

"Talson is in her head, Tina," said Nelco. "He has altered her mind. I don't know if you can help her or not, but you could always try. We can try. He was in my head once, and I survived. I'm sorry I had to tell you this, and that your mom had to drag you here, but it was the only way." There was the slightest hint of self-satisfaction in Nelco's voice.

"What are you going to do?" asked Tina. "You guys want to kill Sela, don't you?"

"There is no way to help her, Tina," said Nelco, "just as there is no way to help the man behind all of this. You're a smart girl, Tina, you know this is the only way."

"What if I'm smart enough to consider the possibility that there could be another way?" asked Tina coolly.

"Your father was murdered, Tina. Talson and Sela killed him."

"I know," said Tina shortly. "Sela's sorry she did it, she told me so."

"It's an act, Tina," said Tracy, her voice was remarkably steady and calm. "She wanted to kill him, just like she wants to kill me. She was just putting on an act to make you feel sorry for her."

"Tina, I have the power now," interjected Nelco. "I took it from Kat's father, and I am going to use it to get justice for your father."

"Kat's father doesn't have the power," said Tina.

"I see Kat never told you that little detail," said Nelco with a sneer.

"That's because she didn't know," said Tina shortly.

"Regardless, I can end this now," said Nelco. "I know you want to think Sela is a good person. You want to have a good big sister, but you have to see the truth. You must know she wants your mother dead."

"Yeah, it's obvious," said Tina, her voice was hushed as if she had just realized something.

"You understand now, don't you," said Nelco. For a moment he sounded excited. "I know it's hard to believe, but you simply can't deny this." His tone grew kinder as he continued. "Talson's world is full of lies, Tina. I know some lies may seem beautiful and kind, while the truth is hard and ugly, but you have to stand up and face reality. That's what your father did, and he died for it. He died trying to expose the truth behind Talson's lies. Most of Talson's followers know that he is lying to them, but they are too afraid to stand up to him. I know it's easy to fall for the wrong side, but we have to face the truth before it's too late."

There was silence in the front room. Kat and Sela looked at each other. Sela shook her head in disgust, but Kat waited, knowing Tina would make some sort of reply.

"You have spent the last however long telling me how Talson is a thief and a liar, but look who's talking?" Tina harsh response seemed to come out of nowhere. "You're stooping to his level and below. You stole power and now you're going to use it to kill the man you used to work for. The way I see it that makes you just as bad as Talson, and probably worse. You keep talking about how Talson uses people, but you are just here to use me. You actually think I'm gonna help you?"

"Tina, Talson and Sela have lied to you, they have felt no remorse for anything they have done," said Tracy.

"Are you two planning on feeling any remorse when you kill Sela and Talson?" asked Tina coldly. "You better not say yes, because there is no room for remorse in premeditated murder."

"Damn, I love her," muttered Sela.

Kat nodded, "I knew she'd see right through Nelco if we gave her the chance."

"How dare you?" Tracy had finally lost control. Suddenly there was a loud crash and Tina screamed.

"Hey, let me go," Tina yelled.

"I don't think so," said Nelco with a cruel sneer. "You may not want to help us, but you will."

"I will not," yelled Tina. "Let me go."

"Not until you decide to join the right side."

The voices were getting closer. It sounded like Nelco was dragging Tina down the hall, but it was hard to tell because Tracy was screaming incoherently.

"They're coming in here," said Sela, quickly withdrawing from the door. Kat stood frozen. The sound of Tracy's screaming had momentarily paralyzed her. "Move," hissed Sela, grabbing Kat's arm. Coming to her senses, Kat dove behind the washing machine and Sela dove behind the dryer just as the door flew open and Nelco threw Tina onto the floor of the laundry room.

Tina's hands and feet were tied together with thin rope. Tracy had stopped yelling and now stood in the doorway with a smirk on her face. Nelco crossed the room and pulled a small towel out of the laundry hamper. He stuffed the towel in Tina's mouth before walking to the back door and turning the key in the lock.

"You can stay here and stay quiet unless you decide to help us," he said in a tone of false kindness. "You can just take your time and decide whose side you're on."

The laundry room door slammed shut and Nelco and Tracy's footsteps receded down the hall.

"I'm sorry Conner," Tracy's voice was still audible. "I didn't think she would react like that."

"I'm sure we scared her, so she'll come around," said Nelco. "We can proceed without her in the meantime. Anyway, I'm off to work, I can't be late getting back from lunch again." The voices faded as both Tracy and Nelco exited out the front door.

Sela stepped casually out from behind the dryer. "Charming man, Conner Nelson, isn't he?"

"And he really needs to clean behind his washing machine," said Kat, coming out from her hiding place and brushing dust off her clothes.

Tina stared up at Kat and Sela, clearly shocked. She tried to say something, but it was muffled by the rag in her mouth."

"Didn't think we cared, did you?" said Kat, surprised by the coldness in her own voice. She wasn't sure why she felt like Tina had just sold her out to Nelco. She knew that Tina had every reason to believe Nelco's story since she didn't know the truth about her father, and Tina had defied Nelco anyway. Despite Tina's loyalty, Kat felt oddly far away from her.

"You were awesome," said Sela walking over to Tina. "I told you, you would have to make a choice," said Sela looking down at her sister. "So while you're laying there, listen to me for a second. You have another choice to make now. You can lay there tied up and gagged and let things happen without you, or you can stay tied up until Nelco comes back and then help him kill a bunch of people, or you can come with us." Sela reached down and pulled the rag out of Tina's mouth.

"Kat," said Tina immediately. "Do you have the power because Talson gave it to you or not?"

"No," said Kat. "I have it because my dad has it, it's in my family. Besides, the power isn't a thing you go buy at the store, it's the ability to experience other people's thoughts. You know I've always been able to do that. You knew I could do it even before I did."

"Why didn't you tell me your dad had the power?"

"Because I didn't know," said Kat somewhat annoyed. "You said that yourself just now."

"What's your problem, Kat?" said Tina coolly.

"I don't know, but I know that your problem is that you're tied up on the floor of Nelco's laundry room."

"Listen, Tina," interrupted Sela. "Nelco has the power now and he is using it to try to kill Talson and me."

"So if I choose a side I'm either going to be used to kill my mother or used to kill my sister. Is that my choice that you were talking about?"

"No," said Sela. "We're not going to use you to kill Tracy."

"Well I don't see any reason to believe that," said Tina. "You're lying."

"There are a lot of lies in this, Tina, but that's not one of them."

"Talson made you kill our father and now he wants to use me to kill our mother. It's obvious that he has a thing against our family."

"Obvious, but incorrect," said Sela.

"How do you know that?"

"I understand how Talson—"

"How he thinks," interrupted Tina, "yeah, you and Conner Nelson."

"Actually, I was going to say that I understand how he feels about your father's death. Listen Tina," said Sela before Tina could say anything, "Conner Nelson is right when he says that the truth is ugly, but he doesn't know the truth about your father and neither do you. Nelco goes on and on about how he is not fooled by the lies, but he has been badly fooled, and he is still living the lie that he fell for. He can't tell you the real truth, but we can."

"Then tell it," said Tina.

"Shall I untie you?" asked Sela.

"That would be nice of you," said Tina sarcastically.

"I can only untie you if you are with us," said Sela.

"You're saying I have to trust you?" said Tina coldly, looking from Sela to Kat.

"That would be nice of you," said Sela with a slight smirk.

Tina struggled angrily against the ropes that bound her.

"Hey, if you can't trust your sister and your best friend, who can you trust?" said Sela.

"You guys work for Talson," said Tina angrily.

"Yeah, we do. What's your point?"

"Nelco worked for Talson once and so did your dad," said Kat.

"My dad did not work for Talson," exclaimed Tina in outrage.

"Yeah he did," said Sela. "How do you think Nelco knew him? The truth is ugly sometimes, Tina." Sela bent down and grabbed hold of the rope that bound Tina's legs. "Listen Tina," she said, looking her sister straight in the eye, "after how well you handled Nelco just now, I want to untie you. The thing is that I won't untie you unless I know you want to face the truth."

There was a silence before Tina spoke. "Fine," she said. "I might as well hear your version of the truth too."

Sela untied Tina legs then looked at Kat who had not moved from where she stood in front of the washing machine. "Do you have a problem with this?" Sela asked. It was not a threat, but simply a question.

Kat wordlessly walked over to Tina and untied the rope around her wrists. Tina glared at her, but Kat did not make eye contact.

"Come on," said Sela, pulling Tina to her feet. "I want to show you something."

"The door's locked," muttered Tina.

"This one isn't," said Sela indicating the door that led to the main part of the apartment. "Let's go."

Sela led the way out of the laundry room and down the hall and opened a door on the left side.

They were standing in a fairly large bedroom that was nicely furnished. It seemed that Nelco had made an effort to make his bedroom much more comfortable than the rest of his house.

"What are we doing in Nelco's bedroom?" asked Tina.

"Here," said Sela, walking across the room and taking a picture from the bedside table and holding it up.

It was a picture of two boys. Kat recognized them immediately as Barty and Nelco. She also noticed that the left edge of the photo seemed to have been cut off so that Barty stood at the very left edge of the photograph.

"He cut it," muttered Kat. "That's the picture of the magic four, only he cut it."

"Exactly," said Sela.

"How did you know it was here?"

"Roco told me," replied Sela. "He saw it when he came to listen in on Nelco's conversation with Remi and Janice. Roco said that Nelco showed them this picture."

"And I bet he failed to mention who he cut out of it," said Kat.

"He showed me that picture too," said Tina. "He showed it to me as soon as I got here with my mom. I asked him who he was, and he showed me the picture to prove that he was a friend of my dad's. Who did he cut out?"

"Roco Ramirez and Talson," answered Kat.

"You've seen the full picture, then?"

"Yeah, Talson has one at the house," replied Kat.

"So does Roco," said Sela. "He used to have the picture hanging over his bed at Headquarters. I remember he wanted to cut Barty and Nelco out of it, so it was only him and Talson, but Talson told him that cutting the picture wouldn't change anything. So then he just took it down so he wouldn't have to look at it anymore. This is the real picture." She reached into her pocket, pulled out the picture of the magic four and handed it to Tina. "Roco let me borrow that," she said in response to Kat's questioning look. "I wanted to show it to Tina just so she'd know."

Tina stared at the picture for a moment. She turned it over. Written on the back in small writing it said, *RTBN, the greatest on the run forever.* Tina turned the picture over again. "RTBN," she muttered. "Roco, Talson, Barty, Nelco. So they were all friends as kids?"

Sela nodded.

"What happened?" whispered Tina.

"I'll bet there's a picture of that in here too," said Sela. She turned around to face Nelco's dresser. "There," she said, pointing to a picture that stood framed on the top of the dresser. It was a picture of a woman with flowing blonde hair and soft hazel eyes. She had a soft mysterious smile and sharp yet kind eyes.

"Who's that?"

"That is Julie Operman," answered Sela.

"Is she Nelco's girlfriend?" asked Tina.

"Was," corrected Sela.

"What's she got to do with this?"

"Pretty much everything. Julie worked for Talson and she was murdered at The Sharktooth Bar fourteen years ago."

"Who killed her?" asked Tina, frowning.

Sela looked at Kat. Kat shook her head. "You tell her," she said.

"Barty Louis," said Sela. "He shot her."

"And he told Nelco it was Talson," added Kat. "Barty lied to Nelco and told him that Talson and Roco had set up the bust at the Sharktooth so that Julie could be killed without anyone seeing who did it."

"The truth was that Barty set up the bust so he could kill Julie," finished Sela. "He lied to Nelco and Nelco believed him. To this day Nelco believes that Talson and Roco are responsible for the murder."

Tina stared at Kat then at Sela as if hoping one of them would refute something that the other had said. "There is no way my father was a murderer," she whispered. "Why would he kill his best friend's girlfriend? Tell me one good reason why he would do that."

"He was jealous, because he wanted Julie and she wasn't interested," Sela answered simply.

"Killing her wouldn't make her any more interested," protested Tina. "He still had no reason to do that."

"He couldn't bring himself to kill Nelco," said Kat. "He knew even if he did kill Nelco, Julie still wouldn't want him. He knew he could never have her, so he killed her and framed Talson."

"Why would he frame Talson?"

"Because he was trying to destroy everything Nelco had," said Sela. "Nelco was

the one he wanted to hurt. By framing Talson he ruined Nelco's friendship with Talson. Then by telling Nelco that Roco had helped set up the murder, he destroyed Nelco's friendship with Roco. At the same time, Barty was trying to destroy everything Talson had too. He lost Nelco, and he lost Julie. Barty still had his friendship with Nelco because he lied to Nelco to keep him on his side. Plus Barty had his friendship with John Carl, which was also built on lies. Barty had planned to keep his relationship with Talson, but that part of his plan failed when Talson found out what Barty had done. That, as you know is what cost Barty his life."

"Are you saying that Talson killed my dad because my dad killed Julie?"

"Yes, Tina," said Sela, "that's the truth."

"I don't believe you," said Tina simply.

"If you don't believe us then I guess you believe Nelco, in which case you should still be laying in that laundry room," said Kat coldly. Kat still wasn't sure why she was angry with Tina. She supposed that she had expected more from her, but she wasn't sure what more she expected.

"I didn't believe it when I was told, either," Sela said in a more understanding tone. "I killed him without knowing what he was or what he had done. I wanted to believe it because it meant that at least I hadn't killed an innocent man. I wanted to believe it and I still couldn't at first."

"Talson made you do it and never told you why you were doing it?" Tina's tone was slightly softer now.

"Yes," said Sela quietly. "He told me afterwards. I knew at some point when Talson was in my mind. I knew everything he knew then, but when he left my mind I no longer knew any of it. It was like having two personalities or something. I had big empty spaces in my memory from the times Talson took over my mind."

"He totally used you," muttered Tina.

"Yes, he did," said Sela. "He was going to leave me to die after it was over, but he changed his mind and he stopped using me in the end. He killed Barty himself and he has paid the price."

"What price?" asked Tina.

"Talson lives with Barty's mind inside his. He has all Barty's thoughts and memories."

"And for that reason I'm supposed to care about what happens to Talson?"

"No," said Sela, "but you have to know that Nelco plans to kill Talson the same way Talson killed Barty, except he's going to use you instead of me. Don't assume that he'll change his mind and spare you the pain the way Talson spared me. If Nelco was left with Talson's mind, it would kill him."

Tina took a deep breath. "Either side of this is the wrong side," she said. "Both sides are evil."

"Choose the lesser of two evils then, I suppose," said Kat. She knew how Tina felt, since she had often felt that same way over the past few weeks.

"Let me make your decision a little easier," said Sela. "Nelco is going to try to use you to kill someone and then he's probably going to kill you. We don't want Talson to die, so obviously we aren't going to use you to kill him."

"Who are you going to use me to kill?

"No one," said Sela.

"Who's going to kill my mom, then?"

"Do you want her dead?" asked Sela. A flicker of surprise crossed her face.

"No," said Tina, "but I know you do."

"I don't care, actually," said Sela. "If someone has to kill Tracy I promise it won't be you. Deal?"

"Fine, deal," said Tina, "but prove to me that my dad murdered Julie."

"Fine," said Sela. "There is a surveillance tape of the night of the shooting. Larry showed it to me once, and I'll make sure he shows it to you if you are sure you want to see it."

"I'm sure," said Tina.

"Okay, then let's get the hell out of here," said Sela. "I'll take you to the Sharktooth."

As they exited the livingroom, Sela picked up a marker from Nelco's desk. On the wall next to the front door she wrote *Nice try Nelco.* And below it she signed with her initials, *S.S.*

CHAPTER 20

THE DOUBLE CONNECTION

As Sela, Kat and Tina drove toward The Sharktooth Bar, Kat leaned back in her seat and closed her eyes. She felt like there was something at the edge of her mind that she could not see. Blurred images kept flashing across her mind, but she could not make out what they were. Every time she tried to concentrate on one image, something else would flash across her mind. She was driving a car, then she was sitting in a desk chair in a small office, then she was sitting on a rock staring out at the sea. The sea turned into a blank stretch of ceiling over her head, then she was standing behind a bar, then the ceiling returned, blank and uninteresting.

As the scene changed so did her feelings. She was confused, then satisfied, then scared, sad, bored. She was sitting, then lying down, then standing, then lying down again. People were talking, glasses were clanking, there was silence, and waves were crashing against the rocks. She was lying on a soft bed, she was bored. There was a distant voice floating through her ears as if from very far away. *Larry, stop, don't.* The voice was angry. *Larry, don't leave me.* The voice changed, it was softer now. *Talson, you're a good man, I know you are.*

Suddenly pain shot through Kat's mind. She felt like her mind was screaming in protest, trying to prevent her from seeing the image that was erupting in her mind's eye. She could not fight it, and the picture slowly became clear. The back room of The Sharktooth Bar was crowded with card tables. Loud music was blaring and there were people at every table. In the roar of the crowd the sound of each individual voice was lost. A haze of smoke hung in the air, obscuring the faces of the gamblers and dealers.

"Good business tonight, huh Romez?" Barty Louis stood leaning against a table.

Out of the haze Kat could make out Roco Ramirez, wearing a fancy vest. He looked much younger and fatter than the muscular, tattooed Roco Kat knew. "Yeah, it's awesome tonight," he said smiling. "Even old Captain John Carl is here. I thought he'd never come back after our little joke last week, but I must say he took it quite well."

"Oh, don't worry about that," said Barty. "He actually thought it was funny, and I gave him the money he lost. It was just a joke between captain and mate, no big thing."

"As long as he's not mad," said Roco, "I don't want him on my bad side."

"No way, he's not mad," said Barty, waving his hand dismissively. "Like I said, he thought it was funny." Kat felt Barty's nervousness, but he kept it from showing on his face. It was hard lying to Roco, but Roco had no idea. Now he just had to wait. His thoughts calmed him, but his heart was still hammering against his chest.

"You okay, mate?" asked Roco. "You look a little nervous or something."

"No, I'm fine," said Barty quickly, as if he was disappointed that he had let his fear show.

"You're not still worried about_," Roco left the end of his sentence unfinished.

Barty paused. "Well, yeah I guess I am still worried."

"Don't be," said Roco. "I think you're crazy to think that he would do that. She is a Silver Shadow and Talson has no reason to hurt her. I mean, hell Barty, he loves her." Roco put his hand on Barty's shoulder. "Don't sweat it mate," he said bracingly.

Kat felt Barty's inward satisfaction. The story had worked, even if Roco had been skeptical at first. He would never suspect anything as long as he executed his plan tonight.

"Hey look, there's Julie," said Roco, pointing to a striking blonde woman who had just sat down at a blackjack table near Roco and Barty. "Hey Julie," said Roco, taking a step toward the table.

She nodded to the two men. "Hey guys, how's it going?"

"Great, in terms of business at least," said Roco.

Barty stood back and said nothing. Kat could feel his anger and disgust, as well as his envy for what he couldn't have. She could feel the gun pressing against the inside of Barty's forearm. Kat suddenly felt a jolt of her own thoughts. She knew what she was about to witness and wanted to block the image from her mind. She struggled, trying to get out of the Sharktooth and back to the reality of sitting in Sela's car.

Kat no longer felt Barty's emotions. She was no longer him, but she could not block the images in her mind. She was now a bodiless witness.

"Go talk to her, mate," Roco said to Barty. "It'll make you feel better."

Barty nodded and walked over to sit next to Julie at the card tables. *Romez is handing it to me.* Kat was back in Barty's body. She could feel Barty's hatred, and his heart hammering in his chest. He kept glancing at the door of the back room, waiting for what he knew was coming.

Suddenly the door of the back room burst open and a much younger Larry ran into the room. "The police are here," he yelled. "We're busted."

Roco turned around and stared at Larry. "What? How?"

Suddenly several police officers came to the door and pushed Larry up against the wall. "Larry James, you are under arrest." The officer cuffed Larry. "Stay against the wall," he ordered. "You have the right to remain silent."

Meanwhile more police officers had stormed into the bar and chaos broke out. People were running for the exits, trying to get out before they were seen. An officer grabbed Roco. "Roco Ramirez, you are under arrest," he said as Roco struggled against him.

"Barty, we have to run," Julie said in panic. "We can't afford to get caught."

Barty sat at the table, making no move to run away. Julie grabbed him by the arm. "Move," she said, "we have to get out of here. We can't be caught."

"Don't worry, we won't get caught," said Barty. His hands were cold and clammy now. He had slipped the gun out of his sleeve under the table.

I don't want to see it. Kat screamed the words in her mind. The scene was gone, and everything was black. Then out of the darkness and nothingness the sound of a gunshot resonated in Kat's head. Then there was nothing but silence and blackness.

You see what I go through, Kat?

Kat felt like her mind was struggling to function.

Talson? What happened? Did you just see—?

Yes, that's why you saw it. I've seen that over and over countless times. Thank you for stopping it when you did. I can't stop it anymore.

I tried to stop it sooner.

So did I. I used to be able to stop it, but I don't think I can anymore. I'm sorry.

Why can't you make it stop now, if you could before?

I don't know. Nelco's work, I expect. He has no idea.

What do you mean?

He thinks he's going to win this way, but he doesn't want what he's going to get. He doesn't want to see what I see, but if he has his way he is going to see it all.

You're going to make him see everything that happened?

Yes, if you help me.

Me?

I thought you wanted to help show people the truth. I thought you wanted Nelco to know what really happened.

Sela says it won't matter. He'll want to kill you anyway.

True, he'll still want to kill me.

Then it doesn't make any difference.

You think it doesn't make any difference? Kat, you know it makes a difference.

But how can I make him see? Why am I seeing what you're seeing?

You are seeing what everyone is seeing, if I'm not mistaken. It is an amazing connection that exists between you and I, Kat. And because of that there are connections everywhere, between Larry and John Carl, and between you and Tracy, even between you and Nelco.

Does that mean they all saw what I just saw?

You tell me.

Tracy saw it, at least part of it. I bet it came as a bit of a shock to her. She thinks you set it up as a trap.

That's an interesting idea. Trust Tracy to find a way to deny the truth when it is staring her in the face.

She thinks it's a fake because the vision disappeared and she didn't see the actual shooting.

Oh well, we can make them all see it again.

I don't want to see it again.

What you want is irrelevant at this point. You can't deny reality no matter how much you don't want to see it. Tracy and Nelco have to see it and experience it to believe it.

But that means you have to see it too.

I've seen it all thousands of times. I can handle a few more.

I feel really bad for you sometimes, Talson.

Don't.

I know you don't want me to, but I can see in your mind, so I feel what you feel.

I don't want that, Kat. I never want you to have to go through what I've gone through. You don't have to see it, only I have to.

No, I need to see it too. It will be harder for Nelco if he has to deal with both of us, won't it?

Yes, but—

But, nothing, I know what we have to do and I'm with you. We have to destroy Barty's mind without destroying yours or anyone else's. I'm not going to just sit here and let you fight Nelco by yourself. I have the power. You think I'm going to just sit here and not use it?

You're strong, Kat.

Not really, anyone would do that.

No Kat, not everyone.

Well, you said we have an incredible connection, so let's use it. Barty was the one who tried to say that you stole the power and now Nelco believes that I only have it because of you. If that's not true, let's prove them wrong.

Nelco talks about the power like it's an object. The power is a living desire. I didn't steal it, it was in my family.

Who was your family?

The car came back around Kat, and she could feel the motion of the car and her back against the seat. She opened her eyes and saw the narrow road ahead and the dim lights that illuminated the run down houses near Headquarters.

"Whoa," she whispered, sitting up straight in her seat and realizing what had just happened.

"Whoa what?" asked Tina leaning forward in the back seat.

"What did you see?" asked Sela.

"It's complicated," said Kat. "Are we going to Headquarters? I thought we were going to the Sharktooth."

"We were, but then Roco called and said we should get down to Headquarters right away. Apparently Nelco is planning to go to the circle when he gets off work at five."

"That's in an hour," said Kat, looking at the clock. "How did Roco know that?"

"Talson," said Sela simply. "Apparently the transfer between Nelco and John Carl was a lot more complicated than we thought. Apparently Talson is able to connect with Nelco's mind now because it's a double connection. I don't know if that's a bad thing or a good thing, but Roco said that Talson isn't telling him anything."

"Well I think it is a good thing, because this way Talson knows what Nelco is doing. This way we can make sure no one is at the circle when he gets there."

"Someone will be there," said Sela. "You think we would let that opportunity pass by?"

"I think it would be too risky," objected Kat. "Who's going to be there to wait for Nelco then?"

"That is being decided as we speak," replied Sela.

"He thinks you're still in his laundry room, Tina," muttered Kat. "I wonder what he'll think when he sees what you wrote on his wall," she added to Sela.

Sela laughed. "He won't be too thrilled, that's for sure," she said as she pulled into the driveway of the old crumbling house that belonged to Milton Roberts.

Milro was waiting for them and came outside as soon as Sela pulled up. "I was sent down here to wait for you guys," he said.

"So who got the job at the circle with Nelco?" Sela asked, as she got out of the car. "Romez?"

"No," said Milro. "You're not going to believe this, but the boss is going down there himself."

"No way, alone?"

"No, one Shadow is going with him."

"Who?"

Milro pointed to Kat.

Sela raised her eyebrows, glancing at Kat.

Kat nodded. She was not surprised that Talson wanted her to come. After all, they had just talked about Kat helping him.

Both Milro and Sela looked surprised by Kat's reaction. "Do you know something we don't know?" asked Milro.

"This is my job," said Kat simply. "I told him I wanted to help him with it."

"Well, he wants to see you in his room," said Milro, still looking surprised.

Talson was lying on his bed with his hands behind his head, and his eyes fixed on the blank ceiling. Kat had never been in his bedroom before. It was a fairly small room, and like his office, it was very simply furnished. "I probably should have told Roco to come with me tonight, as well," said Talson, looking up at Kat who stood awkwardly beside the bed.

"Why isn't he coming?"

"I am afraid that if I let him come we will end up having to deal with another brawl between him and Nelco."

"I'm guessing that fight was pretty nasty," said Kat.

"Has Roco told you about it at all?" asked Talson casually.

"A little," replied Kat. "He said Nelco punched you, and—" she broke off. "Sorry," she muttered.

"Don't be," said Talson with no hint of shame or anger. "Nelco did punch me. Then Roco got into it. They were really beating the hell out of each other, it was really bad, actually." His voice was a remarkably monotone, considering what he was describing.

"Did you try to stop them?"

"Yeah, I did, but as you have probably noticed, Roco and Nelco are both quite a bit bigger than I am. I'm not very strong, but I did manage to break it up after a while. I really don't want to have to deal with something like that again."

"I think Roco can control himself now," said Kat.

"I'd like to think he can too, but I'm not sure I should take the risk."

"What are we going to do when Nelco gets to the circle?"

"You are still sure you want to come?" asked Talson. Throughout their entire conversation Talson had kept his eyes on the ceiling without so much as glancing at Kat.

"Yeah, I'm sure," said Kat, taken aback. She was reminded of the previous day at The Sharktooth Bar when Larry had refused to look at Talson. It was not like Talson to not look at Kat when he was talking to her. "Can you look at me?" she asked quietly.

"No, actually I can't," said Talson, "unless we want Nelco to know what we are planning to do."

"Is that because of the double connection that Sela was telling me about on the way here?"

"Yes, you see, your mind and my mind are easily connected, and since Nelco has access to my mind, he has a window into yours. That is how he got into your head yesterday at the Sharktooth. It is not difficult for me to prevent the connection between you and I if we are not together, however it becomes much harder when we are in the same room talking to each other. It helps me if I avoid eye contact."

"I thought Nelco was only in my dad's head, not yours."

"Being in John Carl's mind means that he is also in mine, because I was in John Carl's mind when Nelco forced the transfer. It was my mistake, but unfortunately there isn't much we can do to fix it now."

"So you're saying that Nelco has your power and my dad's?"

"No, Kat," said Talson. "He just has my power. If I had not been in John Carl's mind at that time, Nelco wouldn't have been able to gain anything."

"But what about my dad's power?"

"He doesn't have the power, Kat."

"Wait, I thought you said—?"

"Have you ever seen your father use his power?" interrupted Talson. "Don't you think you would have a connection to your father's mind? If you have a connection with me, there is no doubt that you would have an even stronger one with your father."

"So, if my father doesn't have the power, why did Nelco think he did?" asked Kat, thoroughly confused now.

"Well, because I told Nelco he did," replied Talson.

"So you lied," said Kat.

"Well, technically, yes, but I told him that a long time ago in the hopes that it would someday be true."

"But my dad knows a lot about the power."

"Kat, I've told you this before, the power is not a gift, and it is not a single entity. It is a desire, an ambition. It is not something one possesses, but rather a desire that comes from within a person. The ability to connect to the mind of another person is a rare gift, but it does not exist without desire."

"So you're saying that my dad has the ability to touch people's minds, but had no desire to actually do it?"

"That's right," replied Talson. Kat thought for a second that she had detected the slightest bit of anger in Talson's voice, at least his tone was not as casual as it had been.

"My dad said to tell you 'I'm not doing it, and he still can't make me'," muttered Kat.

"And now you know what he was talking about," said Talson.

"So that's why you weren't worried about Nelco and the transfer with my dad."

"Exactly," replied Talson, his eyes still fixed on the ceiling as if he was looking at a fascinating picture. "If you can't make your dad use his mental abilities, I know for sure that Nelco can't. Everyone thought I was crazy not to worry about it, but I had a very good reason. I thought Nelco didn't gain anything from John Carl. I'm only taking it seriously now that I know Nelco inadvertently gained my power."

"So when my dad said he's not doing it, he meant that he won't—" Kat paused not sure how to continue.

"He won't let Nelco use him to kill me," Talson finished. "Nice of him, isn't it?" he added with a small smile at the ceiling. "I never could have expected such kindness from him."

"He's not going to help get you killed," said Kat incredulously, "you call that kindness?"

"Believe me, when it comes to John Carl and me, that is the utmost gesture of kindness."

"But he basically just said he won't kill you, that's all," said Kat. She was having a hard time thinking of her father's actions as kind.

"Well, for me and John Carl, I won't kill you is like saying I love you, or something." He shifted uncomfortably on the bed. "It's sad, I know."

"How do you two know each other anyway?" asked Kat.

"That's the part of me that I don't want to remember that Sela talks about," said Talson with a small smile.

"How did you know Sela said that to me?"

"Because I know everything," said Talson with the same sly smile. "At least almost everything."

"Like everything except the fact that Nelco has your power," remarked Kat.

"Don't make me look at you," said Talson smiling slightly.

"So you really are the one Nelco is using now?" said Kat.

"Yes, I am, but fortunately for me, Nelco has no idea what that means."

"Alright, so what's the plan when we get to the circle?"

"This is going to be complicated, so I need you to listen to me for a minute while I explain this. I'm not going to look at you, but I need you to listen anyway. What we are about to do is not going to be easy, and it is going to be somewhat risky. People like you and I have a connection to the mind of every person we come in contact with. The connection is weak, except between certain important people in our lives. That is why we see snatches of people's minds flashing before us. I assume you have experienced that."

"Yes I have," said Kat. "I didn't used to, but lately it's been happening. It happened on my way here in the car. I was seeing a bunch of different things before I saw the night they busted the Sharktooth."

"Yes, and when this happens you can grab hold of one of these fleeting visions by consciously making the decision to concentrate on it. It is easy for you to focus on my mind. You and I connect far too easily, which is why I am so disrespectfully not looking at you.

"However," continued Talson, "if you concentrate very hard on, say for example, Nelco's thoughts, and do not surrender to our connection, then you will be able to get inside Nelco's mind. Once you do that, you can make him see anything you want him to see as long as you remain in control of your own mind and do not allow him to control you. You have to be very careful now, because Nelco will be able to suck you into his control very easily since he is using my power. You cannot let that happen, because if you do, Nelco will have your power and mine together, and sufficient to say, we don't want that."

Kat looked at Talson lying on the bed. He seemed relaxed and casual as if nothing out of the ordinary was happening. "How do we make Nelco see what we want him to see?"

"I seem to have no way to contain Barty's mind anymore, which could easily be my downfall, but I want to use it to my advantage. I can make you see Barty's thoughts, and once I do that, you will be able to concentrate on Nelco's mind and once you are in his head he will see whatever you see. You may or may not actually see the scene at the Sharktooth, but as long as Nelco is trying to take your power, which he will be, he will see it. It is not going to be easy, and the release from Nelco's mind will most likely be painful. I hope that the part of my mind that Nelco currently possesses will somehow come back to my mind. I don't even know if that's possible, but we'll see."

"So you're missing part of your mind?" said Kat in shock.

"Unfortunately, yes," said Talson.

"Can you feel it?"

"At times," said Talson. "I don't really know how to describe it, but it's not a good feeling. I think it is the reason that I am no longer able to control Barty's memories. I was always able to control it before."

"So if we succeed, we'll be able to make Nelco see what really happened to Julie?"

"Yes, and if we repeat it over and over, I am hoping that bits of Barty's thoughts will remain in Nelco's mind and I will lose them."

"Will Nelco die from this?" asked Kat. This had been her question from the beginning. She was sure that Talson would be willing to kill anyone he had to, but she also knew that Nelco and Talson had once been friends.

"Not from the first time," replied Talson.

"But eventually, do you want to kill him?"

"No, I don't want to."

"But are you going to?"

"I don't know," said Talson. He sounded tired. "My hope is that I can use Barty's mind to kill Nelco, but like I said I'm not sure if that's possible."

"Where will Nelco's mind go if that happens?" asked Kat.

"I think it will just be gone, and he and Barty will both be completely dead. Barty's mind can't exist without being inside someone else, so if I can give Nelco all of Barty's thoughts and memories, and then Nelco dies, they will both be gone."

"Do you think that's the only way?" asked Kat.

"No," replied Talson, "it's not the only way, but I think it's the only way that I won't die. It is selfish of me. I should die. I should have already died. But honestly, I'm just not willing to die for this. I suppose that proves I'm cruel, because I'm not willing to die for my friends and family, and I'm reluctant to suffer for them as well. I have always been that way. I suppose I just never really cared, just like Nelco and Barty told me. I always thought I cared, but then I never feel like I care about anything. Nelco and Barty might have been right about me."

"Sela and Roco say you do care," offered Kat. "They might be right too."

Talson sighed, staring at the ceiling. "Are you sure you want to help me?"

Kat looked at that small man lying on the bed. He looked casual, passive, and bored, as if he really didn't care about anything. But Kat knew that he had to care. If he didn't care, he wouldn't even be alive after everything that had happened in his life. Kat felt like she was in the same situation as Tina. She could take a big risk to help Talson, or she could do nothing and Talson might end up getting killed. She was scared, but she also felt determined. Kat didn't know why, but she knew she had to help Talson even if it seemed wrong.

Kat remembered what Sela had said as clearly as if Sela was right there saying it. "Even though I was angry and I thought I hated him, I helped him. In the process I saw a completely different side of him. I realized something that I never knew about him before, and I realized something about myself as well. I hope that someday you will have the chance to realize that same thing."

Kat took a deep breath. "Yeah, I'm sure," she said. "I'm with you."

"Poor Nelco," muttered Talson. "He thinks he knows what he's facing, but he has no idea."

"What about Tina," said Kat, suddenly remembering her friend, who she and Sela had left alone in Milro's house. "Sela had a deal with her."

"Once we get through this insanity with Nelco, you and Sela will have the chance to honor the agreement, and Larry will show her the surveillance tape. I hope that once she sees what happened, you and she will be close again."

"Yeah, me too," said Kat. She didn't have the energy to ask Talson how he knew about something that Kat wasn't sure of herself.

Talson slowly got up, still not looking directly at Kat. "Let's go," he said. "We need to get to the circle before Mr. Nelson."

C H A P T E R   2 1

CHANGE OF PLANS

Tina had been right, there was no right side. Kat felt that no matter what she did, it was going to involve doing something immoral, illegal, or both.

She was sitting in the back of Milro's car, which Talson was driving. Talson had told her she needed to sit in the back on the right side of the car, so that he could not even catch her eye in the rear view mirror. Kat kept her eyes down, looking at her shoes or at the floor. She could feel her mind wandering and knew that meant her mind would connect to another if it were possible. She recognized the feeling now, and knew she had to fight it so Nelco would not discover their plan.

Kat's mind seemed, just as Talson had said it would, to automatically try to connect to another mind. Before, when Kat had been with Sela and Tina, she had seen snatches from different people's minds, but now it seemed that since she was with Talson, the only connection she could make was with his mind. All she could do was sit in silence and stare at the floor, fighting her own mind.

I was wrong, she thought. Everything that had been done was wrong. Tracy, Nelco, Barty, Roco, Sela, Talson, they were all liars, cheaters, traitors, and cold, calculated killers. Kat looked at her own hands, lying limply in her lap. She too was a traitor, a liar, and a cheater, but she was not a killer. Despite this, Kat could not deny the growing possibility that she would become one, or at least become an accomplice. Talson was going to make her into a killer just like Sela. Kat thought of her parents, and how they had been right. Talson had fooled her and now she would either become partially responsible for Nelco and Tracy's deaths, partially responsible for Talson's death, or almost fully responsible for her own death. A million emotions seemed to burn inside Kat's chest, but she wasn't sure if any of them represented how she truly felt. She felt angry or scared or sad or lonely, or a combination of all of them.

"You used me," she said very quietly.

"In what way?" asked Talson. Evidently he had heard her despite how quietly she had spoken.

"I'm not a killer, Talson," said Kat.

"I know that," replied Talson. "You are very lucky. I am personally very impressed by the fact that you are not a killer. It shows that you are a person with exceptional control."

"I'm thirteen," said Kat more forcefully. "I'm a kid, of course I'm not a killer. No one is a killer at my age."

"I wouldn't say no one," said Talson.

"Did you kill someone when you were thirteen, then?" asked Kat somewhat coldly.

"No," said Talson, he had dropped his over-casual tone, his voice was serious now. "By the time I was thirteen I had learned to control my power so that I no longer killed people, but that was only after years of not being able to control it. Years of killing people who I never wanted to kill. Watching people die without knowing how or why it was happening. Just sitting there as they died and their minds became part of me. Seeing their thoughts, their memories, and their knowledge. Living every day with a constant reminder of everyone who had died because I couldn't control my mind. No, Kat, by the time I was your age I had already killed and was done killing. I killed only one person since I was twelve years old, and that was when I was twenty-six and I killed Barty Louis. I tried for a long time to stop killing, I never wanted people to die because of me."

Kat sat staring at the floor in shocked silence, but could no longer prevent the connection.

Get out.

Talson I—

Out.

Kat felt as though she had been pushed roughly away from Talson's thoughts and back to her own shock and horror at what she had just heard. "I don't understand," she began quietly. "You killed people with your mind because you couldn't control your power?"

"Yes," said Talson softly. Kat did not hear any shame in his voice, she heard only sadness.

"But I have the power, and I never killed anyone," she protested.

"You are different from me, Kat. You didn't know what your mind could do when you were younger."

"And you did?"

"Yes, I did. Also, you were not alone as a child. You had contact with many people every day, and as a result you made many minor mental connections with people. If you know what someone is thinking, or what they are about to say, even if you don't realize it you are using your power to connect to their mind. You were able to do this often, all your life. I, on the other hand, was almost completely alone. I spoke to no one. My mind was isolated and unable to make any connections, but I still had the desire to make the connections. When you have very little contact with other people, your mind will cling to the few connections it can make. That means you will quickly be controlling the mind of a stranger who simply caught your eye on the street. If you do not have many people in your life to allow your mind to go from one to the other, your mind will cling to one person until your mind had taken over their mind. Then they die, and you gain all of their knowledge and memories. It actually makes you better because you know more and you suddenly have more memories and experiences. That gain causes the unconscious desire to kill again to gain more. Even if you don't want to kill, it is exceedingly difficult to stop once the cycle starts, especially if you don't understand your mental ability."

Kat sat in silence for a moment. She wasn't sure she would ever understand what

Talson had just said. "I never killed because I wasn't alone, but you were?" she asked after a moment.

"Yes." Talson's reply was emotionless. "I was afraid to try to get close to anyone because I thought I'd kill them. I could never break out of the cycle because I needed people in my life, but I was afraid I would kill them. I had to be alone, but being alone was the problem."

"But you're not alone now," said Kat.

"And I don't kill now."

"How old were you the first time you killed someone?" As soon as the question came out of her mouth, Kat wished she could take it back. She didn't really want to know the answer.

"I was three," replied Talson. The question did not appear to have bothered him.

"I didn't understand it."

Kat could think of nothing to say. "That's horrible," she muttered.

"I know," replied Talson. "All I ever wanted was to make it stop, but I didn't know how. I eventually learned. I had to learn. When I was five, almost six I started to be able to control it. Sometimes I could, sometimes I couldn't. I wanted to have friends, but I was afraid I'd kill them, and I was afraid to tell anyone about what my mind could do. I'll never forget the first time I told someone, when I was eight years old."

"Who did you tell?"

"Roco Ramirez," said Talson softly.

"Roco?" whispered Kat.

"Yeah, my man Romez. The first real friend I ever had, and the best. Marissa was my second friend, then Barty and Nelco. It was only then that my life really got better. My friends didn't save me, but they certainly showed me how to save myself."

"And then you killed one of them," muttered Kat.

"Kat, I'm driving, don't make me crash," said Talson. There was no hint of anger or any other emotion in his voice, and he was staring straight at the road ahead.

"Why didn't you kill me when you could have?" Kat pressed on even though she knew Talson didn't want to talk anymore.

Talson leaned forward and glared at Kat in the rear view mirror. His sudden eye contact startled her. "Are you suggesting that was a mistake?" he asked in a quiet but harsh voice.

Kat looked at the yellow eyes in the mirror for a moment before Talson looked away. She said nothing. They were very near the park now and the hot sun of the afternoon was sinking low, sending long shadows of the trees onto the road.

"Are you still with me, Katerina?" asked Talson, as he parked the car on the street two blocks from the park.

"What would you do if I said I wasn't," asked Kat quietly. "Would you kill me?"

"Do you think I would kill you?" Talson turned around and made direct eye contact with Kat."

"I don't know," she muttered.

"In that case, I suggest you figure that out."

"I don't know you well enough," said Kat. She wasn't entirely sure why she was suddenly doubting Talson.

"You don't trust me," said Talson softly.

"Why should I?" asked Kat sharply.

Talson shrugged his narrow shoulders. "No reason, I suppose. Maybe just because I trust you."

"Well you shouldn't," said Kat. "Nothing is stopping me from selling you out, like Barty and Nelco."

"Actually there is something."

"What?"

"That is something only you can answer," replied Talson smoothly. "I am going to the house to await the arrival of Mr. Nelson, and meanwhile I suggest that you go home. Go home and tell your father what's going on. Do whatever you choose to do. Just know that you will have to accept the consequences of whatever you choose."

"You don't care what I do, do you?" said Kat, glaring at Talson.

"Yes, I do, but I have experienced things that have made me accept the loss of things I care about. I have lost many things, and I have realized that even when you think you can't live without something, that thing will be gone and you will find yourself still surviving without it. There is no way to lose everything.

"I am sure that you will make a good decision about what you should do, Kat. I am sure of it, because I know that you are an intelligent person and I trust your judgment. I'm going to leave you to your thoughts now. You are an incredibly powerful person, Katerina. Don't let anyone tell you different."

Kat sat motionless in the back seat of the car as Talson got out of the car and walked away down the block toward the park and the house where he would wait for a man who had once been his friend and was now trying to kill him. Kat watched Talson until he went behind some trees and disappeared from her view.

The connection was gone, Kat felt it leave her. The feeling of understanding, even closeness, was suddenly gone as if someone had yanked it roughly away. Kat felt lost sitting in the back of Milro's car, despite the fact that she was about five blocks from her house. She felt more alone than she had ever remembered feeling in her life. Slowly Kat climbed out of the car and began to walk very slowly down the street away from the park.

Kat slouched through the front door of her house and was surprised to see her father sitting at the kitchen table doing paperwork.

"What are you doing here?" asked John Carl.

"I don't know," muttered Kat without looking at him.

"Well, maybe you should figure that out," her father replied, flipping through a large stack of sales receipts.

"You sound like Talson," muttered Kat without thinking. "Why didn't you tell me that you had the ability to connect with people's minds just like I do?"

"Because I wish I didn't," said John Carl, still focusing on his papers. "I haven't used it in years."

"How many years?" asked Kat, taking a seat at the end of the table. She couldn't bring herself to ask her father if he had killed anyone.

"Nearly forty, except for a very few times," replied John Carl.

"Did you know Larry had the power?"

"Yes," John Carl replied without looking up.

"Why didn't you tell me?" Kat's tone was no longer angry, she felt too tired to be mad anymore.

"Because I wish he didn't," said John Carl without emotion.

"Why?"

John Carl sighed, looking up from his papers. "Nothing good ever comes from this power we have, Kat, especially not when people like Larry use it. I suppose Talson told you about my mental abilities, then?"

"I actually figured it out once I knew what Conner Nelson had done. I didn't realize that you didn't use it, Talson told me that part."

"I knew you'd figure it out soon enough. It doesn't matter much now, though. Did you tell Talson what I told you to tell him?"

"Yeah."

"What did he say?"

"Typical John Carl," replied Kat.

"He would say that. But he doesn't have much to worry about even if that meathead Nelson uses him somehow."

"Nelco has Talson's power now," said Kat.

"How'd he manage that?" asked John Carl, looking surprised for the first time.

"When he transferred with you, Talson was in your mind, spying on the conversation."

John Carl shook his head. "Typical Talson, can't leave himself out of stuff. He still doesn't have too much to worry about, but at least this might make Mr. Casual sweat a little bit."

"So you don't think Nelco can win?" asked Kat.

"Well, Talson still has you to help him out, so you know—"John Carl shrugged, "he's got it."

"No, actually he doesn't," said Kat. "I just left him to face Nelco."

"Really, why?"

"Well I had said I'd help him, but then I changed my mind and I wasn't sure what to do. He told me to go home and figure it out."

"And you just left him to deal with Nelson?"

"Yeah, is that wrong?"

"Well you left a man to deal with someone who used to be his friend but is now trying to kill him with his own mind. But then again, Talson happens to be a cold hearted, calculating murderer with the power to screw up the lives of everyone on the planet, so you tell me."

"What do you know about Talson's life?" asked Kat.

"More than I need to know," said John Carl. "Where's Nelson? What's he trying to do?"

Kat looked into her father's steady brown eyes. She didn't know why she was telling him, she didn't even know why he cared, but she told him. She told him what Talson wanted her to do, and what Talson faced. She left out any mention of Barty Louis, and his part in the mental connection.

"And you chose not to help with that?" said John Carl, when Kat had finished. He sounded faintly surprised.

"Well, yeah," said Kat, looking away.

"Why?"

Kat was surprised by her father's reaction. "He's using me, and I don't want to become a killer like him. I'd have thought that was obvious to you."

"I thought it was obvious to you that if you don't let Talson use you, Nelco will. Personally, if I know someone is going to use me I would rather it was Talson than Conner Nelson."

"Nelco isn't using me," said Kat.

"You think not?" John Carl challenged. "You think Nelco can just get into Talson's head using a little piece of his power that he stole out of my mind? There is no way. Talson's mind isn't going to connect to a piece of his own mind. Talson will block the connection. He will immediately recognize his own thoughts, assuming that he still remembers who he is. He knows what he was using when he was so rudely spying on me, and therefore he will not allow that part of his mind to connect to him."

"But will he know when Nelco tries to enter his mind?" asked Kat. "I mean he could catch him unaware like he did with the transfer."

"There has to be a double connection with me in all this crap," said John Carl. "That means that Talson will know exactly what Nelson is going to try to do because he can use me, and I'm not stopping him. Nelson doesn't have a chance unless he uses either you, me or Larry. I won't use my abilities, and Larry barely uses his, and even if he does, Larry and Talson have virtually eliminated their mental connection. That leaves you. You have the mental ability, the desire to use it, and the connection to Talson."

"What does that mean, then?" asked Kat.

"Well it means that you could very easily become a killer just by sitting on your ass," said John Carl.

"I think Talson withdrew the connection," protested Kat.

"It doesn't happen that quickly. You can't just decide to throw someone out of your mind. Besides, since Nelco has part of Talson's mind he can re-establish the connection himself. In that case he can use you to enter Talson's mind, and then you're both in big trouble."

Kat stared at her father. "So, if I don't do anything—"

"You'll end up killing Talson and there is a possibility that Nelco will kill you," John Carl said bluntly. "But, the good news is that unless Nelco has someone to dump Talson's mind on, he'll probably die too."

"He's trying to dump it on Tina," said Kat.

"What?" For the first time John Carl looked genuinely concerned.

"Yeah, Nelco had her tied up in his laundry room."

"Son of a bitch," muttered John Carl. "He told me he wanted revenge for Barty, but he's going to sacrifice Barty's daughter so that he doesn't have to pay the price of getting that revenge. The bastard lied to me, he doesn't care about revenge, if he did he wouldn't have waited fourteen years. He just wants Talson's power, so he can use it and be king."

"But if I help Talson—" Kat began.

"He probably won't die, and neither will you, and neither will Tina as long as she stays out of it."

"But I'll end up being partially responsible for Nelco's death, if he dies," said Kat.

"If?" said John Carl raising his eyebrows. "Talson is going to obliterate Conner Nelson. Talson is not going to let some stuffed suit traitor like Nelson gain all that power. Even if he dies, he'll take Nelco with him. You might contribute to Nelco's death if you help Talson, but honestly Kat, who cares? What kind of a man would sacrifice a couple of kids like you and Tina to prove a point against a man like Talson? Even Talson couldn't bring himself to do that."

"I guess you're right," said Kat. "I shouldn't have left Talson, but I just thought I couldn't trust him. I didn't really even think about how evil Nelco is. I just can't believe you're telling me to help Talson," Kat paused. "I know you hate him," she added tentatively.

"Listen," said John Carl. "They're both evil, but from where I'm standing Nelco's worse and he doesn't have an excuse for his actions. Yeah, I hate Talson, but that's not the point right now."

"So you're saying I have to choose between two evils?"

"I don't know if evil is the right word for Talson, but yes, it is a choice between Talson or Nelson."

"And you choose Talson?"

"You could never help Nelco and you know it," said John Carl. "It's just like with Tina, you told her she had to choose between Nelson or you and Sela. She didn't like the choice, but you know she could never choose Nelson after what he did to her."

"How did you—?"

"I can know things about people, Kat, but most of the time I prefer not to know," said John Carl with a small smile.

"You mean know things you shouldn't," said Kat. She was beginning to see her mind as a way to know things about people she had no business knowing.

"I'm glad you realize that your mind isn't meant to do that." For the first time in quite a while John Carl looked at Kat with some measure of pride.

"You're right, it's the same choice, but what can I do now? Go back to the circle? Nelco might already be there."

"Is he?" asked John Carl.

"What? I don't know," said Kat, confused.

"What, are you trying to be like me now? Don't pretend you don't have the ability to use your mind to know things the others say you shouldn't know."

"Talson won't let me into Nelco's mind," said Kat.

"Screw Talson," said John Carl. "Just concentrate on Nelco and it will happen. Talson won't risk blocking you for fear that it will give Nelco a way into his head."

Kat wanted to ask her father why he was using his mind and trying to help her, but she decided against it, choosing to focus on Nelco.

"I have no good reason for doing this, but I don't need one," said John Carl softly. "Just be careful," he added, "don't let him get you."

Kat tried to remember the words Nelco had said to her when he had entered her mind at the Sharktooth. Kat wasn't sure why it happened or how it happened, but she felt excited, angry, and scared at the same time. Kat knew they were Nelco's emotions, and she concentrated on them, losing herself in the feelings. She was staring at the road ahead of her. She was nearly there. What would she find after all these years?

Suddenly, Nelco's thoughts stopped. *You are a fool to enter my mind, Talson.*

Kat was suddenly back with her own thoughts. She tried not to think, she could not let Nelco know it was she and not Talson.

You know you won't win, Talson.

Kat felt like her mind was being pulled toward Nelco's mind. His thoughts were taking over, replacing her consciousness. Kat knew she had to keep her own mind blank, otherwise Nelco would know everything she was thinking. No thought was safe.

A few moments later Kat looked at her father. She felt her own consciousness returning as Nelco's thoughts receded to the edges of her mind. She felt that the ghost of his thoughts was still hanging somewhere in her mind.

"He's nearly at the house," said Kat quietly, "but he's not there yet."

"And he didn't get you?"

"He would have, but he thought I was Talson," said Kat.

John Carl laughed. "That could be a very big mistake for him. You'd better hurry if you want to beat Nelco to wherever."

"You must really hate Nelco if you want me to help Talson."

"I don't want you to help him," said John Carl. "But you have to, and I know that. Listen, I'll drive you to the park so you'll get there before Nelco."

"You will?" whispered Kat in surprise.

"Did I stutter?" asked John Carl sarcastically. He got up and took the car keys off the hook near the kitchen door. "Now let's go, before I change my mind and decide not to help you."

Kat nodded, and followed him outside.

"Talson killed a lot of people, didn't he? I know you know," she added as they pulled out of the driveway.

"Yeah, he did," said John Carl expressionlessly.

"He says I'm lucky it never happened to me," muttered Kat.

"You are damn lucky," said John Carl. "Killing like that is a living hell."

"It happened to you too, didn't it?" said Kat quietly.

"I'm driving, Kat," said John Carl, "don't make me crash."

A minute later John Carl had pulled into the parking lot at the park. He turned and looked at Kat. "Good luck, kid," he said softly. "Don't let Nelco get you, and don't worry about Talson. He's better than he says he is."

Kat nodded. "Thanks Dad," she said. "I thought you hated me and we were enemies."

"Nelco is much more my enemy than you," replied John Carl. "You happen to be my daughter, so the choice between you and him is the easiest choice I've had in years. Just do one thing for me."

"Sure," said Kat.

"Tell Talson I said he's still lucky."

"Okay," said Kat with a small smile. She got out of her father's car and hurried toward the circle of trees. She knew that Nelco was walking toward the house too. He had parked in back of the park and was going to approach the circle from the other side. Kat knew she did not have much time to get inside the house before Nelco saw her.

Kat dashed through the front door of the house and closed the door as quietly as possible. The hallway was very dark. Kat headed for the stairs, hoping there was nothing on the floor that she could not see. Nelco was right outside the door now, gazing at the house. After all his years away from the Silver Shadows it still felt like home to him.

Kat hurried up the stairs as fast as possible and half ran down the hall to the last door on the left. She knocked, hoping Talson would be there. She was not sure that he would even let her in.

"Enter." Talson spoke in his usual lazy voice.

Kat hesitated, then pushed the door open. The room was dimly lit, and Talson was sitting in his usual chair in front of the empty fireplace. The room reminded Kat of the first time she had met Talson. Her life had already changed drastically since their first meeting.

"You came," said Talson, not making direct eye contact.

Kat closed the door behind her. "Nelco is just outside," she said hesitantly.

"I knew he'd be here soon. He didn't see you, did he?"

"No, I got here first," said Kat. "I never saw him, he never saw me."

"That was a risky move, Kat," said Talson, "but I trust that you didn't let him know you were in his mind."

"No, he thought I was you."

"Interesting," said Talson. "Sit down," he added.

Kat sat opposite him. "Just out of curiosity, why did you decide to come back?" asked Talson looking up at her now. "Why did you choose me?"

"Because I realized that Nelco would use me if I didn't, and I'd rather help you than him." Kat felt that although they were looking at each other, she and Talson were not truly making eye contact. It was more like they were looking through each other.

"I told you that already. Besides, Nelco could still use you even if you help me."

"But he won't," said Kat. "You can block Nelco."

"What makes you think that?" asked Talson, looking mildly surprised.

"I went home and my dad convinced me to come back," said Kat quickly. She had thought it might be better not to tell Talson this, but she knew it would impossible not to, now.

Talson's look of surprise heightened. Kat thought he even looked impressed. "Your dad wanted you to help me?"

"Yeah, he did."

"What the hell did that transfer do to him?" Talson shook his head. "Insane," he muttered.

"I couldn't believe it at first either, but he really hates Nelco. He said he'd rather be used by you than Nelco."

"I know he hates Nelco," said Talson softly. "They've known each other a long time and hated each other a long time, but I don't get what's going on with John Carl being so nice to me lately."

Kat shrugged. She didn't really think nice was the word for it. "He said to tell you you're still lucky."

"I hate him," muttered Talson, but his tone did not reflect it.

Suddenly they heard a noise downstairs. "Nelco's here," whispered Kat.

"He's going to the library, just like I thought he would," said Talson. "I knew he could never pass up looking at all those photos."

"I don't know if he'll like what he sees," said Kat.

"Probably not, there are pictures of the good times and the bad times in that room."

"I saw that one of you and Sela," said Kat suddenly. She had had trouble getting that picture out of her mind ever since she had seen it.

"I'm sorry," said Talson. "No one needs to see that. No one, except perhaps Nelco."

You think he'll find it?"

"Well, I know he'll look in the black book."

"Are we gonna go down there?"

"Not yet, we have to wait for the right time, and the right opportunity."

"Can you do it without seeing him?"

"No, I mean, I could, but I would have to connect to his mind and then he could hurt me. If I'm looking at someone, I don't have any problem controlling what they see or hear. When I'm not looking or especially when I'm not in the same room as the person, I find it much harder to be in control. So we will go and face Nelco after he's had time to stroll down memory lane."

There was a silence between them for a moment before Kat spoke. "I'm sorry I

left," she said softly. She really was sorry now that she thought about everything that she and Talson had already done together and everything she had learned from him. She remembered what Sela had said about no one knowing the real Talson. Perhaps the real Talson was not the liar, manipulator and murderer that everyone seemed to know. There were no right or wrong sides. There was no right and wrong between Nelco and Talson, it was much more complicated than that.

"Don't be sorry, Kat," said Talson. "You just needed to have a chance to think about things. This is all very complicated. It doesn't seem fair when you consider all the time I spent earlier today staring at my ceiling trying to figure this out. I didn't give you any time to think."

"You knew I'd come back, didn't you?" said Kat.

"Not really," replied Talson casually. "I certainly hoped you would, and as John

Carl so astutely pointed out, I'm lucky you did."

Kat smiled. "I don't think you really hate each other."

"Think again," said Talson. "It's time to go see Nelco now." Talson rose, "You know the plan."

Kat nodded and stood up.

The door of the library was closed, and Talson stopped in front of it. Kat stood behind him, waiting. Slowly Talson reached out and pushed the door open. From inside the room Kat heard Nelco gasp in shock and something fall to the floor.

"Good evening, Nelco," said Talson so casually he might have been speaking to the ceiling again. He leaned against the doorframe, his posture was slouched and indifferent. Kat remembered how her father had called Talson 'Mr. Casual'. She was not sure that even the prospect of being killed was enough to make Talson sweat.

Kat peered over Talson's shoulder, and could see Nelco standing at the small table in the middle of the small room. The black photo album sat on the table in front of him, and the small picture frame he had dropped lay on the floor in front of him. Clearly Nelco had not expected Talson to walk in on him. As his initial shock faded, Nelco glared at Talson with an expression of the utmost loathing.

"There is quite a story to be told in those pictures," said Talson. His tone was light and almost friendly. "Nothing like taking some time to relive the good old days, don't you think?"

It seemed that Nelco could think of nothing to say. He merely stood completely still, glaring at Talson.

"The truth is in these pictures, Nelco," continued Talson in a more serious tone.

"Truth," said Nelco with a sneer, "you know nothing of the truth."

"Neither do you," said Talson with a half shrug. "Let me show you something."

Kat knew exactly what Talson was going to show Nelco. She felt scared.

You're going to see it, Kat. Nelco is going to try to block me with my own mind, but he won't be able to. Talson's thoughts were intense, and showed the true emotion behind his flat affectation. *Don't let anyone into your mind, even if you think it's me, and don't let yourself feel anything. See it, don't be part of it.*

The memory was playing in Kat's head once again, but this time she had the sensation that she was watching the scene from above, rather than acting out the scene from Barty's point of view. Kat could still see Nelco standing in the library, staring at Talson who was still in the doorway in front of her. The image of The Sharktooth Bar seemed to have appeared in the back of her mind.

Barty sat at a small table in the corner of the back room at the Sharktooth. He was waiting for Nelco. It was the same scene that Kat had experienced when she was at the bar with Talson except now she was not experiencing it, she was only a witness. Kat knew this was what Talson had meant when he had said 'see it, don't be part of it.'

The figures of Talson and Nelco and the library seemed to be fading from Kat's mind. She kept her eyes open, trying to focus on Talson's back, but it seemed to be getting cloudy, as the images of Barty and Nelco at the Sharktooth were growing clearer.

"Nelco, you came."

"Of course I came. What is it? What's going on?"

Kat clasped her hands together trying to focus on the room and herself in that room. She could feel Barty's cruel plan and his twisted lie. See it, don't feel it, she thought to herself as she closed her eyes, blocking out the library and the house so that she could concentrate on being a witness to the conversation between Nelco and Barty. She had to be a witness and only a witness.

"He's going to kill her, Nelco."

Stop it. I know what happens. I know what he said, and I know what you did to him.

I know you know what he said, but you need to know what he thought.

The lie burned like fire inside Kat's mind. She could hear Barty's thoughts and the knowledge of his true plan.

You should have known Barty never really cared, and I should have known too.

You are making me feel this Talson, it's not real. You can't lie to me anymore.

You have my power now, Nelco, why don't you use it to know for sure if it is a lie. You can see what Barty was doing, and what I wasn't doing. The power can show you the truth and then prove to you that it's true.

What truth?

The truth about why I did it, Nelco. Don't you want to know the truth about Julie and I? Don't you want to see who shot her? I can show you, Nelco. You know what I did, but I can show you how I did it, and why.

Don't listen to him.

What is going on?

I'm not Talson, Nelco. My mind exists even if I am gone. Talson is twisting my memories. He thinks he can show you that it was me and not him. He is trying to fool you into thinking he is innocent. You have to help me get out of this prison in Talson's mind. He is trying to change my memories to fit his agenda, but you can stop him.

How?

Use his power, now that you have it. You can use it to take my memories from him.

I can't, he'll block me.

Use the kid. She is not as strong as him, and he won't suppress the connection. That's his weakness. You get to her, you get to him.

And he hasn't realized any of this yet?

Fortunately for us he doesn't know, at least not yet. It is through Kat's mind that I am able to connect to you and be temporarily free from Talson's mind. I want you to have my memories. You were my only true friend. You deserve my mind. Talson betrayed me, he doesn't deserve me.

I have to kill him, Barty.

I can help you succeed. You will have the truth and Talson will no longer be able to lie to you, and you will be able to destroy him. I can help you as long as you take me from Talson. Just help me.

Of course I'll help you. Barlo, I just can't believe this is real; you're dead.

The power is amazingly real, Conner. Talson used to tell us what the power could do, but you never wanted to believe it. You know I've always been the one who had to tell you about the things you never wanted to believe.

Okay, I know. I believe you now. What do I have to do?

You need direct eye contact with the girl.

The library seemed to become clearer before Kat's eyes. Nelco was advancing toward her. Talson didn't stop him, and to Kat's horror, he stepped aside as Nelco approached her. Before Kat could move, Nelco looked directly into Kat's eyes.

Kat didn't understand what was happening. The plan had been for her to enter Nelco's mind so that Talson could show Nelco what had happened to Julie, but it had gone wrong. Nelco was about to enter Kat's mind and she could not stop him. Talson had expressed confidence that Kat would be able to resist Nelco, but Kat realized as soon as Nelco looked at her she knew she could not prevent him from entering her mind. Nelco's eyes looked darker, as if someone else were looking through him. Talson had turned now, and was looking at Kat.

Talson, what's happening?

He can't help you, and you can't help him.

Nelco, you wouldn't. I know you wouldn't.

You're right Talson, he won't, he never could, but I can and I will.

Suddenly Kat's mind was flooded with Barty Louis' thoughts.

Nelco, that fool, he went for everything so easily. Now I can do it, and poor Talson will take the blame forever. No one deserved that hell more than him. Julie would always side with Talson. She was his perfect shadow. It was disgusting, she deserved to die. No one would ever suspect this, why would they? I care too much about everyone to do something like this. But everyone knows Talson has never cared, even when he pretended to. No one will support Talson after this. I will be the one they look to for leadership. That will be the end of Lord Talson the super human, super talent, super genius, handsome, athletic mind reader. He was so clever, so casual, so modest and so classy. Now his life was about to come crashing down, and all the fools who only saw the pretty side of him would know the truth. All the innocent people he killed with his evil power would have justice, and all his followers would see him as the cruel, low, and selfish person that he truly was. They would see him, Barty Louis, as the man who had had the strength to stand up to Talson. If one more person had to die in order to bring Talson down then that was how it had to be. Julie would never go against Talson and she would make sure no one else did. But with her gone, there might be a chance that Talson's followers will all turn against him, and perhaps then they could finish him off completely. They might even think he deserved to die after what he did to Julie. Nelco would certainly want Talson dead for killing the woman he loved. It was all going to be so easy, so perfect.

The night had arrived. Even Romez had been fooled. Poor Romez, he would undoubtedly be arrested and go to jail. But after he got out, even he would go against Talson, thinking he had set up the bust. In the end even Roco, Talson's right-hand man, would go against him. That would serve Talson right.

The back room of the Sharktooth was crowded with gamblers. Barty approached Roco, pushing his way through the crowd. "Good business tonight, huh Romez?"

"Yeah, it's awesome, tonight even old Captain John Carl is here. I thought he'd never come back after our little joke last week, but I must say he took it quite well."

"Oh, don't worry about that, he actually thought it was funny, and I gave him the money he lost. It was just a joke between captain and mate, no big thing."

"As long as he's not mad," said Roco, "I don't want him on my bad side."

"He's not mad. Like I said, he thought it was funny."

"You okay, mate? You look a little nervous or something."

Damn Roco, he notices everything. "No, I'm fine," said Barty quickly.

"You're not still worried about—"

"Well, yeah I guess I still am worried."

"Don't be. You're crazy to think he would do that. She is a Silver Shadow and Talson loves her. He has no motive. Don't sweat it, mate."

Don't sweat it, huh? You have no idea how bad you're going to be sweating it when your bar gets busted tonight.

Julie entered the back room. The gun pressed against the inside of Barty's wrist, hidden under the sleeve of his jacket. Barty sat down beside Julie at the blackjack table.

Then the door of the back room burst open and Larry was there, yelling to warn everyone. Then the police officers ran in, and Larry was up against the wall being cuffed by an officer. Chaos broke out in the bar as three police officers managed to restrain Roco and get him outside.

"Barlo, we have to run," Julie said in panic. "We can't afford to get caught."

"Don't worry, we won't get caught," said Barty, not moving from the table.

It happened in an instant. Barty drew the gun and pulled the trigger in one motion. The shot echoed through Kat's ears as Julie fell to the floor next to the table. Her face registered complete shock. Barty was running for the back exit and was quickly lost in the crowd. Kat had one last look at Julie bleeding on the floor below the table before everything in her mind went blank.

The sound of the gunshot echoed over and over. Kat felt her mind being pulled away from Barty and Nelco. She could no longer see or feel anything. Her mind seemed frozen. Then there was pain, as if her mind was being torn away from the scene at the Sharktooth. Then she realized the pain she was feeling was Nelco's, and she knew he was seeing the shooting over and over in his head.

Stop, stop.

Kat could see the library around her, but she had no thoughts. She could not think of who she was or what was happening. Everything was blank.

C H A P T E R   2 2

UNNECESSARY RISKS

Kat's first thought was that she needed to move. She could feel that she was lying down and that she was uncomfortable. She was lying on her stomach and her right hand was trapped under her body. She tried to move it but her muscles did not obey. It was as if her mind could not reach her body. She struggled to move or just to open her eyes. Finally she managed, with great effort, to roll over and open her eyes.

She was looking up at a rough wood ceiling. The room was very dark except for a narrow beam of silver light coming from across the room, illuminating the ceiling. Kat sat up slowly, looking across the room for the source of the light. As her eyes adjusted to the strange light, she realized she was in a small bedroom that she had never been in before.

"You alright, Kat?"

Kat jumped in surprise at the voice. Then she realized that the light was coming from a chair across the room where Talson sat, holding a small silver light. Kat felt completely disoriented. "Where are we?" she whispered. "What time is it? What happened?"

"We're in my bedroom, it's 9:30, and we succeeded."

"Wow, it's been like three and a half hours. How did we succeed?" Kat was utterly confused. "I thought we failed, I mean I failed."

"No, you did not fail, Kat, and neither did I."

"But what about the plan?"

"Yeah, I changed it," said Talson casually. "I'm sorry, but I really couldn't risk telling you."

"You changed it, just like that?" said Kat incredulously. "What was wrong with the first plan?"

"Nothing, I just thought this one was better. Once we got down to the library and I saw what the situation was, this plan seemed a lot more interesting than my initial plan, so I went for it. I just made it up as I went along, honestly."

"And did it work?"

"It worked phenomenally." Talson actually sounded happy.

"How? I don't get it. Nelco used me, so did Barty."

"No, Kat, I used you. I'm sorry for having to do that without telling you, but there wasn't any other way to do it."

"What are you talking about?" asked Kat. "Barty controlled me, and made me give power to Nelco. Then he made me see all that stuff and hear his thoughts from before he killed Julie."

"No, Kat, I made you give power to Nelco, and I made you see that stuff."

"What?" Kat was appalled and confused. "That's not what happened. Barty was telling Nelco how to kill you, and how he needed to use me. He told Nelco you were impersonating him and making and giving him false memories. Nelco believed his lies, just like he did before. Barty said Nelco could get power through me, and he did. He lied to Nelco again. I couldn't stop him, I'm sorry."

"Don't be sorry, Kat," said Talson. "Barty didn't lie to Nelco, I lied to Nelco while fooling him into thinking I was Barty."

Kat's mouth fell open slightly. "That was you? I thought it was Barty, and that you lost control."

"That was the goal," said Talson. "Nelco thought the same thing. It is important to recognize who is in your head, so that you can't be fooled like that."

"It's so hard to tell," muttered Kat. She had found that in her mind everyone sounded almost the same. The only way she could tell people apart was if she knew what they were likely to be thinking about.

"Yes, it is hard," agreed Talson. "You can't recognize people by how they talk, you have to recognize them by how they think. When you get more experienced you will learn to tell people's thoughts apart just as easily as their voices. I know Nelco is not anywhere near that stage, that's why my plan was effective."

"So what happened to me?" asked Kat. "I thought you said I would be able to block Nelco."

"You did block Nelco," said Talson, fiddling the light in his fingers, "you just couldn't block me."

"Wasn't Barty using me to talk to Nelco?" asked Kat.

"No, Barty can't do that, he's dead."

"So then Nelco just thought he could?"

"Yes, as I've told you before, Nelco doesn't know very much about the power." Talson sounded bored again. "He never really listened when I told him, Barty and Roco about it. Nelco would like to think Barty is still alive and independent, but Barty's mind only exists within my mind. I am the only one who can control his thoughts."

"Yeah, but didn't you lose control of the memories again tonight? Isn't that why Barty was able to connect to Nelco and tell him how to use his power to get inside my head? He said he was using me to get to Nelco."

"Think about that for a moment, Kat," said Talson. "Think about how Barty would be able to enter your mind and then connect to Nelco."

Kat paused. "He used the connection between you and me," she said slowly. "That's how he got from your mind to my mind."

"Kat, that's not possible," said Talson. "In order to do that Barty would have to have the power, and more importantly he'd have to be alive. Dead minds can't just go have conversations by themselves. The world's not that scary."

"So it wasn't really him?"

"No," said Talson. "Like I said, it was me."

"You told Nelco to use me to kill you?" said Kat in sudden outrage. "Why would you do that?"

"I did it because I knew that once Nelco was in your head I would have full control over his mind. Once I had control I was able to make him see everything I wanted him to see."

"Did you tell Nelco that you were trying to twist Barty's memories to further your agenda, or whatever?" asked Kat.

"Or whatever, yes I did tell him something like that. Sounds like something I would do, doesn't it?"

"Screw with someone's mind for your own gain, absolutely," muttered Kat.

"You've been spending too much time with Romez," said Talson with a slight smile.

"What about the part where you told Nelco that our connection was your weakness, is that true?"

"Of course not, it's our strength."

"So you lied to Nelco again, that's not the way he can kill you?"

"I'm getting quite good at it, if I do say so myself," said Talson. "Don't forget that dealing with Nelco requires a lot of lying. Just ask Barty."

Kat was somewhat amused by Talson's ability to turn one of the most serious situations she could ever imagine into something almost funny. "Yeah, you are getting good at it," she said with a small smile. "I was definitely fooled."

"Well, thank you," said Talson smiling. "Like I said, I really had no intention of doing that, but when Nelco used my own power to block me when I tried to enter his mind, I thought I'd take a leaf out of Barty's book and totally fool him in order to, like you said, further my agenda, or whatever."

They both laughed.

Kat wasn't quite sure why she was laughing, and felt somewhat guilty for it. "You just like messing with people's heads don't you?"

"Like you don't," said Talson.

"Why are we laughing? This is serious."

"Everything is serious, Kat," said Talson. "Life doesn't stop being serious just because you laugh."

"I thought we failed," said Kat after a moment's pause. "It felt like we failed, and Nelco thinks we did, but really we succeeded."

"Yes, well sometimes success can feel like failure. I feel like there was a major problem with that plan even though it worked very effectively."

"What problem?"

"I had to use you as a middle man, and I don't like having to do that."

"Yeah, well, better a middle man for you than for Nelco," shrugged Kat. "The only thing I see wrong with it is that even though Nelco saw the truth about what happened, he doesn't believe it because you told him it wasn't the true memory."

Talson nodded. "I know, but at least he's seen it, even if I lied to him about it."

"Do you think you'll ever stop lying to him?"

Talson turned the little light over several times in his hands. "I don't know," he said with a sly smile. "I doubt it."

"Where is he now?"

"I believe he is currently lying unconscious on the floor of the library."

"He's still here?" said Kat, surprised. "It's been hours, what if he wakes up?"

"Well, that was a pretty serious three way connection, and I released it very quickly. Sufficient to say I wasn't very gentle with Nelco, so he might be out for a while."

"So you're just going to leave him there?"

"Yes," said Talson without elaborating.

Kat looked at him. "So what do you think he'll do when he does wake up?"

Talson shrugged. "Whatever it is, I'll know and I'll act accordingly."

"So what happens now?" asked Kat.

"Well, I'm not sure, but I do know that even if I have Nelco fooled right now, this is not over. Nelco is still going to try to do some serious damage, not just to me, but to all of us, including your friend Tina. Plus, we still could have problems where Tracy is concerned."

"But Nelco thinks he succeeded somehow, doesn't he?"

"If I had to guess, I'd say that Nelco will be somewhat confused about what happened. He will think he succeeded in helping Barty to get out of my mind and into his, however he will probably still be worried that I have twisted Barty's memories."

"So he's still going to try to kill you?"

"Absolutely," said Talson. "Barty told him how to do it, so you know he's going to try it as long as Barty keeps telling him how to proceed. And now that Barty is in Nelco's head, he will certainly have control over Nelco's course of action."

"You mean as long as you keep telling him, right?"

"Well, of course," said Talson.

"So you didn't release your connection to Nelco's mind?"

"No, I only released the connection between you and him. The connection between him and me remains. However, Nelco thinks that it is Barty in his head, and technically he's right. He just doesn't know that being connected to Barty means being connected to me. Nelco thinks that Barty is going to tell him how to destroy my mind, but really I am going to tell him how to destroy it, and—"Talson paused. It was as if he was asking Kat to finish his thought.

"And the only part you're going to show him how to destroy is Barty's mind," Kat finished.

"Exactly," said Talson. "I'm really glad you understand the power as well as you do."

Kat shrugged. "I'm starting to learn how people think, even maybe how you think."

Talson smiled and nodded slightly.

There was silence between them for a moment. Talson was playing with the light again and watching the light dance on the ceiling. Kat followed the light with her eyes. It was almost hypnotic.

"He's leaving," Talson said quietly after a few minutes.

"I can't see what he's doing in my mind anymore," said Kat. She had been expecting that she would see where Nelco was going just as she had done before.

"I told you before, you no longer have a connection to Nelco, I'm blocking it."

"Why?"

"I wouldn't be able to fool Nelco if you were in his head. He would see what you and I were doing. We would have to continue to not look at each other, and I know that would never work. Besides, you don't want to see what he's seeing anyway."

"So you're going to just block me so I can't see what's going on with Nelco? He is going after Tina, and I came back and helped you. After all that, you're not even going to let me see what he's doing?"

"You still aren't sure that you did the right thing coming back," Talson's voice was expressionless.

Kat looked directly at Talson. "No, I'm sure."

"Don't look directly at someone when you lie to them," said Talson. "People always feel suspicious if you do that."

"Are you teaching me a lesson in lying or are you calling me a liar?" asked Kat angrily.

Talson shrugged. "Both."

"Fine," conceded Kat. "I'm not sure if I want to be here or not, okay?"

"Okay, figure it out," said Talson. "Do you or do you not want to be here?"

"You knew," muttered Kat.

"Knew what?"

"You knew that I still wasn't sure if I wanted to be here even though I came back. That's why you changed the plan and didn't tell me. You knew I couldn't choose what I wanted to do, so you gave me no choice at all." Kat was surprised to find that there was no anger in her voice, she was simply stating the facts that she knew were true.

"Do you think I am like you, Kat?"

"What do you mean by that?" asked Kat coolly.

"That I don't trust you. You think because you don't trust me that I don't trust you, but I really do."

"I think you're lying," said Kat. This time there was a hint of anger in her voice. Kat stood up, realizing that she had been lying in Talson's bed.

Talson did not answer her or make any move. He just sat, fiddling with the light and following the beam with his strange yellow eyes.

"You used me."

"Really?" said Talson sarcastically. "I had no idea." There was a sneer in his voice that Kat had never heard before. Kat wasn't sure why, but his sarcastic tone, as well as surprising her, seemed to knock all the anger and aggression out of her. She just stood next to the bed, staring at Talson. She was waiting for Talson to say something to make up for his sneering comment, but he said nothing.

Kat stood by the bed, she felt heavy and sluggish as if her brain could not give her limbs the signal to move. She couldn't think of what to say anymore, and she couldn't remember what she was hoping Talson would say. She wanted to leave, but her body didn't seem to be getting the message. Nelco was gone, but obviously Talson didn't care about following him. Kat took a step backward and sank back into Talson's bed.

Talson reached over the wall behind him and turned on a lamp that stood in the corner of the room. Kat blinked as her eyes adjusted to the sudden blaze of light. Kat looked around the room, realizing that Talson's bedroom was probably the room next to his office. It was not a large room, and like his office it was very simply furnished. The bed on which Kat was sitting took up most of the room. There was a small bedside table, a dresser, and a closet. The floor was covered with a nondescript colored carpet that had no specific pattern. The only thing on the bedside table was a clock that seemed to be ticking quite loudly in the silence. Kat lay down on the bed and let her gaze wander upward to the ceiling. There was nothing to see but bare walls, bare carpet, and a blank ceiling. There was nothing to say, nothing to do, nothing to think.

She was standing in a dark hallway looking around for a light. She heard footsteps behind her, and then the beam of a flashlight blinded her. She froze in the middle of the hallway, knowing she had been caught.

"What the hell?" A man's voice spoke from the other side of the blinding light. "Tracy Louis, what the hell are you doing in here?" Slowly the man lowered the light so that she could see his face.

"How do you know me? Who are you?" She looked around frantically, searching for a possible means of escape.

"You first."

"Where are you hiding her?"

The man frowned. "What the hell are you talking about?"

"You know exactly what I'm talking about," said Tracy. She sounded very close

to losing her temper. "You are hiding my daughter somewhere in this house."

"Why do you even care?" A second man had entered the room.

"She's my daughter, how could I not care?" yelled Tracy.

"You tell us," replied the man.

"Just give her to me," said Tracy.

"She isn't here," said the man, casually leaning against the wall.

"Then tell me where she is."

"Tell us where Nelson is," said the first man.

"I don't know what you're talking about," said Tracy, taking a step back from the two men.

"Let's try that again," he said. "Where is Conner Nelson?"

"I, I don't know," stuttered Tracy.

The man advanced toward Tracy. "Cut the crap, Louis, where's Nelson?"

"Who are you? How do you know me?" Tracy sounded scared now.

"Call me Tiro. This is Milro. For the last time, where is Conner Nelson?"

"Why does it matter?"Tracy asked, as she slowly backed away from the two intimidating men.

Tiro grabbed a handful of Tracy's shirt and pushed her against the wall, using his chained hand. "Believe me, it matters."

"Fine, he's going to the Sharktooth," said Tracy. She was trembling now.

Tiro released her. "What's he going there for?"

"Nothing, to have a drink I suppose," she muttered nervously.

Tiro pushed Tracy back against the wall. "No lies, Louis."

"Give me my daughter," cried Tracy. "Why did you kidnap her? Why do you need her?"

"Why do you need her?" asked Milro coldly.

"How can you even—"Tracy began in outrage.

"Shut up," said Tiro. "Why's Nelson going to the bar?"

"Give me my daughter, and I'll tell you whatever you want to know."

"No deal," said Tiro.

"You tell us first, then we'll tell you where she is," said Milro.

"Fine," said Tracy, her voice still shaking. "Conner went to the bar to talk to the bartender, Larry. He thinks that Larry can help him accomplish his goal."

"How is Larry going to help?" demanded Tiro.

"Please, I don't know," said Tracy. "He didn't tell me. Just tell me where my daughter is."

"She not here, she's at our headquarters," said Tiro."Now get the hell out of here." He shoved Tracy toward the door.

"Kat, get up."

Kat awoke immediately, although the voice was not loud. She opened her eyes to see nothing but a blank stretch of wood ceiling. Remembering where she was, she sat up very quickly. Talson was still sitting in his chair, but he was looking directly at her.

"I just saw—"

"I know," interrupted Talson. "We need to follow Nelco to the Sharktooth, but first I'm going to give Larry a heads up." Talson pulled a cell phone out of his jacket pocket. "Larry," he said, "I need you to close the bar now. Get everyone out, and leave the back door unlocked. Sela will call you with more instructions later. I'm going to need you to block everything, no mistakes." He put the phone back in his pocket. "Nelco is going to the Sharktooth to bargain with Larry. I suppose since John Carl won't help him, he's going to try to use Larry to get into my mind. But we are going to completely mess up Nelco's plan."

"So you and Larry have a connection?" Kat asked.

"Had," corrected Talson.

"Well, if the connection doesn't exist anymore, then Nelco can't use Larry, right?"

"That's true, but Nelco doesn't know that," said Talson. "I am not going to inform Nelco that the connection no longer exists, just like I didn't inform him that a transfer with John Carl would not be successful."

"So what is the mistake you were talking about with Larry?"

"Larry and I can't afford to allow a connection to exist between us," said Talson.

"Is that why Larry wouldn't look at you?" asked Kat.

"No, that's not why," said Talson, "but it's a good excuse."

"Then why won't he look at you?"

Talson shrugged. "A number of unimportant reasons."

"Will Larry be in danger if Nelco uses him to get to you?"

"Yes, he would probably die," said Talson expressionlessly.

"You don't sound too concerned," said Kat frowning.

"Well Kat, we don't like each other," said Talson.

"Then why does he help you? He does everything you ask him to do."

"He thinks he has to," said Talson still in an expressionless voice.

"My father said Larry isn't a good person," said Kat. "What does he mean by that?"

Talson shrugged. "Your father has good reasons for saying that, but it doesn't really matter at this point. It's not about whether Larry or Nelco or John Carl or me or anyone is a so-called 'good person'. It just matters what we are going to choose to do, and what we are going to choose not to do."

There was silence for a moment. "Where is Tina right now?" asked Kat finally. "Is she really at Headquarters?"

"No, she's still at Milro's house."

"So Tiro was lying to Tracy, then?"

"I think Tiro wasn't technically lying," said Talson. "I think Sela is at Headquarters, and she is, after all, Tracy's daughter. It's like Tiro to do something like that."

"It's all my fault if Tina gets hurt," muttered Kat. "I have to help her now. I want to tell her the truth."

"I think you have to tell her the truth," said Talson softly. "You are probably the only one she will believe."

Suddenly there were three sharp knocks on the door of Talson's bedroom.

"Come in, Romez," said Talson.

Roco looked from Talson sitting in the chair to Kat on the bed. "What the hell is going on now?" he asked, closing the door behind him.

"Nelco is on his way to the Sharktooth, but I expect he'll wait to see if he gets word from Tracy. We have some time, but I want to get there before he does."

"What is he hoping to accomplish?" asked Roco.

"He wants to make a deal with Larry," said Talson.

"That can't be good.".

"Where's Sela?" asked Talson.

"Headquarters, why?"

"Because I need her," replied Talson without elaborating. "Kat, you go with Roco to the Sharktooth. I will meet you there with Sela."

"But I thought Tina needed to know the truth," said Kat.

"She does, but right now we can't afford to take an unnecessary risk where Tina is concerned." Talson grabbed his coat and disappeared out the door and down the staircase.

So you're still not thinking of working for Nelco, are you?

Get out.

Look who's using their power.

I'm talking to you, that's it.

Just like old times.

Shut up.

It never changes, does it?

No. What do you want?

I wanted to thank you. I wasn't expecting Nelco to pull off a transfer.

You think I was?

Didn't you feel it? How does that happen without you noticing?

I wasn't thinking about it. I never think about the power, I don't care about it.

Well, maybe you'll start caring now that Nelco's trying to make you use it.

So I was right.

Yeah, you were.

I bet it kills you to admit that.

Just a little bit.

Who are you going to let die for you this time?

No one, if I can help it.

But you probably can't help it, can you? You never cared if anyone died for you before, why now?

I have always cared about who died. That's the only reason I could ever stop

killing.

You didn't care when you killed Barty.

I cared more about that than anything else. It shouldn't have ended the way it did, John Carl.

It was always going to end that way, Talson.

According to you, it never should have got this far. Not even close.

Why are you doing this, Talson? Talking to me only makes it easier for him to get more of your power from me. He got to your mind through mine.

You know me, John Carl. I don't take unnecessary risks without a reason.

That means the same thing.

You know how I think.

I don't know why you're doing it. Why take the risk?

That's obvious, either it's a necessary risk or I have a reason.

C H A P T E R   2 3

FACING THE TRUTH

Larry leaned his elbows on the bar, his eyes on the front door. The last of his customers had left and he was alone in the bar. It was a shame, he thought, tonight could have been a good night for business, but his customers certainly didn't appreciate being booted out of the bar by nine o'clock. Larry trusted that he would not have been asked to close if it wasn't important, but nevertheless, he still wasn't happy about it. He was beginning to feel apprehensive, he couldn't help thinking that they could be in for a repeat of the night fourteen years previous. Larry had heard the back door open five minutes earlier, and he knew three people were now waiting in the back room. They were waiting for something, but Larry wasn't sure what.

Suddenly there was a soft knock on the front door of the bar. Larry didn't flinch, he stood up very slowly and made his way toward the door. Larry peered through the blind in the front window closest to the door. Two men stood at the door. Larry recognized them as the two sailors from Captain John Carl's crew who had come in the bar a few days previously.

"Bar's closed, guys," said Larry opening the door a crack, and looking up and down the street to make sure no one was watching. When he was sure no one was watching them, he stepped back to let Sono and Browen into the bar.

"So, do you two have any idea why you're here?" asked Larry as he closed the door behind them.

"Not really," said Sono.

"You better not be here to sweat me for information again," said Larry.

"Well, not unless you want to fill us in," said Browen. "We got a note from the captain saying to meet him here. Where is he, and why are you closed?"

Larry walked slowly back to his position behind the bar. "If I knew anything I'd tell you, but I really have no idea why I'm closed."

"So what happens now?" asked Sono.

Larry shrugged. "You guys want a drink while you wait for your captain?"

A few minutes later there was another knock on the front door. Again Larry moved slowly to the window and looked outside. "The bar's closed," he said again, as he pulled open the front door. When he was satisfied that no one was watching, he pulled the door open slightly wider and let Captain John Carl into the bar.

"Why are you closed?" asked John Carl.

"Because these days I follow orders, Captain," said Larry. He did not look at John Carl, he simply limped back across the room and sat behind the bar. "You want a drink, Captain?"

"On the house?" asked John Carl, his eyes on Sono and Browen.

"You wish," said Larry. "You know my rules, nothing's free."

"Fine," said John Carl. He sat down beside Sono and Browen. "What do you guys want?" he asked.

"What do you mean?" asked Sono. "What do you want? You're the one who wanted to meet us here."

"What about the message you left on my phone?" John Carl pulled his cell phone out of his pocket.

"I didn't call you," said Sono.

"That's your number isn't?" John Carl held the phone in front of Sono. "You left me a message."

"Play it," said Sono.

"Hey Cap, meet me at the Sharktooth at nine," said John Carl, quoting the message. "That's what you said, you remember now?"

Sono grabbed the phone from John Carl and listened for a moment. "That's my number, but that's not me on that message."

John Carl looked at Browen.

"It's not me either," he said defensively

"Listen, you guys," said John Carl, "if this is a joke, it's not all that funny."

"This is what you left on the windshield of my car," said Sono, pulling a slip of paper out of his pocket.

"That's not my handwriting," said John Carl. "Larry, what the hell is this?"

"Something weird happens and you think I did it?" Larry shook his head. "Does it sound like me on that message?"

"No, but I bet you know who it is," said Sono.

"I don't," said Larry coolly. "You know I could have sold a lot more than three drinks tonight. If I had set this up, do you really think I would have picked nine o'clock on a Friday night?"

"Fine, you didn't set this up, I'll give you that," said John Carl reluctantly. "Tell me who did."

"You hacked his phone?" Roco looked at Sela. Sela and Talson had just entered the back room of the Sharktooth where Kat, Roco and Milro were already listening in on the conversation at the bar over an intercom.

"Better than a note on the windshield, Romez," said Sela with a laugh.

"Who is it on the message?" asked Roco.

"Me," said Sela.

"What? How the hell—?" began Roco.

"Technology, baby," said Sela with a smirk. "Voice alteration."

"Why are Sono and Browen here?" asked Milro.

"Because I wanted them to be," said Sela.

"Why them and not Tina?" asked Kat, looking at Talson. "She has more right to the truth than they do. Sela and I had a deal with her, we said we'd show her the truth if she came with us."

"I know," said Talson, "but right now Tina is in danger of being used by Nelco as a sort of mental shield so he can survive killing me. Having her here is too risky."

"What does Nelco have against Tina?" asked Kat. "She didn't do anything."

"She's Barty's daughter, Kat," said Sela. "That's more than enough to get her killed."

"It's my fault if something happens to her," said Kat again.

"No it's not, Kat," said Roco. "It was always going to end this way. Nelco has to face the truth or kill the truth, and he's choosing to kill it."

"Where is Nelco?" asked Milro.

"He'll be here," said Talson. "I suspect he is still trying to figure out what to do about Tina's escape."

"Tracy won't be happy with him," said Sela.

"He won't be happy with her," said Milro. "She came to my place to get Tina back, Nelco sent her."

"Yeah, but he knew Tracy wouldn't get Tina from us," said Sela. "I think he was hoping we'd keep Tracy captive too."

"I'm sure he was surprised that we didn't," said Talson.

"Do you think Nelco will really believe Tina is at Headquarters?" asked Milro.

"He might," said Roco, "but I doubt he would go there. Nelco's too chicken to do that."

There was a pause. Sono, Browen and John Carl had stopped talking at the bar as well.

"Why is my dad here?" asked Kat.

"Because he's part of this," said Talson. "Nelco wants him to help kill me."

Kat couldn't understand why Talson wanted her father present for a conversation with Nelco. He had refused to help Nelco once, but it seemed that Talson was just giving him a chance to change his mind.

There was yet another knock on the front door of The Sharktooth Bar.

"Are we going to find out what's going on now?" asked Browen.

"Who is it?" Sono asked.

Larry peered through the blinds yet again. "Conner Nelson," he said quietly.

John Carl stood up quickly. "You're not letting him in here, are you?"

"If I had the choice I might not," said Larry. He sounded resigned, as if he had known what would happen the entire time.

"What do you mean, you don't have a choice?" asked John Carl in apparent outrage. "What happened to 'my bar, my rules'?"

"It was always going to happen this way, John Carl," said Larry. "I shouldn't have to tell you that."

"You're taking orders from Talson, that's the only reason it has to be this way," John Carl retorted. "Why are you doing it? Because you think if you let him control you it will make up for the things you've done? You know how that will end, Larry, I shouldn't have to tell you."

Larry did not reply. He simply pulled open the door. "The bar's closed, sir."

"Why?" Nelco sounded angry. "It's only 9:30, what's your problem?"

"Evidently, you're my problem," said Larry coolly.

"I need to talk to you," demanded Nelco.

"So do a few other people," said Larry. "Get in here."

Nelco stepped over the threshold, but stopped dead when he saw Sono, Browen and John Carl sitting at the bar. "I thought you said you were closed," he stammered, looking at Larry.

"These guys don't exactly count as customers," said Larry. "What do you want to talk to me about?"

"Good evening, Conner," John Carl interrupted. "Let me guess, you got some bogus message telling you to come here."

"What the heck are you talking about, Thomason?"

"Actually he got a bogus message from Tracy saying she found Tina, and to wait for her," said Sela with a sly smile.

"What kind of a set up is this, Larry?" John Carl sounded suspicious.

"A weird one," said Larry.

"Care to tell us what the hell is going on, Nelson?" said John Carl.

"He'd love to but he doesn't have a clue," muttered Roco.

"You want to know what's going on? Well in that case, you might be interested to know that I discovered the remains of Barton's mind inside Talson's mind," said Nelco. "I have succeeded in capturing his mind, so I now have the benefit of his memories, and Talson can no longer alter them."

"How was he altering them?" asked John Carl indifferently.

"Well, as you can imagine he was trying to make me believe that Barty was guilty of Talson's crimes. Of course, you know Talson, always manipulating people's thoughts to make himself look innocent."

"How did this make him look innocent?" John Carl suddenly sounded interested.

"It's a bunch of crap, John Carl," said Nelco. "Like I said, it's so typical of Talson to screw with people's thoughts."

"Yeah, he tends to do that," said John Carl slowly. He seemed to be thinking very hard now.

"What the hell was that?" asked Roco, looking sideways at Talson. Talson was smiling slightly. "We've got him," he said quietly.

"So, Larry," Nelco's tone was conversational, "I had the great pleasure of witnessing your arrest, thanks to Talson."

"Lucky you," said Larry with the utmost sarcasm. "I don't suppose you happened to notice the event that took place at the table right in front of you at the same time."

"Of course, you always have to remind me of the murder," said Nelco. "Do you just enjoy reminding people of the things that have hurt them the most?"

"Yes, I enjoy it quite a lot," said Larry with mock kindness. "One question, Nelco," he added. "Do you really not know what happened that night or do you just pretend not to because you like living in denial?"

"He's good," muttered Roco. "I swear Larry is brutal if he doesn't like you."

"Tell me about it," muttered Talson.

"The bust was a set up, Nelco, I trust you know that much," Larry continued more seriously.

"Kindly set up by John Carl here, yes I know," said Nelco, his voice full of contempt. "You are responsible for what happened that night, Thomason."

"I'm beginning to think I'm a lot less responsible than I thought I was," said John Carl. "Ramirez cheated me, but it didn't really matter to me that much,"

"Why did you go to the cops if it didn't matter?" asked Larry, coldly.

"Who cares why?" snapped John Carl. He sounded upset now.

"Hey, I went to jail for a long time, so I care" said Larry forcefully. "Just tell me something, why did you bust this place?"

There was a long silence.

"Because Barty told me to," said John Carl quietly. "But if you think that's justification for killing him, you're even crueler than I thought."

"Do you even remember what happened on the night of the bust?" said Larry

impatiently. "The bust doesn't matter, it never mattered."

"The murder, I know," said John Carl, "but what did Julie Operman's death have to do with the bust?"

"Nothing," said Nelco sharply.

"Everything," said a much softer voice at the back door.

"Talson, I knew this was you." John Carl did not even turn to face the back door where Talson, Kat, Sela, Roco, and Milro now stood.

Nelco whirled around to glare at Talson. His face was set, angry, and stubborn. Talson stared back at Nelco with a sort of passive indifference as if he were looking through a dirty window at an uninteresting scene. There was no emotion on his face, and Kat doubted that there were any thoughts in his mind at that moment.

Larry leaned on the bar, looking down at the counter. He did not look at Talson or anyone else in the room. John Carl, too, had kept his eyes down when Talson had entered the bar, but now he raised his head and looked directly at Talson. Kat stared at her father, then at Talson. Talson no longer looked indifferent, but Kat wasn't sure how to describe his expression. Her father did not have the expression of hatred that Kat had expected. His expression seemed unsure and questioning, but Talson's eyes offered no answers.

"Tell me, Talson," said John Carl softly. It seemed to cost him a great effort, and he did not finish the statement out loud.

Talson looked away from John Carl. He walked slowly behind the bar and leaned

on the counter. "Nelco could explain better than I." Talson looked across the counter at Nelco, who still stood apparently immobile halfway between the front door and the counter.

"You killed her," said Nelco his voice shook slightly. "You explain."

"Why did that woman have to die?" asked John Carl. "Who was she?"

"She was one of us," said Talson.

"One of yours, you mean." Anger had returned to John Carl's voice. "Did she

disappoint you, Talson? Is that why you killed her?"

"The only time she ever disappointed me was when she refused to say who killed her. I understand why she didn't, but I have always wished she had."

"You're a liar, Talson," said Nelco. "You knew she'd never rat you out,

even if she was dying. You knew she'd always be too afraid to say it was you who shot her."

"You know I didn't kill her, Conner," said Talson softly. Perhaps it was because Talson had called Nelco by his first name, or perhaps it was just his tone, but Nelco suddenly looked much more afraid.

"Barty knew you were going to kill her and I didn't believe him," said Nelco. There was desperation in his voice now. "Barty knew it was you, so you killed him too."

"It's a nice theory, Nelco," said Talson almost smiling now. "But I openly admit to killing Barty, so why would I lie about Julie?"

John Carl glared hard at Talson leaning against the bar. He still looked angry, and confused.

"Because you loved her," said Nelco more forcefully.

"You've got good answers for everything," said Talson. "Everything except this. Larry, you still have the tape, don't you?"

"Of course," said Larry. "Nelco can have the great pleasure of watching me get arrested yet again." He disappeared into the back room and returned a moment later with an old-looking videotape in his hand.

"I may be a liar, Nelco, but that tape certainly isn't," said Talson.

Sela walked past Nelco and sat down at the bar. For a moment she glanced at Sono and Browen who seemed frozen with shock, then she looked back at Larry. Kat looked at him too. It scared Kat that she didn't understand Larry at all. His mind seemed blank, empty, dead. Kat took a deep breath and sat down beside Sela.

Roco moved over to stand beside Talson behind the bar. He smirked slightly at Nelco. "Ready to see the Sharktooth's finest in surveillance technology?"

Larry stood on a barstool to reach the television above the bar. "Too bad it's in black and white, eh Romez?" He smiled slightly as he reached up to put the tape in the VCR.

Suddenly Nelco leapt over the bar, sending glasses crashing to the floor. He grabbed the legs of the stool Larry was standing on and sent it tumbling to the ground. Larry toppled sideways off the fallen stool onto the floor. Nelco snatched the tape from the floor and made for the back door, but Roco beat him to it. He grabbed Nelco by the front of his shirt and slammed him against the counter, attempting to pry the tape from Nelco's grasp. "Can't face the truth, Nelson?"

"I don't need to see it," yelled Nelco. He swung his elbow at Roco's face, but Roco ducked.

"I need to see it," said John Carl. Like everyone else he had jumped to his feet when Nelco had made for the tape. Only Talson had remained motionless. He still stood, his elbows on the bar, completely unfazed. He made no move to help Larry who had fallen to the floor right behind him. The bartender slowly pulled himself up. He seemed far away. His expression was one of sadness. Kat had the impression that despite the intensity of the current situation, Larry's thoughts were elsewhere.

"Why do you need to see it, John Carl?" Nelco fidgeted with the tape in his hand. "Why do you care?"

"Why don't you?" asked John Carl. There was intensity on his face, and his eyes seemed to burn momentarily.

"It's all lies, John Carl," said Nelco, "you know that. It's just like the memories."

"I'll decide what's a lie and what's true after I've seen it, Nelson," said John Carl. "And just for the record, you can't alter a dead person's memories no matter how much power you have. That was a lie you told me before, to get me on your side."

"So now you're siding with Talson," said Nelco. A strange calm seemed to have suddenly come over him. He reached into his pocket and pulled out a lighter. Roco knocked it out of his hands, but it was too late. The tape had already curled into flames. Nelco sneered as he let the ruined video fall to the floor.

There was shocked silence as everyone in the room stared at the burnt tape on the floor.

"You're a coward, Nelson," said John Carl softly. "I'm far from siding with Talson. Even further than you are from killing him." John Carl turned and walked out of the bar without a backward glance.

Kat stared after her father for a moment, then looked at Talson. His face was still blank, but Kat knew he was smiling inwardly.

Nelco appeared to be enjoying the attention he was being given now that he had burned the only evidence that could prove him wrong. "I think my work here is done," he said calmly. "Thank you for inviting me to this wonderful little party." He turned and exited the bar, leaving only the smell of burnt plastic behind.

The silence that followed Nelco and John Carl's exit stretched on uncomfortably. It seemed that no one could think of anything to say. After a few minutes Sono and Browen stood up from the bar and exited without a word.

The silence was shattered a minute later by a loud and inconsistent knock on the front door. Again Larry moved to the door and peered through the window.

Roco looked over Larry's shoulder. "Just when we thought it couldn't get any weirder," he said. "Tracy."

Larry opened the door, holding it open for Tracy. She looked quickly around the bar room, shock registering in her face.

"Evening Tracy," said Roco, "unfortunately you just missed Nelco."

"Where is he? He knows where Tina is."

"Why do you care about that?" asked Sela looking blankly up at Tracy.

Tracy did not look at Sela. "You stole her," she said angrily. "Where is she?"

"She's safe," said Talson softly.

Tracy took a step back toward the door. Clearly she had not realized that Talson was in the bar. She paused for a moment, taking in the scene. She looked scared. "Larry" she whispered. Apparently, of all present in the bar, Tracy saw Larry as the least frightening. "What's going on?" she whispered.

"We were hoping to show Nelco a certain videotape, but he decided to be difficult about it," said Larry rather casually. He pointed to the remains of the videotape on the floor. "He actually burnt it."

Tracy looked down at the burnt tape, slightly curious. "What was on the tape?"

"It's a surveillance tape from the night this bar was busted," replied Larry, as casually as if the tape had been of a child's birthday party.

"So why burn it?" asked Tracy, looking confused now instead of scared.

"Maybe because he didn't want to see his best friend shoot his girlfriend on camera with all of us watching," said Sela with cruel sarcasm.

"I didn't ask you," snapped Tracy, still looking at Larry.

"Well in that case, I have to say I understand why he burned it," said Larry, matching Sela's sarcastic tone. "I doubt he would have enjoyed being humiliated, horrified, and devastated at the same time. Besides, he couldn't let some old surveillance tape ruin all the hard work he's done to cover up the truth."

"What are you talking about?" asked Tracy angrily.

"Nelco hasn't told you much, has he?" said Roco. "We're talking about how Nelco can't face seeing the truth on that tape."

"That's because he doesn't need a tape," Tracy said almost boastfully. "He can

see the truth in his mind."

Talson chuckled softly. "Can't we all." *Sela we have a problem.*

What problem?

The words in Kat's mind surprised her. *Sela how—? You have the power?*

We'll explain that later. What's the problem?

Tracy is going to let Nelco use Tina.

She won't do that.

Yes she will, Kat. Nelco told her that he won't hurt Tina. She believes everything Nelco says.

So what will happen to Tina if Nelco uses her.

If he succeeds in killing me it will destroy Tina's mind.

What do we do about it? Sela's thoughts came fast and angry.

Kat could feel her heart pounding. *I think I know what we can do. I need to talk to Tracy.*

"Kat," said Talson adopting an authoritative tone. "Take Tracy to the back room. We don't need any more people helping Nelco burn tapes."

Sela and Kat grabbed Tracy's arms before she knew what was happening. Roco stepped out of their way, looking somewhat confused as they forced her through the door into the back room. Sela released Tracy and exited to the front, locking the door behind her.

"What do you want?" gasped Tracy.

The back room was very dark. Kat faced Tracy as her eyes adjusted. "Listen," she said quietly. "Nelco can see the truth in his mind just like you said, but I can see the truth in yours. You would rather make sure Tina is safe than follow Nelco orders, wouldn't you? It's not too late to help her, Tracy. She doesn't want to work for us, she's still on your side."

"Where is she?" There was a hint of desperation in Tracy's voice as she turned to look at Kat. "Kat please, I know you wouldn't let her get hurt."

"There's nothing I can do, Tracy," said Kat. "You are the one who can stop Nelco from hurting her."

"He promised he wouldn't," whispered Tracy, "but, but_"

"But you think he's lying," finished Kat.

"No, I just don't understand. I don't understand what he wants her to do. He says she has to help him for her father."

"You could help him instead," said Kat. "Tina has no connection to what happened, Tracy. She would only really be able to help Nelco if she had really known her father." Kat wasn't sure exactly where she was going, or what she was trying to accomplish, but she felt that Tracy was her best chance to help Tina, Sela, and Talson at the same time.

"I understand the power, Tracy," continued Kat. "What Nelco is going to do is dangerous."

"I know, but I trust him," said Tracy. She smiled slightly. "He would never hurt me."

"You know he would never hurt you," said Kat. "That's why you can help him. It should be you. Your husband deserves it to be you. Tina never had a father, she deserves a mother that's brave enough to do what has to be done."

Tracy gazed at Kat. "Why are you helping me, Katerina?" she whispered.

Kat knew how Tracy thought, and she knew she could use Tracy's own words and values against her now. "I'm sorry for everything, Tracy," said Kat, trying her best to sound sincere. "What I did was wrong. Maybe I can't fix it for myself, but I won't drag Tina down with me. Besides, you already lost one of your daughters to this, you can't lose the other. Tina will be safe. I know you are the only one who can do this."

Tracy blinked. She seemed to be trying to hold back tears. "Thank you, Kat," she whispered. "Just tell me what I have to do."

Kat found the light switch on the wall and turned on the lights. "Sit down," she said.

Tracy looked at her as if slightly intimidated. Kat was not used to adults being scared of her, but it seemed that her mental abilities truly scared Tracy. Tracy backed slowly into a chair without taking her eyes from Kat's face.

"You should wait back here until everyone is gone. Then you can go out to the front. No one will be there except for Larry. He'll make sure you're okay until Nelco comes."

"But he's on Talson's side."

"He only pretends to be," Kat reassured her. "Just stay at the bar. Nelco will

come back."

"He left," said Tracy. "How can you be sure he'll come back."

"How can I be sure? Tracy, you know he'll come back for you."

Tracy smiled slightly. "Of course he will, but what about Tina?"

"I'll bring her here to you."

"You can do that?"

"For Tina, you know I can."

Tracy nodded and put her head in her hands. "I don't know how I'll thank you for this, Katerina."

"Don't worry," said Kat, her hand on the door that lead to the front. "Everything's going to be okay now, it really is."

Tracy smiled weakly. "I trust you Kat."

We got her.

CHAPTER 24

PLANNED MISTAKES

When Kat returned to the front of the bar, she found to her surprise that everyone had left except for Larry, who was stacking glasses behind the bar and Sela who was sitting at the bar watching him.

"Where is everyone?" asked Kat, closing the door to the back room behind her.

"They went to Headquarters," replied Sela lazily. "Nice work in there with Tracy," she added.

"What's going on at Headquarters?"

"I'll tell you in the car, we've gotta go." Sela nodded to Larry. "Make sure you take good care of Tracy for me," she said with a sarcastic smile.

"Of course," said Larry with a smirk. "My best customers get only the finest treatment."

Sela led Kat outside to her car. "Sela," said Kat as they pulled out onto the street, "why didn't you tell me you have the power?"

"I don't really have the power," replied Sela. "It's just Talson's using me so he can do what he does."

"Why?"

"I don't really know, I think he wants to trick Nelco somehow. He has a plan, but as usual I really have no idea what that plan is."

"So are we going to Headquarters, because Nelco can't get to us there?"

"That's what I thought at first, but now I think we're going there because Talson knows Nelco will get to us there."

Kat sat back in silence for a moment. She had felt from the beginning that Talson was playing into Nelco's hands, and now he seemed to be helping Nelco to succeed more than ever. Kat wasn't sure if she should admit her suspicion to Sela, especially since she wasn't sure if she was right

371

or not. It didn't make sense for Talson to be helping Nelco to kill him, but then again Kat had wondered at times if Talson actually wanted to die. The thought that her suspicions might be accurate scared her.

"You okay, Kat?" asked Sela, glancing sideways at her.

"Yeah, I'm okay. I was just thinking how sometimes it seems like_" she broke off.

"Seems like what?"

"Never mind."

"Don't cop out on me like that," said Sela. "You can't just start to tell me something and then go 'oh never mind.' Tell me what's up, Kat."

"Okay, I just feel like maybe Talson's playing into Nelco's hands a little bit, that's all," said Kat quickly. She paused but Sela did not reply. "It just seems like he's giving Nelco and my dad a chance to kill him."

Sela shrugged. "It's possible, but I doubt it," she said finally. "I know Talson pretty well, and he's not going to just let someone kill him."

"Yeah, you're probably right," muttered Kat, unconvinced. "It's just sometimes I feel like maybe Talson doesn't want to live anymore."

"I know what you mean," said Sela, still looking unconcerned. "But I think that when the day comes that Talson wants out, he'll order his own killing. Talson's gotta go in style, you know?"

Kat stared straight ahead at the road in silence, unsure of how to respond.

"Listen, Kat, if Tracy does what you asked her to do and convinces Nelco to use her instead of Tina, it is going to help us all out a lot."

"It doesn't matter," insisted Kat. "It just means that Nelco can kill Tracy, or if he doesn't use her, then he'll end up killing someone else."

"It does matter, Kat," said Sela. "It will be easier to use Tracy than Tina, and Nelco will do whatever's easiest."

"And if he kills her it's my fault."

"If Nelco kills Tracy it's his fault, Kat."

Kat bit back her reply. She knew that Sela didn't care what happened to Tracy, but she didn't want to say it. "I'm just scared," she said quietly.

"I'm scared too," said Sela, although she didn't look it. Her eyes were fixed on the road ahead, her expression blank, her hands on the wheel were steady.

"You've been here before, though," Kat challenged.

"That doesn't mean it's going to be any easier this time," replied Sela. Kat couldn't help thinking that this was going to be a repeat of what had happened fourteen years previously. It seemed that everyone wanted to make sure that the same thing didn't happen again, but no matter how hard they tried it seemed to be happening all over again. Talson had given power to Sela again, and Sela had let him do it again. Kat didn't understand why Talson had asked Sela to kill for him again. After everything he had told her about how he regretted using Sela, he now seemed poised to make the exact same mistake.

"Kat, check the GPS for me," Sela interrupted Kat's thoughts. "See if you can find Nelco. Number 683-225," she added.

Kat scanned the map, checking all the red dots, but she did not see Nelco's number. "I don't see him," she said.

"He must have disabled his tracker again," muttered Sela, sounding somewhat annoyed. "Roco just put a new tracker on his car. It probably doesn't matter, though, they're probably tracking him from Headquarters."

Suddenly the GPS screen flickered and went blank. "What the hell?" muttered Sela, reaching down to push the power button.

"What happened?" asked Kat.

"The system is dead," said Sela. "Hand me the radio, it's down by the floor."

"You guys have radios too? You guys are like the cops."

"Yeah, just like the cops," said Sela sarcastically. "Come in Headquarters," Sela said into the radio.

"Go ahead Sela." Kat recognized Roco's voice over the radio.

"The system in my car just went down."

"Yeah, Nelco screwed up the system.

"He listening?"

"Could be."

Copy, I'll be there in three." She put down the radio.

"What's going on?" asked Kat.

"Nelco disabled the GPS systems from his computer at home. Nelco works with computers and he helped to create the tracking system, so I'm not surprised."

"So the system at Headquarters is down too?" asked Kat.

"Yeah," said Sela. "Luckily we still have the surveillance system within Headquarters. There are cameras everywhere, so if he comes to H.Q. we'll know."

"What if he disables the cameras too?"

"He won't. We created the surveillance system after he left Talson. He doesn't even know it exists. We actually created the system because of him and Barty. Talson was afraid they would come back and try to destroy Headquarters. It's such a big place we needed to have cameras everywhere and someone watching them at all times. Talson never let the security go slack all these years, even though Nelco never tried anything."

Kat looked out the window at the rundown streets and empty crumbling buildings as Sela brought the car to an abrupt stop in front of Milro's house. Milro came outside the house as soon as Sela and Kat stepped out of the car.

"Sela, it's about time. We gotta go," he said, hurrying toward them.

Sela nodded. The three began to walk briskly down the street toward Headquarters. The breeze from the sea blew in their faces as they walked.

"Did you hear any news? Where's Nelco?" Sela asked Milro anxiously.

"He's at Headquarters."

"Damn it," said Sela. "I wanted to get there before him. What the hell is he doing there?" For the first time Sela seemed truly nervous.

"We still haven't figured out why he's there," replied Milro.

"How'd he get in?" Sela demanded.

"Roco said he doesn't see how it could have happened unless Talson disabled the security system." He seemed somewhat intimidated by Sela's sudden intensity.

"Wait a minute," said Sela. "Are you saying Talson disabled the tracking system, not Nelco?"

"It wasn't just the tracking system," said Milro. "It was the locks and the alarms at H.Q. too. Talson's the only one who has access to any of that. Roco said there is no way Nelco could have gotten in unless someone on the inside helped him."

Sela glanced at Kat, then back at Milro. "He has to be doing this for a reason," she said. "How's he doing?"

"Not good, according to Romez. Apparently Nelco got in his head. I don't really understand it though, I thought Talson would be able to block Nelco out."

"I think he could," said Sela.

"Why isn't he? Romez always says that Talson doesn't make mistakes, but it seems like he's making a lot of mistakes with this."

"Talson doesn't make accidental mistakes, he executes planned mistakes."

"I don't see Headquarters," said Milro, as they reached the main highway. "Are the lights out too?"

"Talson's not using his power," said Kat. "The illusion's gone."

"What illusion?" asked Milro.

"Headquarters," replied Kat. "The building being out in the middle of the ocean on an island is an illusion. It's just an image that Talson puts in our heads."

"No way," said Milro. "How do you know that?"

"Come on, Milro. A tunnel under the ocean?"

"I guess, but what's the real Headquarters, then?"

"It's underground. The tunnel goes under the cliffs."

"So that's why there's no windows," muttered Milro.

"Come on, man," said Kat, "how many times have you been here? You never

noticed that the tunnel curves at the beginning and it's sloped downward all the way?"

"I was always too disoriented by the darkness," said Milro defensively.

"Well, that's the point of the darkness."

Milro shook his head. "Shut up Kat, you're making me feel dumb. How did you figure that out so quickly?"

Kat shrugged. "Not everything we see is real. If you can connect to people's minds you can put thoughts in their head, make them see things that don't exist, even make them remember things that never happened."

"Yeah, I know Talson can do all that, I guess I just told myself he didn't use it to mess with us." He shook his head, "I should have known."

Sela, Kat and Milro descended the cliffs as quickly as they could, but the darkness made it difficult. Without the lights from Headquarters the cliffs were in complete darkness. Sela seemed to know the cliff face perfectly, even in darkness, but Milro and Kat struggled down behind her. When they finally reached the tunnel it seemed less black than usual since Kat's eyes were already adjusted to darkness.

Milro stopped short in front of Kat as they emerged from the tunnel. "What is this place?"

Kat peered over his shoulder. They were not standing on a rock island at the bottom of a stone staircase. Instead they found themselves at the top of a long, rather uneven set of sandstone ledges that led to a small crumbling wooden door. The door looked out of place as if it had been built to crudely block the entrance to an underground cave.

"Welcome to the real Headquarters," said Sela.

"The stairs go down, not up," said Milro in disbelief. The whole thing we thought of as Headquarters was a fake," he sounded somewhat angry now. "Why would Talson show us something that wasn't even real?"

"How do we know anything in the world is real?" said Kat.

"What does real even mean?" added Sela.

"Does everything we have inside Headquarters exist or is that all fake too?" asked Milro somewhat angrily.

"I think it's just the structures that are fake. All the technology and possessions we have are real," answered Sela. She didn't seem surprised by the real Headquarters. Kat knew she had seen it before.

The inside of Headquarters had rough stone walls streaked with water stains quite unlike the smooth black walls they were accustomed to seeing. It was still circular and split into two sides, however there was no massive metal column to separate the building. Instead there was a rather large, uninteresting boulder.

"I can't believe this," Milro sounded more disappointed than angry, now. "It's just a bunch of caves, it's not even a building. No wonder we only had those little silver lights, you can't have electricity in an underground cave."

"But there are cameras and computers, and water," said Kat, as they made their way down the much narrower hallway, past the lounge, toward the surveillance room.

"Talson taps city power," said a voice from inside the room. Roco was sitting at a large table with a series of monitors in front of him. The computer room was exactly the way Kat remembered it, all the technology was real just as Sela had said it would be. The only difference was the rough stone walls and floor, which had once resembled those of an office building.

"Welcome to Headquarters without the frills," said Tiro, who was sitting behind Roco.

"Yeah, I hate it," said Milro bitterly.

"Shut up and get in here," said Roco. The room fell silent. It seemed clear that Roco was in no mood for fooling around.

"Where's Nelco?" asked Sela.

"He's on the other side," said Roco.

"What's he doing?"

"Nothing, he's just been looking around at everything. But now it looks like he's headed to Talson's office. I'll bring it up on screen now."

Sela walked into the room and stood behind Roco's chair, Kat followed her. Roco was sitting behind about ten screens all showing a different view of Headquarters.

"There's Nelco," said Roco, pointing to a screen on his right.

"Is that Talson's office?" asked Kat.

"Yeah."

"Where the hell is Talson and how did Nelco get in his office?" asked Milro, joining them at Roco's chair.

"Talson's in the basement," said Roco.

"Well, what does he want us to do about Nelco?" asked Milro. His initial anger upon seeing the less glamorous version of Headquarters seemed to have transformed into panic, now that he realized that Talson didn't appear to have the situation under control.

"That's the problem," replied Tiro, "Talson didn't tell us what to do."

"Did Talson let Nelco in?" asked Sela.

Milro glared sharply at Sela. "Are you crazy? What would make you think he would do that? That's just stupid."

"Stupid, but right," said Tiro.

Milro stared at his brother, apparently speechless.

Kat looked from Milro to Sela. In contrast to Milro's shocked expression, Sela's face was blank. Kat had shared her suspicion that Talson wanted to die, and although Sela had denied it, Kat couldn't help but think that perhaps Sela had lied. It seemed logical that Talson would have shared his true intentions with Sela if he had shared them with anyone. Kat only wished she knew what Sela was thinking, or better yet, how she was able to block Kat from her mind.

Milro was thinking that Talson had betrayed them all, Tiro was thinking that Milro was overreacting to the 'fake' Headquarters, Mevsin was thinking about how Nelco had hacked into their tracking system, and Roco was thinking that he could beat Nelco senseless if he had another chance to fight him, but Kat had no idea what Sela was thinking.

Kat turned her attention back to the screen. Nelco had crossed the office and was now behind Talson's desk. He appeared to be empting the contents of the drawers onto the desk and floor.

"What the hell is he looking for?" muttered Roco.

"Aren't Talson's drawers usually locked?" asked Kat. All the times she had been in Talson's office there had always been padlocks on all the drawers.

"He's lost it," said Milro in panic. "He's crazy. He's going to get us all killed."

"Get a grip, tough guy," said Sela. "Whatever it is that Nelco's looking for, Talson wants him to find it."

"Oh yeah, planned mistakes," said Milro sarcastically. "How could I forget?"

"Shut up Mil," said Tiro. "Check this out, Nelco's looking at a little book."

"Zoom in on it," said Sela.

Roco did not respond. He simply sat, staring transfixed at the monitor.

"Dude, wake up," said Kat. "We all know you could kick Nelco's butt if you had the chance."

Roco flinched in surprise and looked embarrassed.

"I love you, Kat," said Sela, smiling as she reached over Roco's shoulder to adjust the image on the screen.

"It looks like a photo album," said Kat, squinting at the book in Nelco's hands. "He doesn't know we're watching him, does he?"

"No," replied Roco, recovering from Kat's comment. "The cameras were installed after he left."

"I think he's pulling the pictures out," interrupted Sela.

Kat turned her attention back to the monitor. Nelco appeared to be removing each picture from the album and turning it over to look at the back, then placing it back in the album.

"Why is he looking at the backs of the pictures?" muttered Roco.

"I don't know, he must be looking for a date or a name, or something," said Sela.

Nelco paused, staring intently at the photo in his hand. Then he flipped it over and looked at the back for a moment, then he turned it over again. He nodded slowly as if he had just figured out some sort of riddle.

"That's it," muttered Kat. "Sela you were right."

"What's it?" Sela looked confused. "I was right about what?"

"You were right about what Nelco is looking for."

"A date?"

"No, a name. It's the last thing he needs to know."

Sela looked questioningly at Kat. Milro, Tiro and Mevsin looked confused as well, but Roco nodded slowly. "You're right, Kat," he said softly.

"What are you guys talking about?" asked Sela. "What name?"

"Talson's name," said Roco quietly. "His real name. Kat's right, it's the last thing Nelco wants to know. It's the reason he came back to Headquarters. He still wants to win."

"Win what?" asked Sela.

"We had a contest, me, him and Barty, when we were kids to see who would be the first to find out Talson's real name. I've asked him about a hundred times, but he would never tell anyone."

"Does anyone know his name?" asked Tiro.

"I don't know, I thought Marissa knew," said Roco, "but she claims he never told her. I guess he never really trusted anyone that much."

"I don't know," said Sela. "I can understand why someone like Talson wouldn't want people to know his name. He's our boss, he doesn't have to tell us."

"Yeah, well I'm not just 'people'," said Roco, there was resentment in his voice now. "I've known him since he was six years old. He was my brother before he was my boss. He was actually human back then," Roco added. There was a bitterness in his voice that Kat had never heard before.

"Don't be bitter that you lost the contest, Roco," said Sela.

Kat knew in an instant that Sela had gone too far. If Talson had let Nelco find something with his real name on it, something that Talson had never shown to Roco, she could understand why Roco felt angry and betrayed. To Kat's surprise, however, Roco ignored Sela's remark completely.

"He's leaving," said Roco, turning everyone's attention back to the monitor.

"He's still got the picture," said Tiro, pointing to another monitor, which showed Nelco in the hallway outside Talson's office.

"He knows," muttered Roco, more to himself than to anyone in the room. "I'm going down there." Roco pushed back his chair and got to his feet.

"No, Roco, you can't," said Sela. For the first time Kat saw fear in Sela's eyes.

Sela's expression did not go unnoticed by Roco. "What, you're afraid I might screw up your little plan? Guess what, I don't care this time."

"He's going to the lower level," said Sela, there was a hint of panic in her voice now. "Talson is down there. Roco, please, I'm sorry."

"Our camera angles of the lower level suck," said Roco. "Don't worry Sela, I'm not going to mess with him, I just what to see what the hell he's doing."

"Fine," said Sela. Her fear appeared to have vanished. "But wear a mic so you can tell us what's going on, and don't do anything stupid."

Roco sneered at Sela as he grabbed an earpiece. "Don't worry Sela, I won't do anything to get you killed. You're not the only one he cares about, I knew him first," he added coldly.

Kat stared after Roco as he left, then looked around at the others. They all seemed just as confused about the conversation that had just taken place between Roco and Sela.

"Okay, what the hell was that?" asked Tiro.

Sela glared at Tiro.

"What's on the lower level?" asked Kat. She felt that it was important to change the subject.

"Nothing much," said Sela. "Just the heating and air conditioning systems, the water pump, electric."

"Nelco's down there," said Tiro. He had switched the display so the monitors were now showing the lower level of Headquarters. Just as Roco had said, the images were much lower quality than the cameras on the upper level. Nelco was standing in the middle of what appeared to be a rather large, completely empty cave.

"That room looks empty," remarked Kat.

"That's the main room on the lower level," Sela replied. "There are rooms off the sides. Sela pressed a button on a panel below the monitors. "Roco do you copy?"

"Yeah, I'm just outside the main room," Roco's voice came through the speaker. "Where's Nelco?"

"He's in the main room heading toward one of the side rooms."

"Which room?"

"I'm not sure," said Sela. She looked questioningly at Tiro, who shrugged. "It's the one straight across from you as you enter the main room," she replied.

"That's the water system," Roco said slowly. He seemed to be thinking very hard.

"Why the hell is he going in there?" Milro asked.

"Do we have a camera in there?" asked Tiro.

"Yeah," said Sela, pointing to a monitor on the lower left, which displayed a blurry image of a rather small room. "The display sucks though."

"I told you," said Roco. "Aren't you glad I'm here to be your eyes."

"Shut up and figure out what he's doing," said Sela. Her tone was surprisingly cold.

"Sela, you are in no position to give me orders right now," said Roco softly. Roco appeared on the monitor in the main room.

"Where's he going to go where Nelco won't see him?" asked Kat, hoping the question would distract Sela from making an angry retort.

"There's a boiler room next to the room where Nelco is," replied Mevsin, speaking for the first time. "There is a tunnel that joins the two rooms, so he'll probably hide in there."

"What is he doing now?" muttered Milro, looking hard at the grainy image on the screen.

The room Nelco had entered wasn't as small as Kat had first thought. It appeared small because most of the space in the room was taken up by a large water tank that was partially recessed into the stone wall. On the opposite side of the room was a switch to control the flow of water in and out of the tank.

"So that's the water supply for Headquarters?" asked Kat.

"Yeah, the water is tapped from the city and stored in the tank," said Mevsin. "It's

a pressure system that forces the water up to the upper level."

"How do you know all that?"

"I helped fix the wiring once," said Mevsin. "There are pipes underneath us that bring the water up to the upper levels. That's why we have that center column. It hides where the pipes come up from the lower level."

"Talson told you that?" asked Sela, sounding surprised.

"He and Roco explained it to me when I helped fix the system," replied Mevsin.

"Does Nelco know how it works?"

"Unfortunately, yes," Roco's voice startled them. "He and I built it."

"Great," said Sela sarcastically. "Can you see what he's doing now?"

"Yeah, he's at the breaker box," said Roco. "I think he's turning off the power to the pump."

"Why?" asked Sela.

"I don't—" Roco broke off suddenly.

"Roco?" said Sela. "What is it?"

"He's gonna flood the place."

There was a brief moment of stunned silence. "How," Sela whispered after what seemed like a very long time.

"By rewiring the pump system."

"He can do that?" asked Sela, looking at Nelco on the monitor and then at Mevsin.

"There isn't enough pressure to force enough water up to flood us the way the system is now, but if he can boost the power to the pressure system enough, the joints in the pipes will separate," said Mevsin in one breath.

"Are you sure?" asked Sela.

"Yeah," said Mevsin. "That's what happened before when I helped Roco fix the pipes. The pressure was too high and they separated. The lower level flooded."

"So could he get the pressure high enough to flood the upper level?"

Mevsin shrugged, "I'm not sure."

"Roco? Could he?" demanded Sela.

"I doubt it," replied Roco after a moment. "I don't think there is enough water anyway." Roco's tone was convincing, but Kat knew what he had thought just before he spoke. *Yes, he could.*

"Well, what's he doing now?"

"He's taking the wiring apart. I think he's rewiring the system, but I can't see exactly what he's doing."

"Okay, so can he flood us or not?" Sela practically yelled into the speaker. It was apparent that she was not comfortable with Roco rejecting the idea of the flood after he had planted the suggestion.

Roco did not respond despite the urgency in Sela's voice. Instead Mevsin spoke in the same even tone he had had throughout his description of the water system. "There are big pools of salt water on the lower level. At high tide sea water rushes into the caves down there and gets trapped in the pools."

"Yeah, so," said Sela. She seemed distracted as if she hadn't really heard Mevsin.

"Roco," said Mevsin, "if Nelco rewires the system so it draws water not only from the tank but also from the pools would he have enough water to flood us?"

"Yeah, he would have plenty of water, but he still wouldn't have the pressure to move that water up. More water means he would need more power."

Kat watched the monitor. Nelco appeared to be carefully examining some wiring. "What if he rewires the pump to take power from something else?" asked Kat. She felt everyone in the room turn and look at her. "Sorry," she said quietly, "I just thought if—"

"Kat, you're right," said Mevsin. "If he takes power from another system he might have enough power to flood at least one side of Headquarters."

"He could flood Talson's side," said Roco, he sounded scared now. "We've got to warn him."

" Roco, no you can't," said Sela.

"Sela if you think I'm just going to sit here in this tunnel and let Nelco get away with this you really are stupid," said Roco angrily.

"He's not going to flood Talson," said Kat quietly.

"Kat, you can't know that for sure," said Sela.

"Yeah I can," Kat felt a twinge of anger, herself. She wasn't sure if the initial anger had belonged to her or to Nelco, but as she looked at Sela she realized the anger was all her own. "Nelco is down there right now because no one can kill him, and he knows that. He knows he is going to win, Talson is dead and he knows it. He has no reason to flood Talson. He's going to turn off the power to the left side and then he's going to flood us." There was not a waver in Kat's voice. It was just as Talson had told her it would be. 'We don't read minds, Kat. We do not see the thoughts of another, we experience them. In that experience there is no separation between your thoughts and those of the other person.'

Suddenly all the monitors went dark.

"What the hell," said Sela. "Roco, the surveillance just died."

"Told you," said Kat coolly.

"Sela," Roco's voice was hushed, "he's going to turn off all the power to the left side, and we're going to lose the audio connection in a second."

"Okay, Roco," Sela seemed to suddenly become levelheaded, "tell me what he's doing."

"He has the wires to the main system. He disconnected power to the pump. He's about to turn off the power to all of Headquarters, and when it goes off he's going to reroute the power to the pump. I have to go in there and stop him."

"Roco, you can't," said Sela's tone was suddenly pleading.

"Listen, Sela," said Roco, the anger in his voice was gone. "If I don't go in there, you guys are all going to die. Sela, I need you to turn on the back up surveillance system. Once the lights go out you've gotta tell me which wires belong to which system, there is a map of the building plan on the computer."

Sela did not move or respond to Roco. Her face was blank but her eyes seemed to blaze. As usual Kat could not tell what she was thinking.

"Sela?"

"Yeah Roco, I'm on it," said Sela finally, standing up. She crossed the room to the breaker board. It was huge, with dozens of different switches. "Tell me when, Roco," she called across the room.

For a moment there was complete silence then Roco yelled, "Now, Sela."

For an instant Kat saw Sela's hand suspended above the switchboard, then her hand came down and she flipped two switches simultaneously. At the same moment all the monitors came back on and all the lights in the room went out.

For a moment there was silence. "Do you guys hear that?" whispered Tiro.

The sound of soft trickling water reached Kat's ears. "Yeah, it sounds like water," said Kat.

"Did he flood us?" asked Milro, nervously searching the monitors. "I can't see anything, I think the camera we were using is out."

"I don't think it worked," said Mevsin. "That sounds more like a leak than a high pressure flood."

"I guess Roco was able to stop him somehow," said Tiro. "Roco do you copy?"

There was silence.

"Roco, this is Tiro, I repeat, do you copy?"

"He's not answering, let's go down there," said Mevsin, grabbing a flashlight from his desk.

As they all rose to leave, Kat turned to see Sela still standing immobile at the breaker panel. "Are you coming, Sela?" she asked softly.

"Yeah, yeah I'm coming," muttered Sela after a short pause.

They hurried out the door into the main hall, Milro leading the way. Sela brought up the rear. She walked slowly as if she wanted to take as long as possible to reach the lower level. They reached the front of Headquarters and descended a flight of rough, uneven stone steps to the lower level.

"I'll never get used to seeing H.Q. like this," muttered Milro. "I just can't believe it was all fake. Distorting another's perceptions is messed up."

Kat gazed at the rough, water-stained walls around her as the flashlight beam bounced around the stairwell. It seemed foolish now that she had believed that the glossy black walls and the endless undersea tunnel were real. This version of Headquarters was much more believable, but Kat had to agree with Milro, it was disappointing. Kat could not understand why Talson had put so much effort into creating the illusion of a fancy, almost futuristic Headquarters, and she could not help wondering what other illusions he had created.

As they reached the main cave on the lower level, Roco came toward them out of the darkness.

"Roco, you didn't answer us, are you okay?" asked Milro.

"Where's Nelco? He didn't flood anything did he?" asked Mevsin.

"No, no," said Roco softly. "It's just a leak. Nelco didn't have all the pipes connected when the power came on so there wasn't a flood." Roco's voice was emotionless, and his face was set.

"What do you mean when the power came on? The power is off."

"Not the power to the lighting," said Roco stiffly. "I meant the power to the water system." Roco was now staring directly at Sela.

"Wait, where was—" Mevsin broke off, glancing from Roco to Sela. Neither

Roco nor Sela offered a reply. Milro crossed the room to the door of the room that housed the water system and opened the door slowly. He shined the flashlight into the room, but his body blocked the others' view of the room inside. Suddenly Milro drew in his breath and stepped back from the door.

Mevsin, Tiro and Kat hurried across the dark room to join Milro. Roco and Sela remained motionless, however. Kat peered over Milro's shoulder, standing on her tiptoes to see over him into the room. Kat tried to stifle a gasp. Nelco lay on the floor beneath the pump, his body was rigid. The wires that led to the tank were clenched in his left hand.

"The wires were in his hand when the power came on to the pump," muttered Mevsin.

Kat looked around at the Silver Shadows. Everyone looked temporarily shocked, with the exception of Roco and Sela. Roco stood facing Sela, his brow was furrowed and his eyes were cold. Sela was no longer looking at Roco. She had taken a few steps toward the others and was looking at Nelco's stiff body on the floor. Her face was expressionless. The silence was endless.

"One question, Sela," said a soft voice from behind them. "Did you flip the wrong switch?" *Or did you flip the wrong switch.*

Talson stood in the doorway holding his small silver light.

"I don't know, pick one," replied Sela.

"Well in that case I'll give you the benefit of the doubt and say it was an honest mistake."

"More like a planned mistake," muttered Roco. "Are you okay boss?" he added.

"Yeah, but you're not," said Talson. "Thanks for not doing anything stupid."

"Thank Sela for not giving me the chance," said Roco bitterly. "Nelco took something from your office earlier," he added.

Talson smiled in a strained sort of way. "I know, Romez, I know," he said. "I know I let him win your little bet. I'm sorry, but it never should have been so important."

"Yeah, I guess it never should have mattered, but you know it did. We deserved to know, Talson."

"Nelco didn't deserve it." Talson said quietly. He crossed the room slowly to Nelco's body. He reached down, put his hand into the pocket of Nelco's jacket and pulled out the picture that Nelco had taken from his desk earlier. Talson stood looking at the picture in the silver light. The Silver Shadows watched him tensely as if they expected Talson to do something rash, like burn the picture the way Nelco had burned the surveillance tape at the bar. Talson seemed to be temporarily frozen as he gazed at the photograph. Kat wondered what he was thinking, but his mind seemed empty.

Talson turned around very slowly to face the Silver Shadows. "I'm going to the Sharktooth to give Larry the good news," he said softly. "Any of you can come with me if you would like." Talson walked slowly toward the door, but stopped short in front of Roco. He slowly extended his hand holding the picture to Roco. Roco accepted it wordlessly, and without a change of expression, he handed it back to Talson. They looked at each other for a moment. The look could have meant anything, or nothing at all. The two men could have been best friends or mortal enemies, but in that moment it was impossible to tell. Time seemed to stand still, as if the whole world had stopped to try to understand Roco and Talson. Then the moment passed, and Talson was at the door. Sela turned and followed him. Kat hesitated for a moment before she too followed Talson out the door.

C H A P T E R   2 5

THE FOUR WITH THE POWER

"I didn't think it would end this way, Sela," Talson's voice seemed to cut harshly through the silence.

Kat had never been in a situation with such tension as she was in now, sitting in the back seat of Sela's car. Talson sat in the passenger's seat, his posture was relaxed and passive, but his thoughts were chaotic. Sela sat stiff in the driver's seat, her hands gripping the wheel much harder than was necessary. She did not reply to Talson. Her eyes remained fixed on the road ahead of her. Kat had the feeling that Sela had expected it to end exactly the way it had just ended.

"I'm just glad it was you instead of Romez," continued Talson. He seemed determined to get a response from Sela. "Romez would have chosen me and none of you would be alive right now."

Kat was confused by Talson's statement. As far as she was concerned Sela had chosen Talson. She had tried desperately to make sure that Roco didn't do anything that would hurt Talson. Kat tried once again, in vain, to access Sela's mind and heard only the words she spoke a split second later.

"Is Nelco's mind gone?"

"I don't think so," said Talson. "I doubt anything in life could be that easy."

"Tracy has something," said Kat. "I think Nelco transferred some of his power to her, I don't know why." Kat was taken aback by her own statement, she had been focused very hard on Sela, but Tracy's thoughts just came to her.

"He did it so he could control her," said Talson, he didn't seem at all surprised by Kat's statement.

"How can Kat know that and you don't?" For the first time Sela seemed annoyed as she glanced sideways at Talson.

"Kat has much more mental ability than I do at the moment," said Talson. "The power only goes one way, Sela, you know that. My power will stay with those who I have given it to, and those who have taken it from me."

"But Tracy can't have the power, she just can't," said Sela. "That is not how it should have happened." There was fear in Sela's voice for the first time.

"It doesn't matter, Sela, you killed Nelco, you did what had to be done. You knew it was always going to end that way even if no one else did."

Kat stared at the back of Talson's seat. She could make no connection to his mind, and she felt an enormous emptiness inside her chest. Suddenly Kat felt the impact of Talson's words. Kat couldn't connect to his mind because the mind she thought was there didn't exist. The empty feeling seemed to be growing, it was inside Kat's mind and suddenly it was too much to bear. *It cannot end this way.* "It can't end this way," Kat said the words out loud, realizing that otherwise Talson would not hear her.

"Kat, Nelco is dead because I did what he thought I'd never do. I gave up my power."

"That's not true," said Kat. "Nelco died because Sela electrocuted him before Roco had the chance to do anything. Sela, why did you do that?"

"You know why," said Sela.

"No I don't," said Kat angrily. "Did you do it to destroy Talson? I thought you were trying to protect him."

"No, she did it to save me," said Talson softly.

"You said it yourself, Kat," said Sela. "Nelco wanted to kill everyone except Talson. Once everyone else was dead Nelco was going to use that power against Talson."

"What power?" asked Kat. "What are you talking about, Nelco didn't have enough power to kill Talson.

"He never wanted to kill me, Kat," said Talson. "Nelco knew me too well for that. He knew I would probably be happy if he killed me. He hated me much more than that, he wanted to control my mind."

"He had power but he didn't have the power to control your mind. No one does," said Kat.

"He would have been able to after he killed the Silver Shadows," said Sela.

"How, who gave him more mental power?"

"Sela means after he killed you, Kat," said Talson.

"Me?" whispered Kat.

"He thought he might as well take out the rest of us, but you were the main target

of the flood attempt. We couldn't destroy his mind, it would have taken too long."

"I realized his plan too late," said Talson with a hint of disappointment.

"He realized his plan too late," corrected Sela. "Nelco didn't originally plan that."

"So he wanted to use my mind to control you?" Kat asked in disbelief.

"Yes," said Talson.

"Could he have done that?"

"Yes," said Talson again. "The little power he got from me before, and the power he had from John Carl were nothing compared to what he would have if he killed you."

"He wasn't really going to flood us, Kat," said Sela. "He just wanted us to think he was going to. He knew that we were watching him and he knew Roco would try to stop him. He was watching us. He had a camera next to the pump control panel. He tapped into the surveillance system, that's why it went out earlier. He knew where Roco was and he was going to shoot him the second he walked into that room. He knew that Tiro, Milro, and Mevsin would come down as soon as Roco didn't respond. He would have killed them too."

"What about you and me?" asked Kat.

"He had other plans for us," replied Sela. "Kat, you and I are the only two people in the world who could ever destroy Talson's mind. And it would have taken both of us. Nelco knew Talson well enough to know he isn't one man with one mind, but he never thought—"

"Because he never thought Talson would give up his power," said Kat solemnly.

"No one ever does," said Talson shaking his head slowly.

"So you two had a plan all along," said Kat. "You just pretended not to know what was happening, and pretended to make a mistake with the breakers. You planned it all."

"Of course we did," said Talson. "If Sela makes a mistake, you have to know it was a planned mistake. You should have realized that by now," Talson added with a slight hint of a laugh.

Kat still did not find the situation funny. "But you lost your power this way too, so it doesn't matter," she said.

"It matters to me, Kat. All the people that matter to me would have been killed and I would have been made to live with their minds. There are things I could never live with, and when faced with those things there is nothing I can't live without."

The silence that followed Talson's statement was broken by the sound of Sela's phone ringing.

"Larry," said Sela picking it up from the cup holder between the seats. "Yeah,

we're on our way, we'll be there in like three minutes," she paused. "I didn't do anything. He's dead. I did, but I'll explain when we get there."

Sela put the phone down shaking her head. "Larry," she muttered with an expression that was almost a smile. "He asks a million questions. Where are you? What did I do to Tracy? Where's Nelco? Who killed him?" She laughed. "Typical Larry."

"Of course," said Talson. "If you tell Larry that someone died, the first thing he asks is who killed him. The man always assumes it's murder."

"Well, with our track record it's a pretty safe assumption," said Sela.

"That's true, there's been more death in my life than life." The sadness of Talson's statement was eclipsed by his indifferent tone.

They had arrived at the harbor, which was well lit despite the late hour. The lights of many boats reflected on the calm water. "I'm parking in front," said Sela. "I'm just too lazy to hide the car around the block. What's the plan, Boss?" she added in a more serious tone.

"No mind, no plan," said Talson. "Let's go."

"Works for me," said Sela as they got out of the car.

"Isn't that Milro's car?" said Kat, pointing at a dark blue car parked a little way down the street.

"It looks like it, but it can't be," said Sela. "Milro's still back at H.Q."

"It's Marissa," said Talson softly.

A second later Marissa stepped out of the car, her long gray streaked hair seemed to glow in the light of the street lamps. Marissa was not dressed colorfully the way she had been the day Kat had met her. Tonight she was dressed in black, which made her seem much darker than Kat had remembered.

"What is she doing here?" asked Sela. Kat could not tell if Sela was scared or just surprised to see Marissa.

"Dude, Kat, what are you doing here?"

Kat could hardly believe her ears as she turned to see Tina step out of the car. "Tina, how—?" began Kat, jogging down the street to meet her. "Are you okay?"

"Yeah, I'm good," said Tina. "Marissa's cool." She glanced past Kat to Sela and Talson. In the dim light of the street lamps Kat doubted Tina would recognize Talson from a distance.

"Yeah, I'm glad you're okay," said Kat distractedly. "I think your mom's inside."

"Yeah, Marissa said she would be here. I need to talk to her, and I didn't know where to find her."

"Oh yeah, we came to find her too." Kat wasn't sure if this was completely true, but it seemed like the only real reason she could give for why she, Sela, and Talson had come back to the Sharktooth. But somehow Kat doubted that Talson really didn't have a plan. Mental power or not, she knew he was prepared for every situation.

Tracy sat slouched over the bar with her back to the door when Kat and the others entered the bar. She did not look up as they approached her. Kat looked sideways at Tina. She was staring at her mother, looking scared and confused. Sela's face was blank, and her eyes were cold as she glared at Tracy. Talson stood back in the doorway as if he was hesitant to enter. This was the first time Kat had seen him in the light since Nelco's death. Kat was so taken aback by Talson's appearance that she momentarily forgot all about Tracy and Tina, or anything else for that matter.

Talson looked even smaller and paler than Kat remembered as he leaned against the doorframe. But it was his eyes that stunned Kat into silent disbelief. They were no longer the flaming shade of yellow for which Talson was so famous. His eyes were now a dull shade of greenish yellow mixed with brown. It was an unnatural color, which made Talson look even less human than he had before. His gaze seemed vacant, as if all the life in his eyes had vanished. Talson noticed Kat looking at him. He met Kat's eyes, and for a fleeting moment she thought she could hear him in her mind saying 'no need to stare, I'm not that interesting' but a second later she knew she had imagined it. There was nothing in her mind except her own thoughts and Talson's emptiness. She knew he had nothing, no thoughts, no memories, just the scene in front of his eyes.

Suddenly, Kat saw the scene that was happening behind her through Talson, and was brought abruptly back to her own mind. She turned around just in time to see Tracy pull out a gun and point it at Sela's chest. Her eyes were unfocused and wild.

"Where's Conner?" Tracy demanded, the gun shaking slightly in her right hand.

For a moment no one answered. Sela looked Tracy in the eyes, ignoring the gun pointed at her chest.

"I said, where's Conner?" Tracy raised her voice.

"Do you want to kill me, Tracy?" asked Sela finally.

"You? Hardly," said Tracy with a hint of contempt. She shifted the gun and pointed it at Kat. "You, Katerina, you had a deal with me. You said you would bring Nelco here and you didn't. You lied to me, Katerina."

"I was going to, I swear," said Kat convincingly. She had not been scared until the moment Tracy had turned the gun on her. Although Kat could now feel her heart hammering against her chest, she somehow knew what to say. "Don't blame me, it was Sela. She killed him."

"Shut up," snapped Tracy. "I've had enough of your silly games, Kat. Tell me where Conner is right now or I swear to God I will kill you both." She pointed the gun back at Sela, then at Kat, her hand still shook slightly.

"Fine, you win," said Sela, picking up where Kat left off. "We'll tell you where Nelco is, no more games. He's at our headquarters, and he's dead."

"That's a lie," said Tracy.

"You know I'd never lie to you," said Sela. For the first time she seemed to truly be enjoying herself. Kat had the feeling that this was not the first time Sela had been threatened at gunpoint. "I've never lied to you, Tracy, I've neglected to tell you the truth, but I've never lied to you."

"No," whispered Tracy, "it can't be true." Her hand was shaking more violently and her eyes seemed unfocused. "It can't be true," she said again, her voice shaking now. She turned the gun back on Kat. "How could you let this happen, Kat. We had a deal, you promised me, how could you?" Her voice rose suddenly.

"I guess I lied," said Kat with a half shrug. "I guess I shouldn't make promises I can't keep."

"Kat tried," said Sela casually. "Don't blame her."

Suddenly Tracy seemed to calm down. Her calm was somehow more threatening than her rage. "How did it happen?" Tracy whispered. "How did he die?"

"Technically he was electrocuted by a water pump," said Sela with a hint of a smile. "Tragic, really."

"Well that's a convenient cover story," said Tracy with cold sarcasm.

"Well, no, it wasn't actually as convenient as it sounds, but it'll do."

"It'll do?" Tracy repeated with disgust. "Of course it will do, *you killed him*," her voice rose once again. "A water pump? Was that the best you could do?"

Sela sighed deliberately. "Sadly, yes," she placed her hand on her chest in a gesture of mock sincerity. "I apologize for my gross lack of creativity, but if you must know the truth, he really brought it on himself."

"He did not," Tracy's voice rose in anger again and this time she pointed the gun at Talson who had crossed the room to stand behind Sela and Kat. "You killed him," she pointed her index finger at Talson. "You killed them all, my husband, Julie Operman, and all the others. You turned my daughter and Katerina into killers."

For a moment Talson merely looked at Tracy as if he was trying to decide whether to reply to her or not. Kat wondered if Talson would have killed Tracy if he still had his mind intact. He had said Tracy was a problem that they would have to deal with. Talson had said that she, Kat, would be the one to take on that problem. Kat knew that Talson could not use his mind to kill Tracy anymore, and that meant that she would have to do it. It seemed that any moment he would give her some sort of signal and expect her to do something.

Talson, however, did not look at Kat, instead he kept his eyes on Tracy and spoke in a soft slow voice. "Put the gun down, Louis," he said. No one moved. It was as if time had stopped when Talson spoke. "Think about it, Tracy, what are you really going to do? Kill your daughter? Kill your other daughter's best friend? Kill your husband's best friend?"

"You weren't his best friend, you killed him."

"I thought I was his best friend, Tracy," said Talson. "Barty lied to me every day from the first day I met him when I was nine years old. And he lied to everyone else every day for his entire life. He told me that he ran away from home, but he still lived with his parents. His brought me food from his house and told me he stole it from his father's café. One day Barty showed me the dead body of a boy behind a dumpster. He said that he just found the body and he pretended to be upset, but I knew he killed that boy. He worked for John Carl for years and lied to him. He lied to you Tracy, he told you he worked nights, but he really worked for me. He told you and John Carl that he hated me, and he told me that he really hated John Carl. He pretended to disapprove when Sela joined me, but it was really his plan all along. He brought John Carl here to the Sharktooth and told him the games were rigged. The games at the Sharktooth were always fair, and Barty knew that because he worked here. He told John Carl to call the cops so that he could use the bust as a diversion. He lied to Nelco and told him that I was planning to kill Julie Operman, and then in the chaos of the bust he shot her. He lied to everyone, but he was an incredibly smart man and he was able to keep all those stories straight in his head and fool a lot of people.

"I killed your husband, Tracy; I didn't want to, but I thought I had to. I was angry and I acted on my anger by destroying what I saw at the time as the source of my anger. When it was done I realized that the source of my anger wasn't Barty Louis. It was never him. The source of my anger has always been myself. I could have stopped Barty thirty years before I did, but I didn't want to. Even though I knew he lied, he acted like my friend.

If it weren't for my mental abilities I never would have known he was lying, so when he was with me I pretended I didn't have the power. I pretended I didn't know he was a liar and a murderer. I pretended until I believed it all because I wanted a friend. Because I pretended not to have the power when I was with him, I never killed him with it. He was how I learned to control my mind. After he shot Julie I stopped pretending, and I did what I should have done years before, I killed him. In the end I wasn't angry with Barty for being who he was, I was angry with myself for not allowing myself to see who he truly was.

"After I killed him I had to live with the truth of who he was every day. I have lived with his mind for nearly fifteen years. Barty lived to see how elaborate of a lie he could pull off without drawing suspicions. He believed he could fool everyone, and he died the day I stopped letting him fool me. You can say whatever you want, but your mind always tells the truth if you let it. You know who he was. We know why you're really holding that gun."

Tracy stared at Talson. Her hand was shaking again, now worse than before. A sort of madness seemed to have come over her as Talson finished speaking.

"Tracy," said Talson, "prove me wrong and put the gun down."

"She won't," said Sela softly.

"Mom, please," said Tina, "what are you doing? Please don't kill them."

"She's not going to kill us," said Kat quietly.

In the same moment Tracy raised the gun as if she were going to fire at the ceiling. "I'm sorry Selena," she said softly.

Kat shut her eyes but she could not block out Tracy's frenzied mind. She heard Tina gasp somewhere in the distance, but her mind was with Tracy. Nelco had betrayed her, just as she knew deep down that Barty had betrayed her. Her own daughter knew what she was about to do and would do nothing to stop it. Talson was right, but there was no way to live knowing that her husband had been no better than Talson. Kat screwed up her face against the tidal wave of emotions, words and images that filled Tracy's mind. Even her last thoughts were not her own, it seemed unfair. Suddenly everything was gone as the shot rang out, echoing around the room.

Kat opened her eyes to see Tracy slumped over the bar with the gun still stuck in her hand. The blood from her head was already flowing onto the bar and onto the floor. Kat turned to see Tina shaking, her face buried in her hands. Sela simply stared blankly at the pool of blood that was forming on top of the bar. Despite Tracy's last words, Sela's face was as blank as ever. Kat didn't know what to do. She wanted to do something to comfort Tina, but she knew nothing she could say would make a difference. No one moved or spoke. The Sharktooth Bar seemed temporarily lifeless.

Larry awoke with a start to the sound of a gunshot. For a moment he thought he was dreaming. The gunshot that destroyed Larry's bar and his life had haunted his dreams for almost fourteen years. Larry opened his eyes and stared absently at the ceiling of his small bedroom. As much as he hoped he had imagined the shot, Larry knew it was real. He knew he needed to go downstairs, but he did not move from his bed. Larry knew the damage had been done, but he was not sure he could face seeing another bloody scene in The Sharktooth Bar.

"Kat, where are you going?" Sela took a step toward Kat.

Kat did not turn around or reply to Sela as she headed into the back room of the bar. "Kat, don't leave," she heard Tina cry, as she closed the door behind her. Kat knew Tina was probably afraid of being left alone in a room with Sela, Talson and the rest of his followers especially after what she had just witnessed, but now was not the time for Kat to be sensitive.

Kat squinted through the darkness in the back room, pulling her penlight from her pocket. She turned on the light and found the small door that was almost completely hidden by a stack of chairs and a table that were pushed against it. Kat pushed the chairs away from the door just enough so she could open it a quarter of the way. She squeezed through the opening with some difficulty and found herself standing at the foot of a narrow staircase that seemed to curve halfway up. Kat ascended the stairs and paused on the landing. In front of her stood a single rough wood door. Slowly she raised her hand and knocked.

There was no answer. Kat knocked again, slightly louder this time. "It's not locked," a lazy voice came from inside.

Kat hesitated for a moment, then pushed the door open. Kat was standing in a small loft apartment that consisted of a single room. In the far corner to Kat's left, a large bed took up a considerable amount of space in the room. The rest of the room was taken up by several bookshelves, and every inch of the rough walls was covered with pictures, newspaper clippings, and the like. Despite this, the room was minimally furnished, and besides the walls, it was very neat. The only furniture in the room was a small, but very organized desk that stood against the wall near the bed, and a large, very comfortable looking leather chair that sat in front of a large television at the other side of the room.

At first Kat did not see anyone. The room was completely silent and appeared to be empty.

"Katerina Thomason, my first visitor in about fourteen years."

Larry's voice startled Kat. Larry had been lying so motionless in bed that Kat had not immediately noticed him. Now she saw him laying flat on his back on the bed, his eyes at the ceiling. His posture reminded Kat so strikingly of Talson that Kat took a step back into the doorway.

"Larry," she said softly.

"Yeah, who died?" asked Larry, still looking at the ceiling. He was dressed in plaid pajama pants and a black T-shirt, which added to his look of complete indifference.

"Tracy," said Kat quietly.

"Sela shoot her?"

"No," said Kat, slightly taken aback. "She shot herself."

"Sela really kill Nelson?"

"Yeah, that's why I'm here," said Kat. "Nelco's dead and now Talson's mind is lost, he has nothing left, it's like he's empty or something."

"What's that got to do with me?" Larry still remained stationary on his back, staring at the ceiling.

"But we can't just let him die. There has to be something we can do."

"And you think I can help you, why?"

"I know you have the power, Larry. Maybe you don't like Talson, but after everything he's done he doesn't deserve to die like this. You know it shouldn't end this way."

Larry pushed himself up on one elbow and finally looked at Kat. "Who told you I didn't like Talson?"

"It doesn't matter, I know you know him, and I know you have the power, so you can help me."

"Yeah," said Larry rather bitterly, laying back down. "Yeah, I know him."

"And you have the power, right?" Kat said more forcefully.

Yes, I have the damn mind thing.

Okay then, help me help Talson. There has to be a way.

"Yes, there is always a way Kat, but that doesn't mean we should use it."

"So, what, you're just going to lay there and do nothing?" said Kat somewhat angrily. "Talson told me that you would never let the mistakes of the past repeat themselves."

"In the past Talson has let others die so he could live. He won't do that this time. The past has already been repeated here, Kat, there is nothing I can do to stop it anymore. It is Talson, not me that won't let the past be repeated."

"Are you saying someone would have to die to save Talson?" asked Kat.

Larry sat up fully, looking Kat directly in the eye for the first time. "You know how it works, Katerina. The mind is supposed to be the thing that makes us human, but for people like us the mind is what makes us less human. Minds like ours don't create great things, they destroy them. No one is supposed to have our ability."

"So you're like my dad, you think we shouldn't use it?"

"It takes a great deal of strength and effort to control the power to invade the minds of others, but it takes even more strength not to do it at all," replied Larry. "I do it not by choice, Kat," he continued. "I have never had the strength to stop using the power. I have always used it, but I have never found a way to use it for anything good. The power we have is dark, Kat."

For a moment Kat was not sure if Larry had spoken aloud or if she had simply heard his thoughts. His mind was perfectly clear, as if nothing but their dialogue existed in his head. Kat could hardly believe that Larry had no other thoughts.

"It's mental control, Kat, and it too is evil," said Larry, before Kat could put her thoughts into a spoken question. "I have near perfect mind control."

"When I talk to someone I have no other thoughts in the back of my mind. When I see something happening in front of me at the bar it's the only thing in my head in that moment. That's why I have a perfect memory for what I see."

"But why is that evil?"

"Being able to hear the thoughts that go through people's heads everyday depressed me when I was younger because while I was hearing people's thoughts I was judging them. I allowed myself to have emotions toward a person based only on how they thought, rather than how they spoke or acted. I hated everyone no matter how great they were to me because I knew what they thought about in the privacy of their own minds. So I trained my mind to be blank whenever I talk to someone or hear their thoughts. I don't allow myself to have an emotional response or to judge them for their thoughts, only for their words and their actions. It's evil because it means I don't really have much response to words and actions either, any more."

"Is that what Sela does?" asked Kat. "She's always blank."

"Yeah, I think Sela does do something along those lines."

"But she doesn't have the power, does she?"

"No," said Larry, "she does it so people like us can't tell what she's thinking. You've probably noticed that it's easier to hear people's thoughts when they are having an emotional reaction. Thinking about the past and the future gives us an emotional reaction to the present moment, an opinion, a prediction, a wish, an intention. That's the human mental experience. If you take everything as is without connecting it to the past or the future, without judging it, and without an opinion, then all you have is a scene in front of your eyes. It consists of pieces. If someone tries to hear what you're thinking about the situation all they will hear is an objective piece by piece analysis of the objects and people in that situation. Chances are they won't find out anything they don't already know.

"I think Sela started doing it as a way of helping Talson. When he was weak she took care of him, but she didn't want Talson to know how many doubts she had about helping him. She never stopped doing it after

Talson got better, so now Talson can't read her and neither can anyone else, but it's made her into a robot. It's sad to see what it's done to her. She used to be so open and expressive, but you would never guess that now."

"Do you think she wants it that way?"

"I don't know if she can control her control anymore, if you know what I mean. I've let myself have some mental dialogue recently, but only when I'm alone. It's hard to deal with your own mind once you get used to suppressing it."

Kat looked at Larry sitting on this bed in his pajamas, his curly light brown and gray hair matted and out of place. His dull brown eyes made him look slightly insane. He looked like an old bartender, a man who could snap at any moment, certainly not an articulate man with perfect control of his mental states.

"Tell me something, Kat," said Larry. "Why do you want to save Talson?"

Kat wasn't sure how to answer. She couldn't honestly say why she wanted to save Talson, she just felt like it was the only right thing to do.

"Fair enough," said Larry without waiting for Kat to speak. "Tell me this, why come to me for help?"

"Because Talson trusts you," said Kat. "And I thought if anyone could find a way to fix this, it would be you."

"You know me better than I thought," muttered Larry. He sighed. "Normally it is not possible to save the mind that has been as fragmented as Talson's. I mean, technically he should already be dead, but as it has always been, he's not dead because of his incredible power. Talson could live entirely through the minds of others. The question is whether he will choose to lose himself or lose his life. It's not my place to choose for him."

"So you're not going to do anything?" asked Kat.

"I never said that," replied Larry. "I'm going to go downstairs, make sure my bar hasn't been bombed, and then go back to sleep." Larry rose slowly from his bed and grabbed a gray bathrobe that hung on a hook next to his bed. He walked out the door without a backward glance, pulling the robe over his shoulders.

The light was dim in the bar as Larry entered, followed closely by Kat. "Well, look who it is," said Roco's unmistakable voice through the gloomy air. "It's the boss."

"What are you doing in my bar, Ramirez?" Larry pretended to sound angry.

"Your bar," sneered Roco, "it was mine before it was yours."

"It is mine and it was yours, enough said," said Larry with a chuckle.

"You know while you're laughing there is a dead body in here," said Talson, who was leaning against the bar.

"That's why I'm laughing," said Larry with a cruelly sarcastic smirk. He glanced at Tracy's limp body without interest. "She owed me fifty bucks from the night she passed out in here."

"A woman kills herself in your bar and all you're worried about is the tab she ran up before she died?" Kat couldn't tell if Talson was genuinely angry with Larry or just joking with him.

"Wow, Talson's being sensitive," said Larry loudly. "Have you lost your mind?" He grinned cruelly. "Oh that's right, you have lost your mind." Larry glanced out the window. "Look who's coming, it's the man with the mind he's too cool to use."

Kat looked out the window in time to see her father standing outside the bar. Larry's sudden contempt and insensitivity toward Tracy, Talson, and John Carl was far from his usual unassuming demeanor. "I'm not sure I want to witness this again, I'm going back to bed. You look like you could use some sleep yourself," he added, looking at Talson. "Don't forget to get rid of the body before I open tomorrow. Sela, you owe me fifty bucks," he added as he headed back through the door and up the stairs.

There was a shocked silence for a moment. Kat could still see her father standing outside the door, apparently torn about coming inside.

"One question," said Roco. "Is Larry serious?"

"Yes," said Sela.

"No," said Talson at almost the same moment.

"So I don't owe him fifty bucks?" asked Sela. It was the first attempt at humor Kat had heard from Sela in a long time. Kat kept thinking about what Larry had told her about Sela. She wondered what it would be like to live completely objectively with no emotions or judgments. It didn't seem worth it.

"No, he was serious about the fifty bucks," said Talson, "but not much else. He's up to something."

Kat took a peek out the window again, then made her way slowly to the door. She looked uncertainly over her shoulder at Talson.

"Don't look at me, go."

Kat stepped out into the night, closing the heavy door behind her. Kat's father was standing a few feet away, leaning against a wooden post.

"Hey Kat," he said casually as she approached.

"Hi Dad," said Kat apprehensively. She had no idea what to expect from him.

"Is Nelson dead yet?" John Carl asked in the same casual tone.

"Yeah," said Kat without elaborating.

"And Tracy?"

"Yeah," said Kat again.

"You guilty?"

"No." Kat was slightly taken aback.

"Talson?"

"No."

"You gonna try to save him?"

Kat stood for a moment unable to think of anything to say. "How? How did you know—?" she broke off. She could not imagine how her father could have known what had happened to Talson let alone that she was planning to try to help him.

"How did I know?" her father chuckled. "Have you seen him?" he added with sarcasm that bordered on cruelty.

"His eyes, yeah I know," said Kat, choosing to answer the question and ignore the tone in which it had been asked.

"You didn't answer the more important question," said John Carl. "Are you gonna save him or not?"

Kat looked at her father. She was unsure of what to say and afraid of how her father would react to anything she did say.

John Carl sighed as if he had resigned himself to do something very unpleasant. "You don't have to be afraid to tell me that you want to save him just because you think I'd rather you didn't. Even if you don't know why you want to help him, you should just tell me the truth."

Kat continued to look at her father, completely lost for words.

"What? I can do the mind thing too, remember?"

"Yeah, but you didn't do anything all those times when I was in your head trying to force you to tell me stuff," said Kat dropping her gaze. "And you said that as long as I was with Talson then we were enemies."

"I said that, but you should know better than to think I meant it. I don't always mean what I say, Kat, in fact I rarely do. In fact, most people rarely mean what they say. They think what they mean, and say something different. It's only people like Talson who don't say or think what they mean."

"People say what they mean, Dad," said Kat. "Thoughts don't matter unless you say it."

"That's not true, Kat, that's convenient."

"You're the one who always used to tell me that."

"Yes, and I told you that in the hope that it would save you and others from your mind."

"But people think horrible things, even good people," protested Kat. "It's not always the truth."

"Good people are terrible sometimes, just like terrible people sometimes do good things. Thoughts hold the potential for both sides. Words represent a preliminary decision toward one side, and actions are a more decisive choice. What you think about what you've done in the aftermath of that action is the truth of who you are. I said we were enemies, and I acted like we were, but I never thought it was true."

Kat nodded, "me neither. Do you think Talson should have the power? Even though he hurt people with it, he hated himself for it."

"What do you think?"

"I don't know," said Kat, looking away.

"Really?" challenged John Carl. "That's not what you're thinking. You're thinking you need him to have it, whether it's good for him or not."

"But—" began Kat, but she stopped herself. Her father had said exactly what she had been thinking. "It's just that he's the only person who can help me to control my mind. I need him."

"You're right, Kat. Talson is the only person who has ever managed to control the power of his mind while still maintaining complete use of it. He has control to the point that he can totally take over someone's mind without killing them. But people deserve their own thoughts. There are just some things that no one was ever meant to see and hear."

"Yeah, I know, I feel like I shouldn't have heard Tracy's last thoughts before she killed herself," muttered Kat.

"Exactly," said John Carl. "Our thoughts are supposed to be private, they are our last true freedom. People like us have the power to take that freedom away. Without mental freedom there is little reason for anyone to live. Talson is the only person who has ever been able to truly control the power, and he is the only one who can truly help you to control your mind, but that's not a reason to save him. You shouldn't save Talson because you need him. If you're going to help Talson it should be because you know he needs you."

"I don't think he really needs me," objected Kat.

"He gave up his power to save you, the Silver Shadows, and even me. Nelco was going to kill me, and I thought he was going to kill you. I used my mind to try to destroy him before he could get to you. Talson gave part of his mind to Sela, and she carried out his plan. Talson and Sela saved us all."

"Don't give me too much credit, you might hurt yourself," Talson's voice startled them both.

Kat stared from her father to Talson as he approached them. She wasn't at all sure what to expect from either of them at the moment. For a brief moment Talson and John Carl looked at each other, then they both looked away at the same time.

"I should have known that the day I used my mind would be the day you lost yours," muttered John Carl.

"Be careful what you wish for; I suppose that's the lesson I'm supposed to have learned," said Talson dryly.

"Wow, you have lost your mind," said John Carl with a smirk. "The real Talson would never admit that he ever wanted me to use my power."

"You're the one saying 'Talson saved everyone, he deserves your help, Kat, he needs you'." Talson did a rather cruel and accurate impression of John Carl's gruff voice. "Do you hear yourself?"

"It's the truth, you did save everyone," said John Carl. "As much as I wish I didn't have to, I'll give you that."

"You don't have to give me credit, Sela did everything."

"Yeah, but you were behind it, just like last time. Sela's work is your work."

"Regardless, it's not me that needs help. It's Larry."

"Oh that's clever," said John Carl coldly. Suddenly Kat sensed anger from her father toward Talson, although his mind was blank.

"I mean old man Larry, what the hell is wrong with you?" Talson looked momentarily disgusted.

"What's wrong with Larry?" interrupted Kat, somewhat confused.

"If anyone knows it's you," said Talson. "What did you talk to him about?"

"Helping you," replied Kat.

"What he say?" asked Talson.

"No."

"What did he think, though?" asked John Carl.

"Nothing, I'm sure," said Talson.

"Yeah," said Kat. "He told me that's how he controls his mind."

"Yeah, it makes him nearly impossible to read and gives him near perfect memory," said Talson. "He may have said he wouldn't help me, but he's putting my mind back together."

"What?" said Kat and John Carl together.

"You can't just put people's minds back together," said John Carl, sounding annoyed. "No one has that kind of mental control. You can't piece together someone's mind, that would be like reliving their entire life for them. You'd have to get every memory exactly right or you'd change the way the person remembered his own life. No one has that kind of memory."

Talson looked momentarily disappointed. "Larry does. Do you remember nothing?"

"Even if he could put the pieces of your mind back together there is no way to pass them to you. Your mind would be inside him, so you would be living through Larry's mind."

"I'm essentially living through his mind right now, without it I have no past."

"But you can't live like that forever. I still say it's impossible," John Carl said, shaking his head.

"For those who have lived alone, possible and impossible are very clear, but for those who have lived lives with others the lines are blurred. I see what is possible in the minds of others, even if those things don't exist in my mind."

John Carl looked at Talson without speaking. Kat knew they were communicating without speaking, but she could not penetrate their thoughts. By 'lived with others' she knew Talson meant living with the minds of others, but she still didn't understand what Larry was doing.

"You were right about one thing, John Carl," Talson sounded sad. "I would be nothing without the others, but I am much more without myself."

For a second as the two men looked at each other, Kat was afraid that her father would attack Talson in some way, but then they both turned away from each other. John Carl walked away silently into the night, heading across the street toward the docks. Talson headed back into The Sharktooth Bar.

Kat stood outside in the near darkness, staring blankly at the shabby exterior of the Sharktooth with its barred windows and rough, paint chipped walls. It had a haunted appearance under the yellow glow of the streetlight.

Kat walked back to the front of the bar, pausing with her hand on the doorknob. She wasn't sure if she wanted to go back inside and see Tracy's bloody, lifeless corpse slouched over the bar. She didn't even want to see Tina, because she knew nothing she could say would make the situation any easier. Kat withdrew from the door slowly and walked around the side of the building. Sparse grass crunched loudly under her feet, breaking the silence of the night. Kat could never remember the harbor being so silent. The street was always busy with people and cars, but tonight it was silent and deserted. Kat made her way to the small parking lot behind the bar and sat down on the curb. She stared blankly into the darkness, and for the first time Kat had no thoughts, no emotions, no judgments, nothing but space and silence.

Suddenly a narrow beam of light fell across Kat's back. "What are you doing out here," the voice made Kat jump. She turned around to see Larry standing in the doorway to the back of the bar, still wearing his gray bathrobe. The light was coming from a lamp that sat on a table behind him.

"I don't really know what I'm doing, to be honest," said Kat.

"Well, I came to ask you to help me," said Larry. All of the sarcasm he had had earlier was gone and Larry appeared calm and completely serious.

"Me, help you? How?"

"I'm trying to help Talson, but I need you to help me. To put it simply, I need your mind to fix his mind."

"I thought you were going to bed and you weren't going to help Talson."

"You really take people too seriously Kat, you know I didn't mean any of that crap, right?"

"I wasn't sure," said Kat defensively.

"Yeah, well I owe Talson one," said Larry. "Actually, I owe him more than one, and I'm really not as lazy or as mean as I pretend to be, at least not anymore."

"Did Talson try to kill you, once?" asked Kat softly. She had wondered what the connection was between Larry and Talson and this was the only thing she could think of that would explain their odd relationship.

"Yes, he has tried several times, actually," Larry replied blankly. "But I killed him a little bit every day of his life for years, so I deserved it. Talson has been through hell, Kat, his whole life he has never been happy."

"He seems happy sometimes," said Kat.

Larry shook his head, he looked overwhelmingly sad all of a sudden. "In his mind he can create whatever feelings he wants, but that's not his real self."

"Who is he really, then?" asked Kat. "Where did he come from?"

"Nowhere he wants to remember," said Larry in a hollow voice. "The only reason I wouldn't help Talson is because I don't really want to see his mind, I don't know if I can handle it, that's why I need you."

Kat didn't see how she could possibly handle it any better than Larry would, but she agreed to help him anyway. She stood up and followed him into the back room. "My dad said it wasn't possible to put someone's mind back together, is he wrong?" she asked, as Larry closed the door behind her.

"Well, it's a little easier to put something back together if you've already taken it apart once before," said Larry softly.

Kat wanted very badly to see the thoughts behind Larry's words about Talson, but she doubted there were any.

Larry sat down at a small table. Kat sat opposite him. "Talson wouldn't want you to see what you're going to see, Kat," said Larry, "but it's the only way, just be prepared."

Kat nodded, "I'm ready."

Kat did not see anything. There were no images or memories flashing through her mind. There were only words, the words inside Talson's mind as he walked down the street toward Kat's own house. His intentions were in those words, and they did not match what he had described to Kat. *He would kill John Carl if he refused to use his power, and even if he did use it he would still deserve to die. His daughter would be just like him, he would make sure she was.*

The words became so jumbled in Kat's mind that she could no longer understand them. She could only feel Talson's anger, his sadness. Bits and pieces of other situations, other memories of Talson's life, came into Kat's head, but they were fragmented and out of chronological order, the jumbled pieces of a broken mind.

Larry had to be killed, but he knew he would never be able to do it. If only he could make Larry care, make him think, he never would. Sela had made herself just like him. Kat, he wanted to tell her everything, but he was too ashamed, it didn't matter anyway. She would hate him. If she knew, she would have no reason to look up to him. Talson's emotions washed over Kat's mind, anger, sadness, hatred, hatred for others who didn't understand him, hatred for John Carl and Larry, but mostly hatred for himself. He wanted so badly to think the way the others thought, so simply. They were all so happy, in their own world. He would never be like them.

Finally Kat saw. She saw Talson's life, but it was blurred. There was a woman with long black hair and green eyes, and there was an angry looking little boy with brown hair. She saw the cliffs by Headquarters, and watched as a car went tumbling down the cliffs. Two boys ran through the streets being chased by three angry men. There was an old rundown schoolyard where two boys played basketball. There was Marissa as a much younger woman, and there was Roco, Barty, and Nelco laughing together at the bar. The images in Kat's mind became more and more jumbled and chaotic. She could no longer tell what she was seeing. She was no longer seeing Talson's thoughts, she was inside them. She was the boy in the car as it tumbled down the bluff top, it was her fault. She was a killer. She wished she were dead. She wanted so badly to get out, to make her thoughts stop. And then they did, and everything went completely blank.

Kat could hear voices around her, but she could not understand them. Slowly she could make out Sela's voice. "Did she really see everything in your mind?"

"Not everything."

Kat recognized Talson's voice. Her eyelids felt heavy, but slowly she forced them open. She was still sitting slumped over the table in the back room, but Larry was gone. Roco, Sela, and Talson were standing around her.

"I can't believe you did that, Kat," said Sela.

"I can't believe you executed Nelco with a water pump," Kat mumbled, pushing herself up on one elbow. "It was all Larry's plan anyway."

"I told you he wasn't serious," said Talson, looking at Sela. Then he turned and looked at Kat. His eyes shone green in the soft light.

Kat stared at him for a moment. "You have my eyes," she whispered.

Talson smiled slightly. "No, Kat, *you* have *my* eyes."

Kat stood up slowly and saw her father standing a distance away in the doorway. She looked at him then at Talson. "You two are related, aren't you?" she said.

"What?" Roco's eyes widened.

Kat looked directly at her father, ignoring Roco. "He's your brother who you said died, isn't he?"

For a moment John Carl said nothing. Then he nodded very slightly.

Kat turned to Talson, he nodded in the same noncommittal sort of way.

"Why didn't you tell me?" asked Kat.

"Because I officially died," said Talson softly.

"In the car, I know, but you're not actually dead."

"No, but I should be," said Talson. "If not then, I certainly should be now."

"What's your real name?" asked Kat.

Talson shook his head slowly.

"He'll never tell you that one, Kat, trust me," said Roco.

"I bet Larry knows," said Kat.

"Where is Larry?" asked Roco.

"He's upstairs," said Sela turning away.

"Is he okay?" asked Kat. She looked at Talson, but he, too, avoided her gaze.

"I never wanted him to do this," he said softly. "He shouldn't have helped me."

"You didn't deserve to die like that," said Sela

"Yes I did," said Talson. Suddenly he sounded angry. "I have always deserved to die like that. I should have died so many times, but someone always stopped it." Talson caught John Carl's eye for a fleeting second. "People have always risked their lives to save me, and—"Talson's breath caught in his chest.

"That's because there have always been people who cared about you," said Sela.

"No Sela, the people who have saved me did so under the misconception that I would someday find it in myself to return the favor." He turned without another word and headed up the stairs toward Larry's room.

For a moment no one moved, then John Carl slowly made his way across the room to the staircase.

"You're crazy to go up there, Thomason," said Roco.

"No, Ramirez," said John Carl, "I'd be crazy not to." He paused on the bottom step. *Kat, come with me.*

Kat stood still for a moment. She wanted to ask her father why, but she decided against it and followed him up the stairs.

Larry was laying on his bed in the exact same posture he had been in when Kat had last visited his room. Looking at the clock on the wall in Larry's room Kat could scarcely believe that only an hour had passed since she had last been there. It felt like ages. The lamp on the desk sent a soft glow of light on his pale face as he lay perfectly motionless.

Talson stood a few paces from the bed, looking down at Larry. He did not acknowledge John Carl or Kat as they came through the door to stand behind him.

"You shouldn't be here," said Larry suddenly. "I would deserve to die alone."

"So would I," said Talson seriously, "but you made sure that didn't happen."

"You don't deserve that," said Larry. "If anything is wrong with you it's because of me. You know that. You know people always talk about wanting to die surrounded by family. I was always convinced that would never happen to me. In fact I never thought I'd want that."

"Is it worse than you imagined?" asked John Carl. He sounded like he was trying to make light of the situation, but Kat wasn't sure that was possible.

"No, it's just about as terrifying as I thought it would be," said Larry with a weak smile. "But seriously, you shouldn't be here, J.C."

Kat stood back from the door, feeling too scared to enter. The phrase 'surrounded by family' kept replaying in her mind. She knew what it meant, but somehow she could not accept that there was any truth in it.

"I'm here because of Kat," John Carl said. "Whether or not you think you deserve us to be here or not isn't the point. The point is telling the truth before it's too late. That's why we're here."

Kat looked at her father knowing that until she spoke what she knew was the truth, it would never seem real to her. "Larry is my grandfather, isn't he? He's your father, that's why we all have the power," she said very quietly.

John Carl gave the same noncommittal nod he had made when Kat had asked if he and Talson were brothers.

"Yes, Kat," said Talson more forcefully.

"But why didn't you tell me," asked Kat. "Why would you hide who you really are? Does anyone else know?"

"No one knows," said Talson.

"Not even Roco and Sela?" asked Kat. "What about Barty or Nelco. Barty worked with you both, didn't he know you were brothers?"

"Roco and Sela never knew," said Talson. "I showed Romez that picture of us tonight, so I think he knows something now. Nelco figured it out in the end, but Barty never knew, not even when he died."

"He was a liar, he never really deserved to know," muttered John Carl.

"Who are we really?" Kat asked. "Why did you all hide your identities?"

"We are a broken family, Kat," said Larry softly, after a short silence. "We all have incredible talent that we allowed to destroy us in different ways. When we were together we were always a family full of hate. The best way for all of us to live was to live as if the family didn't exist. I made my sons hate me, and each other. I couldn't live with that truth, so I pretended they weren't my sons."

Kat looked to her father, wanting to hear an explanation from him. "Why didn't you tell me about Talson all those times I asked you, you could have told me, why didn't you?"

"I was afraid, I suppose," said John Carl. For the first time he looked ashamed. "I knew you would have the mental abilities, and I was afraid your mind would destroy you. I didn't know what to do about it, so I ignored it. I told you that the things people think don't matter, so you wouldn't take your skills seriously. I'm sorry I wasn't brave for you Kat, you deserve better."

Kat ignored her father's apology, and turned to face Talson. "You didn't tell me because my dad didn't want you to, right?" she said, remembering something Talson had once told her.

Talson nodded. His eyes shone a milky shade of green, not so dark as Kat's, but still the resemblance between them was evident. Kat wondered for a moment why she had never seen her own face in Talson before now. She looked at Larry, and the realization that he was her grandfather still seemed unbelievable, despite the resemblance she now saw between Larry and her father.

"I killed a lot of people, Kat," said Talson quietly. Although he had confessed this to Kat before it seemed to take him a great deal of effort to admit it this time. "I didn't want you to be like me. I wanted you to be better, stronger, kinder, and less angry. I didn't want you to hate yourself. I thought I couldn't help you if you knew who I was, I thought you'd just end up like me. But I should have known better, I suppose you were never going to become the killer I am."

"But you really wanted to tell me everything, didn't you?" protested Kat. "You hated my dad, so why did you do what he wanted?"

Talson shook his head slowly, but said nothing.

Kat continued to stare at Talson, waiting for him to say something to defend himself or explain himself, but he said nothing. *Doesn't he have anything to say for himself? He can't admit to being afraid of my dad. He wanted me to be better than him. It wasn't even a real answer.* She expected more of Talson.

"Kat," said John Carl forcefully. Kat felt suddenly as if a giant hand had grasped her brain stopping her thoughts. "Whether or not Talson and I once hated each other, or even still do isn't the point.

The point is that you saved Talson for the wrong reasons. You saved him because you wanted more answers out of him. You did it for yourself, just like I did when I was eight years old. There was a time when I would have said that was all this man deserved, but today he deserves better."

Kat was completely taken aback by her father's defense of Talson. Talson himself looked just as surprised.

"I've waited a long time for that," whispered Larry. He looked glassy eyed now, leaning on his pillows. "If you are going to hate anyone it should be me, anyway."

"No, it shouldn't," said John Carl. "You did what no one else would."

"I stopped hating you a long time ago, Larry," said Talson softly.

Larry smiled slightly and closed his eyes, "just promise me one thing, both of you, actually all three of you. Just don't kill each other," said Larry slowly.

John Carl moved to stand next to Talson at the end of Larry's bed. "I'm not a killer," he said with a slight smile, "it's all on him," he gestured to Talson.

Talson smiled slightly, "alright, I promise I won't let Kat kill me when she changes her mind about saving me. No, seriously," Talson reached out and touched Larry's hand. "I'm done killing."

Larry, lay back against his pillows with a smile on his wrinkled face. "Thank you, Larry," he said softly. His eyes closed all the way and he lay limp on the bed.

There was silence. Kat felt Larry's last moments, but this time she forced herself to concentrate on the clock on the wall so Larry could have his last thoughts to himself. For the first time she didn't care if she missed out on some information she wanted. Her father was right, some things were meant to be private.

Talson withdrew his hand and took a step back from the bed.

He'll still try to kill me. He just said that to make Larry's last moment a happy one.

Talson suddenly glared at John Carl. "I dare you to say that out loud," he said. Kat could not tell if he was truly angry with John Carl for his accusation, or if he was just pretending to be mad.

"I think you lied," said John Carl flatly.

"You have the power, though," interjected Kat. "You know he was telling the truth."

"Ah ha, busted," said Talson with a slight laugh. "I see why you never wanted to use your mind. Until you use your power you're free to think what you want about people. Once you see their thoughts you can't deny the truth about them."

John Carl looked angry for a moment then he cracked a small smile. "Alright, I guess it's just hard to believe that Lord Talson won't try to kill me again."

"And live with your mind inside my head? I'm crazy enough without it. And don't call me 'Lord'."

"You should call him Larry," said Kat. "That is your name, isn't it?" she added, looking at Talson.

"I'm dead, remember? I don't have a name."

"You're a liar," said Kat smiling slightly. She looked at her father, but John Carl shook his head.

"Don't look at me," he said with a chuckle. "I know better than to get involved with that."

"For all the hatred between the three of you, you guys were actually pretty funny together," remarked Kat.

Talson shook his head, looking sad. "It was Larry, he was a funny man when he wanted to be. We can't let his humor die with him."

"I'm sorry," said Kat suddenly. "I didn't mean this to happen. I wanted to do the right thing. I didn't really mean what I said before. I know. I don't know what I was thinking, and I was being selfish, it was wrong."

"You mean, you didn't really just save me for answers?" said Talson, pretending to look disappointed. He smiled. "I know, Kat," he said more seriously. "I know why you did it. No one means what they say, and most people don't even mean what they think. Don't take your thoughts too seriously."

CHAPTER 26

LAWRENCE JAMES

Kat looked out over the sea, watching the clouds swirl around in the dark sky. It was late afternoon, but it was dark enough to be night. Kat looked at her father who stood a few feet away staring out to sea. He had asked to come with her to Headquarters, but she knew he didn't really want to be there. He was afraid.

"Can you see it?" asked Kat softly.

"Yes, I've always been able to see it," muttered John Carl.

Kat looked out at the large rock that stood empty in the middle of the sea. "I can't see it anymore," she said.

"Talson must trust you," said John Carl. "He was always proud of Headquarters. Creating something so complete and extensive that fooled everyone. It must have been hard for him when all his followers saw it for what it really is."

"I guess," said Kat. "I think it bothered them more than it bothered him."

"Talson says that he, Larry, and I all have the same power, but it's not true, Kat. Talson is leagues more mentally powerful than Larry or I ever was. I mean look at Headquarters. He can make you see anything. He has the power to control people's perceptions and he abuses it."

"Yeah, I guess he does," muttered Kat. "But I don't know, I don't really think Talson is a bad person."

"That's debatable," said John Carl with a slight smile. "I guess he is a bad person, but he wishes he wasn't, so in that sense he isn't as bad as he could be."

"Are you going to come with me?" asked Kat.

"No, you just go, Kat."

Kat started down the bluff slowly, looking back at her father on the cliff top. She wished he would come with her. Kat wasn't sure why, but going into Headquarters alone seemed scarier than anything that had happened. It had been nearly a week since the events at the Sharktooth, but Kat had not seen Talson or any of the Silver Shadows. She wasn't sure she was ready to see Talson and she had the feeling he wasn't ready to see her, but Kat knew better than to try to postpone the inevitable. As much as Kat struggled to accept it, Talson was family.

As Kat entered the tunnel, the complete darkness momentarily disoriented her. She pulled out her flashlight even though Sela had told her lights wouldn't work. To her surprise the beam of light shone brilliantly off the walls of the tunnel, illuminating the path ahead. Kat wondered absently why Sela had lied to her, but somehow the lie didn't surprise her. She was beginning to doubt whether anything Sela said was true.

Headquarters looked shabby with its rough sandstone walls and uneven rock staircases. Kat suddenly wished she could see the old Headquarters with its smooth black walls and handsome staircases. She tried to imagine it the way it had looked before, half hoping that it would trick her mind into seeing it the way Talson had made her see it. Her attempt was in vain however, and the rough stone walls remained as she arrived at the door to Talson's office.

She raised her hand and knocked softly. "Come in Kat," Talson's voice sounded far away.

Kat entered cautiously. Talson's office looked as it always had, full of books, shelves and photo albums. Talson was not in sight, but the door to his bedroom was slightly open. Kat peeked through the door and saw Talson lying in his bed.

Kat stood in the doorway without speaking. She had thought of so many things she wanted to say to Talson, but now that she saw him none of them seemed important anymore.

"How are you doing?" she asked softly.

"I'm alive," answered Talson, his eyes at the ceiling. "Are you doing alright?"

"Yeah," said Kat. "I'm fine, I just came to—" she paused. "Well I don't know."

"I want to show you something, Kat." Talson rose slowly from his bed. He was dressed a lot like Larry had been when Kat had entered his room. Kat was about to remark to Talson on his resemblance to Larry, but was afraid Talson wouldn't appreciate the comparison.

"No, I know I look like him," said Talson. "No offense taken."

"I never saw it before I knew."

"Well, we all tend to only see the things we know, because we generally don't believe our own judgment when we see things we don't know." Talson pulled on his full-length black coat and wordlessly headed for the door. Kat followed him, somewhat confused.

Talson led Kat outside and back through the tunnel. "Sela told me lights don't

work in this tunnel," said Kat, shining her light in front of her.

"Sela lies," said Talson without elaborating.

"I always believed what she told me, but now_"

"You think she lied about everything," Talson finished Kat's sentence.

"Did she?" asked Kat as they emerged from the tunnel.

"I doubt it. I lied to Sela a lot, she tells those same lies to others. Sela's mother and father were both extraordinary liars, so she has inherited the gift of dishonesty. But despite that, she always finds it within herself to tell the truth when it really matters."

They had climbed the cliff and began to walk toward the streets. Kat looked around, but her father was nowhere to be seen. Talson led Kat to Milro's apartment and climbed into his car. Kat got in beside him. "Where are we going?" she asked.

Talson did not answer. After a few minutes Talson pulled the car in front of a small cemetery. Talson got out of the car and led Kat through the graveyard. The cloudy weather made the silent graveyard seem eerie. Talson paused in front of a small headstone. Kat stopped and stood behind him, looking down at the gravestone. The stone read 'Lawrence James Thomason Junior.' Kat's eyes shifted to the headstone beside it on the same plot, which read "Linda Katerina Thomason."

"Your mom?" Kat whispered.

Talson nodded.

"My dad named me after her, didn't he?"

"Yes," said Talson. "You look like her, too."

"She's the only one who really died in the car accident, right?"

Talson nodded again.

"You pretended to be dead, why didn't my dad do the same thing?"

"I knew I was going to run away before it happened, I was just waiting for the right time to do it. The accident gave me the chance to disappear. I knew my brother wanted to run away too, he just never believed that he could survive."

"But you were three, how did you survive?"

Talson shrugged slightly. "The same way I do now, I guess. One second at a time, one thought at a time."

"Does it ever bother you?" Kat gestured to the gravestone, "I mean having your own grave, even though you're alive?"

"Not really," said Talson softly. "The grave isn't really a lie. I believe Larry Junior really died in that car. The crash was my fault. My father hit my mother. He did that a lot back then, but that particular time I just thought I had to do something about it. I finally told him to stop. He turned around to hit me and took his eyes off the road. We swerved and went off the cliff right by Headquarters."

"That doesn't make the wreck your fault."

"That's what your dad told me, but I never believed him. I picked the wrong time to stand up to my father, that was my fault." Talson looked down at the graves. "It's not my grave that bothers me, it's that one." He gestured to Linda Thomason's gravestone. "My mother deserved better than this. They say you only live once, and you die once, but everyone dies many times in their lives. Part of you dies every day and something else is born, but you live through it. Larry James Thomason Junior really did die in that car. I never wanted to remember who I was ever again. I wanted to be someone else. That's when I realized that I could use other people's minds and hide from my own mind. I became Talson, the man of many minds. I took over people's minds so I could forget what was in my own mind. I killed a lot of people, and I tried to kill my father to get revenge for my mother. Then I tried to kill my brother because he would never fight against our father the way I did. But even through all that I always knew that the only person I really ever wanted to kill was myself, Larry Junior. But you know, he was the only one I could never kill, because he's already dead. "

"Do you really hate my father?" asked Kat softly.

Talson shook his head. "No, Kat, I don't hate him. He made a lot of mistakes and did a lot of cruel things, just like I did. He almost killed me, I almost killed him, but it's over now."

"When did he almost kill you?" asked Kat.

Talson unbuttoned his coat and shirt to reveal a long scar on his chest. "Larry was drunk, he got mad at my brother and took a knife from the kitchen. He was in a rage, swinging it all over the place. John Carl thought Larry was really going to cut him with it so he grabbed me and said 'cut Larry instead, he's the one who hates you.' John Carl grabbed me and used me as a shield. He pushed me toward my father and the knife cut my arm. I guess my dad realized what had happened and he dropped the knife. John Carl pushed me down and I fell on it."

Kat looked up at Talson, horrified. "He told your father to cut you instead of him?"

"He did that all the time. He always told my father to beat me up instead of him. My brother always told Larry that I was the only one who hated him. I think Larry really believed that until I showed up to visit him in prison about fifteen years after the accident."

"Larry was in jail that long?" said Kat

"Twenty-five years was his sentence," said Talson grimly. "He served seventeen. I visited him a lot and I helped him to control his mind, that made him hate people less."

"He told me he hated everyone because he judged them for their thoughts."

"Yes, that was his whole problem. That's why he was violent, and that was why he drank. But he changed. Larry was a great man as long as he didn't let his anger get the better of him."

"You forgave him even though he killed your mother?" said Kat softly.

"I killed my best friend, Kat, and I never forgave myself for that, just like I never forgave Larry for what he did. I didn't forgive him, I just understood him. He acted like he hated everyone, but he really just hated himself, he was no different from me."

"You shouldn't hate yourself, Talson," said Kat softly, "you deserve better than that."

Talson smiled slightly. "I know, Kat, but my mind never wants to believe that. I need you though, Kat, I really do. I've always needed my friends. It used to be Barty, and Nelco and Romez, but Romez is the only one who didn't turn against me. I never act like I appreciate anyone, but believe me, Kat, I would die without people like Roco and Sela, and you and the rest of the Silver Shadows. Even Larry, I needed him in the end, he's the last person I ever wanted to have help me and now I have to honor him."

"Is he going to be buried here?"

"No, he wanted to be cremated, no service, no nothing, but I'm going to spread his ashes at the circle."

Kat nodded, "He was my Grandpa even if I only knew it for like two days. I'll come with you."

Talson smiled, "Alright, let's go."

They drove in silence, but Kat knew Talson was thinking about his life and what he was going to do now that the war within his own family was over. They arrived at the park and Kat followed Talson around the pond to the circle of trees. Roco, Milro, Tiro and Mevsin were already there and seemed to be deep in conversation. They immediately fell silent as they caught sight of Kat and Talson. Kat half wanted to know what they were talking about, but she resisted. After everything that had happened, Kat wasn't sure she wanted to know others' thoughts anymore.

"Hey kid," Roco nodded to Kat, "you okay?"

"Yeah, you?" said Kat.

Roco nodded wordlessly and looked at Talson. *He left me the bar.*

"The Sharktooth was always yours, Romez."

"Just curious, what do the cops think happened at the Sharktooth?" asked Mevsin.

"Tracy killed Larry, killed herself, something like that," said Milro.

"Based on what evidence?"

"The evidence in their minds, of course," said Talson lightly.

"That's wrong, you can't just make the police believe whatever you want," objected Mevsin frowning.

"And what would you suggest, Melvin, shall I tell the police that I'm Larry James Junior who died thirty six years ago, and my father destroyed his own mind in a successful attempt to rebuild my mind after it was fragmented when Conner Nelson was electrocuted by a water pump in a building that no one can see?"

"Point taken, jackass," said Mevsin with a smirk.

"My apologies, Mevsin," said Talson seriously. "That was my tribute to Larry, it's what he would have said." Talson turned away and poured the ashes around the base of the old house.

No one spoke for what seemed like an eternity. Finally Roco turned to Kat. "Your friend's here, you know," he indicated a clump of trees on the far side of the house. "She's been hiding there the whole time."

"What?" Kat hurried over and peered between the trees. Sure enough, she found Tina crouched below the tangled undergrowth. She was staring up at Kat looking sad and scared, rather like a lost puppy. Kat, however, was not enthusiastic to see her. "What the hell are you doing here, and why are you hiding like some coward?"

"I was hoping to see Sela, she said she wouldn't be here but I guess—"Tina broke off awkwardly. For the first time Kat thought Tina seemed scared of her.

"She lied, good guess," said Kat coolly, "but she must have actually told the truth this time, for once. When did you see her, anyway?"

Tina stood up to face Kat, the fear Kat had seen seemed to have been replaced by contempt. "She came by the child services place where I've been for the last six days,"Tina gave Kat a significant look. Clearly she had expected Kat to come, and possibly take her in. "I'm an orphan, Kat, my mom killed herself, and Sela's the only one who came to check on me. Sela, the person who is the least capable of caring about others, even she felt bad for me."

Kat looked over her shoulder. Roco and the others seemed to have taken a few steps further away from where Tina and Kat stood. If they were eavesdropping they were making a point to act as if they weren't.

"Tina, I'm sorry, I haven't left my house at all. I just didn't want to have anyone else's thoughts in my head. I just needed to rest. I'm glad Sela came though, she's your sister."

"Well whatever, Sela's gone so it doesn't even matter," said Tina, looking away.

"No, Tina, she wouldn't have just left like that for good. She'll be back, I mean, Talson's here. She'll come back for him."

"Who cares, Kat," Tina suddenly looked resigned to the worst. "Sela was evil and so is Talson. You used to know that before you decided that your mind makes you better than me and everyone else. You joined Talson and I supported you, but you said in the beginning that we still needed revenge for my dad."

"I said that before I knew what your father did. I don't think I'm better than you. You just don't want to face what really happened. I know you want to believe that your dad was a good person who was brutally killed by some evil, mind-destroying monster, but that's not how it happened. Your dad was a murderer and Talson killed him over it. I know you wanted me to join Talson so I could avenge your dad's death. I also know that you wanted Sela to hang around and be your big sister and make peace with your mom so you could live happily ever after. What I don't understand is why you ever thought that could actually happen. Your mom was manipulative and angry, and in the end, she was a coward. You said it yourself, Sela doesn't care, that's just who she is. Is the truth so hard to see?"

Tina shook her head, tears on her face now. "No, Kat, you don't understand. For people who can't see into other people's minds the truth *is* hard to see, and life still has mystery. People who can't tell what other people are really thinking are free to dream and imagine people the way they want them to be." Tina's voice broke as she finished. She pushed past Kat and walked away through the trees, wiping her eyes.

Kat stood motionless, watching her go. Kat knew it would never be the same between her and Tina. She knew she could never fix it, but she could not accept that this was the end of their friendship. *Tracy killed herself, Sela's gone, Tina's life is over, and I can't fix it.*

Try anyway.

Kat still did not move.

I said try anyway.

Kat suddenly sprinted toward the sidewalk at the edge of the park. "Tina, wait," she cried.

Tina slowed down slightly, but kept walking away from Kat. Kat paused, realizing she had no idea what to say. "Tina, I'm sorry," she began uncertainly. "I don't care what you think of me right now, even though I know what you think, it doesn't matter. I know its over, I know we'll never be friends again, but you can't hate me. Please, we have to fix this."

Tina stopped walking now and turned to face Kat. "No, we can't fix it. We can't fix it because you know that right now I think you're an evil, selfish person. You know I blame you and Talson for destroying my family. But what's worse is that I let you do it. I trusted you, and I made a deal with you and Sela. I let you try to help me. You know what you did to me and you know everything I think about what happened, so why bother trying to pretend it doesn't matter. You can't pretend Kat, you can't fix anything because you know too much."

"But I don't want to know. I've always known what you were thinking, you thought it was cool."

"Yeah, well, I didn't know it could kill people."

"Tina, just listen, I'm sorry, but this is too important to me to not try, even if I know you won't forgive me."

Tina looked at Kat for a moment, her gaze steady. "You know I'm thinking of forgiving or at least not blaming you, right?"

"Yeah, I know but you shouldn't forgive me, it was my fault."

"Fine you're not forgiven, but—" Tina looked at the ground, ashamed. "All those

things you said about my mom, and my dad, and Sela, and about happy endings…you were totally right."

Kat nodded, "I wish I wasn't. I hate being right."

"Yeah, I hate when you're right too, but that's just the truth so I can't argue with it."

Kat nodded, looking away. She still wasn't sure if Tina was going to accept her apology, and part of her was too scared to ask the question to which she so badly wanted an answer. *Are we even?*

"Yeah, we're good," said Tina.

Kat looked up at Tina, completely taken aback. "Did you just—?"

"Nah, lucky guess," replied Tina with a slight smile. "Come see me sometime at the house of the unwanted, abandoned, and otherwise unfortunate children awaiting foster homes."

"Wow, you inherited Sela's dark humor, didn't you?" Kat tried to conceal her happiness and relief.

"Yeah, well, my mom killed herself, so I have permission to be dark now." Tina turned and walked away without another word.

Kat watched Tina walking toward the bus station. She stood motionless in the middle of the sidewalk for several minutes before she slowly headed back to the park.

"I knew you could fix it, Kat." Talson was waiting for her at the edge of the park.

"Yeah, I wasn't sure I could." Kat paused. "So what happens now? What are you going to do?"

"I don't know, I want to go somewhere I've never been, see something new. I've been in this city my entire life. What about you Katerina, what will you do?"

Kat shrugged, "go to school, play basketball."

"Be normal?" said Talson with a slight smile.

"I don't know if that's possible," said Kat. "I'll just try not to kill anyone."

"I'll try to do the same," said Talson. He paused and looked at the sky. *Thanks for everything, Kat. Whether you wanted to or not, you really helped me when no one else could.*

Yeah, well, you helped me when no one else would, so we're even. "Will you come back?" Kat added aloud. She wondered if Talson would leave the city and his past behind for good.

"Of course I'll come back," said Talson. "And even if I don't, I know our paths will cross again someday. But until we meet again," he extended his left hand.

Kat nodded, "I know, we shake lefty." They shook hands and stood staring at each other for a moment. Then at the same moment they both turned and walked side by side along the sidewalk to the corner. Talson pulled the hood up on his coat and turned right, heading toward the house where Kat had first met him and Kat turned left. She didn't look back and she headed up the street toward her house, but she knew that Lawrence James Thomason Junior was watching her over his shoulder as she turned the corner and disappeared from view.

EPILOGUE

The full moon hung above the sea, casting dancing strips of light over its calm surface. The air was still, and the only sound that could be heard was the dull slap of the waves washing lazily over the rocks. A small car was parked at the side of the road near the cliff top. Two men stood on the rocks just below the top of the bluff. They stared out across the calm water with the same steady, expressionless gaze. Then in unison they both lowered their eyes to a small rock ledge many feet below, as if they could both see something that was invisible to the rest of the world.

The taller of the men reached into his pocket. "This is yours, Larry," he said softly. Holding out what looked to be a very crinkled piece of paper.

The smaller man took the paper and unfolded it. It was a very faded and battered five-dollar bill. Larry looked at the bill with his strange milky green eyes. "Is this the same one?" he asked softly.

The man nodded slowly. "Thirty-six years."

Larry smiled slightly and placed the bill carefully into his pocket. "Thanks J.C."

They stared out to sea in silence for a moment. "What's next for Talson?" John Carl asked.

"I don't know," replied Larry. "I guess I'll go somewhere and try to find something. I'm not sure what, but I think I'll figure it out eventually."

John Carl nodded. "I won't bet against you."